Derek Robinson grew up in Bristol, was a fighter pilot
in the RAF, read history at Cambridge, and then spent
eleven years working in advertising in London and New
York before becoming a full-time writer.

Artillery of Lies is his seventh novel and is a sequel
to *The Eldorado Network*. All his novels have in common
a certain debunking of the myths of war. He has also
written books on squash and rugby and broadcasts for
both radio and television on sport and the arts.

DEREK ROBINSON

Artillery of Lies

PAN BOOKS
IN ASSOCIATION WITH MACMILLAN LONDON

First published 1991 by Macmillan London Limited
This edition first published 1992 by Pan Books Limited,
Cavaye Place, London SW10 9PG
in association with Macmillan London Limited
1 3 5 7 9 8 6 4 2
© Derek Robinson 1991
ISBN 0 330 32366 0
Typeset by Macmillan Production Limited
Printed in England by Clays Ltd, St Ives plc

To Robin and Mary

'And there's no fog,' Luis complained. 'You said there would be fog.' He managed to make his voice both sour and savage.

'Not all the time,' said Templeton. 'I never said England was foggy all the time.'

'Damned swindle.'

'I could sing you a bit of fog,' Julie said. Luis was standing at the window with his hands deep in the pockets of his great-coat. She stood behind him and slid her hands into the pockets, but he refused to link fingers. She rested her chin on his shoulder and crooned: '*A foggy day . . . in London town . . . It had me blue . . . It had me down . . .*' He hunched his shoulders and frowned even harder at the shifting image of parkland. The rain blurred the glass and made the bare black branches twitch and flicker like bits of early cinema film. He blinked, changed focus, and saw his own reflection. Handsome young devil, he thought. Dark eyes, high cheekbones, strong brows: thank God for a bit of Moorish blood in the family. He flashed his shy smile, just to keep in practice. Irresistible.

'No orange juice for breakfast either,' he said bitterly.

'For God's sake, Luis, there's a *war* on,' Julie said, and walked away.

'Nobody told me I wouldn't get any orange juice. I always have orange juice for breakfast, I'm no good without orange juice, I can't work.' He kicked a radiator. 'Wouldn't have left Lisbon if I'd known it was like this.'

'Tell you what, I'll lay on some nice juicy prunes tomorrow,' Templeton said.

1

'I shit on your prunes,' Luis said.

'No, it's the other way around,' Julie told him.

'I suppose the shortage of fog is also because there is a war on,' Luis said.

'Be fair, old chap,' Templeton said. 'You can't expect to have fog *and* half a gale of wind and rain.'

'You will tell me next there is no pageantry in England. No pomp and ceremony. Because there is a war on.'

'I'll take you to the Changing of the Guard,' Templeton promised. 'Just as soon as it stops raining.'

Luis sighed and took his hands from his pockets to raise them, palms upwards. 'I should live so long,' he said.

Templeton looked to Julie for help, but she shook her head. 'He wasted his youth in the cinema,' she told him. 'He thinks life is a B-movie. Does this thing work?' She had found a gramophone and was sorting out the records.

'This severe shortage of fog and orange juice,' Luis said, 'is very significant and I shall inform Herr Hitler at the earliest possible opportunity.'

'I'll go and organize some tea,' Templeton said.

As he went out, Julie was dancing to a slow foxtrot with Luis, her arms inside his greatcoat.

'Earl Grey!' Luis called out.

'Wrong,' she said. 'Duke Ellington.'

Which at least made him laugh. I suppose that's your volatile Latin temperament for you, Templeton thought. Give me good old English phlegm every time. You know where you are with phlegm.

Templeton needed a stiff cup of tea.

Julie Conroy was American and she could take the stuff or leave it alone, especially before lunch; Luis Cabrillo was Spanish so his choice was simpler: he left it alone. Templeton was English and in the face of adversity he automatically thought of tea. There had been no lack of adversity on the journey from Lisbon.

This was December 1942. Portugal was neutral, perched

2

uneasily on the elbow of Spain, which was also neutral but not too neutral to send a division of troops to fight for Hitler on the Russian Front.

Because nearly all the rest of Europe belonged to Hitler, neutrals like Portugal and Switzerland and Sweden were immensely useful to both sides. Portugal was especially popular with the various intelligence agencies. The climate was pleasant, you could get a decent cup of real coffee for next to nothing, and the Portuguese secret police didn't throw their weight about. Not unless you were stupid enough to embarrass them by not even pretending to be, for instance, the Assistant Cultural Attaché at your nation's embassy. There were more spies in Lisbon than in any other capital. Demand attracted supply: detailed and startling information, some of it quite accurate, came from a shifting army of paid informants. In particular the Lisbon agents of the Abwehr, German Military Intelligence, always got advance notice of arrivals and departures by boat or plane. Despite the war, there were scheduled commercial flights between Portugal and Britain. If Luis Cabrillo had taken one of those planes, the Abwehr would have known and would have been painfully surprised, since they believed he had been in Britain for many months, working for them.

The British embassy had a department called Quarantine Control to handle this kind of problem. At three in the morning, during a cold drizzle, in a sad and semi-derelict corner of Lisbon docks, Quarantine Control smuggled Luis, Julie, and Templeton on to a rusting gutbucket of a British freighter only minutes before she sailed. It was a three-day voyage to Gibraltar. The weather got worse. The boat lurched and plunged and thumped and butted the Atlantic as if looking for a fight. She was loaded and overloaded with a cargo of carob pods, her skipper taking the view that if you were going to be torpedoed you might as well go down big. The carob pods put out an overblown supersweet smell that no gale could disperse. Luis had never been to sea before, and he was very sick. He lay in his bunk, a martyr to every heave and shudder, and raged feebly against the British government. 'Is this the best you can do?' he demanded of Templeton. 'This slow death?'

3

'I'm afraid it is, old chap.' Templeton had once served in the Royal Navy, and now he was enjoying a thick ham sandwich with plenty of mustard. Julie slumped in a chair, pale as an empty plate.

'That filthy stench . . .' Luis clung to the bunk as the freighter groaned under the wallop of another wave. 'It chokes me.'

'I'm told carob makes splendid animal feed. Cattle fight each other for it, apparently.'

'Eldorado Network,' Luis whispered. 'Best damn network in Europe. All that work. Suppose I die?'

'Oh, can it, Luis,' Julie said. 'D'you think I'm enjoying this?' Against all advice from her stomach she had eaten a bowl of stew and she knew that if she relaxed her attention for an instant, her stomach would send it back. 'Anyway, the Eldorado Network doesn't exist, so you can go right ahead and die and see if anyone cares.'

They glared at each other. Templeton sighed. He was a bachelor; he had never understood love.

'Think I'll take a turn about the deck,' he said. 'Can I get anyone anything?' Neither of them even looked at him.

Quarantine Control had a man waiting for them at Gibraltar. 'Good news,' he said. 'I've got you on a plane for England tonight.' The plane was a Sunderland flying boat and it took off as soon as night fell, carrying them high above the route the freighter had taken. When Luis discovered this he took malevolent pleasure in telling Templeton.

'Only a couple of hours and we shall be back exactly where we started,' he shouted. (The Sunderland made a lot of noise.) 'Isn't progress wonderful?'

Templeton nodded and got on with his leg of cold chicken. He had made this flight before and he knew that the best approach was to fill yourself up with food and drink and hope to sleep the rest of the way. Julie was already wrapped in blankets with a bottle of wine for company.

Luis had never been up in an aeroplane before and he could not rest. On the other hand there was nothing to see, nothing to read, nothing to do, and the booming roar of the engines made conversation difficult. The fuselage was dimly lit. As the plane climbed the temperature fell. He couldn't find anywhere comfortable to sit or lie or sprawl. His eardrums hurt.

The pilot flew far out over the Atlantic in order to avoid German aircraft operating from France. The Sunderland was not built for speed. It cruised at 150 or 160 miles an hour, churning stolidly through the night, hour after hour. Luis had never been so bored in his life. This was worse than prison; if he were in prison he could make trouble; inside this deafening, freezing machine was nothing, nothing. He found his penknife and began scraping his initials on a black box while thinking savage and brutal thoughts about Templeton for persuading him to leave Lisbon. A crewman came and shouted and took the penknife away. Luis hated the crewman too.

The flight lasted ten and a half hours.

It was still night when they landed at Plymouth harbour. They were given breakfast – charred bacon and a slab of reconstituted dried egg – and then put in a car. Luis fell asleep. The first time he saw England by daylight it was grey with rain. He asked Templeton where they were. 'Salisbury Plain, I think,' Templeton said. 'Not far now.' Luis asked him where they were going. 'Big house called Rackham Towers, just outside London. You'll like it there.'

'Don't bet your pension on it,' Julie said.

It was mid-morning when they arrived. Rackham Towers was a Victorian pile set in five hundred acres of parkland and built of rain-blackened granite. It had battlements. It had round turrets with arrow slits, and overhanging square turrets with cannon ports, and smaller square turrets growing out of the bigger square turrets. A besieging army would have died of hunger until it worked out how to get in through the French windows.

They stood in the rain and looked at it.

'Fortunately, the light is bad,' Luis said.

'Unusual place, isn't it?' Templeton said. 'I'm told the architect shot himself.'

'Before or after?' Julie asked.

'It's quite nice inside.' Templeton and Julie made for the door,

5

leaving Luis standing and staring at the house. 'Why on earth is he being such a pig?' Templeton murmured.

'Why not? There he was in Lisbon, having a lovely war, running the whole show, praised and admired by all and making a killing too, when down came the British Secret Service and took all his toys away.'

'Not quite. We just want him to let us play with them.'

'He says it's a rotten swizz. Is that the phrase?'

'In my country,' Luis shouted at them, 'in Spain, we would pay our enemies to come and bomb a thing like this.' He turned 'thing' into a piece of airborne graffiti.

Templeton carried in a tray of tea and biscuits, and found Luis and Julie on the sofa, reading the morning papers. Her eyes were half closed. 'If you want to go to bed,' Templeton said, 'your rooms are ready. Just say.' She smiled, looking as lazy as a cat in the sun.

'Listen,' Luis announced, 'I didn't realize this Stalingrad business was so awful.' He winced as he read on. 'My God,' he muttered.

'I haven't seen a paper.' Templeton looked over Luis's shoulder and scanned the story. 'That's not so bad, is it? I'd say it was quite good. German Sixth Army's still trapped and the Russians are breaking out on all sides. Nothing for us to worry about there.'

'What? It's a disaster. It could become a catastrophe.' Luis gave him the newspaper and began bouncing on the sofa, using up his excess of nervous energy, until Julie complained and he stood up. 'The OKW must be desperately worried,' he said. 'I mean, where is it going to stop?'

Fatigue was beginning to catch up with Templeton. 'Sorry, old chap,' he said. 'Not quite with you. OK what?'

'Oberkommando der Wehrmacht.' Luis snapped out the words. 'Hitler's High Command.' Templeton put milk in his tea, and waited. 'You remember Hitler?' Luis said. 'Looks like Charlie Chaplin, only not so funny?'

'With you now, Luis. So tell me why I should worry about OKW's ulcers.'

'Because the largest office in OKW is the Abwehr. When OKW catches a cold, the Abwehr runs a fever. It needs to be soothed.' Luis was pacing up and down, gesturing. 'Luckily I have just the medicine. The British War Cabinet is unhappy about this Soviet success, very unhappy.'

Templeton was more tired than he knew. 'Where does it say that?' he asked. He gave the newspapers a shake.

'Perhaps not the entire War Cabinet. No. But a powerful minority is very, very apprehensive. The danger is . . .' Luis walked all around the sofa and ended up looking at Julie. 'What is the danger?' he asked, like an actor at rehearsals, seeking a cue.

Julie yawned and curled herself around a cushion. 'I guess the danger is the Bolsheviks will sweep across Europe like a red tide,' she said sleepily.

Luis clicked his fingers. 'Of course. And we don't want that, do we?' he said to Templeton. 'So we're going to reduce the number of Arctic convoys we send to Russia. We must stop feeding the bear before he gets too big and gobbles us all up. That's it. That's what several influential members of the War Cabinet are demanding. Yes. Far too many ships are being sunk in the Arctic. Britain must stop bleeding herself white for the greater glory of Uncle Joe Stalin. Ha!' He jumped in the air, clicked his heels and clapped his hands. 'You see? Stalingrad is not all doom and disaster. There is a bright and optimistic side to Stalingrad, if you know where to look. Where to listen.'

'And where exactly did you see and hear all this?' Templeton asked.

'Um . . .' Luis gave it some thought, pursing his lips and shrugging as he selected his source. 'Pinetree,' he said at last.

'Pinetree? Refresh my memory. Whose codename is Pinetree?'

'British civilian employee in the American embassy.'

Templeton finished his tea. 'Well, Pinetree would know, if anyone does.'

'Exactly. I'll draft something for transmission. The Abwehr will

7

love it, they must be gasping for good news. Can we get it out tonight?'

'I'll see.' Templeton heard the crunch of tyres on gravel and he went to the window, in time to see a man in a blue rain-coat run up the steps. Freddy Garcia. Thank God. For the first time in a week, Templeton felt he could afford to think about relaxing. Eldorado was Freddy's pigeon now.

'How is Lisbon? Don't tell me, I can't stand to know,' said Freddy Garcia. 'London's ghastly. The Americans have got all the taxis and ever since we had a bomb in the back garden, I can't make the hot-water system work. Not that it matters, because I virtually live in the office, which is another madhouse. The Director won't hire a secretary unless she's in *Debrett* or *Burke's Peerage*; he says in this racket loyalty counts more than efficiency, so there are debs everywhere. Charming gels with perfect manners but the files are in chaos. You don't know how lucky you are, Charles.'

'Actually, it was raining in Lisbon too. I think it's raining everywhere. Not in North Africa, perhaps.'

'What? It rains harder and colder in North Africa than anywhere outside Burma.'

'I'll take your word for it, Freddy,' Templeton said. 'I mean to say, you've been everywhere, haven't you?'

They were warming their backsides at the library fire. Garcia was about forty years old. He was Anglo-Spanish. His face was olive skinned, smooth, straight lipped, with a polished axe-head of a nose and black hair that he brushed straight back, no parting. But he dressed like an English countryman, perhaps a successful vet or a stud-farmer: whipcord trousers, tweed jacket of a soft and faded pattern with leather patches on the elbows, rust-red woollen tie. His father had been a minor Spanish diplomat, his English mother a very good painter of watercolours. For work and pleasure the family had travelled around the world, ending up in London, where MI6 (the public label of the British secret intelligence service) recruited Freddy the day after Hitler invaded Poland.

He was recruited in a fashion typical of the day. He was in Brown's, a club which had a lot of members who were obviously decent chaps, and someone he occasionally played backgammon with came up to him at the bar and asked him if he might be interested in doing something interesting. Freddy said he might. It all depended on what and where and why and how long. Hard to say, the man said. We do lots of different things in lots of different places, all for the same reason, and we'll go on doing them as long as this war lasts. It's not boring. They had lunch, then Freddy went with him, and by tea-time he was a spy.

He had dual nationality, and until the fall of France he floated around Europe on his Spanish passport, doing harm and good by stealth and subterfuge. What he mainly did was help talented Jewish scientists escape from Germany. The man in Brown's had been right: it was not boring. After the fall of France, he joined MI5's new B1A section, which ran the Double-Cross System.

'They tell me your Mr Cabrillo is a bit of a handful,' Freddy Garcia said.

'Two handfuls, actually,' Templeton said. 'You don't get Luis without Julie Conroy. Very pretty, very American, very head-screwed-on.'

'Damn. Where on earth did he pick up Miss Conroy?'

'Madrid, and it's Mrs Conroy.'

'Double damn.'

'It's all in the Eldorado file,' Templeton said. 'I suggest you read the file before you make any judgements.' He hoisted a fat bundle of papers from his briefcase.

'Crikey.' Garcia weighed the bundle on his palms. 'He's been busy, hasn't he?'

'The Abwehr certainly think so. I'll get the kitchen to send you up some sandwiches at lunchtime. It's a jolly good read.'

Templeton went out. Freddy Garcia put the bundle on a table and tugged at the ends of the tape around it until they came loose. The first page was headed *Origins*. He found a deep armchair and began to read.

CODENAME: 'ELDORADO'

AGENT: Luis Jorge Ricardo CABRILLO
NATIONALITY: Spanish
AGE: 24 (b. 9 September 1918)
LANGUAGES: Fluent English (self-taught), some French
POLITICS: None (anti-Fascist and anti-Communist)
EDUCATION: Varied. Cabrillo claims to have attended 27 different schools in 13 towns and to have been expelled from 23 of them. (As an employee of Spanish State Railways, his father moved from town to town.)

Spanish Civil War

Having left school at the age of 15 and tried many jobs, Cabrillo was a taxi driver (aged 17) in Granada, specializing in tourists, when the Civil War broke out. He soon found profitable work as chauffeur/interpreter for English and American war correspondents. Cabrillo claims he became expert at 'discovering' appropriate news to suit the political slant of any reporter's newspaper (e.g. Guernica was destroyed either by German bombs or by the dynamite of Republican saboteurs); for this he got well paid. The work took him back and forth through the Republican and Nationalist lines and grew increasingly dangerous. Both sides suspected him of spying. He was nearly arrested in Guernica shortly after the bombing but escaped. In the course of his escape a Nationalist Army officer chasing him was killed (accidentally, Cabrillo says) and Cabrillo somehow acquired a very large sum of money.

He went into hiding for the next four years. The first two, he spent moving about northern Spain, keeping clear of areas of the fighting, always travelling on foot and pretending to be a poor peasant. When the war ended (March 1939) he moved to Madrid and rented a small apartment. He claims not to have left it for the next two years – he was still on the wanted list of Franco's police in 1939 and 1940 – and spent all his time reading books in English, thus acquiring a huge, if miscellaneous and secondhand, knowledge of life in Britain.

Introduction to intelligence work

By May 1941 Cabrillo's money had run out. He emerged from hiding and applied to the British embassy for work as a spy. As he had no experience apart from his job with the war correspondents, no contacts in Occupied Europe and no knowledge of German, the embassy turned him down.

Cabrillo immediately went to the German embassy and offered to spy for the Axis cause. (He now asserts that this move was intended to give him valuable inside knowledge of the workings of German military intelligence which he could later offer to British Intelligence.) It seems that Madrid Abwehr were impressed by his initiative and imagination and agreed to train him. This they did, very thoroughly: he learned codes, secret writing, gunmanship, unarmed combat, Morse transmission, radio maintenance and repair, technique of microdots, landing by rubber dinghy, principles of military intelligence, conversion of British systems of weights, measures, and currencies, how to recruit sub-agents, the psychology of espionage. According to Cabrillo he scored well in everything except gunmanship and radio.

The Abwehr must have been confident of Cabrillo's value because he survived two potential disasters. The lesser involved his friendship with an American woman, Mrs Julie Conroy, whom he met at the German embassy; she was seeking information about her husband, an American journalist, thought to be somewhere in Europe. Their friendship ripened but so did Mrs Conroy's anti-Nazi views, which she expressed openly. This disturbed Brigadier Christian (then head of Madrid Abwehr); however, Cabrillo persuaded him that a vehemently anti-Nazi girlfriend was excellent cover for an Abwehr agent. In any case Mrs Conroy left Madrid for America (or so Christian believed) and the crisis passed.

More serious was the involvement of Freddy Ryan, an MI6 agent who was infiltrated as a potential Abwehr agent. Ryan trained alongside Cabrillo until something (or someone) betrayed him. The Abwehr shot him, in Cabrillo's presence. Cabrillo might have been considered guilty (or at least suspect) by association; in the event Christian seems to have decided that Ryan's death had so frightened Cabrillo that he had been cleansed of any possible disloyalty.

Madrid Abwehr planned to land Cabrillo in England by rubber dinghy from a U-boat. He took strong exception to this, pointing out that since he was a Spanish neutral he could go by ship or air to Britain, travelling as a businessman. He further persuaded them that he had arranged a method of communication which was better than radio: he would use friends in the Spanish embassy in London to send his reports by diplomatic bag to Lisbon, where another contact would forward them to Madrid. Christian agreed to these arrangements and Cabrillo left Madrid for England, travelling alone, on 23 July 1941.

Cabrillo went no further than Lisbon. He rented an office and an apartment and began sending his reports to Madrid; the first arrived only a week after his departure and was warmly welcomed. As he got into his stride he maintained a steady output of two, sometimes three, extensive reports per week, covering virtually every aspect of the war in which the Abwehr was interested, from Atlantic convoy patterns and scales of food rationing, to secret tank trials and new airfields, as well as political intelligence about the strategic policies of the various Allied governments. Quite rapidly, Abwehr HQ in Berlin began to attach considerable importance to Eldorado reports. Digests and analyses of them were routinely forwarded to the German High Command and even to Hitler's headquarters.

Cabrillo has described how he was able to maintain such a continuous stream of apparently high-grade 'intelligence'. He names three factors:

(1) His wide knowledge of English life, the product of two years' ceaseless reading in Madrid.

(2) His use of three works of reference which he had found in Lisbon, namely: the 1923 Michelin Guide to Great Britain; Holiday Haunts, published by the Great Western Railway in 1937; and a school geography textbook, Exploring the British Isles by Jasper H. Stembridge, Book 4.

(3) His creative formula, which consists of looking at what is actually happening in the war, then asking himself the question: 'What would the Germans most like to hear?', and shaping his answer into something that resembles military intelligence.

Cabrillo wasted no time in recruiting sub-agents and communication assistants. The latter were codenamed BLUEBIRD and STORK, minor officials in the Spanish embassies in London and Lisbon; the former were SEAGULL, a Communist foreman in the Liverpool docks, and KNICKERS, a travelling soft-drinks salesman in south-east England. In due course at least seven more sub-agents were supposedly recruited:

GARLIC – a Venezuelan medical student in Glasgow
NUTMEG – a retired Army officer working for the Ministry of Food
        in Cambridge
WALLPAPER – a lecturer at the University of Birmingham,
        probably homosexual

HAYSTACK – manager of a London hotel
PINETREE – British employee in the American embassy
HAMBONE – telephone operator in Plymouth
DONKEY – telephone engineer in Belfast

Naturally, all these members of the Eldorado Network had to be paid for the information or services they provided, as did Cabrillo himself. Before he left Madrid, the Abwehr had opened accounts for him in Switzerland and Lisbon; now they rewarded him generously. By the end of 1941 he had received almost £50,000.

During the summer and autumn of 1941, MI5 began to receive intercepts of some of the Eldorado reports. At that time, these appeared to be authentic and it was assumed that Eldorado was in fact operating from Britain. All attempts to locate the agent were of course doomed to failure.

Mrs Conroy

In Lisbon there were several interesting developments. Mrs Conroy stumbled across Cabrillo's path and tracked him down. It says something for the persuasiveness of his reports that when she first read them (after breaking into his office) she was so convinced that he was a German agent that she tried to shoot him, using an old revolver she had found in a file cabinet. Fortunately, she missed; Cabrillo was able to convince her that he was a freelance operator working entirely for his own benefit and that if anything he told the Abwehr was true, this was pure coincidence. Thereafter Mrs Conroy joined him; they lived and worked together. She provided a useful double-check on his reports and was instrumental in detecting and correcting several mistakes which might well have betrayed him.

Bradburn & Wedge

At the same time the Portuguese Ministry of Taxation took note of the fact that Cabrillo seemed to be running a business of some kind, and required him to supply details. To satisfy the Ministry, and to create a cover, Cabrillo and Conroy set up a genuine business called

Bradburn & Wedge, a name they had found in the 1923 Michelin, and began trading in such items as lemonade crystals, de-greasing patents, and soap. (An accountant was engaged to handle their tax returns and the company flourished, albeit on a small scale.)

Cabrillo continued to expand his imaginary network. He had every encouragement from Madrid Abwehr whose payments and questionnaires served as guides to those areas of intelligence in which they were especially interested. However, Mrs Conroy became concerned about the mounting risk that the flood of intelligence emerging from Eldorado would sooner or later contain an element of truth (for instance, details of a convoy route) with disastrous results for the Allies (e.g. interception by U-boats). She therefore persuaded Cabrillo to apply again at the British embassy and volunteer his services for the Allied cause.

Rebuffed by MI6

Cabrillo did volunteer. Through sheer bad luck he was interviewed by William Witteridge. We know now that Witteridge was totally unsuited to work in an intelligence agency, given his almost complete lack of imagination and a profound distrust of his colleagues. Shortly after his meeting with Cabrillo he was transferred to the Khartoum office, but from his brief notes of the interview it seems that Witteridge demanded Cabrillo's undivided loyalty: i.e. if he wished to join the British Secret Service he must first resign from his German employment. Witteridge was apparently incapable of getting his mind around the concept of a double-agent, and so for a second time Cabrillo's offer was rejected by British Intelligence.

Abwehr agent 'Eagle'

Meanwhile one of the Abwehr controllers in Madrid, Otto Krafft, had recruited another agent in Britain, an American businessman codenamed EAGLE. This led to a crisis in Cabrillo's operations when Eldorado submitted a report on the British output of light alloys which directly contradicted a report on the same subject received from Eagle. Brigadier Christian ordered the two agents to meet on a specified date at a given rendezvous – Manchester railway station – in order to resolve their disagreement. This was obviously impossible and at first Cabrillo thought his network had been blown. Then he discovered that someone in Lisbon was trying to intercept the Abwehr's order to him concerning the rendezvous. Cabrillo succeeded in following the man to business premises in Oporto and asked him to explain his behaviour. The man attacked him and in self-defence Cabrillo killed him. When Cabrillo searched his office he learned that the dead man was Eagle, and that Eagle was the brother of Otto Krafft. It seems certain that Otto Krafft had seen the potential for earning large sums of money by selling invented information to the Abwehr and that he had established his brother as a fictitious agent, supposedly in England but actually in Oporto. (Phoney agents of this kind have, of course, always been the bane of intelligence agencies. Eagle had one great advantage in that Otto Krafft could advise him what to write; it was pure bad luck that he chose to write about British light alloys.)

When Eagle (as Eldorado reported) failed to keep the rendezvous, Christian's faith in Eldorado was restored. Cabrillo had had a lucky escape. His response to this was to work harder than ever in order to fill the vacuum left by Eagle. He added more sub-agents; his appetite for creating fake intelligence seemed limitless. At the same time his relationship with Mrs Conroy, always variable, became occasionally stormy as she recognized the mounting risks of swindling the Abwehr on such a scale, while he talked of becoming the first spy millionaire.

MI6 again: no joy

The next development, early in 1942, came about because Cabrillo had met Charles Templeton (MI6, Lisbon), whom he trusted to some extent – they had shared hazardous experiences in the Civil War. Templeton persuaded him to apply yet again to work for the British. By now Witteridge had gone from MI5 and the fact that Cabrillo was Eldorado had begun to sink in. Unfortunately Witteridge's replacement also took completely the wrong line with Cabrillo. His tone was brusque and impatient; he insisted that Cabrillo had no choice but to join the department. Cabrillo thought otherwise. The meeting was a failure.

Abwehr request rendezvous

Almost immediately Cabrillo got a summons to meet Brigadier Christian in a Lisbon hotel in four days' time. The great risk inherent in keeping this appointment was obvious: if the Abwehr had cause to suspect Cabrillo then Christian would seize him and he would face interrogation and almost certain death. Partly as a reaction against his treatment at the British embassy and partly because he was loath to abandon his network when it was so profitable, Cabrillo decided to meet Christian. He was astonished to be awarded the Iron Cross, Second Class, for his services to the Reich.

The occasion was all the more remarkable as Christian was accompanied by Wolfgang Adler, an Abwehr officer who had never concealed the fact that he disliked and distrusted Cabrillo. After Christian and Adler left, Mrs Conroy joined Cabrillo and they celebrated the award. Then Adler unexpectedly returned, announced that he wanted to go over to the British, and asked Cabrillo to help him.

Adler's thinking was that a German victory was impossible, the war must end to avoid further atrocities, and he (Adler) could tell the British everything about the Abwehr organization and operations. Behind Adler's request was the implication that he knew Cabrillo to be a double-agent and therefore able to get in touch with British Intelligence. When Adler became insistent, Cabrillo reluctantly contacted Templeton, but Templeton's reply was that British Intelligence had no use for Adler since there was nothing new he could tell them. At the same time, Mrs Conroy pointed out to Cabrillo that if Adler was allowed to defect he would effectively destroy the Eldorado Network since the Abwehr must assume that he had betrayed its existence to MI5.

Cabrillo now tried to delay Adler, saying the British were not ready for him and he should wait in Madrid. Adler rejected this. He said that he must go to England at once as he had just murdered Brigadier Christian (by strangulation) in the German embassy. (Cabrillo believes that Adler was not altogether mentally stable, a condition aggravated by his recent service on the Russian Front. Also, murdering Christian may have been a way of burning his boats.) Thus Cabrillo – by now highly anxious – was left with no choice but to take Adler to the British embassy. Before they could arrive there, Adler collapsed in the street and died, apparently from a heart attack but actually from the effects of a fast-acting poison administered by one of our men using a hidden syringe. Templeton was on the spot; he took Cabrillo and Conroy to the embassy, where at last a deal was struck and the Eldorado Network was absorbed into the Double-Cross System.

Eldorado and Torch

Cabrillo and Conroy remained in Lisbon. From now on their work was integrated with the overall Allied policy for disinformation –

principally the deception plans preceding Operation Torch, the Allied landings in North Africa. Here, Eldorado's reports seem to have been highly effective in persuading the enemy that an invasion of Greece was being planned; indeed, German military resources were transferred to the eastern Mediterranean shortly before Allied troops landed at the western end.

This, it was assumed, would mark the end of Eldorado: surely the Abwehr would cease to trust an informant who had so completely pointed them in the wrong direction. In the event, this did not happen and we can only assume that Madrid gave Eldorado credit for faithfully reporting a major Allied diversionary exercise which was meant to deceive the enemy; as such it was sound military intelligence and Eldorado would have been at fault if he had not detected it. In any event, the Abwehr continued to pay Eldorado and therefore we saw no reason to wind up the Network; quite the reverse. This being so, it was decided to transfer Cabrillo and Mrs Conroy to England where they could more easily be integrated with the rest of the Double-Cross effort.

Appendix

The attached appendix provides a summary of all Eldorado reports . . .

The appendix was at least two hundred pages long. Freddy Garcia polished his reading glasses and settled down to a good long read.

'Crumbs!' Freddy Garcia said. He rarely swore; schoolboy slang was usually his limit. 'Also crikey,' he added. He tied up the Eldorado file in its ribbon and hid the bundle on a high library shelf. Rackham Towers was staffed and guarded by MI5 but Garcia trusted nobody.

He found Templeton. They took their coats and went for a walk in the grounds. The rain and wind had stopped, and in the dusk everything was as still as a tapestry.

'He's got nerve, I'll say that for him,' Garcia said.

'He's only twenty-four. When I was twenty-four, I had nerve too.'

'Ah. You don't much like him.'

Templeton thought. 'He can be quite likeable,' he said. 'He can also be quite difficult. Bloody impossible, sometimes. On the other hand, you've got to admire his achievements, especially as he did it all himself. He's a one-man-band who sounds like a symphony orchestra. What's more he writes the music, too.'

'Then what makes him so difficult?'

'Oh, he's obsessive. This network is his whole life, he really worries about his motley crew of sub-agents and whether or not they're pulling their weight. Who should get a bonus, who should get the sack. That sort of thing. Quite absurd, really.'

'And Mrs Conroy?'

'She's OK. Young, sharp, nice to look at. I think they love each other, in a cockeyed fashion. Julie's quite a healthy influence on Luis. She kicks him in the balls when he goes off the deep end.'

'When you say they love each other . . .'

'Twice nightly, with matinées Wednesdays and Saturdays.'

'I want to get this straight, Charles. You're saying they enjoy sexual intercourse.'

'If they don't enjoy it, they're martyrs to suffering.' Templeton couldn't keep a tinge of envy out of his voice.

'Never mind, Charles,' Garcia said. 'You were twenty-four once. I just hope the Director doesn't get to hear about their martyrdom. He doesn't like sex between agents.'

'If he doesn't like it he needn't join in.'

'You know what I mean. Tell me . . . Are you absolutely convinced, in your own mind, that Eldorado is everything he claims to be?'

'He got the Iron Cross, Freddy. And pots of Abwehr money.'

'I wasn't thinking of the Abwehr. I just wondered . . . I mean, this Eldorado Network is such a professional job, isn't it? Maybe Luis Cabrillo was assisted by . . . I don't know . . . the Americans, or the Russians.'

They walked back in silence towards the house.

'No,' said Templeton. 'Sorry, Freddy. I haven't had a proper night's sleep in four days and my brain feels like congealed suet. I can just about get it around the idea of the Eldorado Network being the creation of a mad Spanish freelance who's too young to know better but I honestly can't find room for any Yanks or Ruskies. Sorry.'

'It's possible, though.'

'Anything's possible with Cabrillo. I wouldn't be surprised to discover that he's really the bastard son of Rudolf Hess by a lady flamenco dancer. That's how he learned Morse, you see: through playing the castanets. Ravel's "Bolero" is really the Italian Army Order of Battle. Which reminds me . . .' Templeton took a couple of sheets of paper from an outside pocket. 'He couldn't wait to start work. He says this is an urgent message from sub-agent Pinetree.'

They went inside and Garcia scanned the paper. 'Definitely not,' he said.

Templeton had found an armchair to sprawl in. 'Personally, I think it's rather good.' He allowed his eyes to close.

'Good? It's brilliant. Full marks for style, and I'm sure the Abwehr would love the content. What Hitler wants right now is fewer Allied convoys to Russia. Unfortunately, that may well happen.' Templeton opened his eyes. 'His U-boats are sinking our ships in the Atlantic like billyo, whatever billyo is,' Garcia said. 'Sinking them faster than we can build them. At this rate, we shall have to cut the Russian convoys whether we like it or not.'

'Ah. That's different.' Templeton made a supreme effort and stood up. 'Sherry? And then I really must go to bed. Which, incidentally, is what Luis and Julie did an hour ago. Ingenious young devil, isn't he?'

'He has a knack for stumbling on the truth.'

'He's going to hate you for killing it.'

'Oh no. He's going to hate *you* for killing it. Then I'll catch him on the rebound and he'll love me. I'm his case officer, Charles; I can't afford to let him hate me. Whereas you will soon be off to Lisbon. You are emotionally expendable.'

They went in search of sherry.

'Prune juice,' Templeton said. 'Remind me to tell you about prune juice.'

The MI5 report on Eldorado was wrong in one important respect. Wolfgang Adler had not murdered Brigadier Christian by strangulation, as he had told Luis Cabrillo. Adler had been convinced that he had killed the Brigadier. Later, an appropriate obituary notice had appeared in the Berlin newspapers. MI5 knew that a Brigadier Wagner had taken over as head of Madrid Abwehr. Christian's death seemed to have been confirmed on all sides, but in fact he was still alive. Adler had chosen the wrong way to kill him.

As a cause of death on the Russian Front in 1942, strangulation came well down the list. Those who died in action usually got shot or shelled. Those who died from other causes either froze or starved. Hardly anybody got throttled, whether by an enemy or by an angry friend. To do it properly you had to take your gloves off, which nobody wanted to do; and even so, it could be a lengthy business, making you a standing target for any third party with a rifle.

So, although Wolfgang Adler had witnessed death in many forms during his spell on the Russian Front, he had no experience of strangulation. When he had followed Brigadier Christian, chief of Madrid Abwehr, into the lavatories of the Lisbon embassy, smashed a large bottle of disinfectant over his head and (as he thought) strangled him with his tie, he had bungled the job. To begin with, a lot of blood streamed from Christian's head. It made Adler's fingers slippery. He tried to pick bits of broken glass off Christian's neck and shoulders, not wanting to cut himself, but his fingers were too slippery to grip the shards. He began to panic: at any moment someone might come in. He grabbed Christian's tie and tried to rip it off. That was a mistake: all he did was tighten the knot. And then his fingers were so greasy with blood that he couldn't unpick the knot. He rolled Christian on to his face, took one end of the tie in each hand, crossed the ends at the back of Christian's neck and heaved on them and kept on heaving until

20

all the strength had drained out of his arms through his fingers and he let go. Christian lay like a sack of wheat.

Still nobody had come in. Adler got up, washed his hands, dried them, went back to the basin and, unhurriedly, washed his face. The pool of blood around Christian's head was congealing. By this time Adler was irrationally confident that nobody would come in. He felt very sure of himself; he had done it. He combed his hair. He left.

When the door clicked shut, Christian staggered to his feet, lurched to the nearest cubicle and locked himself in. He felt faint. He had just enough strength to sit on the floor before he fell down. When he woke his head was resting against the toilet bowl and he knew he was about to be sick, so he made the most of the facilities. Perfectly normal, he told himself. You get hit on the head, you throw up. Correct response. His recent lunch smelled disgusting; he wondered why on earth he had eaten it. He flushed the toilet. The gushing waters sounded wonderfully clean and healthy, so he flushed the toilet again. He had an idea. Next time he flushed the toilet, he washed his face and neck in its rushing torrent and felt a lot better.

Christian was alive because he was strong and Adler was sloppy. If Adler had been better organized, he would have carried a knife or an axe and that would have been that. Instead he had improvised with a bottle of disinfectant which merely stunned Christian. He had come to just as Adler was fumbling and cursing at the knot of his tie. Christian kept his eyes shut. As Adler rolled him on to his face, he guessed what was coming and clutched a handful of his own shirt front and dragged it down. When Adler heaved on the ends of the tie, Christian's right arm took much of the strain. He also had unusually strong neck muscles. He had been an above-average athlete (discus, shot, wrestling) and he had kept fit; often, in the middle of a meeting, he would wander away from the table and do a quick dozen push-ups. Adler should have remembered that. When Adler started strangling, Christian's neck muscles were braced. Adler didn't notice. Christian couldn't keep up the resistance for long, and when Adler finally stood up, panting, he was semi-conscious. But only semi. Adler should have

21

rolled him over and tested his breathing or his pulse. Come to that, Adler should have used his own tie and damn the expense. But Adler was too impetuous, too sloppy, too disorganized.

After five minutes' deep breathing Christian felt strong enough to leave the lavatories. He reached the office of the embassy doctor without meeting any Abwehr staff and went straight into the examination room. The doctor, who had learned to be unsurprised by anything the Abwehr did, followed him.

'Lock the door,' Christian said. 'I'm dead. Murdered. Now I want you to get me on a plane to Berlin.'

'Sit down.' The doctor examined the pupils of his eyes and took his pulse. He had already noticed the patches of black blood matting Christian's hair. 'How were you killed?'

'Knocked out and strangled. Watch out for broken glass.' He winced as the doctor searched his scalp. 'What's that awful stink?'

'Disinfectant. You're soaked in it. Whoever killed you was very concerned not to contaminate the wound.'

Christian found that funny. He laughed so much that he reopened the cut. Eventually the doctor stitched it up. That evening Christian's coffin, packed with sandbags, was flown out of Lisbon. Christian was on the same plane, wearing a mask of bandages and carrying a passport that said he was Albert Meyer, fruit importer.

Next day he telephoned Abwehr headquarters. Admiral Canaris, its head, was not there but his second-in-command, General Oster was. Christian got through to Oster's secretary and after some insistence, bluff, threats, and the casual use of a few high-powered codewords, he got to speak to Oster himself. 'Good morning,' he said. 'Very sad news about Brigadier Christian.'

'Ah.' There was a signal lying on Oster's blotter. It had come from Madrid Abwehr and it said that Christian's body was being flown home for interment and would be held at Tempelhof airport mortuary, pending instructions. Nothing more. Oster had tried to telephone Madrid but the lines were down somewhere in France: Allied bombing or French sabotage, or maybe non-aligned mice. 'Sad indeed,' he said. 'You are perhaps a relative?'

22

'Very close. If you meet me beside the coffin in an hour perhaps we can discuss it.'

Christian was waiting at the airport mortuary when Oster arrived. Oster took his hat off. 'Might we be alone for a few minutes?' he asked the attendant. The man left them to their grief. 'I hope you won't be offended,' Oster said, 'if I ask to see your papers.'

'I can do better.' Christian unwound the bandages and gave his unshaven cheeks a vigorous massage. 'Sorry about the stubble, sir,' he said. 'Sorry about the secrecy, too. I'm afraid I didn't completely trust your telephone.'

Oster knew Christian; indeed he had recommended his promotion to brigadier. 'I'm glad you're not in this box,' he said. 'I thought I recognized your voice. Now what's going on?'

'It's all rather squalid,' Christian said. 'But in a nutshell, I believe that my Abwehr section has been infiltrated by the SD.'

The SD was the intelligence and espionage arm of the SS, the Nazi security service, which Heinrich Himmler controlled. In theory the SS and the SD were responsible only for the internal security of the Third Reich; that was why Himmler also had charge of the Gestapo. Military intelligence was a totally separate area. That was the Abwehr's responsibility. It was the Abwehr's job to run spies in foreign countries and to collect military intelligence for the German armed forces. But Himmler was the most ruthlessly ambitious of Hitler's ministers. He could never be satisfied with what he had. He wanted the Abwehr too. The rivalry between his SD and Admiral Canaris's Abwehr was an open secret. It was a small war within the big war.

Oster took a little stroll around the coffin and ended up where he began. 'I've always assumed the SD are constantly trying to penetrate us,' he said. 'God knows they hate our guts.'

'Hate is one thing. Attempted murder is another,' Christian said. 'The man the SD put into my section was on the verge of destroying my top agent in Britain, Eldorado. When he realized I knew what he was doing, he tried to kill me. In fact, he thinks he succeeded.'

'This wouldn't be Adler, would it?' Oster asked.

23

'Yes.' Christian, forgetting his stitches, scratched his head and winced. 'How did you know, sir?'

'Why didn't you have him arrested?'

'I thought of it. Then I thought: No, far better to see what he does next. Give the SD plenty of rope and maybe they'll hang themselves, and Adler too.'

'Mmm.' Oster, who was an inch or two shorter, stood on tiptoe to see the injury. 'Nasty . . . Well, Adler's beyond hanging, I'm afraid. Just after you phoned I had another signal from Madrid. Young Adler suffered a heart attack yesterday and passed away.'

'Heart attack?' Christian said. 'At thirty-one?'

'He was rash and impetuous. Perhaps he couldn't wait. What's in this box?'

'Sandbags. Good Spanish earth, soaked in good Spanish blood from the Civil War, I shouldn't be surprised.'

'I'll have those. They'll do my roses a power of good.'

Christian went to Abwehr headquarters in Oster's car, with the curtains closed. On the way they talked about how best to fight off the SD.

'You know, sir,' Christian said, 'when I think of the sheer volume of intelligence we've been getting out of the Eldorado Network, and the shining quality, then I'm appalled the SD should try to destroy it. I mean, that's nothing short of treachery.'

'Himmler doesn't think so. Himmler thinks our existence is a kind of treachery.'

'What on earth does the man want?' Christian asked. Occasionally a whiff of disinfectant crossed his nostrils, and the phrase 'Death in Madrid' passed through his mind like the name of some absurd new perfume. 'The Party can't run *everything*.'

'Who says? It does in Russia.'

'Very badly, by all reports. Anyway, military intelligence is no job for a bunch of Party hacks. It needs imagination, flair, quick wits.'

'I wish I could say they were stupid,' Oster said. 'That's the trouble with the SD: they're not at all stupid, they're bloody clever and they catch a lot of spies, real spies. The SD's got so many people inside the Resistance movements, they make them look like Swiss cheese. I've got some hard types working for me, but . . .' Oster sniffed. 'Madrid isn't the only Abwehr station the SD has broken into,' he said. 'Brussels, Brest, Oslo, Paris, Hamburg. We kick them out, but it never stops.'

Christian nodded. He didn't care what happened to Abwehr Brest. Only a month ago, one of his reports from Nutmeg, an Eldorado sub-agent, got mistakenly routed by teleprinter to Brest instead of to Berlin. Brest pinched it and claimed it as their own work. The SD could have Abwehr Brest, as far as Christian was concerned. 'I'm sure Admiral Canaris gives as good as he gets,' he said.

Oster seemed to find this simple remark very encouraging. He gave a smile of huge enjoyment that energized his face until he looked like a middle-aged baby in the middle of a damn good breast-feed. 'Canaris holds a fistful of aces,' he said. 'He knows what Hitler likes. Hitler likes spies, and we've got the best. As long as the Abwehr can tell Hitler what's happening on the other side of the hill, the Abwehr's safe, believe me.'

They drove into the basement garage of Abwehr headquarters and took the lift to the top floor. Oster had the keys to a spacious apartment. 'The kitchen's well stocked,' he said. 'Stay inside. And don't shave. I like you like that. Terribly tough.' He went out and locked the door.

Christian made himself an omelette and drank a bottle of beer. He spent the afternoon on the balcony, enjoying the view and the crisp, bright weather. For dinner there was an excellent goulash and an apple tart. There was even some Spanish wine; a tangy Rioja. Had Oster arranged all this specially for him? Christian liked to think so. He went to bed, relaxed and content.

Admiral Canaris and General Oster came in as he was having breakfast.

'My dear Christian!' Canaris said. They shook hands. 'Madrid sent us a signal saying you were dead.' He gave Christian the piece of paper. 'You might like to have it framed. Hang it in the lavatory as a conversation piece.'

Christian tucked the signal into his dressing-gown pocket. 'From now on, I plan to stay out of lavatories as much as possible, sir.'

'Very wise. Oster says you got brained with a bottle.'

Christian nodded. 'Disinfectant.'

'I know exactly how you feel, only in my case it was champagne.' Canaris touched a small white scar above his left eye. 'The work of a jealous husband. The poor man was insane with rage, which is just as well because if he had stopped to think he would have used a steak knife on me.'

'You were in a restaurant?' Oster asked.

'The Tour d'Argent, in Paris. Why?'

'Oh . . . I just wondered who paid for the champagne, that's all.'

'Oster is enormously practical,' Canaris told Christian. 'After I've done something he tells me whether or not it's possible, the man's invaluable, without Oster I'd be helpless.' He lifted the coffee pot and found it empty.

'Who did pay?' Oster asked.

'She did. Famous actress, worth millions. Besides, I was unconscious. Splendid fellow,' he said as Oster carried the coffee pot into the kitchen.

Christian was amused by the Admiral's chatter and impressed by his suit, which was grey flannel, double-breasted, sleekly tailored. Canaris seemed to him enviably polished and elegant, not like a sailor at all, too slim, his face too lively, his voice too rich and varied. He made Christian feel like a scruff; but a favourite scruff. 'I've been thinking about that bottle of disinfectant,' Christian said. 'It doesn't seem quite right.'

'You're right, it doesn't. And I'll tell you something else . . .' Canaris ate a piece of sliced salami. 'I've been thinking about the lavatory, and that seems all wrong.'

'Too public,' Christian said.

'Far too public.'

26

'Unless, of course, Adler didn't plan it, he just acted spontaneously. Impetuously.'

'That's even worse.'

'I agree, sir. But I think it's what happened: Adler saw his chance and grabbed the nearest weapon. Whereas if he'd used his brains and done it properly, he'd have hit me with the marble ashtray next to the hand-basins and I wouldn't be here now.'

'Big ashtray?'

'Like a soup bowl.'

'Ah.' Canaris touched the scar on his forehead with the tip of his little finger. 'I didn't really get this from a champagne bottle, you know. I just said that to tease Oster. I fell down a companionway when I was a midshipman. So the question is . . .' Oster came in with a fresh pot of coffee. 'What is the question, Oster?'

'Was Adler really working for the SD, and if so why did they let him make such a hash of a simple murder, and if not who was he working for and why did they kill him, since he obviously didn't die of a heart attack?'

'No, no, no. That's not the question at all.' Canaris took a cup of coffee and perched on the arm of a settee. 'I mean, it might be the second, third, or fourth question but it's not the first. The first question is why did the SD – assuming Adler was working for the SD – want Christian dead? What were they hoping to achieve?'

Christian opened his mouth to speak and then decided to eat a piece of toast instead. He had been going to say that Adler's purpose was to discredit the Eldorado Network, which had been his, Christian's, creation. But of course, Eldorado wouldn't go out of operation just because its creator died. Christian felt a slight flush of shame at his own vanity, and hid behind his napkin.

'Suppose,' Oster said, 'just suppose that we've been misreading the SD's motives. Perhaps they weren't acting from rivalry or professional jealousy, you know. Just knocking us down to make them look bigger. Perhaps they're scared of something that Eldorado is reporting.'

Canaris rolled his eyes until they looked at the ceiling. 'Well,' he said.

Christian waited, but apparently that word was both the beginning and the end. 'Doesn't seem very likely, does it?' Christian said. 'I can't imagine Eldorado's stuff making anyone sweat in the SD.'

'I can,' Canaris said.

'So can I,' Oster said. 'Remember Hasselmann?'

The name rang a faint, cracked bell in Christian's memory. He thought hard. Arno Hasselmann. Some sort of scandal in . . . Where was it? Denmark? Belgium? 'Hasselmann the Gauleiter?' he said.

'Hasselmann the ex-Deputy Gauleiter. He shot himself six months ago in Rotterdam.'

'Yes, of course. Some sort of scandal. He'd been taking bribes.'

'Oh, they all take bribes,' Canaris said. 'Bribes don't count any more.'

'It was what he was doing with the money,' Oster said. 'Nobody minded if he wanted to dress up in women's silk underwear, I'm told it's very comfortable, but he shouldn't have collected such a harem of pretty blond Dutch boys. It was unpatriotic. There are still plenty of good-looking blond German lads available.'

'You know how people gossip,' Canaris said. 'It even reached the Japanese embassy in Helsinki. One of our Swedish agents mentioned it in a signal. The SD were furious when they heard about that. It made them look so stupid, you see. They can't stand looking stupid. Terribly sensitive lot, the SD. They'd have shot the agent if they could.'

'Eldorado hasn't reported anything remotely like that,' Christian said.

'I know. Oster has been up all night, going through the files. Which leads us to examine Theory B.'

'Theory B,' Oster said, 'is that Adler did not bash you over the head on orders from his masters in the SD, but panicked for reasons we may never know.'

'But if the SD didn't know what he was up to,' Christian said, 'why did they kill him?'

'Right first time,' Canaris said. 'So out of the window goes

28

Theory B. Theory C says that Adler penetrated Madrid Abwehr on behalf of the SD but then got mixed up with yet another organization. The Czechs have an excellent network in Spain, for instance.' He meant the Czech government-in-exile. 'And the Poles. Plus the Italians. Not to mention the Hungarians. But of course you know all this.'

'Adler wasn't the sort of man to let himself be recruited by a foreign agency,' Christian said. 'I never liked him, but he was a thorough-going patriot, I'll grant him that. Loyal to the core.'

'Why have the Hungarians got spies in Spain?' Oster asked. 'They're supposed to be on our side.'

Canaris blinked sadly. 'Fish gotta swim, birds gotta fly,' he said. 'Hungarians gotta steal secrets. It's in their blood. Why didn't you like Adler?' he asked Christian.

'It was nothing personal, Admiral, at least not on my part. Adler became strangely jealous of Eldorado.' Christian rubbed his jaw: the two-day growth itched. 'It affected his work, I had to step in and tell him not to be so stupid.' Christian suddenly wondered: Did I miss something? Adler was no fool. What could I have missed?

'Jealous,' Canaris murmured. 'How curious.'

'Especially as Eldorado's in England,' Oster said.

'What I meant was,' Christian said, 'jealous of his success.'

Canaris said, 'It doesn't sound right, does it? If the SD infiltrated Adler into Madrid Abwehr, they'd want him to work hard and be trusted, not sit around brooding and sulking. Did he brood and sulk?'

'Oh, endlessly.' A tiny idea formed at the back of Christian's mind and rapidly grew. 'Well . . . not endlessly. He was quite perky a week or two ago, but that was because he thought he'd found something not quite right in the Eldorado Network.'

'Indeed?' Canaris said. 'What, exactly?'

'One of the sub-agents. Adler reckoned he was faking his intelligence.'

'Which one?'

'Damned if I can remember,' Christian said miserably. 'There are ten or a dozen in the Network. Adler mentioned several names

29

but only one that he could make any case against, and frankly I wasn't paying much attention. I had more important things on my mind, and now this bang on the head hasn't done my memory any good, so . . .' He shrugged, and busied himself with the last of his coffee. When he glanced up, Canaris and Oster were looking at each other.

'It's what I would do if I were running the SD,' Oster said.

'What?' Christian asked.

'Infiltrate the Eldorado Network,' Canaris told him. 'What if Adler discovered that an Eldorado sub-agent is working for the SD? He tries to tell you but you send him away. Why would you do that? Adler can't make sense of it. Then he suddenly thinks: maybe *you*, Christian, are on the SD payroll too! So now Adler is in real trouble, big danger, because *you* know that *he* knows. So he kills you. Or does his best.'

'I see,' Christian said. 'And who then kills Adler? The SD?'

Canaris unexpectedly laughed. 'You're right. We end up with an SD man behind every lamppost. Absurd.' He looked at his watch. 'I'm late. Look here: don't give yourself a headache, but . . . try to remember that name.'

They left. Christian lay on a couch and told his brain to project that name on to the ceiling. It projected many names, including those of pretty adolescent girlfriends he had not thought of in twenty years; but not the name he wanted.

It was snowing in Madrid.

The snow clouds had hustled down from the Bay of Biscay until they hit the Guadarrama mountains and began to dump their load. Nearby Madrid, set in the high plateau of New Castile, rapidly turned white and, in the diplomatic district, the German embassy at No. 8 Calle de Fortuny got rather more than its share.

Brigadier Wagner stood on the balcony of the third-floor office he had taken over when Abwehr HQ in Berlin sent him to succeed Brigadier Christian. Wagner let the snow blow through the door and speckle the carpet. Flakes settled on his cheeks, his brow, his eyelids; he opened his mouth and tasted the snow on his tongue.

Good stuff, crisp and clean. The skiing in the mountains would be excellent tomorrow. He was fit, he'd exercised regularly, and he had a new pair of skis, given to him on his last trip to Berlin by a cousin, a major who ran a unit that tested equipment for mountain troops. Wagner flexed his knees and swayed. Snowflakes pelted his face. In his imagination he was skiing like the wind.

Behind him, voices mumbled and somebody coughed. Bloody Eldorado, Wagner thought. The only thing that stands between me and a week in the mountains is bloody Eldorado. He went inside and closed the window. 'Anything new come in?' he asked.

'Nothing, sir, I'm afraid,' said Otto Krafft.

'Damn. What the hell's happened to him?' Wagner took the chair at the head of the table. 'He's never done this before, has he?' He waved at the others to sit. 'I've got better things to do than hang around waiting for Eldorado to deliver.'

'Yes, sir?' Dr Hartmann said.

The others looked at him. Hartmann was small and wore rimless spectacles and he had never been known to laugh. If he smiled it was a thoughtful smile, as if someone had misplaced a decimal point and thus made a tiny unintentional joke. He was the section's technical expert, very good on things like radar and torque and low-temperature lubricants, but it was not like him to ask slightly provocative questions of the new boss.

'What d'you mean, "yes sir"?' Wagner said gently.

'What do I mean?' Hartmann nudged the papers in front of him, squaring them off. 'My apologies. I assumed you were about to tell us what better things there are to be done.'

'Well, you've all been here longer than I have. What d'you suggest?'

'I suggest, sir,' said Otto Krafft, 'that we sit tight for another forty-eight hours. I mean, there's no need to panic yet.'

'I wouldn't dream of it,' Wagner said. 'But when the need arrives I hope we shall all panic together, as one man. Teamwork counts, in panic as in all things, don't you agree?' They grinned dutifully and were glad when he ended the meeting and went skiing. Too snide by half.

31

*

'Eldorado has been silent for the best part of a week,' Freddy Garcia said. 'Madrid Abwehr must be very worried. It's essential we send them something meaty, damn quick.'

'I'm flying out to Lisbon tonight,' Templeton said. 'I'll take it.'

'Good,' Luis grunted. 'You can write it too. What are these?'

'English pork sausages,' Julie said.

Luis cut one open and sniffed it. 'A holy miracle!' he announced. 'The pork has turned to bread!'

'Have some bacon,' Templeton suggested. 'I think you'll find it attractively pork-flavoured.'

Luis took quite a lot of bacon and plenty of scrambled egg and began eating. 'Scrumptious!' he said. 'Yippee. Or is it yummy?' He looked at Garcia.

'Yummy for grub, yippee for general high spirits.'

'And yarooh?'

'Yarooh indicates pain or dismay.'

'No, no,' Templeton said. 'Surely it's cripes for dismay.'

'Blimey!' Luis said. 'Or do I mean crikey?'

'He's been reading *The Adventures of Billy Bunter at Greyfriars School*,' Julie said. 'They all talk in code. That's what appeals to him.'

'A classic of English literature,' Templeton said. 'It's stiff with over-eating, beatings, and hero-worship. I'm surprised it's not a bestseller in Germany.'

'Pass the butter,' Luis said.

There was a fairly brittle silence while he buttered some toast. Templeton picked up crumbs with his fingertip and examined them for dangerous political tendencies. Garcia watched him, ready to offer a second opinion if asked. Luis munched.

'Maybe this wasn't such a hot idea,' Julie said, 'coming to England.' They all looked. 'I mean, if he's going to be permanently bloody temperamental about his work, I might just go home to the States.'

She got up from the table and walked to the window. A little

32

sunshine was leaking in, cautiously, as if this might be the wrong room. It touched her long black hair and found shades of the deepest red in it. Her hands were plunged in the patch pockets of her skirt and when she turned her face to the sky, she looked twenty-four going on sixteen. Luis, secretly watching her, remembered the first impression she had made on him, long ago in Madrid. With people milling around her, she had seemed to him totally calm and in control, like a leopard among some gazelle. She still did. He envied that strength.

'Is it OK if I take a walk?' she asked.

'Yes, of course it's OK,' Garcia said. 'Stay inside the estate, won't you? There's miles and miles of walks. You might find some chestnuts. We could roast them after dinner.'

Luis cleared his throat. 'The British must be in a pitiful condition if they have to scavenge for nuts.' He switched his glance from Garcia to Templeton and back.

'Nice touch,' Templeton said.

'I like it!' Garcia said. 'Let's use it. Let's use it today! Where d'you want to work? The library? Good. Splendid. Let's go.'

Brigadier Wagner came back to Madrid after some very satisfactory skiing. He was tanned, clear-eyed, five pounds lighter, and thoroughly at peace with himself. Now, as he rode up in the lift to his office on the seventh floor, he was looking forward to having his staff on the carpet and, when they admitted failure, pulling the carpet from beneath their feet for the pleasure of watching them bounce on their backsides. Then Richard Fischer met him and spoiled everything.

'Eldorado has delivered,' Fischer said. 'He's had flu. That's why we didn't hear from him. It's a big report, one of his biggest. Nearly all his network is involved – Seagull, Knickers, Pinetree, Nutmeg, the lot. We're still working on it.'

Fischer was a lanky, sandy-haired ex-journalist who had suffered under many editors; he was ready to smile if Wagner did; until then he kept his serious professional face.

Wagner took off his coat. 'My office,' he said. 'The whole team.' Already he had forgotten his disappointment.

The gang trooped in and sat down: Fischer, followed by Otto Krafft, a trim, pleasant-looking, youngish man who was so blond that his eyebrows seemed almost silver; Franz Werth, pudgy in plus-fours and a cardigan; and Dr Hartmann, the jacket of his dark blue suit thoroughly buttoned from top to bottom. All carried files and bundles of paper and large yellow legal notepads.

'So,' Wagner said. 'What's new?'

'The Yanks are restless,' Richard Fischer began.

'That's not new,' Wagner scoffed. 'All Americans are congenitally restless. They can't sit still for five minutes.'

'Ah.' It was a tight, clipped sound: a note of punctuation. Fischer closed his file. He put his pen away. He sat back and looked at Otto Krafft.

'The French are suspicious,' Otto said. He waited three seconds, until Wagner's mouth opened, and then added: 'But there's nothing new about that either.'

'As for the Canadians,' Franz Werth said, 'the Canadians are far from happy.' He cleared his throat. 'As usual,' he said.

'The Russians,' Dr Hartmann announced. 'What can one say about the Russians that has not been said before?' He made a weak, middle-aged gesture of despair. 'Greedy and grasping, grasping and greedy.'

Brigadier Wagner smiled. He had a good smile but it did nothing to these men. They sat and looked. None moved. There was nothing challenging or even questioning in their attitudes. They simply occupied their places and waited.

'So this is what the great Eldorado report amounts to,' Wagner said, still smiling. He had been down a similar alley years before when he had been an amateur actor and the entire cast had taken a severe dislike to the director. At rehearsals, everyone did everything slightly wrong. The director raged, sulked and finally quit. Wagner learned then that even in a dictatorship you must lead by consent. He had forgotten this and they had now reminded him. 'Tell me, Richard,' he said, 'exactly how are the Yanks betraying their restlessness?'

34

'Oh . . .' Fischer flicked through a few pages. 'It's probably not . . . I expect Pinetree just . . . I mean, this sort of thing's happened before often enough, hasn't it, Franz?'

'Pinetree is like Nutmeg,' Franz Werth said. 'He sings beautifully but on one note only.'

'Same with Hambone,' Otto Krafft remarked. 'Hambone's on a par with Nutmeg, really.'

'Seagull too,' Dr Hartmann said.

'Oh well . . .' Fischer studied the ceiling. 'We all know about Seagull, don't we?'

'I sometimes wonder,' Dr Hartmann said, 'if Seagull hasn't got more in common with Pinetree than Nutmeg.'

'I think I know what you mean,' Krafft said. 'I know just what you mean.'

Werth raised a finger. 'In a sense,' he suggested, 'would it not be true to say that Seagull is to Pinetree as Nutmeg is to . . . Haystack?'

'Haystack,' Fischer said. 'Haystack. Now there's a thought. Haystack.'

Brigadier Wagner said, 'Refresh my memory. Which sub-agent is Haystack?'

They looked at each other, as if wondering who was best qualified to answer such a tricky question. Eventually, Franz Werth half-raised his hand. 'Yes?' Wagner said.

'He's the one in London,' Werth said. Fischer nodded.

Wagner felt his temper start to smoke, so he took it for a slow walk around the room. 'So is Pinetree,' he said. 'Isn't he?'

'West London,' Werth said. 'Pinetree is in west London. Haystack is in *north* London.'

'I have a map of London,' Werth offered. 'If it would help.'

'This is all very entertaining,' Wagner said, 'but it does nothing to help bring nearer the victory of the German nation, does it? Furthermore, I need hardly remind you that you are commissioned officers in the German Army, subject to military discipline and bound by the oaths of loyalty and allegiance to the Führer.' He let that sink in. 'Now then, Fischer, you were telling me about the American attitude.'

Fischer gave his notes a quick glance. 'Eldorado has forwarded a report from Pinetree, who is a British civilian employed by the US embassy,' he said. 'Pinetree says a major disagreement is taking place between the commanders of the American and the British armed forces. In brief, the Americans want to get on with the war but the British say it's far too early to start operations in Europe.'

Wagner raised a finger. 'Sounds like the usual high-level bickering,' he said. 'What difference does it make to us? Surely that's the question.'

'Eldorado says Pinetree says the Americans are worried sick about the war in the Pacific. The Japanese seem unstoppable. They've captured virtually everything north of Australia except Guadalcanal, and the battle for Guadalcanal is ferocious. So the Americans in London are saying . . .' Fischer read aloud from his notes: 'Quote: *If we're not gonna fight in Europe then for Chrissake let's go help our buddies in the Pacific,* unquote.'

'The Russians won't like that,' Dr Hartmann said.

'Pinetree also sent us a lot of stuff about the North African invasion,' Fischer said. 'Sundry cock-ups and disasters at sea: capsized American landing-craft, collisions between British and American warships, et cetera. The sort of thing nobody wants to repeat in a hurry. It all reinforces the Pacific-versus-Europe argument.'

'Right,' Brigadier Wagner said. 'Fine, good, splendid. Now what is the gist of the French discontent, Otto? And who says so?'

'Donkey is the main informant, sir,' Krafft said, 'with Wallpaper backing him up.' He saw Wagner furrow his brows and said, 'Donkey's the Belfast telephone engineer and Wallpaper is the pansy lecturer at Birmingham University. He fancies Frenchmen.'

'Are there a lot of Frenchmen at Birmingham?'

'A full division in the area, Eldorado says. Twenty thousand.'

'Ah.' Wagner's brow cleared. '*Embarras de richesses,* as they probably never say in Birmingham. Twenty thousand . . . I hope Wallpaper isn't exhausting himself on our behalf.'

'He keeps tremendously fit, sir. Gymnastics, water polo, even rugby football.'

Wagner sniffed. 'I have my doubts about grown men who scamper about in their underwear and grapple so enthusiastically.'

'No doubts about Wallpaper, sir. He's as bent as a fiddler's elbow. I suppose that's why he's interested in French politics.'

'And he's sent us the latest de Gaulle anecdote,' Wagner said.

Krafft was surprised. 'As a matter of fact, Wallpaper did send us a new de Gaulle joke . . . Um . . . Here it is: What is the difference between Napoleon and General de Gaulle?' He glanced at the others.

'All right, tell us,' Wagner said.

'Napoleon is the small one,' Krafft said.

'That's not very funny,' Richard Fischer complained.

'I never said it was funny,' Krafft told him, 'I said it was a British joke. You know what the British are like. They're all convinced they have a great sense of humour, but in fact they only laugh at bodily functions.'

'What – sex?' Werth asked.

'Certainly not,' Krafft said. 'Bowel movements. The British find defecation irresistibly funny.'

'What an extraordinary race,' Werth said.

'Oh, I don't know,' Dr Hartmann said. 'It offers them the chance of a healthy guffaw once a day.'

'So de Gaulle is unpopular in England,' Brigadier Wagner said firmly.

'Yes, sir. Also in France, parts of Algeria and Tunisia, Syria, French West Africa, and various other outposts of the French Empire,' Krafft said. 'Senior officers on de Gaulle's staff have opened their hearts to Wallpaper. They share a common interest in good wine, apparently. He reports that de Gaulle is determined to lead the liberation of France and become its new ruler, but others disagree.'

'Where does Donkey come into all this?' Wagner asked. 'He's in Northern Ireland, isn't he?'

'That's where the disagreement is, sir. A lot of French troops refuse to take orders from de Gaulle – so many, in fact, that the British have sent them to Northern Ireland to avoid trouble. Donkey listens in to their telephone conversations. He says the French are too busy arguing with their allies and with each other to fight us. For instance, most of them are disgusted that they weren't included in the invasion of Tunisia and Algeria. Donkey says it's all France to them and they think Churchill's trying to steal it. What's more, a lot of them say they won't get involved in any attack on the south of France because that's not Occupied Europe, it's Vichy France; the Vichy government's entitled to defend it and who wants Frenchmen fighting Frenchmen?'

'Logical,' Wagner said.

'The Russians won't like it,' Dr Hartmann said.

Wagner sniffed. 'Everyone else has to put up with the idiocy of the French, so why not the Russians? Thank you, Otto. Who's next?'

'I've got a lot more, sir,' Otto said. 'The French in Britain are so unhappy about food rationing that they've taken to collecting chestnuts to supplement their diet but this has brought them into conflict with the natives, who want the nuts for themselves.'

'Splendid,' Wagner said. 'Nothing like fighting over a handful of nuts to work up an appetite. Now then, Franz. Canada frets. Why?'

Werth shuffled his papers and blinked a bit. 'Unlike the French confusion, the Canadian dilemma is remarkably clear-cut, sir. They had one disaster at Dieppe, they don't want another like it, and if the British War Office keeps insisting, then the Canadian troops may well mutiny.'

'More dissension in the ranks,' Wagner murmured. 'How encouraging . . . Mind you, I wouldn't be sorry to see a few more Dieppes. As raids go, it was a large and self-inflicted wound.'

Fischer said, 'The Canadian force suffered seventy-five per cent losses, so I heard. A very bloody nose.'

'Knickers puts the figure even higher,' Werth said. 'Knickers reckons that half the survivors who got back to England were totally useless after that.'

Wagner said, 'Knickers is . . . ?'

'A travelling salesman in soft drinks,' Werth said. 'Lemonades and ginger beers and the like. He visits a lot of army camps in the south of England. Knickers says that many Canadians have deserted, following rumours that a similar raid is being planned. As a result, crime has increased – burglary, theft, hold-ups – because even deserters have to eat. Knickers himself was robbed by Canadian deserters only last week.'

'Good God!' Wagner said. 'Not hurt, I hope?'

'No, no. They took his wallet. Fifty pounds.'

'Be sure he gets repaid out of expenses.'

'Yes, sir. Knickers also reports that Canadian units are being isolated as much as possible to avoid contact with British troops so that their morale will not suffer from accounts of the Dieppe shambles. This follows a severe fall in recruiting for commando units.'

'The Russians won't like that,' Dr Hartmann said.

'Your Russians don't seem to like anything very much, Doctor,' said Wagner.

'They are consistent in that respect, sir. What they want is an offensive in the west. Preferably several offensives. Virtually all the war – all the land war, certainly – is being fought in the east. The Russians want their allies to take some of the pressure off them. Eldorado has a more or less direct line to the Kremlin in the form of sub-agent Seagull. Seagull is a foreman in Liverpool docks and a lifelong Communist. Unless the British and the American Armies start fighting in Europe soon, Seagull says there will be Communist-led strikes in Liverpool docks and elsewhere. Seagull's analysis is short and sharp: Stalin is running out of men, munitions, and, above all, patience.'

'If Stalin tries to bully the Yanks, they'll turn their backs on him,' Richard Fischer remarked.

'The French can't agree on a leader, let alone a plan,' Otto Krafft said.

'You know where the Canadians stand,' Franz Werth added. 'Well to the rear.'

'Thank you, gentlemen,' Brigadier Wagner said. 'I feel sure

39

that Berlin will read this latest bulletin from Eldorado with great interest.'

They got up and filed out, but Wagner signalled to Fischer to stay. 'Tell me,' he said. 'Why should a dedicated English Communist docker like Seagull give intelligence to the Abwehr?'

'That's simple, sir,' Fischer explained. 'Eldorado told him he's working for the Communist Czech Resistance.'

Wagner nodded. 'I knew there was a reason. I just wanted to know what it was.'

Down the corridor, Krafft and Werth were watching Dr Hartmann make coffee. 'The old bastard seemed pretty pleased at the end,' Krafft said.

'So he should be,' Werth said.

'Rubbish!' Hartmann snapped. 'What's there to be pleased about?' His spectacles misted in steam from the electric kettle and he growled in annoyance.

'Well . . . for a start, the Wehrmacht can relax in the west,' Krafft said. 'The enemy doesn't seem to know whether he's coming or going, does he?'

Dr Hartmann polished his spectacles on the large silk handkerchief he kept in his breast pocket. His face was compressed into a grimace that almost closed his eyes. The other two men were a soft, wavering blur. 'So it seems *on the surface*,' he said, 'everyone arguing, nobody agreeing. But what is the subject of all the argument?' He put his glasses on. Krafft and Werth sprang into sharp relief. They looked puzzled. 'Heavens above!' he said. 'If you were the enemy, how would you define your intentions?'

'Hostile,' Werth said lamely. 'I suppose.'

'De Gaulle wants to attack. The Americans want to attack. The British want to make commando raids. And the Russians don't give a damn who does what as long as someone does something aggressive soon. If Eldorado's intelligence means anything, it means we'd better reinforce our western defences and do it *now*.'

Richard Fischer came in. 'I heard that,' he said. 'For Christ's sake don't tell the Brigadier. He's just promised us all promotion. Provided.'

'Provided what?' Otto Krafft asked.

'Provided we recruit another Eldorado and install him in England.' Fischer took a sugar-cube and chewed it, noisily and cheerfully. 'Or better yet, two Eldorados.' They were all gazing at him in amazement. 'Thus making three in all. One on, one spare, and one in the wash. Just like army socks.'

The air-raid sirens wailed as Admiral Canaris's car made its way across Berlin, and his driver glanced over his shoulder. Canaris gave a small, weary gesture: go on. There were so many air-raid warnings nowadays that people often ignored them. 'Probably just a couple of photo-reconnaissance Mosquitoes,' Oster said. 'We can't allow the RAF to disturb your funeral, can we, Christian?'

Christian said nothing. He was glad of his beard, for it hid his expression. He felt uneasy. He had eaten no breakfast and his stomach rumbled like a bowling alley; he hoped the noise of the car muffled it but worrying made him even more uneasy. Going to your own funeral should be a joke. Oster was certainly amused. Canaris was distant, preoccupied.

It was Canaris who had pointed out that Christian had been declared dead for some time now and the SD might think it odd that he had not been buried. So the Madrid coffin had been found; appropriate notices had been put in the Berlin papers; and here they all were, on their way to pay him their last respects.

It was a pleasant day, with more sun than cloud and a taste of oncoming spring in the air. That, too, didn't seem right; somehow Christian had always pictured himself being lowered into the ground on a grim and blustery day, with a knot of close friends clustered together in silent grief. Instead, to his shocked surprise, a small army of Prussian guardsmen was drawn up at the graveside.

Christian took in the crisp uniforms, the gleaming leather, the glittering buttons. 'Was all this really necessary?' he whispered to Oster.

'You Navy types don't appreciate a good funeral,' Oster said. 'You just wrap him in his hammock and slide him over the side. We send the chap off in style.'

Muffled drums began a distant throb and the coffin came in

41

sight, borne on the shoulders of slow-marching soldiers. They took for ever to arrive. Christian's stomach had ceased rumbling and was setting like cement. He saw his dress-cap resting on the coffin, and his decorations – how on earth did they get hold of those? – and a wreath as big as a lifebelt, and next to it, winking in the sunlight, a bronze plaque with his full name engraved on it. Christian couldn't take any more. He shut his eyes. He heard gruff orders, stated rather than shouted, and after much shuffling the chaplain began to speak. Christian opened his eyes and looked up, and there, far away and very high, was a great formation of silvery aircraft. They had to be American, almost certainly Flying Fortresses. At that height they looked like tiny fish, a school of extremely well-drilled minnows all holding their places in the current. The engines created a soft, sensuous rumble.

Canaris said a few words, praising a career which sounded very ordinary to Christian until he realized that it was his own. Then the riflemen did their bit. They aimed at the sky and Christian had the silly idea that they were trying to shoot down his immortal soul before it reached heaven. The volley banged. Firing squad, Christian thought. Does the victim hear the rifles that kill him? Probably not. Who cares, anyway?

More orders. Christ, would this business never end? A bugler stepped forward and began to write his musical signature in the calm air, just as the grunt of remote explosions reached them. Christian saw a thin, black curve of smoke that must have come from a dying Fortress and he thought: Oh well, the bugler's efforts aren't completely wasted.

He followed Canaris and Oster and threw a handful of earth into the hole. His hand felt black and sticky; his face felt white and sweaty. As he turned away, Oster took his arm. 'We all come to it in the end, old chap,' he said softly.

'I feel such a fool.' Christian got out his handkerchief and wiped his hands and blew his nose. 'I haven't done anything and yet I'm exhausted.'

'You haven't died. That's an achievement. Any fool can die, it's easy. Not dying is a full-time job. Very demanding.'

The car rushed them smoothly and quietly back to the centre of the city. Christian relaxed and watched the fire engines charging in the opposite direction, their crews hanging on like sailors in a storm. The excitement had made him drowsy, and when Oster shook him awake, the car was stopped outside a restaurant. 'On this special occasion,' Canaris said, 'I felt that we all deserved a good funeral breakfast.'

Christian forced a smile. The last thing he wanted was food. But his appetite returned as soon as they were shown into a private room and he smelled *sauerbraten mit knödel*, his favourite dish when he was a boy. Fresh crusty bread was put on the table; he ate a fragment and found that he was hungry. A good Rhine wine was poured; he drank a little when Oster proposed some absurd toast and the lightly chilled, slightly dry liquid went down like a glorious salute to all the good things of life. It was perfect for the smoked trout, too.

'Simple food is best,' Admiral Canaris said. 'The less fuss, the more taste. The French never know when to stop.'

'And the English never know how to start,' Christian said.

That amused them, and from then on the conversation flowed freely. Christian's stomach gratefully accepted all donations; he felt sure of himself again, so sure that he chose *rahmschnitzel mit champignons* instead of *sauerbraten*. The wine was a delicate rosé from Provence.

'The French get some things right, sir,' he said.

Canaris smiled and proposed a toast. 'To the truth!' he said. 'Always supposing it exists, that is.' They touched glasses.

'Did you see the uninvited guest at your ceremony?' Oster asked. Christian shook his head. 'An SD man was trying to resemble a tombstone, without much success,' Oster told him. 'The chief spotted him at once.'

'They follow me everywhere,' Canaris remarked, not complaining.

'That's outrageous, sir,' Christian said.

'Is it? I suppose it is. I find it oddly reassuring to be outraged. At least they think I'm still dangerous.'

'Any man with a fully functioning brain is dangerous to them,' Oster said cheerfully.

'Himmler disapproves of original thought,' Canaris said. 'He wants to make it illegal; then his Gestapo would have a field-day. They'd hang everybody who couldn't prove he was a congenital idiot.'

They laughed; although Christian wondered whether or not it was such a joke. 'How does an idiot prove he's an idiot?' he asked.

'It's not easy,' Oster said. 'You have to be very, very clever.'

Canaris glanced sideways at Oster. 'But not too clever,' he said. 'That would be really idiotic.'

It was a mild rebuke. Christian sensed it, if he didn't understand it. Oster had the shadow of a strangely impish expression, but he said nothing. He took a piece of bread, tore it in half, fitted the halves together.

'Anyway,' Canaris said, 'Hitler admires brains. He likes arguments.'

Oster poured more wine. 'Wouldn't it be more accurate to say that he likes others to have arguments? So that he can play A against B, and C against both of them, and wind up doing what he wanted to do in the first place?'

The restaurant owner came in with a cherry tart and some cheeses, and went away.

Christian said, 'It's a great pity everyone can't stop arguing and backbiting and just unite to get on with the job.'

'No cream,' Canaris pointed out. 'War is hell.'

'It's not quite as simple as that,' Oster told Christian. 'First you must define the job.'

Christian was surprised. 'Well . . . winning the war, obviously, sir.'

'Which war?' Canaris asked. He was serving the cherry tart. 'And how do you define success?'

'Perhaps I'm very stupid, sir, but there's only one war that I can see.'

'Come, come, old chap,' Oster said, 'you don't really believe that. Look: when we went into Poland, it was a completely different war from what we're fighting now. Everything has changed since then. Everything. Utterly changed.'

44

'Germany hasn't changed,' Christian insisted. 'We're all fighting for the Reich.'

Oster found a cherry-stone and used his tongue to work it on to the bowl of his spoon. 'That's an interesting idea,' he said. 'We must talk more about it at some time.'

'I would agree with you that the Reich must be defended,' Admiral Canaris said. 'We in the Abwehr must be aware and alert. We owe it to—' he patted his lips with his napkin, — 'to the German people.'

'Did you know, for instance,' Oster said, 'that a couple of months after we invaded Poland, we were *that* close' – he snapped his fingers – 'to an Army coup?' Christian's mouth was full, which saved him from answering. 'Some of our more old-fashioned generals, and a few marshals too, disliked what we were doing in Poland. Not so much the fact as the style. Poor taste, they thought. Not the way a gentleman behaves. Do what you like to soldiers, but women and children . . . The way some of our Action Groups behaved was pure self-indulgence. Were you there?'

Christian swallowed. 'No,' he said.

'I was,' Canaris said. 'Sordid.'

'The Army thought it was time for a change,' Oster said.

'My God,' Christian said. 'That was when the bomb went off in that beer cellar in Munich, wasn't it?'

'The Führer left the meeting twenty minutes early. Quite unprecedented. Nobody could understand why. Of course the bomb was the work of the British Secret Service.'

'Scoundrels,' Canaris said.

'One wonders . . .' Oster gave a gently smiling, helpless, speculative gesture. 'Just suppose: if the enemy had been less incompetent, what would have become of us?'

Christian said, 'I suppose—'

'A rhetorical question, no doubt,' Canaris said. 'We must all be grateful that our beloved Führer survived to lead his people onwards to . . . um . . . to . . .' He tugged at an earlobe. 'What's next, Oster?'

'Coffee, sir?' Oster suggested.

'That'll do,' Canaris said. 'Coffee.'

*

In his first month at Rackham Towers, Luis Cabrillo worked very hard. He behaved like a pig towards everyone, but he churned out a steady flood of good stuff for Madrid Abwehr. He had help: in London two researchers, sometimes three, serviced the Eldorado Network with raw material for both truth and lies – accurate information about the Allies' war effort which it was considered worth giving away to the Abwehr, in order to sugar the important disinformation which it was hoped would seriously mislead the enemy. The Eldorado files grew thicker in the offices of Madrid Abwehr. Brigadier Wagner's team worked long hours, analysing and annotating, cross-referencing and extrapolating and projecting, so that they could encode their findings and radio them to Berlin, along with copies of the original Eldorado material. The radio operators were soon decoding Berlin's acknowledgements, followed by Berlin's comments and questionnaires, all to be referred to Eldorado without delay (thus forming the inspiration for much of his future reports). The Eldorado Network had always been big business. Now it was a small industry.

And the products of the industry found a ready market in the German military leadership. Berlin Abwehr automatically sent summaries of the Eldorado reports to the OKW, the High Command of the Armed Forces. If a report was juicy enough it went straight to the Commander-in-Chief, the Führer himself. Admiral Canaris knew that Hitler was impressed by this intelligence because Hitler sometimes congratulated him on it. Also because it changed Hitler's thinking. Two months after Dieppe, Hitler had taken offence at some Allied misbehaviour or other and had threatened to put in chains all prisoners of war captured in that raid. Churchill, naturally, had threatened to respond by putting German prisoners of war in chains. So far, fairly predictable. Then Hitler publicly ordered that all captured British commandos should be executed. The British government protested, of course: a crude and barbaric breach of the Geneva Convention and all that. But it was Eldorado who discovered that a secret Anglo-American committee had recommended a wide

46

variety of retaliations if Hitler's orders were carried out. For every commando executed, the British would hang a captured German general. When they ran out of generals they would work their way down the ranks. Alternatively (so Eldorado reported), for as long as Hitler's order remained in force, the British would put five hundred German prisoners of war on board every freighter that crossed the Atlantic. That might give the U-boat commanders something to think about. Or . . . There were ten proposals in all, ending with the suggestion that an English town be renamed after each martyred commando. Eldorado himself took credit for this piece of espionage but it was buttressed by the work of Seagull and Knickers. Knickers had overheard two commando sergeants discussing, with approval, their CO's idea that every man should fight to the death rather than surrender. Seagull's contribution was the Russian view. He said the Russian leadership were pleased to hear that British troops were getting a taste of raw battle as Soviet soldiers had been fighting it since invasion by the Nazi murderers.

'The Führer isn't going to like this, sir,' said Major Schwartz, the duty officer at Berlin Abwehr, when he showed the Eldorado report to Admiral Canaris.

The Admiral read it, twice. 'You're mistaken, Major,' he said. 'The Führer won't enjoy it but he will undoubtedly be glad he has seen it.' Canaris was right. Hitler thought again. He didn't give a damn if the Allies hanged every captured German general twice over – he had total contempt for failure – but he didn't want to bolster Soviet morale by executing British commandos. He let the idea slide.

When Brigadier Christian came across all this in the files of Berlin Abwehr, he felt a little surge of pride. He had taken an unknown, untrained, penniless, cocky young Spaniard off the streets of Madrid, groomed him and polished him and kept faith in him, and now his faith had paid off. Now Eldorado led one of the most important spy rings in Europe; perhaps *the* most important, with Eldorado signals landing on the Führer's desk! Actually, the truth was that Christian had not found Eldorado on the streets of Madrid; Eldorado had walked off the streets into the Madrid embassy and had used his initiative and persistence to find the Abwehr department. What's more, far from keeping faith with him, Christian had had so little confidence in Eldorado that as soon as the agent was sent to England, Christian had begun to think of sacrificing him by ordering him to carry out some particularly reckless piece of sabotage. Still, that was all ancient history now. Christian looked on Eldorado as his baby, and he said as much to General Oster.

'Of course you do, old man,' Oster said affably. 'Of course he is, and personally I think you deserve to be carried shoulder-high down the Unter den Linden by bevies of big-breasted blonde beauties.'

'Oh, I don't know about that, sir.'

'If the chance comes, take it. You get a perfect view down the fronts of their dresses.'

Christian wasn't sure how to react to that. Oster was handsome, almost too handsome for a soldier and certainly more elegant than any general Christian had met. What was even more unmilitary, he seemed ready to find a joke in everything. This was disconcerting at times. Christian played safe. 'Anything to serve the interests of the Reich,' he said.

They were drinking beer on the terrace of a café in the Tiergarten. It was a chill afternoon, with a sky as cold and hard as an upturned steel bowl. Somewhere out of sight, dead leaves were being burned and their scent tinged the air with a merciless nostalgia. Christian revelled in it. At last his beard had thickened enough for him to be allowed to go out in the streets. He was disguised in German naval officer's uniform – the Abwehr had given him a new identity as Commodore Albert Meyer – and there was even a pfennig coin in his left shoe to remind him to limp. Nobody in the SD (or even in the Abwehr) was likely to recognize him now. So he enjoyed the comfort of concealment while he rediscovered the pleasures of Berlin, always his favourite city.

Oster said, 'The best way you can serve the Reich is by making sure the Eldorado channel is always open for traffic.'

'No difficulty so far, sir. He uses the Spanish diplomatic bag, both ways.'

'Yes.' Oster made rings on the table with his beer mug. 'Which means the Spanish foreign ministry reads his reports before we do.'

The same thought had occurred to Christian many times. 'We can't stop them looking, I suppose, although I must say the seals are always intact.'

'Proves nothing.'

'Agreed. But everything Eldorado sends is in code.'

'So what? We knew the British Admiralty code for years.' Oster dipped his finger in his beer and made a Mickey Mouse face out of the rings on the table.

'Even so, there's nothing to worry about, is there, sir? Spain's on our side. Last year Franco damn near let us take Gibraltar. The Admiral himself came down to plan the raid. I was all set to lead a sabotage unit.'

'Oh, I know.' Oster gave Mickey a foolish smile and immediately rubbed it out. 'Canaris had the time of his life. He's always wanted to be a masterspy. I helped him pick out that ludicrous black hat he wore everywhere in Spain. Remember? For concealment, he said.'

'It was somewhat on the generous side.'

'No bigger than an elephant's ear. British Intelligence loved him for it. They must have been quite disappointed when we didn't have a go at Gib.'

Christian was beginning to be irritated by Oster's flippancy. 'I still think the operation stood a damn good chance, sir,' he said.

'Franco didn't. Franco looked at the odds and like a good gambler he said to himself, "Sod it, I don't have to bet yet, I'll wait and see." Cunning bugger, Franco.'

'He sent his Blue Division to fight with us in the east.'

'Volunteers,' Oster said. 'Part of the great and holy crusade against Bolshevism.'

'It's all one war,' Christian said.

'Ah, now that's where you're wrong. It's actually several wars.' Oster abandoned his finger-painting; at last he had found

49

something serious. 'Take North Africa. The Americans don't really care about that. The British do. Suez matters to them. Take Greece. Does Greece matter to us Germans? Of course not. So why did we go there?'

'To get Mussolini out of trouble.'

'Right! Greece is Mussolini's war. He wanted a bit of cheap glory, he fucked it up and we had to do the job for him. Take Poland.'

'We already did,' Christian said.

'Not all. We gave half to the Russians, remember? But England and France *started* this war because of Poland. Now they're fighting alongside Russia and where's bloody old Poland? Lost in the shuffle.'

'Great wars are bound to be complex affairs,' Christian said. He was beginning to feel stiff and cold.

'I bet you General Francisco Franco doesn't find it complex. Francisco Franco looks around and says to himself: "Does poor, battered, shattered Spain really want to fight the British Empire, the United States, and the USSR all at once?"'

Christian drank some beer but it was flat so he threw the rest away. 'You don't paint a very optimistic picture, sir,' he said.

'Depends what you mean by optimism,' Oster said briskly. 'Come with me, Christian, and I'll show you what this war is really all about.'

Oster's car took them across Berlin. A faint sunshine had broken through the steel-grey overcast and there was just enough breeze to move the huge swastika flags and pennants that hung from every large building. The display gave Christian a great sense of patriotic unity: of a calm and quiet determination; very sturdy, very *German*. He was about to comment on this and he glanced at Oster; but Oster's head was half-hidden behind the raised collar of his great-coat and his eyes were almost closed. Christian saved the thought for later.

The car stopped at the Brandenburg Gate and the driver hurried to let them out. Oster waved his gloves at the massive pillars of the monument, topped by a giant Goddess of War with a chariot drawn by four horses as tall as elephants.

50

'Ever been up there?' he asked. 'I thought not. Stunning view. Come on.'

They entered by a low steel door tucked away in a corner of the monument. It was a long dark climb up a tightly spiralling staircase but Oster was right: the view was worth it. Christian found himself looking out at an apparently endless boulevard, straight and broad, cutting clean across the heart of Berlin. Of course he had seen it before – but always at ground level. Now he saw it as its designer must have imagined: emerging from infinity, testing the imagination. This was much more than a road. This was a *statement*. 'Thank you, sir,' he said. 'Memorable is hardly the word.'

'Oh, it's just the beginning,' Oster said. 'This runs east–west. Picture an even greater street crossing it, north–south. You've seen the Champs-Elysées?'

'Once or twice.'

'Three hundred and thirty feet wide, so I'm told. Feeble, isn't it? A miserable alley. Our north–south avenue is four hundred feet wide! And five miles long! The widest, longest avenue in the world. How big d'you think the Arc de Triomphe is?'

'I'm afraid I've no idea, sir.'

'Oh, it's stunted, believe me. Tiny. No more than a hundred and sixty feet high. Makes you wonder what all the fuss is about, doesn't it? Now, *our* Triumphal Arch is more than twice as high! Three hundred and eighty-six feet! You can fit their piddling little hoop in the opening of our Arch and still leave room for a squadron of Heinkels to fly through! See?' Oster pointed at an empty bit of landscape.

'Um . . . no, sir,' Christian said.

'Well, we haven't built it yet. Have patience, Christian, have patience. Anyway, the piddling little French hoop, or 'oop as they would say, has no place under our Triumphal Arch – which, incidentally, will bear the names of our glorious dead in the last war, all one million eight hundred thousand of them, carved in granite, which you must agree will make the glorious dead feel much better . . . Where was I?'

'Under the 'oop,' Christian said.

51

'Ah yes. Now, on a clear day when you look through the arch you will see, three miles down the grand avenue, something really rather large, called the Great Hall. It's next to the Reichstag. See the Reichstag?'

'Yes, sir.' There was nothing large next to the Reichstag.

'Well, you can fit the Reichstag into the gents' cloakroom of the Great Hall. It's got a dome shaped like St Peter's in Rome. You've seen St Peter's? Seen the Capitol in Washington?'

'I have.' Christian was wondering if all this was some bizarre, long-winded, private joke of Oster's.

'You could get the Capitol *and* St Peter's under the dome of our Great Hall several times over. Makes you think, doesn't it?'

'It must surely be the biggest in the world.'

'Of course. That's the whole point. Biggest and tallest. Crowned with a German eagle holding the swastika in its claws, nearly a thousand feet in the air.'

Christian decided that enough was enough. 'Evidently this is not a clear enough day, sir,' he said. 'I see no such Great Hall.'

Oster patted him on the shoulder. 'Never mind. Look over there: Adolf Hitler Platz! Room for a million cheering people! On one side: the new Chancellery, Hitler's palace, seventy times bigger than the present Chancellery! Twenty-two million square feet! That is where the Führer receives foreign diplomats, Christian, provided their little legs are strong enough, because they'll have to walk more than a quarter of a mile to reach his reception room . . . What else? To the right there's the Soldiers' Hall, I think that's a sort of tomb for field-marshals, slightly smaller than the Jungfrau. Over here you see Goering's new Air Ministry, eight hundred feet long. Over there the new Town Hall, fifteen hundred feet long . . . War Academy . . . Navy Building . . . about a dozen separate ministry buildings – Interior, Justice, Colonies.' Oster kept pointing to these phantom structures with apparent recognition. 'Plus a couple of new railroad stations, a few ornamental lakes, aerodromes . . .' He was running down at last. 'And a very big building for the Gestapo, and the Gestapo, and the Gestapo,' he said. 'Not forgetting the Gestapo.'

Nothing more was said until they were down on the street and in the car, heading for home. Oster sprawled in a corner of the back seat, head in hand, staring out of the window.

Christian cleared his throat. 'I have to say, sir, that I understood none of that.'

'Join the club. Only two people understand it: Hitler and Speer. And now Speer tells me he's not so sure.'

'Reichminister Speer? Minister of Arms Production?'

'And formerly Hitler's architect.' Oster straightened up and turned to Christian. 'We were on the same plane about a month ago, coming back from the eastern front. He'd been . . . Well, it doesn't matter where he'd been. Or me. Anyway, the plane had to land in Poland. Bad weather. We were stuck in this God-awful dump. Nothing to do but drink and talk. He told me about Hitler's plans for a new Berlin. Speer designed nearly all of it. Great Hall, Triumphal Arch, Chancellery, all those colossal buildings. Perfectly feasible, he said. Might take billions and billions of marks, but . . .' Oster shrugged.

'It is the capital city,' Christian said. 'Surely it deserves great architecture.'

'And the rest of Germany too? Speer said all our other cities are to be rebuilt on the same heroic scale. Hamburg, Düsseldorf, Essen, Hanover, Munich, Cologne, everywhere.'

'Well, clearly that's not feasible.'

Oster laughed. 'Hitler thinks it is. Those Royal Air Force Lancasters and American Flying Fortresses: they're simply carrying out necessary demolition work for the greater glory of the Third Reich.'

When they got back to Oster's office, Christian had had time to think.

'We were speaking of optimism, sir,' he said. 'Although it seems rather a long time ago.'

'And before that we were talking about Eldorado and the crucial importance of keeping the Eldorado channel open to traffic,' Oster said.

'Yes.' Christian tugged at his lower lip. 'I must seem very dense, sir. It's just that I'm still trying to work out the link between the Eldorado Network and Reichminister Speer.'

Suddenly Oster became impatient. 'Look, Christian: when d'you think this vast architectural extravaganza was planned? I'll tell you. All the designs were drawn long before we went into Poland. There are scale models hundreds of feet long hidden away in the Chancellery! It's one of the reasons Hitler wanted this war – let him conquer Europe, conquer Russia, conquer the world or if he can't conquer it, then at least *dominate* the bloody thing, and he can afford to build everything he damn well pleases! This is a war to satisfy Hitler's vanity and make him famous. Armies are dying so Hitler will be remembered.'

Christian was shaking his head. 'I cannot believe the Führer would lead us into war unless it was for the benefit of the German people.'

Oster anticipated the last words and spoke over them. 'In that case forget everything I've said,' he told Christian briskly. 'Remember this instead. Sooner or later, every war comes to an end. Agreed?'

Christian felt uncomfortable about agreeing but he could see no alternative. 'I suppose that's true, sir,' he said.

'And when it comes to doing a deal with the west, Eldorado is one of the best go-betweens we could have.'

'Eldorado's not a go-between,' Christian protested. 'He's a spy, he collects intelligence.'

'Call him what you like,' Oster said. 'Just keep him warm and comfortable and happy in his work.'

'Madrid runs Eldorado. I'm dead.'

'Then you watch over Madrid. Do it from a safe distance. As a good ghost should.'

The Twenty Committee met in London once a week. Its name wasn't the cleverest idea ever. In the early days of the war, a committee had been set up to manage the business of running double-agents and someone had written XX on the cover of the minutes of the first meeting: XX for double-cross. That was a little too obvious, so it was translated to the Twenty Committee. An utterly meaningless, irrelevant name would have been safer: the

Peachtree Committee, say, or better yet something really boring, such as the Reserve Stocks Sub-Committee; but after a couple of years the name had stuck.

It was an interestingly high-powered group, spattered with the initials that are spawned by modern war. The two British security services were represented: MI5 and MI6 – the first because its job was to catch spies in Britain and the second because its job involved knowing what foreign intelligence agencies were up to – and there were also men from HDE (Home Defence Executive), NID (Naval Intelligence Directorate), AMI (Air Ministry Intelligence), DMI (Director of Military Intelligence), CCO (Chief of Combined Operations), GHQ Home Forces, and a few more. The Twenty Committee did not decide on the strategic goals for its deception operations. Those goals came down to them from an even more high-powered outfit, known as the 'W' Committee. The 'W' Committee went all the way to the top. When, for instance, the Allies planned Operation Torch (the Anglo-American landings in North Africa), it was the 'W' Committee that ordered the Twenty Committee to use its double-agents to mislead the enemy into preparing for raids elsewhere: Norway, Greece, France, wherever could be made to seem plausible. That was strategy. Just how the Twenty Committee did it was their business. That was tactics.

Much of the weekly meetings was spent discussing what their agents should tell the enemy that was false and what they might tell him that was true. The Abwehr was not stupid. If an agent persistently pointed the Abwehr in the wrong direction it would rapidly stop believing him; what was worse, it would start suspecting that he had been turned by the other side. So the Twenty Committee had to keep sugaring its disinformation with some genuine intelligence; and it had to be useful, original intelligence, not snippets of news that anyone could collect from the daily papers. Running a double-agent meant cultivating the faith and confidence of the enemy. It was a very delicate swindle.

The Twenty Committee's decisions were passed on to the various case officers, such as Freddy Garcia. The committee members never met an agent. In the case of Luis Cabrillo, they should have been grateful. Six weeks after arriving at Rackham Towers he was still behaving like a pig.

It was just before midday. Luis was in bed. Freddy was at his desk, reading a draft of Luis's latest report. Julie was sitting at the other side of the desk, checking through the claims for expenses incurred by Eldorado sub-agents.

'Buranda,' said Freddy. 'Where's Buranda?'

Julie didn't look up. 'Beats me,' she said. 'You had it last.'

He got an atlas and began searching.

'I wish he wouldn't do this,' Julie said. Freddy grunted, and turned to the index. 'Plus twenty-five per cent?' she said. 'I mean what the hell *for?*'

'Who is it?'

'Nutmeg.'

'Bonus, maybe?'

Julie made a face. 'Can't be. It's backdated to cover all payments over the last six months.'

'Including expenses?'

Julie nodded. Freddy thought about it and went back to his atlas. 'Buranda, Buranda,' he murmured. 'Could it be an airport?'

A log burned through, collapsed, and provoked a brief fit of enthusiasm in the fire. The fit subsided. The door opened and Luis shuffled in. He was wearing pyjamas, dressing-gown, and slippers, and was reading a document typed on pink paper. Freddy recognized the latest memorandum from the Twenty Committee.

'This is shit,' Luis said. A page fluttered to the floor. He shuffled to the window, still reading. He had not shaved and his hair was a mess. There was a long silence. 'That is shit too,' he said. Another page fell from his fingers.

Freddy got up and went out of the room. Julie checked her watch, went to the sideboard and poured herself some sherry. 'Want a drink?' she said. 'The bar's open.'

Luis said nothing but went on reading. The more he read, the further away he held the document, until it was at arm's length and he was frowning to focus. He reached the end of the page and twitched his thumbs, and the page slipped away. 'More shit,' he said. He raised his eyes without moving his head and saw the glass in her hand. 'This is shit and that is piss,' he said.

'You should know,' Julie said evenly. 'It's your national drink, after all.'

Luis sniffed. 'We sell that treacle to the stupid English. Real sherry does not leave Spain.'

Freddy came back in with half a dozen pink pages. 'I followed the paper trail to his room,' he explained to Julie as he picked up the three pages lying on the floor. 'You really mustn't do this, Luis,' he said. 'You know the stuff is classified.'

'Don't shout at me,' Luis said in a low, grim voice. Freddy had not been shouting. 'I don't write for people who shout at me.'

'Anyway, what's wrong with it?' Julie asked.

'It's shit,' Luis said.

She looked wide-eyed at Freddy. 'It must be wonderful to have such mastery of the English language,' she said.

'We take what we're given, Luis,' Freddy said. 'If the Twenty Committee wants us to work on Atlantic convoy routes then we do it, because that's what matters.'

'Not to the Abwehr. The Abwehr ask me about tanks and bombers, not about merchant ships.'

'So surprise them,' Julie said.

Luis handed Freddy the remains of the memorandum. 'Give this toilet paper to your Archbishop of Canterbury,' he said. 'Let him pray for a miracle.'

'You told me you didn't believe in God,' Julie said.

'There is no God.'

'So how can you expect a miracle?'

Luis reached inside his pyjamas and scratched his ribs while he thought. 'With so much religion in the world,' he said, 'it would be a miracle if there were no God.' He liked that. For a moment he seemed gloomily pleased with himself. 'I believe in an ex-God. God was so ashamed of himself for creating Creation that he committed suicide.'

57

'Funny nobody noticed,' she said.

'There was a press release, but it was all in Latin.' Luis stopped scratching. 'I feel thin,' he said.

'You know,' Freddy said, and he tapped the draft Eldorado report on his desk. 'This is damn good. Thin?' He craned his neck to examine him. 'Thin? We can't have that. D'you think he looks thin, Julie?'

'No, I think he looks fat. Sort of gross but consumptive. Wheeze for us, Luis. Shake your flab.'

'I didn't say I look thin. I said I feel thin. It's this lousy diet. I need fresh sardines.' Luis hugged himself and hunched his shoulders as if trapped in a blizzard. 'Sardines and oranges.'

'One does one's best,' Freddy said, 'but there are certain obstacles, I'm afraid . . . Never mind, this is a splendid report although there *are* one or two small points.'

Luis screwed his eyes tightly shut and curled his toes.

'I'm afraid your exploding turds will have to go,' Freddy said. 'Brilliant idea. Truly brilliant. Well done, Drainpipe! Also the one-man submarine. That's out.'

Luis opened his eyes to glare at Freddy. 'Perfectly feasible,' he muttered.

'That's the trouble, old chap. They're both too true. German soldiers all over France have to watch their step in case what they tread in goes off bang.'

'Shit,' Luis said wearily. He drifted towards the door.

'Before you go,' Freddy said, 'is Buranda a city or a country?'

'Yes,' Luis said, and shuffled out.

They looked at each other. 'I don't like his mood,' Freddy said.

'What you might call shitty,' she said. 'Who's Drainpipe?'

'Didn't I tell you? New sub-agent. An angry Welshman. The Army requisitioned his farm and now they test experimental munitions there. He could be very useful.' Freddy spread his arms along the mantelpiece and warmed his backside. Beyond the windows, a bored and impatient wind chased the same few dead leaves around the lawns. The day was as light as it was ever going to be, which was a chilled and smoky gloom. Freddy said,

'What's wrong with him, Julie? Nothing pleases him, and yet he's turning out first-rate stuff. I mean, just take a look.'

She perched on the desk and read the exposed page of the draft report:

> is confirmed by GARLIC who says that police have confiscated all binoculars and telescopes owned by private individuals living within sight of the Clyde estuary. This is to prevent them from seeing horrific damage to convoys arriving after crossing the Atlantic. Some ships are so badly damaged, burning, etc, that dockers refuse to work on them and massive numbers of troops are unloading cargo instead. (Numerous accidents and wastage due to incompetence.) PINETREE reports heavy signals traffic London–Washington prompted by British Army decision to postpone/cancel raids on Le Havre, St Malo, Brest; also unspecified targets on Belgian/Dutch coasts. This decision directly caused by docks crisis (see above). WALLPAPER however has alternative information which indicates that the planned operations were much further north, probably in the region Denmark–Norway, with the aim of disrupting iron ore supplies from Sweden to Hamburg. I do not question WALLPAPER's intentions but I suspect that his informants (largely Free French officers) are concerned to minimize damage to their homeland by campaigning for military operations elsewhere.
>
> HAYSTACK reports that a stolen document from the Ministry of Economic Warfare is circulating in London, revealing that contrary to official statements the average output per man/week in the semi-skilled sector has failed to reverse a decline which cannot be attributed to such negative factors as . . .

She skimmed the next few paragraphs. 'God!' she said. 'This is boring.'

'I know. That's what makes it so beautiful.' Freddy came and looked over her shoulder. 'It's so boring it's got to be true. Nobody but a government department could come up with anything so boring as that. He's a genius.'

'It's not true? All this Ministry stuff?'

'Certainly not. It's all hokum. But it *rings* true, doesn't it? And if you believe it you're more likely to swallow the rest of the report

– burning convoys and bolshy dockers and cancelled assaults on Fortress Europe.'

Julie flicked through a few pages. Freddy was right; Luis had a special style: a mixture of B-movie adventure, travellers' tales, gossip, scandal, and dense thickets of bureaucratic prose. She had forgotten how impressive it was. 'Has the Army really cancelled any raids on Europe?' she asked.

'I've no idea. Doesn't really matter, does it? As long as the Germans think we might attack, they'll keep lots of men in the west. Where Luis is so clever is in making bad news look like good news . . .' The flicker of white pyjama trousers caught his eye. 'For heaven's sake,' he said. 'What is he up to now?'

Luis, still in his dressing-gown, was trudging across the grass towards a clump of pines. The wind blew his hair sideways. He stopped to pick up a piece of dead wood; tucked it under his arm; walked on. 'He'll freeze,' Freddy said.

'I'll go,' she said.

By the time she caught up with him, he had crossed the pines and was tramping resolutely down a muddy path into a great sprawl of woodland. Treetops creaked and rocked. The air was raw with the threat of an oncoming storm. She was in gumboots and overcoat and was carrying boots for Luis and an old army cape. 'Put these on,' she said.

'Don't need 'em.' He had not looked at her.

'Luis . . .' She was about to say: *Don't be such a schmuck, you schmuck*, but she swallowed the words. 'It could get pretty cold.'

'I'll light a fire.' Without stopping, he showed her the piece of wood. It was thick and mossy and black with damp.

'That's good. Got any matches?'

He nodded.

The track narrowed and she had to walk behind him. They followed a stream, crossed it, climbed a long slope that was broken with jagged outcrops of stone. All the time the air grew colder and the light got worse. Half-way up the slope a fallen tree blocked the path. Luis scrambled over it and lost his slippers. Julie ducked underneath. 'Sit,' she ordered, and pointed to a flat rock. Luis sat. She shoved the gumboots on

60

his muddy feet and spread the cape over his shoulders. 'Lead on,' she said.

Half a mile away he came upon a place where a rocky overhang created a shallow cave, high above a stand of magnificent beeches. 'Fire here,' he said. He still had his piece of black, mossy wood. He looked at it as if deciding which end to light first.

She took it out of his hands and threw it as far as she could, so it went sailing down between the tall, clean-cut trunks of the beeches. 'You're a nice guy, Luis,' she said, 'but it's obvious you were never a Girl Scout.'

'I can light a fire.' He was angry, but he was also shivering.

'Oh, sure. In Spain you can light a fire, where it's hot and dry. Who can't? Scratch a Spaniard and start a fire, isn't that right, Luis? But this is soggy old England, so give me the matches.'

Luis refused. He folded his arms and put one foot crosswise on top of the other. His nose was running and he wiped it with the back of his hand. 'They're *my* matches,' he muttered.

'Shit!' she said. 'To quote an eminent writer.' There was deadlock while she stared at him and he stared at nothing. 'OK, I tell you what,' she said. 'You light the fire, right? I *make* it and you *light* it. Deal? Terrific.' Before Luis could respond she had grabbed his arm and pointed him at some trees. 'Get dry wood, thin as your finger. Look for dead branches still on the tree.' She gave him a shove and turned and went the opposite way. 'This is *fun!*' she cried. *You dumb schmuck*, she added silently.

Julie built a fire on good Girl Scout principles. Luis shuffled back and dumped a huge armful of dry sticks beside it. She pointed to the spot where he should apply flame. 'Put it there, partner,' she said. He broke three matches before he got one to light, but its flame spread like magic and the blaze was a beacon in a dark and wicked world. 'Now all we need is marshmallows,' she said.

'For what?' he asked.

'To stuff up your nose!' she shouted. 'What else?' She found that very funny and when she laughed, he blinked with bewilderment. His cape had fallen off; his dressing-gown hung open; his pyjamas were unbuttoned; he was a walking disaster. Yet nothing could

61

disguise his slim and clean-limbed grace. Julie wiped her filthy hands on his chest. It was an action that slipped easily into a hug, and the hug became an embrace. 'Is that a bottle in your pocket,' Luis asked, 'or am I glad to see you?'

It was half a bottle of sherry: all that Julie had been able to grab on her way out. 'Genuine treacle,' she said. 'The poor bloody Spanish aren't allowed to get their sticky hands on this.'

Luis took a long swig. 'Only wonderful,' he said, and burped. 'No breakfast,' he explained.

They sat in the radiance of the fire for the best part of an hour, talking easily, and sometimes not talking, just as easily. In the end, odd spots of rain fizzed into the embers. 'We ought to go,' Julie said.

'I'm not going back there.' He picked up an old branch and whacked it on the ground. It snapped. 'Rotten,' he said. The tension and gloom were seeping back again.

'What's wrong, Luis?' she asked.

'I'm bored,' he said.

She had heard this before, more than once, but still she was not sure how to handle it. 'I can see how you would be,' she said. 'What with a world war raging all around you, a fight to the death between freedom and Fascism, I mean it gets sort of tedious and—'

'Yes, yes, yes, I know,' he said. 'I know I know I know I know. Don't tell me I should be grateful I'm alive and not hungry and in England, I know all that. Makes no difference.' Luis hid his face in his hands. 'I can't write if I'm bored. I hate it. There's no point.'

'But you *are* writing,' Julie pointed out, 'and Freddy likes it. Freddy reckons it's hot stuff.'

'That's not *writing*.' The word came out like a kick on the shins. 'That's hack-work. Somebody in London picks out the music. I'm just the monkey that dances for them.'

Julie said nothing. Against such self-contempt there was nothing to be said.

'We should have stayed in Lisbon.' He removed his hands and looked into the gold of the fire. 'I was happy in Lisbon. It was

62

bloody hard work but it was a marvellous game. Just me and them. Every day I got out of bed and I thought: What can I sell them today? And I invented something, I made up Eldorado, nobody else did that, just me, I created Eldorado, I recruited all his pals and I christened them, Seagull and Pinetree and Knickers and Garlic and Nutmeg, they all came from me. Just me.'

'That reminds me,' Julie said. 'About Nutmeg . . .'

'And it was *fun*,' Luis said with a kind of savage desperation. 'It was *exciting*.'

'It was damn dangerous. You nearly got killed.'

'Now . . .' Luis sucked his teeth and spat into the fire. 'Now I have to get permission before I can turn around and fart.'

'Come on.' She got up, and pulled him to his feet. They set off into the dusk. 'So you're not a one-man band any more. So what? You're properly organized now, Luis. Eldorado really makes a difference to the war. You're bigger than ever, kid.'

'You don't understand.' Luis stumbled along behind her, his bare feet sliding and slipping in his gumboots. 'Eldorado was my secret. Just me, and later you but you didn't count because we were in love and so we were like one person.'

'Gee, thanks,' she said.

'Now they've taken my secret away. Eldorado's just another department of the British War Office, for the love of Sam.'

'Mike,' she said. 'Love of Mike.'

'Why not Sam?'

Julie could think of no reason. 'You win,' she said.

They said little more until they came in sight of the house, when she remembered Nutmeg. 'Luis . . . Why is Nutmeg getting twenty-five per cent of his last six months' earnings?'

'Income tax demand,' Luis said.

'Tax? That's crazy. How did the Revenue get into the act?'

'He told them about his extra earnings. He said he got the money by selling paintings. Nutmeg is a gifted artist.'

'The Abwehr isn't going to buy that, Luis. The Abwehr's going to want to know why Nutmeg couldn't keep his fool mouth shut and save them twenty-five per cent.'

'Nutmeg is a retired officer of the British Indian Army,' Luis declared, with a tinge of reproach in his voice. 'He is an honourable man. He wouldn't cheat on his taxes and I for one would never dream of suggesting that he should.'

'Pardon me all to hell and back,' Julie said.

They went inside.

Dr Hartmann surprised everyone, including himself, by being the first to recruit a new spy.

Hartmann wasn't much interested in people. He wasn't even excited by war. What gripped him was science, especially the science of radio, and barometric fuses, and what blast-waves did to concrete buildings, that sort of thing. He approved of the war because it gave him so much opportunity to develop his interests, and he enjoyed analysing Eldorado's contributions, especially as the fellow wasn't there to argue. But apart from that, Hartmann preferred chess to people. It was at a chess club in the old part of Madrid that he met Laszlo Martini.

Laszlo was about thirty, thin and bearded, and he dressed like a crook who had bought the local police chief and doesn't care who knows it: snakeskin shoes, midnight-blue suit with cuffs on the sleeves and a little too much flare in the lapels, hand-painted silk tie that looked like an explosion in a Chinese paint factory. Dr Hartmann disliked him on sight and when he saw the fingernails – too long and not clean enough – he despised him. But then he overheard Laszlo speak a few words of English to the barman: 'That's OK. And keep the change.' Later Hartmann introduced himself and invited Laszlo to play. They tied after five games: two wins each, one stalemate. So the fellow was not stupid. Whether or not he was foolish was something else. His use of English suggested he might be vain. And perhaps lonely, if he had to go around impressing barmen with his superiority.

'Please forgive me if I intrude,' Hartmann said (they were speaking Spanish), 'but yours is a name I have not often encountered in Spain before.'

'My family is not originally Spanish,' Martini said. 'The full name is Martini-Hoffman-de-Seversky-Danacek.'

'With your permission I shall confine myself to Martini.' Hartmann cranked up a small, respectful smile. 'Does it relate perhaps to the great Italian house of Vermouth?'

'On my mother's side, alas. I shall never inherit.' He shrugged one shoulder: what was a lost fortune to a man like Martini? 'And you, señor, unless I mistake myself, you are not a native of this country?'

Hartmann explained that he was a commercial attaché at the German embassy.

Martini leaned back and looked at him with sudden interest. 'Deutschland,' he said. It came out like an incantation.

'That's the place,' Hartmann agreed. '*Uber alles*, as the saying goes.'

'You know, Herr Doktor, we have more in common than chess,' Martini said, and took in a deep breath as if to brace himself for a major statement. 'I volunteered for the Blue Division,' he said. 'I wanted to march against the Comintern, to fight with the last drop of my blood to stop the Red menace crushing western Christian civilization.' Hartmann stared: either the words or the clothes were wrong; they did not fit each other. 'One of the greatest tragedies of my life,' Martini went on. 'At the medical examination they discovered that I am colour-blind. Their standards are high. I was rejected.' He made a small gesture of helplessness and looked away: for him, the war was over.

Hartmann said carefully, 'No doubt you would still like to stand alongside the German soldier and help him to victory?' Martini nodded. 'Perhaps I can arrange something,' Hartmann said. 'Not the Blues versus the Reds, what with your eyesight, but maybe something in the grey area.' He gave Martini his card. 'Come and see me in the morning. Shall we say ten o'clock?'

Laszlo Martini arrived at ten to ten, dressed as soberly as a banker. By eleven his English had been tested (and found to be American) and he had agreed to become an interpreter and translator; by twelve they were talking about his willingness to travel and work alone; before lunch he was a full-time trainee intelligence agent, keen to be parachuted into England. Dr Hartmann was slightly alarmed by the speed of his recruitment. 'You do

realize, don't you, that this work is really quite dangerous?'
he asked.

Martini almost smiled. 'I am ready to live and die for the cause,'
he said.

'Oh, you mustn't die,' Hartmann said. 'That would be no good
to anybody.'

The other controllers were impressed by his find. 'How did you
do it?' Richard Fischer wanted to know. Otto Krafft and Franz
Werth stopped what they were doing and waited for the answer.

'It's not easy to explain,' Hartmann said. 'All I can tell you is
new agents don't walk in off the street. You've got to go out and
search.'

'But where?' Krafft asked.

'Yes,' Hartmann said contentedly. 'It's difficult, isn't it?'

Fischer worried at it for the rest of the day and half the night.
He went to sleep with the question *Where do you get a good spy in
Spain?* chasing itself around his brain. His subconscious did its
stuff and he awoke with the answer: ask Belasco.

Mario Belasco was a major in the Spanish secret police. In the
past, he and Fischer had done some favours for each other. During
Luis Cabrillo's training, a fellow-trainee, Freddy Ryan, had had to
be killed; Fischer got the job of disposing of the body. He tried
to get it cremated, didn't have the right documents, and was glad
when Belasco had them faked for him in a hurry – the corpse was
beginning to get ripe. In return Fischer passed Belasco a list of
anti-government agitators which the Abwehr had acquired while
looking for something else; Belasco smoothly scooped them up,
them and their dynamite too.

Fischer found Belasco in his office, being shaved by a little
old man who had a head like a dried walnut and spidery hands
that never stopped shaking. 'My dear friend!' Belasco said. His
lips moved; his head did not. 'Take a seat. Have a coffee. Have
a shave.'

Fischer had to look away from the trembling razor. 'I'm not
brave enough,' he said. 'Aren't you afraid of losing an ear?'

'Terrified.' Belasco was still and silent while the quavering steel
tackled his upper lip. 'The consolation is that after this, nothing

more frightening can happen to me for the rest of the day.' He held his breath as the razor harvested the last few patches of lather. The old man gave him a towel. 'Thank you, God,' he said, looking at the ceiling. 'I'll do something for You one day. Now what can I do for you, Richard?'

Fischer described his needs.

'Easy,' Belasco said. He finished drying his ears and neck and tossed the towel to the old man. He unlocked a desk drawer and took out a folder. 'How about a couple of Egyptians? They're freelancing around the city and I know their rates are very reasonable.'

'No.'

'Fluent English.'

'I can't send Egyptians to England, Mario.'

'No, I suppose not. What about a Czech?'

'If you mean the fat drunk with the glass eye, we sacked him last year. Dreadful man. Never washes.'

'True,' Belasco said. 'Let's see . . .' He worked down his list. 'He's dead . . . He's working for the Americans . . . They're in prison . . . She's got no English . . . He's got no brains . . . He's in prison . . . He's got the pox . . . Ah, here's someone: a Dutchman. Fair English, lots of brains, no pox, and quite handsome.' He held up a photograph.

Fischer looked at it. 'Don't I know that face?' he said.

'He had a career in films until the war came along.'

'If I recognized him, so will half of England.'

'Could be useful. Nobody suspects someone famous. And he could grow a moustache.'

'He can grow asparagus, I'm still not risking him.'

'Mmm.' Belasco turned a page. 'It's not so easy, after all. Your best prospects are all in jail.'

The little old man said, in a voice full of dry rot, 'Then get one out.' He finished packing up his shaving gear and left.

'I suppose we could always get one out,' Belasco said.

'What are they in for?' Fischer asked.

'Fraud. Nearly always fraud and deception.'

'Yes. It would be, wouldn't it?'

67

They went through Belasco's list and picked out a thirty-four-year-old Hungarian called Ferenc Tekeli. He had sold military secrets to Russia, France, and Spain. Now he was serving five years for fraud and ten years for impersonating a policeman. Fischer visited him in a Madrid prison that afternoon. It took less than five minutes to do a deal. Fischer thought he had never seen such a surprised and happy man; but then equally he had never known such a foul and rancid stink-pit of a prison. He could still smell it on his clothes next day.

That left Otto Krafft and Franz Werth still without any recruits.

'Nobody said that everybody has to come up with a second Eldorado,' Franz said to Otto. 'If that happened, Wagner would have five Eldorados. I mean to say, there isn't that much military intelligence to be found in England, is there?'

'I don't advise you to take that line with the Brigadier,' Otto said. They were walking in the embassy gardens. The weather was bleak: the trees looked black as iron, the paths were treacherous with ice.

'I keep looking in the personal advertisement columns of the Spanish papers,' Franz said. 'What I want to see is: *Young man, observant, intelligent, hardworking, and brave, fluent English, seeks interesting employment, willing to travel, anything considered, danger no object.* You used to see that sort of ad all the time before the war. Not now. What's wrong with young men nowadays?'

'I blame the cinema. People have forgotten how to entertain themselves.'

Franz was not listening. 'I suppose there's nothing to stop me advertising,' he said broodingly. 'You know: *International firm seeks young man, observant, intelligent*, et cetera. Might work, mightn't it?'

'I can guarantee you at least one reply.'

Franz worked at it for five seconds and gave up. 'Who?' he asked.

'The British Secret Service.'

'Oh. You think they'd recognize . . . Yes, I suppose they

would. And then of course they'd try to infiltrate one of their men in the hope that we'd send him to England.'

'In which case the consequences would be dire.'

'Appalling. Catastrophic. I don't think I'll advertise.'

They paused at a frozen goldfish pond. 'What baffles me,' Franz said, 'is knowing where to start looking. I mean, what *is* a spy? A good spy.'

'Someone who doesn't look like a spy. Luis Cabrillo didn't look like a spy, did he? He looked like the kind of young Spanish buck you wouldn't leave in the same room with your wife, whatever the time of day. Come on, I'm freezing.'

They turned back. 'So why do they do it?' Franz wondered. 'Perhaps, if we can work that out, it might give us a clue about where to look for one.'

'The worst ones do it for vanity,' Otto said. 'The best ones do it for love. And in between—'

'Wait, wait! Love, you say. The best ones do it for love.' Franz beat his gloved hands together as if to prompt his brain. A pigeon took flight and clattered away. 'I have had an absurd idea,' he said. 'But then, war is an absurd idea, so why not? Especially if it gets us off the hook. There's a young woman in the Press Office called Stephanie Schmidt. Shortish, rather podgy, thick horn-rim glasses, hair in a bun. Have you met her?'

'No,' Otto said, 'and I don't think I want to.'

'She's madly in love with you.'

Otto was silent. He was blond and blue-eyed, there was nothing wrong with his face and his body was slim and athletic: it would not be the first time a stranger had fallen in love with him. Good looks could be a curse. 'How do you know?' he asked.

'Oh, everyone knows. She's even asked for a transfer to the Abwehr. I'm told her English is excellent. Why don't you have a word with her?'

Otto stamped his feet, hard, to vent some anger. 'Why don't you?' he said.

'She's not in love with me.'

'And I'm not in love with her.' But that was no answer, and he knew it.

'Listen: Eldorado Mark 2 doesn't have to be a man,' Franz said. 'In fact there's a lot to be said for using an ugly little woman as an agent. Less conspicuous. Nobody notices her.'

'Sure, sure. And when they catch her and shoot her I expect she dies very quietly. No fuss, no embarrassment.'

'I don't know why you're being so touchy. For all you know she may be itching to become an agent.'

In fact the idea had not occurred to Stephanie Schmidt and when, a couple of hours later, Franz gently suggested it to her, she was astonished. They talked it over for quite a long time before he played his ace. 'We attach great importance to the relationship between an agent and her controlling officer back here at Madrid Abwehr,' he said. 'They must trust and understand each other, utterly and completely. Your controller would be—' he consulted a file, '—Otto Krafft. Would that suit you?' Fraulein Schmidt indicated that it would suit her. When Franz told him this, Otto muttered that it wouldn't be any fun for her if she went to England. Franz said, 'It's not going to be any fun for her if she stays here, is it? And this way, her love isn't completely wasted. What do you want, Otto? War served up with ice-cream and chopped nuts on top? Spare yourself some grief. It's never going to be like that.'

'It stinks,' Otto said.

'Of course it stinks. Whoever won a war with roses?'

Next day an Irishman called Docherty proved Dr Hartmann wrong by walking in off the street and volunteering to be a German agent. He had a little difficulty finding the Abwehr because Laszlo Martini (whom he had met in a bar) had simply told him to ask for the commercial attaché, and the embassy had a genuine commercial attaché as well as the cover position held by Hartmann. Docherty kept hinting at the great military secrets he could reveal only to the right man, and eventually he ended up in Richard Fischer's office, Hartmann being unavailable. Docherty had no secrets to reveal but he told gory stories of his involvement in the Anglo-Irish Troubles of 1916–1922 and after, when he had killed Englishmen by the dozen, or even the score. Fischer found him hugely entertaining and sometimes even semi-convincing.

'Why do you want to spy for Germany?' he asked.

'It's purely a matter of principle,' Docherty said. 'You see, I need a thousand pounds by Tuesday.' Compared with the Stephanie Schmidt affair, this was irresistibly straightforward. Docherty's name was added to the list. That made four, which should be enough.

'Yes, it's a fascinating idea, Luis,' Freddy Garcia said, 'and we all love it madly, but it's not *convoys*, is it?'

'Boring bloody convoys,' Luis grumbled. 'All I write about is convoys. Week after week, convoys, convoys, convoys.'

'That's in the nature of things, Luis. Convoys never stop. They're always crossing the Atlantic.'

Julie said, 'And you never stop eating the food they bring.'

Luis scribbled furiously and deliberately broke the point of his pencil. 'Look at that,' he accused. 'Cheap and nasty. How can a chap write with such rubbish?' He flung the pencil in the fire.

'You're childish,' she said.

He gave her a sideways look that was half-roguish, half-loutish. 'Let's go to bed,' he said. 'I'll show you whether I'm childish or not.'

'We just got out of bed.' It was mid-morning.

'And was I childish last night?'

'Shut up, Luis.'

'What's the matter? Embarrassed? I thought all you modern Americans were frank and free about sex.'

'In your case there's not a hell of a lot to say, is there? In and out, in and out.'

'Just like the convoys,' Freddy said, and wished he hadn't: at that moment, Luis's slim olive face was frozen with anger at Julie. Freddy hurried to distract him.

'If you want to know what I honestly think, Luis, I think your Petrified Bog is too good an idea for this report. You've already given the Abwehr your splendid Very Low Level Extreme Delayed Opening Parachute and they're always fascinated by secret new equipment, aren't they? And Hitler . . . Didn't you tell me that

71

Hitler is obsessed with paratroops?' Luis nodded. 'Why is that, d'you think?'

'Oh . . . he likes to strike from the sky, it satisfies his godlike idea of himself.' Luis wandered over to the curtains and worked the drawstring, opening and shutting, opening and shutting. 'And he likes to play with secret weapons, just to prove to his generals how clever he is.'

'But surely Crete . . .'

'Yes, I know. Crete gave me the idea.' By now Luis had forgotten about Julie. 'Hitler sent his paratroopers to capture Crete and the British shot half of them dead while they were floating down.'

'So they did. Perfect targets. And you thought—'

'I thought . . . Well, I'll tell you exactly what happened, Freddy. I remembered a movie I saw where one guy is going to throw another guy off a skyscraper, and the first guy says to the second guy, "Don't worry, it's only the last six inches that hurts." '

Freddy laughed. 'Jolly good. Quite true, too.'

'And I thought, why not invent a parachute that opens at the bottom of the jump instead of the top? Say, two hundred feet from the ground?'

'And you've done it,' Freddy said. 'Brilliant! I'm sure Jerry will be tickled pink, and that's exactly why it would be a mistake to put your Petrified Bog in the same report. We mustn't spoil the Abwehr, must we?'

Luis said nothing. He was looking in a mirror and trying to waggle his ears. The harder he tried, the more his eyebrows fluttered. It was very discouraging.

'Incidentally, I see you've made another reference to the delegation from Buranda,' Freddy said. 'Where exactly is Buranda?'

'On the Peruvian border. Very rich in manganese.'

'Ah. Let's add that, shall we?' Freddy wrote it in the margin. 'Nice touch,' he said, 'but it's still not convoys, is it?'

Luis slumped in an armchair. He was looking towards Julie but his eyes were not focused on her and he never blinked, so that he almost seemed blind. She knew this expression. Luis was dreaming again. After a while he hooked both legs over one arm of the chair. Freddy was working at his desk; the only sounds were the occasional crisp shuffle of paper, and the flicker of the fire, and the patter of rain on glass. Luis slowly raised his legs again until they pointed up and his head and shoulders hung down. Finally he blinked. 'This position encourages the flow of blood to the brain,' he remarked.

'A long and lonely expedition,' she said. 'Pack sandwiches.'

Luis slid further down and let his head rest on the floor. 'I see a special convoy,' he said.

Freddy waited. 'What's special about it?' he asked.

'It's upside-down,' Julie said.

Freddy frowned at her, but Luis said: 'Hey! I like that! Make a note of that, it's better than what I had in mind.' He relaxed his legs and tumbled gracefully on to the carpet, head-first. 'An upside-down convoy. See? You put the ships under the water! Isn't that a terrific idea?'

'No,' Freddy said. 'Tell me what you thought of first.'

Luis crawled over to Julie and rested against her legs. 'Eldorado hears about a special convoy going to India. Much better target, right? For weeks and weeks we've been trying to sell the Abwehr a lot of phoney routes and sailing dates for transatlantic convoys. I am fed up with all that. The Abwehr is fed up with it. It's boring. Now Eldorado discovers there will soon be a special convoy sailing south, much closer to France, much easier for the U-boats to find. So the U-boats leave the transatlantic convoys! They go and lie in wait for . . . for . . . for a very special convoy with *a very, very special passenger*.' Utterly delighted by his own invention, Luis hid his face in Julie's skirt.

'Oh, yes?' Freddy said. 'Who?'

'King George VI,' Luis said, muffled but happy.

'Why is the King of England going to India?' Julie asked.

Luis emerged. 'He's Emperor of India. He can do what he likes.'

'Not in wartime,' Freddy said.

'Prince of Wales, then.'

'There isn't one. The King has no sons.'

73

Luis thought about it. 'In that case I shall send the Prime Minister,' he said. 'And you can't stop me.' He got up and left the room and went to the library and wrote until lunch. When he came out he handed the draft Eldorado report to Freddy and said: 'If you don't let me out of this dump I shall never write another word. How can I write about a country I never see?'

'I've got a meeting with the Director this afternoon,' Freddy said. 'I'll raise the matter then, I promise.'

The Director was a cheerful and energetic Scots widower aged fifty. He looked like the deputy headmaster of a prosperous boys' school: lean, tweed-suited, and easily forgettable. His wife Peggy had died, suddenly and inexplicably, a year before Britain went to war. His grief had soured to bitterness and even rage: there were times when he had found himself flinging the smaller bits of furniture around their silent house. Then he had a dream. He rarely dreamed. This was a powerful and dramatic dream, in which Peggy flew down the chimney of his childhood nursery and caught him refusing to get out of his bed because his porridge was cold. She said nothing; simply sat at the foot of the bed and looked at him. She was just as she had been when they first met. Soon he couldn't tolerate her look any longer and he woke up. It was twenty to four. He couldn't stay where he was but he felt utterly exhausted. *It's only twenty to four*, he complained to himself. *It's too early to grow up*. That didn't seem right. He got up, had a bath, made some breakfast. It marked the beginning of the end of his bitterness and rage. When war came along and recruited him out of the publishing industry into the intelligence industry, he welcomed the work. It was something fresh and interesting to tell Peggy when he got home to the flat in the evening. Nobody else in the business could talk to his wife or his girlfriend about his job, and many couples were split by the strain of that silence, but the Director chatted endlessly – if silently – to Peggy. Often, when he had finished telling her about some new problem, he saw it (and sometimes even the answer) much more clearly than when he had begun. The dull, pragmatic side of him said that he was talking to a shadow, a memory. The funny side said: *So what? I deal in ghosts all day long. What's wrong with adding another?* The Director was a balanced man.

When Freddy Garcia told him that Eldorado wanted to be allowed to leave Rackham Towers, the Director said, 'Well, he can't. It's out of the question. And if he tries to escape, you have my permission to shoot him. More than permission: orders.'

'This is the same Eldorado whose network is going great guns, is it, sir?' Freddy asked.

'The very same. The man is a marvel. And now you want to know why he can't be trusted on his own.'

'Um . . . yes.'

'It's because he knows, or *thinks* he knows, that the Double-Cross System runs every German agent in Britain.'

This was news to Freddy. 'Does it really?' he asked. 'I knew we had a lot of them in the bag, and I assumed we'd turned a high percentage, but I never imagined we might be running the lot.'

'And you needn't exercise yourself over it now,' the Director said. 'It doesn't matter, not to you anyway. The point is, young Eldorado thinks what he thinks. Why? Because when he was in Lisbon, someone told him so.'

'Very ill-advised,' Freddy said.

'Well, to be fair, which is a habit I try to avoid, I suppose they reckoned the Eldorado Network would soon be wound up. Obviously the Abwehr wouldn't trust it after they got cheated blind over the North African invasion, so it was only a short-term investment. As it happened the Abwehr did go on trusting it. And in all the consequent agonizing reappraisals, what with hustling Eldorado off to England and reshuffling our own men in Lisbon, nobody thought to tell me that Eldorado knows too much for anybody's good, his or ours, until last night, when the relevant file reached me. Small bombshell, I can tell you.'

A secretary came in with coffee and biscuits.

'I was a Boy Scout,' the Director said, 'back in the fourteenth century, and one of the things we were taught when pitching camp was to imagine how it would look in the worst possible weather. Well, we've pitched our camp. What's the worst that could happen?'

'Eldorado escapes, goes back to Spain, spills the beans to the Abwehr, we lose everything.'

The Director sipped his coffee.

'I can do worse than that,' he said. 'What if Eldorado gets nobbled by a passing Abwehr agent in this country, tells him everything and we don't know he's done it. We continue to operate the Double-Cross System but now the Abwehr sees right through it. In fact they read it backwards and work out all our deception plans.'

'Yes, that's worse than nothing,' Freddy said. 'Far worse.'

'Oh, it's unthinkable,' the Director told him. 'It must be made absolutely and utterly impossible.'

'What d'you want me to do, sir?'

'I've no idea, Freddy. None.'

'We could bung Luis and Julie inside the Tower of London, sir.'

'We could, but we can't. I need Eldorado. He's indispensable.'

'We can't keep him buttoned up at Rackham Towers, sir. He'll go potty. Equally obviously, we daren't let him out. I mean, suppose he takes it into his head to do a bunk, and he vanishes. We shan't know whether he's done us any damage or not.'

The Director nodded.

'Golly,' Freddy said.

'Golly indeed,' the Director said. 'And I need a solution by this afternoon, if you would be so kind.'

Much of Madrid had taken a beating during the Civil War and the damage was still there to be seen, especially in the poor areas: gutted houses, potholes, filthy streets, rusted sheets of corrugated iron that flapped and throbbed in the wind. It was wretched, and the weather was wretchedly cold, so Laszlo Martini had dressed suitably in calf-length leather boots, aviator's fleece-lined jacket, and astrakhan hat, plus a white silk scarf to protect his throat.

His mission was to make his way across Madrid, noting what he saw at a dozen scattered points, and to report. As the area was unknown to him he had bought a street map. Even so, the twisting course was hard to follow and half the stupid street signs were missing. He was standing in the middle of an especially dreary, empty street, studying his map, when a man in a black rain-coat came out of nowhere and said in English: 'Identity card, please.'

Martini stared. This was nobody he knew from the German embassy. He said, 'Identity card?'

The man stared back. Martini tried to fold up his map. The wind hampered him and he cursed. At least he remembered to curse in English. 'Damn, damn,' he said. The map tore and he ended up folding it badly.

'Anything wrong?' the man said.

'Bloody weather.' Martini grinned, and glanced to see if the man showed any sympathy, while he stuffed the map in a pocket with one hand and searched for his identity card with the other.

The man took his time examining the card. He chewed his lip, he briefly creased his brow, he sniffed once, compared the photograph with the real face, sniffed again. Martini watched, and wondered what it all meant. The man returned the card. 'Where were you born?' he asked.

'Birmingham,' Martini said.

'Ah.' The man nearly smiled; certainly his face lightened. 'A Scouse, eh?'

Martini nodded. Now the man did smile, and Martini smiled back. Why not? 'Mind how you go,' the man said.

In the hills north of Madrid the weather was worse. The wind went hunting down the valleys, driving thin flurries of snow before it. Nothing else moved. The streams were frozen and the rocks were black with ice. There was absolutely nothing up there to interest anyone but a suicidal geologist.

Otto Krafft drove an embassy Mercedes deep into the hills until he found a place to park. Stephanie Schmidt was sitting beside him, stoutly shod and warmly dressed. They had not spoken since they set out. Now he said, 'You have the message?' She nodded.

He said, 'Carry on, then. Transmit as much as you can in the space of ten minutes.' She took a leather suitcase from under her feet and got out.

At first the climbing was easy. The wind in her face was refreshing and the slope was nothing to worry a fit young woman. Still, before she had gone fifty yards, Otto noticed how the burden of the suitcase made her lopsided. He was not surprised; it weighed forty-five pounds. Then she reached a steeper gradient, studded with outcrops, and soon she was struggling. Struggling to keep her feet, and struggling to keep the suitcase from whacking against a rock.

The car looked like a toy when Stephanie Schmidt stopped beside a flat slab, half-way up the slope. She had been determined to reach the top because she knew transmission would be better at height, but the hill was far worse ahead and her lungs were fighting for air like a couple of small wild animals and there was a widening pain around her heart. Also her right arm was one long ache. She placed the suitcase very carefully and peeled her fingers off the handle. Already the chill of the wind was working through her clothes; she knew she had to start transmitting soon, before the cold made her shiver; but she must get her breath back first.

She opened the suitcase, switched on the transmitter, made all the checks. It was encouraging to see the little lights glow and to hear the soft buzz in her headphones. Good. Time to call up base.

She made five attempts before she got an acknowledgement. By now the cold was attacking from all quarters, numbing her legs on the rock and bringing tears as the wind whipped her eyes. She slipped the message under the clips and began sending. Her wrist felt rusted and her fingers were stiff and clumsy. The message looked enormously long. She tapped and tapped and tapped. The wind rattled the message-sheet, blurring the words. Tiny pockets of snow gathered inside the suitcase.

'Bang!' Otto Krafft said. 'You're dead.' He was sitting on a rock, higher up the hill. Stephanie Schmidt was so startled that she stuttered the key and made a nonsense of that transmission. 'Sign off now,' he said. 'Switch off. Pack up.'

He carried the suitcase back down to the car. There was a flask of hot coffee for her. They said nothing on the way back to the city. She did not dare look at his face so she glanced often at his hands on the wheel – the manliest hands in the world – and worried because she had not reached the top. Why had he said *Bang! You're dead*?

No coffee for Ferenc Tekeli. He sat on a bench by a tram stop outside a factory in a part of Madrid the tourists never saw, and he worked his muscles, clenching and squeezing and pressing, to keep some of the cold at bay. The discomfort didn't much bother him – he had suffered worse, and longer, in jail – and anyway he was well wrapped up in an ex-army great-coat, so patched and dirty that its original colour was lost. The trams came and went, screeching and sparking on the battered track. Tekeli had been sitting for an hour and his rump was numb, but if needed he could sit for another hour, or two. Jail taught patience.

From time to time people came and sat until their tram arrived. Few spoke.

The man Tekeli had been waiting for looked just like the others: stained overalls, scuffed boots, needed a shave. The difference was that when he sat he said in English: 'More bloody snow on the way.'

Tekeli scratched his forehead and yawned. 'Bloody weather,' he said. 'Freeze your balls off.'

They sat hunched, facing the road, not seeing each other, while several trams went by.

'Been waiting long?' the man asked.

'Good bit,' Tekeli said.

Another pause, before the man gave a snuffling chuckle and said, 'Makes you laugh, doesn't it? Spend all day making something that flies at four hundred miles an hour and then you have to hang about for a sodding tram.'

Tekeli chuckled too and said, 'What is it, a new fighter?'

'Well, it's not a lousy tank.'

'Four hundred . . .' Tekeli sniffed. 'Doesn't seem possible, does it? Not on one engine. I bet it's got two engines.'

'Dunno. Not my job.'

79

'Oh.' Tekeli rested his elbows on his knees, and waited. Nothing came. 'Hasn't it flown yet, then?'

The man leaned away and blew his nose through his fingers.

'What I don't get,' Tekeli said, 'is how do they know it can do four hundred if it hasn't flown yet?'

'You ask too many fucking silly questions,' the man said, 'and for that you will be hanged by the neck until you are dead.' He got up and trudged away.

Two miles outside the *Estacion del Norte* the railway lines passed under a major road, and Docherty was painting the bridge. To be strictly accurate he was preparing to paint it: chipping away old bits of flake, cleaning off any rust, covering the patches with red lead. It was a long bridge, made of many girders, and clearly he had weeks of work ahead. Docherty, in paint-stained overalls and with a torn beret pulled down over his ears, just got on with it. Even when a policeman paused and remarked that it was about time someone did something, this whole damn bridge was rusting away, Docherty only grunted and kept chipping. At 1 p.m. he collected his pots and brushes and left.

The post-mortem began at 3 p.m. in a large room at the German embassy. All four Abwehr recruits were present, plus their controllers and several instructors. Brigadier Wagner sat at the back and watched.

Dr Hartmann spoke first. 'The mission involved visiting six locations on foot and gathering intelligence,' he said. 'The agent was caught and shot.' He looked at Laszlo Martini. 'Is that right?'

Martini had turned very pale. 'No, it's not,' he said, too loudly. 'I followed my orders, I found three locations and I have absolutely no doubt—'

'Why were you dressed like that?' Hartmann asked. 'Flying jacket, expensive hat, silk scarf?'

'It was damned cold. Did you want me to freeze?'

'An agent should be inconspicuous. You walked down the centre of the street, dressed like a peacock and waving a street map.'

'What should I do? Knock on doors and ask the way?' Martini was trembling with indignation.

'You should have studied the map and mastered the route before you set out. And when Joachim here asked for your identity card you reacted very badly.'

'He surprised me, he made me jump.'

Joachim stood up and said, 'You repeated my words, which made you look nervous. Then you panicked when you folded the map and tore it. Worst of all, you looked straight at me when you gave me your identity card and continued to look at my face, my eyes.'

'We have told you,' Hartmann said, 'at a checkpoint, when you have to show your papers, *always look away*. Look indifferent. Look bored. It's a routine, you have shown your papers a thousand times, it's not important, you don't care.' By now Martini seemed crushed with shame.

'And finally,' Joachim said, 'a man from Birmingham is not known as a "Scouse". That is for Liverpool.'

'Failed the test,' Hartmann said, and sat down.

Otto Krafft stood.

'Simple task,' he said. 'Morse transmission by short-wave set. The agent was probably captured and shot.' He looked at Stephanie Schmidt. 'Why did you climb the hill?' he asked.

It was the last question she expected. The longer she stared at him the more foolish she felt until the silence became an intolerable ache and she blundered into speech. 'I didn't climb it all,' she said, 'I only climbed half of it.' Even to her, that sounded feeble. Worse than feeble: stupid.

'In that case,' Otto said, 'why did you climb only half of the hill?' He pitied this poor young woman and he hated her mute adoration, but nobody except Franz Werth would have guessed it from his manner.

'The wind and the cold,' she said. 'The radio was so heavy that . . .' She rubbed her right arm. 'I'm sorry. I'm sure I'll do better next time if only—'

'Not a chance,' Otto said. 'No next time. You're dead, I shot you. The British have detector vans. You know that. The longer

81

you transmit, the greater their chances of finding you. You were on the air for nearly twenty minutes. I said ten.'

'I forgot.' That sounded dreadful. 'I mean I remembered at the start but it was hard to use the Morse key, I couldn't get any speed and some mistakes happened so . . . so I had to . . . to correct . . .' Her voice dried up.

'Your wrist was stiff because you carried the case in your right hand,' Otto said. 'That's an elementary mistake. You've been told a dozen times. It was freezing cold up there so your fingers were numb. There was no need to climb the hill in the first place. You could have transmitted from the back of the car; the signal would have been perfectly strong. I didn't tell you to go up there. It was your idea. And supposing it had been essential, you could always have asked me to carry the set.'

'I'm sorry, I'm sorry,' she whispered.

'What's more, the message was needlessly long.' Otto produced the paper and read aloud: *In response to your previous communication dated last Thursday . . .* You could have cut all that.'

'It wasn't my message,' she said, pleading.

'It was your life,' Otto said. 'You lost it and you bungled the message too. Failed the test.' As he turned away he looked briefly at Franz Werth, a look that said *Don't blame me, it was your lousy idea in the first place.*

Richard Fischer came forward. 'The mission required the agent to hang around an aircraft factory and gather intelligence about a new fighter. The agent was probably arrested, in Bruno's opinion.'

Bruno stood up. 'You pressed too hard,' he said to Tekeli. 'I gave you an opening and you charged into it, demanding further detailed information. Is it a new fighter? How many engines? Has it flown yet? Bang-bang-bang. It wasn't a chat at a tram stop, you were kicking the door down.'

'That's prison for you,' Tekeli said. 'It destroys the art of civilized conversation. What should I have said?'

'The trick is to talk *to* the man *about* the man,' Bruno said. 'Leave the aeroplane aside, you'll get to it eventually. Flatter him, get him relaxed, let him chat about the most important

82

subject in the world: *himself*.' He turned to Fischer and adopted the workman's accent. 'I wish they made bloody trams that go at four hundred miles an hour.'

'You said a mouthful, chum,' Fischer said. 'That's the best idea I heard all week.'

'Sooner I get home, sooner I get to bed.'

'I expect you've earned it,' Fischer said.

'Too bloody true.'

'I couldn't do your job, and that's the honest truth,' Fischer said. 'All that responsibility. I'd be scared to death.'

Bruno smirked. 'You've got to have broad shoulders, I suppose. Strong eardrums, too, come to that.'

'Eardrums?' Fischer looked quaintly puzzled. 'Strong eardrums?'

'Engine-testing,' Bruno explained. 'Bloody deafening it is. Still, you got to expect a bit of noise from two thousand horsepower, haven't you?'

'*Two thousand* . . .' Fischer rolled his eyes.

'And that's just the one engine,' Bruno said. 'You should hear both of them going! Blast the laces out your boots, it would.'

'You see?' Fischer said to Tekeli. 'He *wants* to boast a bit. All you need to do is make admiring noises and wait. Don't press. Pressing annoys him. He gets suspicious. You failed the test.'

He gave way to Franz Werth. 'The mission was to sabotage a road bridge by planting explosives under the central arch. The agent survived but so did the bridge. No explosives were planted.'

'They will be,' Docherty said. 'Give me another five days.'

Everyone laughed. After three depressing failures, Docherty was an entertaining flop. 'Five days?' Werth said. 'I was rather hoping for five hours.'

'You didn't say five hours. You didn't say any time.'

'I assumed that urgency was implicit in the order.'

'Well, now. D'you want it fast or d'you want it good?' said Docherty. That silenced Werth. 'It takes time and care to destroy a great big bridge like that. The police come and go on top. The trains come and go underneath. Suppose a driver suddenly sees a strange man crawling in and out the steelwork. What does he think? But if a man starts painting that bridge on Monday, by Friday nobody even sees him any more. Him and his big pots of paint. Which are really full of dynamite. Am I right?'

Werth nodded. 'You've done it before.'

'I've done it before,' Docherty said. 'And never failed.'

'Thank you, gentlemen,' said Brigadier Wagner. 'And, of course, Fräulein Schmidt.' They all turned to listen. 'I have one thing to add. At the end of this course, only two agents will be sent to England. Obviously they must be the two best qualified. As for the other two . . .' Wagner smiled like an undertaker. 'A painful decision, a very painful decision. And now I think we might have some refreshments.'

The four recruits came together into a defensive huddle. 'Why do they humiliate us?' demanded Laszlo Martini, softly and savagely. 'I offer them my life and they treat me like an idiot.'

'You behaved like an idiot,' Ferenc Tekeli said through half a chocolate biscuit. 'They seem to like you,' he told Docherty. 'How do you do it? The rest of us are hopeless failures.'

'Oh, it's easy.' Docherty waited until they were all listening. 'Fake everything,' he said. 'Lie, cheat, and swindle at all times. Never let an honest word pass your lips.'

Martini was disgusted, Schmidt was startled, Tekeli was intrigued. 'Really?' he said.

'It's the honest truth. Would I lie to you?'

The controllers were grouped around Brigadier Wagner, who was saying: 'No, no, no. You haven't been listening, Fischer. I never told you they were ready to go. Any fool can see that such is not the case. Ready to go? Two of them couldn't find the menu in a restaurant, for God's sake.'

'But you said they were going in, sir.'

'And so they are.'

'All?' Krafft asked.

'Probably. When I said only two would go, that was to buck up the other two, make them train harder.'

'The woman is a born victim,' Krafft said. 'She can't win, ever.'

84

'Maybe, maybe. It's surprising what resources people discover inside themselves when they are tested to the full. In any case I've found that it boosts the morale of the rest of the group if they regard one member as a loser. No winners without losers. And besides, Berlin is anxious to get some radio sets into Eldorado's hands.'

'Ah,' Fischer said. 'I begin to understand. We send the sets in with our new agents.'

'Through Ireland, probably,' Wagner said. 'Rendezvous with Eldorado one week from next Tuesday.'

This was startling news. It meant doing a ton of work in a great rush. It also meant the training course would be cut very short.

'Two of them stand a chance,' Dr Hartmann said. 'The Irishman and the Hungarian are natural survivors, I think. The other two . . . I'm not so sure.'

'I am,' Franz Werth said. 'The British will shoot them within forty-eight hours.'

'Maybe, maybe,' Brigadier Wagner said. 'It makes little difference. If they don't go we should have to shoot them here. I can't risk allowing a couple of chumps like Martini and Schmidt to run free in Madrid with all their knowledge of the Abwehr.'

Otto Krafft said, 'But you don't mind if they tell it to the British?'

Wagner was getting bored with the discussion. 'Betrayal to the enemy is an everyday hazard. I can cope with that. Local gossip is worse. It's like dry rot: it spreads back up the system. The only solution is to cut it out.' He fell silent as Laszlo Martini approached them.

'I am a crack shot with a pistol,' he announced harshly. 'I can shoot Winston Churchill for you from fifty yards. I can do it now, I need no further training. I shot for Italy in the Olympic Games.'

'Churchill,' said Brigadier Wagner. 'What an interesting idea. Of course, Churchill is not Stalin.' Martini's mouth twitched: he was not sure what that remark meant. 'I understood that your main concern was to aid the anti-Bolshevik crusade,' Wagner explained.

'Churchill is Stalin's puppet in the west,' Martini said.

'How true. Well, why not? Of course, you will have to lose your beard.' Wagner glanced around him. The others nodded.

'Is it essential?'

Fischer said, 'The English think that anyone with a beard has a bomb in his back pocket.'

Martini hesitated. 'I see . . . When may I have a pistol?'

'Now, if you like. Bruno! Bruno, kindly escort Mr Martini to the armoury, would you? Thank you so much.'

They watched him go. 'According to Eldorado, Mr Churchill is on a warship in a convoy to India,' Otto Krafft said.

'Oh well,' Wagner said. 'Maybe he'll shoot Sir Stafford Cripps instead. Cripps is, I believe, the Minister for Aircraft Production, a much thinner man and therefore a more challenging target.'

'Martini never shot for Italy,' Fischer said.

'Nor did Inocencio Slonski,' Dr Hartmann said.

'Slonski, Slonski,' Werth said. 'That name sounds unfamiliar. Why have I never heard it before?'

'Because our tame assassin hates it. He calls himself Martini-Hoffman-de-Seversky-Danacek but his real name is Inocencio Slonski. Russian father, Spanish mother. I gave his fingerprints to the Spanish police and they gave me a dismal list of convictions for minor fraud.'

'Explains a lot,' Otto Krafft said. 'He's living in a dream world.'

'Aren't they all?' Wagner asked; but nobody answered.

Later, Richard Fischer came to the Brigadier's office with a small problem. 'I'm trying to draft the signal to Eldorado for the rendezvous with our new agents, sir,' he said. 'We don't know where Eldorado lives, of course. He's always insisted on that and it's good policy. What we don't know can't slip out. All our communications with him are via the Spanish diplomatic bag. Now, I'm very reluctant to send him details of the new agents – photographs and so on. It's tempting providence. One leak and we lose the lot. On the other hand, how are they to meet?'

Wagner said, 'We have pictures of Eldorado?'

'Yes, sir.'

86

'Then this is what you do. The new agents memorize his face. You signal Eldorado to be . . .' Wagner strolled over to a wall map of Britain. 'To be in Liverpool at the railway station, platform one, at noon. Don't say anything to him about the agents. Let *them* find *him*.'

'He'll think it odd if we don't give any sort of reason, sir.'

'Oh, tell him . . .' Wagner thought about it for ten seconds. 'Tell him Winston Churchill will be there.'

'But Churchill is on a convoy to India, sir.'

'Exactly. That is why it is essential for Eldorado to check out a report that he's going to be in Liverpool.' Wagner took Fischer by the shoulders, turned him round, and gave him a gentle push towards the door. 'Forget about the truth, Richard. Do what works.' He watched Fischer leave. 'Sometimes I think you're too pure for this job,' he called after him.

Define the problem, Freddy Garcia told himself as the soup was served. How can you get an answer until you're sure what the question is? Very well. The problem is in two parts. Luis Cabrillo won't work unless we let him out, and we daren't let him out because he knows too much. Ditto Julie Conroy. OK. Nothing we can do to alter Part One. He's got to work, we can't drop him, far too valuable. So the only variable has to be Part Two.

The simple solution was to provide total round-the-clock protection for the pair. Hugely expensive and they would rapidly grow to loathe it.

For a wild minute of utter fantasy Freddy considered plastic surgery. Make Luis unrecognizable and the Abwehr could never find him. The fantasy disappeared with the soup plate.

Over some sort of mackerel pie – Freddy disliked mackerel but there was a war on – he wondered whether it might be possible to persuade the Abwehr that Eldorado, while generally sound and reliable, was neurotic about the possibility that the British might have turned a few German agents. Immunize the Abwehr against the truth by injecting them with a drop of it.

No, no, no. Rotten idea. Highly dangerous and it might

87

raise suspicions that didn't at present exist. Forget it, forget it.

The rest of the mackerel pie produced nothing but fishbones.

The steamed currant duff contained very few currants. Freddy thought of convoys torpedoed in the heaving, freezing mid-Atlantic and told himself he was lucky. A small panic squeezed his lungs: he was running out of variables. Couldn't change the protection. Or the appearance. Or the Abwehr's preconceptions. What was left? Hypnosis? Brain surgery?

A five-watt light bulb flickered feebly in a dim corner of his mind and went out. He shut his eyes and worked very hard at making it come on again.

An hour later he was standing in front of the Director.

'It seems to me, sir, that our whole difficulty arises because someone told Eldorado about the supposedly universal scope of the Double-Cross System,' Freddy said. 'Someone told him we run every German agent in Britain, and he of course believes it. Therefore the solution is to make him un-believe it.'

'Tell him he was misinformed? Think he'd swallow that?'

'No. It's got to be a lot stronger. Eldorado's got to convince himself that we don't control all the Abwehr agents. I can think of only one way to achieve that. He must meet some Abwehr agents who are quite obviously *not* under our control.'

The Director blinked rapidly for about four seconds and then laughed. 'Nasty shock for young Eldorado.'

'It could be made into quite a dramatic occasion.'

'Do it,' the Director said. 'Bamboozle him. Scare the Spanish pants off him. This is a serious business, Freddy. It deserves a code name.' He opened a folder and ran his finger down a list. 'Shoelace,' he said. 'That's the next allocated word. Operation Shoelace.' He wrinkled his nose so that his spectacles bounced. 'Shoelace . . .' He stared across the desk. 'Bit feeble.'

'How about "Bamboozle"?' Freddy suggested.

'Operation Bamboozle.' The Director let the sound hang in the air. He liked its punch and rhythm. 'Bamboozle,' he repeated. 'Yes.'

88

'Doubly appropriate,' Freddy said. 'Eldorado's been doing it to others for ages. Now it's going to be done unto him.'

Brigadier Christian never succeeded in remembering the name that Wolfgang Adler had identified as the bad link in the Eldorado Network.

The more he studied the files at Abwehr headquarters, the less confidence he felt in his ability to re-create his conversation with Adler. The names of the sub-agents jostled in his mind – Nutmeg and Knickers, Haystack and Garlic, Pinetree and Seagull and Hambone – until they were all utterly interchangeable. Christian finally abandoned the chase and went back to the raw material, the files of agents' reports. If Adler had spotted something incriminating it must still be there. Christian went on the hunt. If the SD had infiltrated their man into the Eldorado Network, it could only be in order to discredit the network and eventually destroy it. Steal the jewel from the Abwehr's crown and you were half-way to stealing the crown itself. Christian did his best to suppress his anger but that sort of treachery enraged him. He had heard Admiral Canaris say that Eldorado was worth at least one Panzer division to the Wehrmacht, and here was Himmler's SD trying to sabotage that Panzer division while it was fighting its very hardest, and all to feed Himmler's political jealousies! Christian prided himself on being a plain soldier – he certainly wasn't a member of the Nazi party – and he had a simple code of honour. All those helping Germany win this war deserved the best. All the rest deserved to be shot.

He saw little of General Oster. After that bizarre and bewildering guided tour of Great Architectural Triumphs that Hitler Never Built, Christian had worried whether the General was suffering from the severe strain of his job. To be Chief of Staff of the Abwehr, a vast organization responsible for German military intelligence throughout the world – that was enough to crack any man. In particular Christian worried about Oster's sarcastic, sneering remark directed at the Führer: *This was a war to satisfy Hitler's vanity and make him famous.* What on earth was that

89

supposed to mean? It made no sense. On the other hand as soon as Christian had spoken up for sanity and had had the courage stoutly to defend the war which was, as he had said, 'for the benefit of the German people', Oster had changed tack.

But his new tack had been almost as strange: *Sooner or later, every war comes to an end.* Followed by something about doing a deal with the West, and Eldorado being a very good go-between, so keep him warm and happy.

That puzzled Christian. He tried to look at it from every angle and he got nowhere. There was nobody he could trust to ask for an objective opinion. He even wrote out a complete transcript of Oster's conversation, as well as he could remember it. On paper it looked even worse. It was almost too bad to be true. What in God's name did Oster think he was playing at?

Christian stared at his transcript. It was laid out like the pages of dialogue in a play. And suddenly he realized: that must be the answer. That explained everything.

Oster had been playing a part. Christian had arrived in Berlin in very peculiar circumstances. Oster had decided to test his strengths and check his loyalties. Was Christian the sort of man who could be tempted to drift under pressure from the powerful opinions of a superior officer? Did he have a mind of his own, or would he agree to anything just because Oster said so? Lean on Christian, and how did he react? That was obviously what Oster had been trying to find out.

But how about Eldorado, 'the best go-between we could have'? Christian solved that one in no time.

When the Führer unleashed his secret weapon – or weapons, because the news was full of the ceaseless efforts of brilliant German scientists to place revolutionary means of victory in the hands of the fighting man – then hostilities would end overnight. The enemy's resolve would crumble like a sugar-lump in a rainstorm. How best could the Führer negotiate with a nation like Britain that was in a state of collapse? (And of course without Britain, America was helpless.) Fast, reliable channels of communication would be essential. Who better than Eldorado? That was obviously what Oster had been driving at, and it was a brilliant idea.

Christian acted. He signalled Madrid Abwehr to get some radio sets into Eldorado's hands pretty damn quick. When the crunch came, he didn't want to have to depend on the Spanish diplomatic bag.

While he was at it, Christian sent a few more signals to Madrid. German naval intelligence had failed to find any sign of the special convoy. *Query Eldorado re his Churchill India-bound report,* Christian ordered. Luftwaffe intelligence had been sceptical about another item. *Query Eldorado re report on Low-level Parachute,* Christian ordered. *Query Eldorado re Buranda: who/what/where?* He signed the signals *Oster* and went off to a well-deserved lunch.

One thing that had seriously worried Eldorado's Abwehr controllers when his first reports began reaching them was his sloppy accountancy. Obviously he didn't fully understand the British monetary system. The classic case was his claim for a rail fare of £1 23s 18d. Richard Fischer had kept that claim and now he showed it to the four recruits. 'This should be a death warrant,' he said. 'Anyone in England who thinks this price exists is asking to be caught and shot. What's wrong with it?'

They all looked at Docherty.

'The letter "s" means shillings and the letter "d" means pence,' he said. They were all speaking English and Docherty enjoyed delivering his words in an Irish brogue as thick as shoe-leather. 'You get twenty shillings to your pound and twelve pence to your shilling.'

'So what's the correct statement for this rail fare?' Fischer asked, and waved at Docherty to be silent.

Stephanie Schmidt thought like mad and got there first. 'Two pounds and four shillings and six pennies,' she said, and held her breath until Fischer nodded.

'You are in London and you enter a pub and ask for a large whisky,' he said. 'The barman serves it, you ask how much, he says eighteen pence. Is he too a spy?'

'Either a spy or a spycatcher,' Martini said.

Ferenc Tekeli said, 'He could just be a foreigner. There must be thousands of foreigners in London now.'

'No, he's English,' Fischer said. 'Eighteen pence is a common way of saying one shilling and sixpence when that is the full price. Similarly a price may be quoted entirely in shillings, without reference to pounds. Twenty-three shillings for a coat, for instance.'

'Jesus Christ,' Martini said angrily. 'What have the British got against the decimal system?'

'And don't forget,' Docherty warned them, 'there's four farthings to the penny, as well.'

'In everyday speech,' Fischer went on, 'a pound is known as a quid, a shilling is a bob and there is a half-crown coin worth two-and-six that is commonly called half a dollar. Perversely the British have no such coin as a crown. Or a dollar. Is that all clear? Now then: weights and measures. Forget the metric system. Twelve inches make one foot, three feet one yard, and one thousand seven hundred and sixty yards equal one mile.'

'We can't remember all that,' Martini protested.

'British schoolchildren master it without difficulty,' Fischer told him.

'Chinese children talk Chinese,' Martini pointed out. 'So what?'

'I was in China last year,' Docherty said. 'Bought a small Chinese infant for half a dollar. Spoke perfect English.'

'Moving on to the British system of weights,' Fischer said. 'We start with the ounce. Sixteen ounces make one pound. Fourteen pounds make one stone, eight stone one hundredweight, twenty hundredweight one ton. Right, let's go over those. Here's an actual example. Butter costs half a crown a pound but your weekly ration is only three ounces, so how much should you pay?' Fischer gave an encouraging smile. Everyone but Docherty looked blankly helpless.

Schmidt said, 'Three ounces?'

Docherty sucked in his breath. 'And lucky to get it,' he said.

'Put it another way,' Fischer said. 'How much change would you expect from a pound note?'

Next day there was a written examination on British currency and systems of measurement. Schmidt accused Laszlo Martini of cheating by looking at her answers. He denied it, she slapped his face, he bloodied her nose, she kicked him in the balls. It was not the only angry dispute. They all competed fiercely – for practice time on the Morse keys; at the firing range; in the explosives department; in the gymnasium, where they learned how to kill without weapons. There were many squabbles. Brigadier Wagner approved. 'Aggression!' he said to Dr Hartmann. 'That's what war's all about, isn't it?' Hartmann returned a bleak smile. As far as he could see, war was all about terrifying danger in squalid discomfort and he intended to stay as far away from it as possible.

Freddy Garcia found Luis and Julie on the terrace, enjoying a rare spell of sunshine. 'Good news!' he announced. 'You're out of jail. Quarantine is over. Where would you like to go?'

'Templeton said he'd take us to see the Changing of the Guard,' Julie said, 'but then he went away.'

Luis climbed on to the top of the terrace wall. 'I want to meet the King,' he said. He began walking, arms outstretched. 'Also the Queen.'

'Don't know about that, old boy.'

'You're bloody useless, Garcia. I bet the Abwehr could get me to meet Herr Hitler.'

'Let's go and see the Oxford colleges,' Julie said.

'Oh, Oxford!' Luis scoffed. He reached a corner and made a tricky turn. 'Nowadays it's just the Latin Quarter of the Cowley Motor Works.'

'How d'you know? You've never been there. You read that in a book.'

'I've read all the books,' Luis said. 'Listen, I'm hungry. What's for lunch?' He jumped down.

'I'll find you some jolly good pageantry,' Freddy promised. 'You'll like that.' But as they went indoors the phone was ringing. It was the Director. Freddy went to his office and took the call on his scrambler.

'Something odd has happened,' the Director said. 'Madrid Abwehr has sent a signal saying they want Eldorado to go to Liverpool next Tuesday. They've never done that before, have they?'

'Not since we brought him to England, sir.' Freddy thought hard. 'They once tried to set up a rendezvous with another agent but that was a long while back. Anyway, it flopped. Do they say why?'

'Report from a normally reliable source that Winston Churchill is going to be at Liverpool railway station on Tuesday at twelve noon. Platform one, so they say.'

'I see.' Garcia's mind bounced rapidly off the various implications. 'I wonder why they want Eldorado to go, sir? I mean, Seagull is in Liverpool. They know that.'

'Yes. But it was Eldorado who recently reported Churchill *en route* to India.'

'Um.' Freddy scratched his nose. 'Can we find out if the Abwehr's information is correct, sir?'

'Probably. To what end?'

'Well, sir, if the Prime Minister is *not* going to visit Liverpool on Tuesday, we've nothing to worry about. Eldorado can simply tell the Abwehr he went there and nothing happened.'

'What if someone who looks like Winston Churchill arrives on platform one? To my knowledge at least two men who could pass as Churchill's double are in circulation. What then?'

'Yes, but . . . I mean, the Abwehr aren't going to know that.' Silence from the other end. 'Are they, sir?'

'Look, Freddy: my guess is Eldorado's controllers in Madrid are less than happy. Eldorado promised them a convoy. No convoy, and it seems they've got wind of a visit by the Prime Minister to Liverpool instead. Now, if you were the Abwehr, what would you want?'

'I'd want to know what the dickens was going on, sir.'

'Quite. And you might even want to reassure yourself that your man in England was absolutely straight. That he wouldn't lie to get himself out of an awkward corner. How would you do that?'

'Um . . . How would I do that? I suppose . . .' Freddy was

talking to gain time to think. 'Well, I suppose I'd . . . Let's see . . . Yes, I think the best way would be . . .' His brain came galloping to the rescue. 'Would be to have *another* agent on Liverpool station next Tuesday. Watching Eldorado, to see what he sees.'

'And that's why Eldorado's got to go to Liverpool,' the Director said. 'He must be seen to be there. It's too risky, otherwise. Do you agree?'

'Oh, absolutely, sir,' Freddy said. 'The whole network might be at stake.'

'You can use this Liverpool expedition to promote Operation Bamboozle,' the Director said. 'I don't want him coming back still believing we control every Abwehr agent in Britain.'

'Yes, sir.' There was a pause while they each reviewed the situation. 'Of course, I may come back not believing it either.'

The Director grunted, and hung up.

Luis and Julie had begun lunch. 'Toad in the hole again,' Luis complained. 'Tastes even more disgusting than it sounds.'

'Never mind,' Freddy said brightly. 'I've just arranged a super outing. We all go to Liverpool on Tuesday!'

'Not me,' Luis told him. 'I'm not going anywhere. I've decided to become a recluse.'

'You'd hate it, old chap. And think how much Madrid would miss you.'

'Fuck 'em.' Luis put his elbows on the table and put his head in his hands.

'OK. You stay, we'll go,' Julie said. 'Has Liverpool got much pageantry?'

'Liverpool has *everything*,' Freddy said. 'It's the gateway to England. It has a cultural heritage you simply can't find anywhere else. Its ambience is absolutely . . . um . . . unique.' Freddy thought hard. 'We have a saying: "The man who is tired of Liverpool is tired of life." '

'Dr Johnson,' Luis said. 'And it was London, not Liverpool.'

'He was misquoted.'

Luis looked at him with suspicion. 'Can I get fresh sardines in Liverpool?' he asked.

'Luis, if you can get them anywhere in Britain you can get them there,' Freddy said. 'That's my solemn promise.'

Luis pushed his lunch away, only half-eaten. The tip of a sausage poked through a crust of batter, like a whale breaking the surface of a golden brown sea. The longer Luis looked at it, the lower his eyelids sank. 'Mr Churchill did not sail to India in a convoy,' he said softly. 'The British Navy cancelled the convoy when they discovered that so many U-boats had been diverted to intercept it.' He prodded the sausage with his fork and made it submerge.

'Of course they did,' Freddy said. 'Will you write it?'

Luis stood. 'I might,' he said.

Everyone noticed that Laszlo Martini was in much better spirits since the Abwehr armoury had issued him with a pistol. What gratified him as much as the weapon was its silencer, an attachment as big as a beer bottle. He wore the gun in a huge holster that dangled under his left armpit. It made him feel tremendously strong.

Laszlo had never shot anyone in his life; indeed he had never even struck anyone. He was small and not muscular; it was wise to stay out of fights. The night after he got his pistol he went out and shot two men. Their names were Stefano and Joaquim. They were large men who made a living as debt-collectors: they beat up people who owed money. It was a family concern. Stefano's uncle lent the money at high rates; when repayment was late his nephews found the borrower and hit him. Laszlo had suffered at their bruising hands more than once. Now he found them in a bar and invited them to come outside. In the alley behind the bar he shot one of them in the shoulder and the other in the leg. They fell down. The pistol made little noise, just a gasp like suppressed surprise. It was all so easy. Laszlo wished he had done it long ago. Nevertheless he took no further chances. He went straight to the German embassy and stayed there until the end of the agents' training. Then Brigadier Wagner decided that they all deserved one last night out on the town, at the Abwehr's expense.

He took them and the controllers to an expensive restaurant.

Laszlo felt fairly secure there. Ferenc Tekeli ate and drank hugely; Docherty was relaxed and amusing; Stephanie Schmidt became tearfully patriotic and offered to sing the Horst Wessel song. That was when Brigadier Wagner suggested they move on and see a bullfight. Laszlo was reluctant to show himself in public but he really had no choice, and so he put a good face on it. 'I was a matador once,' he announced. 'I was the youngest matador in Spain.'

'Good for you,' Franz Werth murmured.

'They awarded me both ears *five times*,' Laszlo said. 'Once I got both ears and the tail.'

'A meal in itself,' Ferenc said.

'That's nothing,' Docherty said. 'In Dublin cattle market I could have got you the ears and the tail and both kidneys with a good pound of ox liver thrown in at no extra cost. They know me well in Dublin cattle market,' he told the Brigadier.

'Very gratifying, I'm sure,' Wagner said.

Five of the eight advertised bulls had been killed by the time they reached the ring. It was very early in the season and the experiment of holding midweek bullfights in the evening was not hugely popular, so the Brigadier's party was able to get good seats. The sixth bull was a disappointment: stupid and slow and speedily brought to its end. A disgruntled shower of seat cushions and oranges flew into the arena, and the band played a *paso doble* very loudly. Ferenc Tekeli went off and came back with whole trays of salt peanuts and blood oranges and sugar doughnuts. He was having a wonderful time.

Laszlo was nervous. He felt dreadfully exposed, surrounded by all these people. Any one of them might be an enemy, or might report his presence to his enemies. He began searching for someone staring at him, for the fatal flicker of recognition.

Richard Fischer saw Laszlo looking about him and said, 'Quite like old times for you, I suppose.' Laszlo needed a couple of seconds to understand the remark.

'Yes,' he said. 'I killed my last bull over there.' He pointed to a distant stain in the sand. 'He was colossal, the greatest bull in Spain.' Then he fell silent. He was convinced that someone was watching him. Anxiety made his heartbeat skip and stamp.

The gates swung open as the seventh bull came hurtling into the ring like the shaggy wrath of God. Clearly it was in a ferociously bad temper.

Everyone cheered up. The picadors tried a nervous bit of bloodletting and a horse got smashed sideways. Now everyone was gripped by the spectacle; everyone except a young peanut-vendor in the aisle a few rows below the Brigadier's party. He was looking upwards. He was staring at Laszlo, or so it seemed to Laszlo when he noticed this solitary face amongst all the backs of heads. He looked hard and long at the youth, and the youth turned and walked away. Strolled away. No hurry.

You don't fool me so easy, Laszlo thought, you cocky little pipsqueak. The face was unfamiliar but that meant nothing. Blow holes in a couple of Madrid's gorillas and all their pals were out looking for you. Laszlo stood up and squeezed past the knees of the Brigadier's party. 'Have one for me while you're at it,' Ferenc said.

The peanut-vendor was wearing a bright yellow coat which made it easy to track him. He went down a flight of stairs and turned left into a wide, curving corridor ribbed with girders that had been white once, back in the days of El Greco when paint was cheap. Laszlo kept pace with him while bits of paper, chocolate wrappings, and trampled pages from old newspapers kept pace with Laszlo, urged along the corridor by one of those quirks of ventilation that inhabit large arenas. Every few seconds the crowd roared, and the roar filtered down to the corridor as an oddly random, pointless noise, like the sound of wild weather outside a castle. The kid was taking off his yellow coat as he walked. He went down more steps, turned to the right into another corridor and stopped at the window of a little office. As Laszlo walked past he was handing in his coat and his peanut tray. Now the sporadic roars were dulled and distant. Laszlo's footsteps echoed off the white-tiled walls like constant warnings. This is not wise, he told himself. This is not necessary. This is a terrific risk. Which produced the answer: Sure it's a risk. But it's terrific, it's irresistible, and it's too late to turn back now.

He stopped at a barred window with a broken pane. It gave a dusty view of a flaking wall. The more he looked at this nothingness the sillier he felt, and it made him angry.

The kid left the office and came towards him, whistling. Laszlo waited until he was about to pass and then turned, cleverly revolving on his heels, and said, 'OK, junior. What's the message?'

The kid was a lot younger than he had seemed upstairs. The big yellow coat had hidden his boney shoulders, which were like wire coat-hangers inside a too-small, too-old jersey. He was fourteen, maybe fifteen. But Laszlo didn't scare him. 'Beats me,' he said. 'What is the message?'

Laszlo stared into his eyes. Grey eyes, high cheekbones, big lower lip, pointed chin, needed a haircut. There were ten thousand kids like this in Madrid. Maybe gypsy, maybe a touch of Moor in the Arab nose. And the olive skin. A born liar, this one. Been stealing since he could walk. Since he could run, anyway. 'You know what happened to Stefano,' he said.

'Sure I know. Stefano got caught.'

'Don't make jokes with me.'

Now the kid seemed puzzled. 'Which Stefano? You mean Stefano the waiter? He got six months, didn't he? Why? Did he owe you—'

'Cut it out. You saw me upstairs.'

The kid shrugged. 'I saw a thousand people upstairs. You, I don't know from a hole in the ground.' He walked away.

Laszlo followed, anger burning like acid. 'Listen, you little piece of piss,' he said, and shoved the kid's shoulder. The kid stumbled and bounced off the wall.

'Hey, hey, hey,' he said. Fear made his voice crack. 'I don't know you. Get away from me, you lousy lunatic.' It was a very grown-up word and he stuttered a little over it. This encouraged Laszlo.

'You tell Stefano's uncle something from me,' he said, and began poking the kid in the chest to emphasize his words. 'You tell—'

99

'I wasn't looking at you, for Christ's sake!' The kid had worked out where Laszlo came from. 'It was the guy who bought my peanuts. He bought the whole damn tray! I never saw anyone do that before.' Upstairs, the roars of the crowd were following each other like heavy surf.

'You find Stefano's uncle,' Laszlo said, 'and you tell him from me to lay off.' He took out his gun, just for display.

The kid jumped away and his throat made a high, squeaking sound.

'Lay off, remember?'

'Yes. I'll tell him.'

Laszlo scratched his head with the muzzle of the big long silencer, the way they did in the movies, and stared the kid in the eyes until he made him blink. 'You lying piece of pigshit,' he said. 'You're not going to Stefano's uncle. You're going to the cops.'

The kid instantly ran, pigeon-toed and head back, arms pumping like pistons. Laszlo chased him. There were stairs at the end of the corridor. The kid went down them three and four at a time, much too fast, until his heel skidded off the edge of a step and he finished the rest in a whirling fall, an ugly blur of arms and legs and a shuddering head that only stopped when it whacked against some crates of empty bottles. Even then the kid got up, or nearly: one knee had quit. Laszlo was a fuzzy silhouette at the top of the stairs. Pointing. Aiming. The kid threw a bottle. It smashed half-way up. He threw another. Same result. Laszlo fired. He put three bullets into the kid's chest, all within a hand's span, just like that: *phut-phut-phut*.

As he sheathed the gun, he turned and saw Otto Krafft standing twenty yards away, watching.

'It's done,' Laszlo called out.

Otto came towards him and looked down the stairs. 'Business or pleasure?' he asked.

'A man like me has many enemies,' Laszlo said.

'That doesn't answer the question,' Otto said. High above could be heard the tramp of feet. Some people were not waiting to see the final bull. 'It was probably a silly question so I expect it would

100

have got a silly answer. Come on, let's get out of here. No more gunnery. Keep the artillery out of sight. Understand?'

'I need it,' Laszlo said. 'A man like me—'

'Yes, I know, I know. Many enemies.' He took Laszlo's arm.

'Not as many as before,' Laszlo said contentedly.

Christian was not stupid, and he was certainly not lazy, but he was not accustomed to doing much tough, original thinking. He could solve a complex problem by boiling it down to its essentials and then applying the standard treatment as taught at Staff College. Christian had done quite well at Staff College. Later, when he was put in charge of Madrid Abwehr he found the work straightforward provided he stuck to Staff College principles, one of which was: Don't look for the answer until you've defined the problem. Sounds obvious, but he had seen many officers so enthusiastic that they rushed into action before they knew exactly what it was they were trying to achieve. Christian had never made that mistake. He had always known exactly what target he was trying to hit, and why.

That, however, was before he came to Berlin and learned from Oster that this was not one war but several wars all rolled into a sprawling, confusing conflict. For the first time Christian had to think hard about the purpose of this conflict. What target must they hit in order to win? Was it America? Obviously not. The Luftwaffe didn't have a four-engined bomber, let alone one that could bomb New York or Washington or Boston and fly home again. Yet Hitler had declared war on America. Why? At that point America wasn't at war with Germany, Pearl Harbor was still burning, and Roosevelt had his hands full, so why did the Führer go looking for more trouble? To help Japan, because Japan was a partner with the Axis? Japan hadn't helped Germany when Hitler invaded Russia. All right, everyone thought the Russians would collapse and give up after six weeks, but surely the Japs could have attacked Stalin in the Far East when it became obvious that Germany could do with a bit of help . . . The more Christian brooded over it, the more it puzzled him. The aim and object of war was victory by conquest. Surely nobody in his right mind believed that Germany and Italy would force the USA to her knees? And you had to be pretty optimistic to expect the conquest of Britain.

These and many other thoughts wheeled around inside Christian's mind. Back in the beginning, in 1940, everything had gone so well and so quickly: the capture of almost all of Europe from the Pyrenees to Greece to Norway in just a year was a good start by anybody's reckoning. Even now Christian found it hard to believe it would not end in total inevitable triumph for the Third Reich, the Reich of a Thousand Years.

But if not victory, what was the alternative? A deal with the Allies? Christian tried to imagine Hitler at a great round table, haggling with Stalin and Churchill and Roosevelt. *Let me keep Poland and you can have France back. No, I want Greece. Who gets Bulgaria?* It was not a convincing picture and it soon faded. Christian was left looking at a war which could never be won, could only be lost. That idea he found intolerable.

Something else he couldn't understand was Oster's unfailing cheeriness. The General was, as usual, brisk and breezy when he took Christian off to lunch in the officers' dining-room at Abwehr HQ. 'Beefsteak today,' Oster said. 'One of the perks of tyranny.' He chose a table where a tall, red-headed man was sitting. Oster introduced him as Stefan Domenik. 'Watch out,' Oster said cheerfully. 'He's a wicked, corrosive influence.'

'You look very well on it,' Christian said. Domenik had a strong, suntanned face, with untroubled eyes and a wide, generous mouth that slipped easily into a smile.

'I'm happy in my work,' Domenik said.

'He tells jokes,' Oster said from the side of his mouth.

'Is that so terrible?' Christian asked, putting on a look of innocence for Oster's benefit.

'Show him,' Oster said.

'Italian Army manoeuvres,' Domenik said, and raised his arms in surrender.

'Heard it. We'll have the beefsteak,' Oster told the waiter. 'Haven't you any new jokes?' he asked Domenik.

'Mussolini goes on to a balcony to make a speech,' Domenik said. 'Thousands of Italians below. Mussolini says, "Perhaps you're wondering why you lot are down there while I am up here. Well, let me remind you of the old Neapolitan saying: If you want to keep the flies off one end of the table, put a bucket of shit on the other." '

Oster laughed so much that he dropped his napkin. 'I'm not sure I understand it,' he said, 'but it's very funny.' Christian had not laughed. 'Don't mind him,' Oster said. 'He's in deep mourning.'

'It's a very Italian joke,' Christian said safely. 'Wouldn't you say?'

'Know any good naval jokes?' Domenik asked him.

Christian shook his head. He was glad of his beard because it helped to hide his astonishment. You just didn't poke fun at any Fascist leader in Berlin. Even in Abwehr HQ. God alone knew who might be listening. Yet Oster was encouraging the man; asking for more.

'There's a new Luftwaffe joke,' Domenik said. 'A Luftwaffe mechanic in a fighter squadron goes to the stores and says to the storeman: "Can you give me a tailwheel for a new Messerschmitt 109?" And the storeman thinks for a bit, and then says, "Yes, that sounds like a fair swap." '

'Ah!' Oster said. 'Nice. Bull's-eye. Where did you hear that one?'

'Northern France, Abbeville airfield.'

'Yes. Of course. That's where our 109s have been coming up against their Typhoons.'

'Coming up,' Domenik said, 'and going down.'

The wine waiter appeared and Oster began discussing vintages. Christian leaned towards Domenik and said softly, 'It's a clever joke, but surely our Messerschmitts aren't as bad as that?'

'No, of course not. Excellent little plane, the 109. The trouble is the enemy's got a better one, and when you're a fighter pilot that's what concerns you.'

Oster eventually ordered a pre-war claret. 'Boring but reliable,' he said, and then noticed Christian's expression. 'Beneath that

103

grizzled beard there lies a grizzled face,' he told Domenik. 'What seems to be the trouble?' he asked Christian.

'Nothing, it's just that . . .' Christian fiddled with his cutlery. 'Well, sir, it's just that, to be completely honest, I don't think it helps the war effort to make disparaging jokes.'

'All jokes are disparaging,' Domenik murmured.

'And *repeating* such jokes is . . . is . . .'

'Try "unpatriotic",' Oster said.

'Criminal?' Domenik suggested. 'Treasonable?'

Christian shook his head. 'I don't see what good it does, that's all.'

'Canaris does,' Oster said. A plate of mushrooms fried in butter with garlic arrived, and he speared one with a toothpick. 'The Admiral made Stefan his official joke-collector. Eat, eat.'

'I get them from all over Europe,' Domenik said. 'Even Russia. Where's the best place to dig a slit-trench when the Russians attack?'

'Give up,' Oster said.

'Italy. Not exactly hilarious, I agree, but then the Eastern Front isn't a very amusing place, is it? I expect you'd like to know why the head of the Abwehr is interested in soldiers' jokes. It's because jokes provide a glimpse into the true morale of the armed forces.'

'They tell us what the men are really thinking,' Oster said. 'No point in listening to the generals, they don't know.'

The beefsteaks came. Domenik asked for English mustard. 'We get it from our man in Switzerland,' he explained.

'Stefan and I are the only people here who use it,' Oster said. 'The others disapprove, on principle.'

'You can carry patriotism too far,' Domenik said. Christian eyed the mustard a couple of times, but in the end he left it alone.

Later, with plenty of good meat and wine inside him, Christian felt more relaxed and cheerful. He even made them laugh. The conversation had wandered through many topics and returned to Italy. 'It's an absurd alliance,' Domenik said. 'How on earth has it lasted so long?'

'Goebbels says it's all a matter of trust and understanding,' Oster said.

'Exactly,' Christian said. 'We don't trust them and they don't understand us.'

'There you are!' Domenik told Oster. 'I knew he had a sense of humour.'

Christian tasted the thrill of risk and immediately wanted more. 'As a matter of fact I do know one Navy joke,' he said. Domenik took out a small notebook. 'Naval officer has been stationed in the north of Norway for a year and a half,' Christian said. 'Finally he gets some leave, flies home to his wife in Berlin; the first thing they do is jump into bed. Half an hour later, completely exhausted, they both fall asleep. The dog comes and scratches on the bedroom door. The officer wakes up in a panic and says, "Oh my God, it's your husband!" but his wife just turns over and says' – here Christian put a yawn into his voice – ' "Don't worry, darling, he's in the north of Norway." '

'Splendid.' Domenik was still writing. 'Very tasty indeed. There are a lot of infidelity jokes going around, but that's the best.'

'Glad to be of help.'

'Censorship never really does any good,' Oster said. 'People always find a way around it. They tell jokes. That's the loophole in censorship.'

'A nation breathes through its loopholes,' Domenik said.

Christian went back to his office feeling enlivened and encouraged, although he wasn't sure why. He felt purposeful. The walls were covered with different coloured cards, each colour representing an Eldorado sub-agent, and on the cards Christian had summarized the important elements of their reports. For days now he had been moving the cards about, grouping those with a common theme, tracking a story as it drifted from the red cards which were Wallpaper to the green of Garlic, the brown of Pinetree, the white of Nutmeg, the blue of Seagull. Each wall was a frozen splash of colour, and Christian was convinced that somewhere in all that mass of information was hidden the dirty secret that the late Wolfgang Adler had discovered. Christian prowled around the room, searching for something, he didn't know what but he knew he would recognize it when he saw it. Not just a mistake, you expected an agent to make mistakes. It had to be much worse. On that day in Madrid, Adler had come to Christian in a state of suppressed delight, convinced he had evidence of serious fraud, perhaps of treachery. But where did it lie?

'If anybody asks, tell them you work for the BBC,' Freddy Garcia said. 'Say you're an assistant producer, or something.'

'What about me?' Julie asked.

'American journalist. You can fake that, can't you?'

'Not assistant producer,' Luis said. 'Chief producer, me.'

'Holy shit,' she said wearily. 'He's off again.'

Freddy parked the car and they got out. All through supper Luis had grumbled and complained about his impossible work and his lousy employers, he didn't know which was worse, the Abwehr or MI5, they were both like pigs at a trough, gobbled up all you gave them and snorted for more . . . And the food, he said, was inedible, I mean look at it . . . And nobody could sleep on his bed which had more lumps than the gravy and why wasn't there any decent drinkable wine instead of this vinegar? On and on and on.

Finally, to shut him up, Freddy took them both down to the village pub, the George and Dragon.

The moonlight was brilliant, and it showed up the hanging inn-sign. Luis pointed. 'See that?' he said, sneering. 'Bloody saints, they're all the same. Let the poor little dragon have his fun, I say. It's only a woman, after all.'

'Keep practising,' Julie said. 'One day you'll be a total creep.'

The pub was full. Freddy bought beer for everybody; it seemed to be all there was to drink. When he got back to them, they were quarrelling. 'You two have a great talent for disagreement,' he said. 'It makes me wonder—'

'She lost us the table,' Luis said flatly. 'Typical.'

'You were too damn dithery,' she said.

Freddy said, 'Tell uncle.'

'Two tables become empty, at the same time,' Luis said. 'I say, "Quick, grab that table." She wants to know what's wrong with the *other* table. I say, "Who the hell cares? A table is a table! What d'you want? An illustrated prospectus?" By the time she makes up her mind both tables are taken. Both!'

Julie, in a voice like slowly tearing paper, said, 'I'm happy to stand.'

'You see what I have to live with? Nothing is ever right first time with this woman. Take a bus, she wants to know why you don't take a taxi. Take a taxi, she—'

'Listen, dummy, if you want to sit, then sit! It's your stupid life and get this: *nobody has to live with anybody*.'

'No? No?' Luis's forefinger began stabbing accusingly. 'So who was chasing who in Lisbon? You're the great memory. Try and remember *that*.'

'Chasing whom,' Freddy suggested, but it was wasted.

'Chasing? Where d'you get this chasing? I was hunting the silly bastard,' she explained to Freddy. 'I was going to kill him. Pity I didn't.' Several nearby drinkers had begun to take an interest. Freddy smiled hugely, as if it were all just a joke. Nobody was fooled.

'She wanted to marry me. You wanted to get your female hooks into me, didn't you?'

'You keep pointing that dirty digit and I'll break it off, so help me God.'

'Now I'm puzzled,' Freddy said, working his smile-muscles hard. 'I thought you were already married?'

'Sure. That's what Luis can't stand. Drives him wild to think he can't have everything he lays his horny hands on. Jealous.'

'Me? Jealous of your alcoholic hack of a husband? Spends his life sitting in hotel rooms making up lies about the war?'

'And what the hell d'you think you're doing?'

'Luis works for the BBC,' Freddy told the listening drinkers.

'That a fact?' one man said. 'There's a bloke over there who's in the BBC. Him in the red scarf. Jimmy somebody.'

'Good heavens!' Luis said. 'Fancy finding old Jimmy in here!' He took his beer and set off through the crowd.

107

Freddy and Julie looked at each other for several moments. His smile had gone but she was still pink with anger. 'Oh well,' Freddy said. 'Maybe he'll like Liverpool.'

'Don't hold your breath,' she said.

He took her arm and they moved to a more private corner. 'This isn't easy for you, is it? He seems determined to find fault everywhere. The peculiar part about it is that his work is so bloody brilliant. That's not just what we think, the other side says so too, they can't get enough of it, Madrid's given him another bonus. I mean, you'd think that would make him happy, but . . .'

'Have you told him?'

'Yes.'

'What did he say?'

'Said nothing about the bonus. Began talking about the Civil War. Told me the only party he could support was the royalists because he was a descendant of the ancient kings of Spain.'

'That's garbage.'

Freddy nodded. 'But if it makes him happy, who cares? Where is he now, anyway?'

Luis was talking to Jimmy somebody.

'You work for the BBC, *ja*?' he said.

'That's right. I'm a driver.'

'That is very interesting. Would you like to earn five pounds? I am a captain storm-trooper in the Adolf Hitler Division of the SS and I want to buy some big secrets.'

'Fancy that,' said Jimmy.

'Can you get me some big secrets? About five pounds' worth.'

Jimmy drank some beer and studied Luis through the glass. 'You don't look big enough to be a Nazi storm-trooper,' he said.

'All right then, ten pounds,' Luis said. *'Verdammter Engländer!'*

'Tell you what,' Jimmy said. 'You stay here and I'll see what I can lay my hands on.' He was soon lost in the crowd.

Freddy Garcia said to Julie, 'Perhaps if we gave him another medal . . . I might be able to wangle a George Cross for him. D'you think that would make him feel any better?'

'Forget it, Freddy.'

'You're right, he'd probably want to know why it wasn't a knighthood. Well, he can't have a knighthood and that's that.'

'Forget knighthoods. Forget anything to do with patriotism. Luis gets no kick out of patriotism. It's not his style.'

Freddy frowned. He swirled his beer until it came dangerously near the top. 'What a strange fellow he is,' he said.

Luis had drifted through the drinkers until he came to a man who looked like a caricature of a hunting squire. He wore faded, baggy tweeds and he had a powerful, hooked nose above a cavalry moustache that was turning silver at the ends. A copy of *The Times* poked out of a jacket pocket, and he was drinking beer from his own engraved pewter tankard. A spaniel sat at his heels. '*Sprechen sie Deutsch?*' Luis asked him.

The man examined him unhurriedly while he thought about the question. 'As a matter of fact I do,' he said. His voice was a courteous growl.

'*Das ist gut.* Allow me to introduce myself. I am SS-Sturm-bannführer von Rundstedt.' Luis clicked his heels.

'Are you, indeed? I'm Colonel Plunket. Retired, of course.' They shook hands. 'According to my newspaper von Rundstedt is a field-marshal and he's in France.'

'A dodge.' Luis tapped the side of his nose. 'To deceive the British Secret Service. Now then: you look like a chap who knows his way about. Where can I find the Allied Order of Battle?'

'My goodness,' Plunket said. 'That's a tall order.'

Luis edged closer. 'You won't be the loser,' he said, and nudged his elbow. 'I've got fifty gold sovereigns sewn into my underpants.'

'Have you, by God?' Plunket finished his beer. 'How frightfully resourceful . . . Look, old chap, you wait here and I'll go and get the . . . um . . . Order of Battle. Come on, dog.'

Freddy Garcia, standing on tiptoe, saw some of this encounter. 'He seems to be enjoying himself,' he told Julie. 'Maybe he just needs company. It's too quiet up at the house.'

'I'd certainly like some freedom. Being in Rackham Towers is like being in solitary at the country club. Why don't you let us loose? We're not going to run off and join the gypsies.'

109

'Wish I could, old girl. My hands are tied.'

She took one hand and gently shook it. 'Gosh,' she said. 'So they are.'

'*Achtung! Achtung!*' Luis said, smiling warmly at a gloomy man in the uniform of a Home Guard sergeant. 'I am the official representative of the Luftwaffe in the south of England and I wish to purchase a Spitfire.'

'Get fucked,' the sergeant said.

'May I buy you a drink?'

'Pint of mild, Fred!' the sergeant shouted. 'This kraut's paying.' Several other Home Guards turned and stared.

'Drinks for all these brave Tommies too,' Luis told the barman. 'How much is a torpedo?' he asked a passing sailor. 'Have a drink. I need secrets. The Führer pays top prices. Drinks for everyone! We are all in this war together, *ja*?'

Freddy and Julie had found seats. 'Can you still see him?' she asked.

'Don't worry. I've got a couple of men outside. He won't wander off.' Their heads were close together, their voices low.

'You're really married to this job, Freddy.'

'Oh, well. It's a big job. And my other marriage is sort of past tense now.'

'Mine too. Not that it was ever a stunning success. I guess I married Harry because my parents didn't like him as much as I did. I sometimes wonder if I was really in love, or just in love with the idea of being in love. I was only a kid, what did I know about anything? Harry was a big-shot journalist and that was very romantic, or so I thought. You know, always at the centre of the action, making the headlines. But *Harry* wasn't romantic. Passionate about news, sure. And ready for a roll in the hay once in a while, although if the phone rang, then step aside. You don't know what marriage to a journalist is like until you've experienced the thrill of lying underneath him while he talks to his editor a thousand miles away and you can feel his interest in you steadily shrinking in proportion to his growing enthusiasm for his next scoop.' Freddy heard a savage sadness in her voice. He reached for her hand. 'I've got no right to complain,' she said. 'I knew what

I was doing. No, dammit, that's not true. I hadn't the faintest idea what I was doing.'

They were completely hidden by the crowd. Freddy put his arm round her shoulders and whispered, 'You may think your love-life is none of my business but believe me it is. Eldorado and his network are developing into something really crucial. Could save thousands of lives. Maybe tens of thousands. Luis is worth a battleship. Two battleships.'

'I'll see your battleships,' she murmured, 'and raise you a brigade of tanks.'

'I'm serious. Luis has got to be kept happy. I can't afford to let him get depressed. He might go off the boil. You can help. You understand him.'

'Do I? He's impossible.'

'He's certainly difficult. The question is . . .' Freddy hesitated for a moment, '. . . do you love each other?'

Julie hunched her shoulders, and Freddy squeezed her arm reassuringly. Suddenly the pub seemed to be full of policemen. There was much shouting; a table went over and glasses broke; and Luis was being frog-marched through the drinkers, shouting '*Donner und Blitzen!* I demand to see the German consul!' The crowd fell back, and Luis, held by two constables, stared down at Freddy and Julie. 'Treacherous bastard,' he said with great feeling.

'Is this the man you came here with, sir?' a police inspector asked Luis.

'Public enemy number umpteen,' Luis said. 'Take him out and shoot him.'

'I'll explain all this outside,' Freddy told the inspector. But before they could leave, the barman had a drinks bill for three pounds two shillings and twopence that he wanted someone to pay. Freddy gave him a fiver and told him to keep the change.

The Heinkel 59 touched down on the black water and her floats carved a pair of long creamy wakes. It was four in the morning. The seaplane had taken off from Brest, on the north-west tip of

111

France, at midnight. She was a big strong machine, a biplane with twin engines, designed to rescue German aircrew from the sea, so she had plenty of room for four Abwehr agents from Madrid and their four suitcases.

All had dozed (and Ferenc Tekeli had slept) during the flight, but they came wide awake at the jolt and the sudden vibrant rush of water. In half a minute it had slackened almost to nothing. The pilot taxied softly and gently, the engines throttled back to a dull throb, and it was possible to feel the slight heave and dip of a swell. 'Get ready,' a crewman said to the agents. He began to unlock a door.

They went ashore in a large rubber dinghy. Leaving the Heinkel should have been easy: they had practised it several times; it was just a matter of climbing down a ladder, reaching one of the massive floats, and stepping into the dinghy. But Laszlo Martini's legs were stiff. Getting into the boat, he stumbled and trod on Stephanie Schmidt. She cried out in pain. 'Move over, can't you?' Laszlo said angrily.

'I'm in the right place, you stupid fool,' she hissed.

'What's up?' Docherty asked.

'Quiet, quiet,' the crewman said softly.

'It's all very well for you,' Stephanie grumbled.

Ferenc was the last to get in. 'My goodness, it's cold, isn't it?' he said. 'And dark.' The moon was down; there was no horizon; everything was black on black. 'Who's got the brandy?' he asked.

'Start paddling,' the crewman whispered.

'What?' Laszlo's ears had not recovered from hours of engine-roar. 'Who's that?' he said. The crewman thrust a paddle towards him and banged his wrist. 'Sweet Jesus!' Laszlo cried.

'Paddle, for God's sake,' the crewman whispered.

'You broke my arm,' Laszlo accused.

It took them fifteen minutes to reach the shore. At the end the crewman jumped over the side and dragged the dinghy on to the sand, so they stepped ashore with dry feet. Without a word the crewman shoved off and climbed in. The dinghy disappeared.

'Welcome to Ireland,' Docherty said. 'Peaceful, isn't it?'

They walked inland a long way until they found a road. Stephanie was already tired from carrying her suitcase, so they stopped for a rest. 'I thought Ireland was neutral,' Ferenc said. 'I expected to see lots of lights. There isn't a single, solitary light to be seen. Anyone want some chocolate?'

'This is the west coast of Ireland,' Docherty said. 'Hardly anybody lives here, and they're all in their beds now, aren't they?'

'Bloody radio.' Laszlo rubbed his wrist. 'Weighs a ton.'

'The west coast,' Stephanie said. 'That's the left-hand side, isn't it?'

'I could do with some breakfast,' Ferenc said through his chocolate. 'What's the chance of getting some breakfast soon?'

'I'm not carrying this bastard suitcase all the way to Liverpool,' Laszlo said. 'What do they take me for? A labourer?'

'Give it to me,' Stephanie said. 'I'll be happy to serve the Fatherland twice over, if I can.'

This was so painfully heroic that it silenced them, and they set off again, with Laszlo still carrying his case. But they had walked only a short distance when a vehicle came along the road and stopped. 'You're a long way from anywhere,' the driver said.

'Our car broke down a couple of miles back,' Docherty said. 'Could you give us a lift, maybe?'

'Where are you going?'

'We'll go where you're going.'

'Is that so? Well, I'm going to the Luftwaffe seaplane base at Brest, if that's any use to you.'

It took Docherty about five seconds to realize what had happened, and he laughed. The others reacted according to character. Ferenc was puzzled, but pleased to know that breakfast was not far away. Laszlo was angry because he had been tricked and made to look a fool, or so he thought. Stephanie simply didn't understand, even when Richard Fischer (who was driving) explained. 'It's just a rehearsal, Stephie,' he said. 'A dry run.'

'Then where have we been?'

'Nowhere. Out into the Atlantic and back.'

113

'But that doesn't make sense. We might as well have stayed here. What's the point?'

'The point was to make you *think* you were in Ireland.'

'But we were bound to find out. They don't even speak the same language.'

'Shut up, you female idiot,' Laszlo snarled.

'You kicked me,' Stephanie said. 'He kicked me,' she told Fischer, but Fischer was not interested. 'Next time you kick me,' she warned Laszlo, 'I'll kick you back. *Twice*.'

After breakfast at the seaplane base, Fischer told them to keep their mouths shut while they were in the rubber dinghy. 'Sound carries a long way across water,' he said. 'I heard every word you said. Ireland's neutral but there is still smuggling. Suppose I'd been an Irish coastguard? You'd all be in an Irish jail by now. What have you got to stay to that?'

Nobody had anything to say.

'Get plenty of sleep,' Fischer advised. 'Tonight we're really sending you into Ireland.'

Christian was dashing up the stairs, taking them two at a time with no thought for his supposed limp, when he suddenly lost confidence, turned, and hurried back to his office. He stared at the coloured cards pinned to the walls and his confidence returned. He had been right. It was all there. This time he unpinned a dozen cards and took them with him.

Oster already had a visitor: Domenik. Nevertheless he was pleased to see Christian. 'Try it out on the Commodore, Stefan,' he said genially. Christian wasn't interested in Domenik's jokes but he had no choice. He forced himself to be patient.

'Question,' Domenik said. 'How much does it cost to become a U-boat Captain?'

'Don't know. How much?'

'How much have you got?'

Christian shuffled his squares of cardboard while they watched him. 'Is that it?' he asked.

'That's it,' Oster said.

'I see.'

'That means he doesn't see,' Oster said.

'It's all about U-boat losses,' Domenik said. 'There's a certain lack of volunteers. If you want the job, it's yours. Get it? That's what the joke is about.'

'Oh.'

'Try him with the air-raid joke,' Oster suggested.

'You are in the middle of a one-thousand-bomber raid. Huge bombs are exploding all around. The city is an inferno. What, according to the official advice, should you do?'

Christian shrugged.

Domenik said, 'Place a paper bag over your head and walk, do not run, to the nearest bunker.'

'Why not run?' Oster asked immediately.

'You don't want to start a panic, do you?' Domenik said. They both laughed.

'Very good,' Christian said. 'Most amusing. I have something you ought to see—'

'Tell him the one about the eighteen-franc note,' Oster said.

'Man walks into a bar . . .' Domenik began.

'It's Garlic,' Christian said very firmly. 'He's the joker in the pack. It's all here.'

'Thank you, Stefan,' Oster said. 'We'll have lunch, yes?' Domenik smiled and left. 'Garlic,' Oster said. 'Show me.'

'You have to take a long, broad view. Each individual report could be explained away, but . . .' Christian was spreading his coloured cards on Oster's desk. 'It's what happens when you relate Garlic's work with the stuff coming from elsewhere that gives the game away.'

'Which colour is Garlic?'

'Green. For instance, look at last September's report, sir. All that stuff about convoys leaving the Clyde and so on. As you know, the details turned out to be wrong.'

'Not necessarily Garlic's fault. The British could have changed the sailing orders after the convoys left.'

'It's possible, I agree. Our friends in naval intelligence were not impressed, though, were they? However, that's not my point, sir.

My point is that Garlic couldn't have been anywhere near Glasgow or the Clyde last September, as he and every other medical student at Glasgow University had already been transferred to Newcastle. Why? Because three large unexploded bombs had been found next to the medical school. Six weeks the students were away. It was reported in the English newspapers. The bomb-disposal officer was given a medal.' Christian gave Oster a cutting of the story. 'I must have been blind to have missed it for so long,' he said.

Oster read the report. 'I grant you it looks odd,' he said, 'but there may be an explanation. What else have you got?'

'A lot, sir. Just compare each Garlic card with the one beside it. Here . . . Garlic on commando training in the Scottish Highlands, which he claims to have observed. There . . . Haystack reports a ban on travel by foreigners of more than thirty miles. Garlic is Venezuelan.'

'Haystack could be wrong.'

'Yes, but could they *all* be wrong, sir? Look there: you can't believe Garlic on minefields if what Seagull says about railway sabotage is true. Garlic says *this* about food rations, Nutmeg says *that*. Garlic's report on oil tankers doesn't make sense if you believe what Hambone says about fuel stocks. And so on and so on. Is everyone out of step except Garlic?'

Oster said nothing. He continued to say nothing for about ten minutes, while he read and reread the coloured cards. Christian went and sat on a couch. Once, the telephone rang and Oster, without looking up, took it and said: 'No calls,' and put it back. An aeroplane droned somewhere out of sight. Eventually it came into view, very small and slow. Christian watched it until it flew behind a tiny fault in the windowglass, was lost, then reappeared. By moving his head slightly he put the plane back in the fault and kept it there, a helpless, unseen prisoner. Domenik's last line sidled into his head: *Man walks into a bar.* It sounded like the absurd title of some absurd modernist painting. Christian's head would move no further: the plane appeared and escaped.

'Yes,' Oster said. 'Yes indeed.' He linked his hands behind his head and looked down at Christian.

116

'I should have brought the relevant files,' Christian said. 'Stupid of me. I can easily—'

'Forget the files. We're going to see the Admiral and, believe me, Canaris won't waste time checking your paperwork. Come on!' Oster was through the door and heading down the corridor at a quick jog-trot.

Admiral Canaris heard the news without a blink. 'And you really think the SD is behind all this,' he said.

'Who stands to benefit except Himmler?' said Oster. 'Not Eldorado, obviously. The last thing *he* wants is a rotten apple in his barrel. Not us. Not the OKW. No, the only explanation that adds up is that Garlic was infiltrated by the SD so that in due course Himmler can expose Garlic and denounce us, thus scoring points twice over – first for discovering a traitor inside the Abwehr, and then for saving the Reich from the consequences of our alleged monstrous folly. Next step: the SS takes over the Abwehr.'

Canaris took off his wrist-watch and carefully, thoughtfully, wound it up. 'There is one other possibility,' he said. 'The British Secret Service may have stumbled across Garlic and turned him.'

'Yes, sir, they may,' Christian said. 'But Garlic was recruited by Eldorado and he reports to Eldorado. If the British grabbed Garlic they would never be satisfied with one sub-agent. They would roll up the entire network.'

'Like a carpet,' Oster said.

'And we'd spot it,' Christian said, 'and they'd know that we'd spotted it, and so the game would be over before it began.'

'It was just a thought,' Canaris said. He was still holding his watch, following the second hand as it marched stiffly around the dial, sixty paces to the minute. 'What now?'

'What do you suggest, sir?' Oster asked.

'Kill him quick,' Canaris said.

Even when the police had taken them all to the stationhouse, Luis treated his arrest as a huge joke. The police were not amused. They could tolerate his rant-and-rave speeches in German – if it

117

was German – but when he tried to steal the inspector's pistol they promptly locked him in a cell. 'I'll give you a good price,' Luis shouted. 'Thirty feet of salami and all the sauerkraut you can eat.' They ignored him and got on with questioning Freddy and Julie. Soon Luis fell asleep.

When he awoke it was daylight. Freddy had made the necessary phone calls; the police had satisfied themselves that Freddy really was in MI5; apologies all round; they could go. Luis demanded breakfast.

'Don't be such an idiot,' Freddy said wearily. 'There's plenty of breakfast just up the road.'

Luis looped his arms around the bars of his cell and hooked his fingers together. 'Breakfast,' he said. A policeman tried to unhook his fingers.

'Don't damage him, for God's sake!' Freddy said. 'He needs those to write with.'

In the end Luis got his breakfast: fried bread with Daddies sauce and a mug of tea. 'What's wrong?' Julie asked from an uncomfortable armchair. 'Gone off your sauerkraut?'

'Mother?' he said, turning his head like a blind man. 'What on earth are you doing in a dreadful place like this?'

It was not a very funny joke; not at that time of day; not after a long, dreary night. Even so, Luis might have got away with it; but he had woken up feeling fresh and then the victory over getting served breakfast had made him cocky. Now he found his own remark irresistibly clever. He tittered at it. Tittered like a schoolboy.

There was a brief, frozen silence.

Julie got up. 'I'll wait in the car,' she told Freddy.

Nobody spoke during the short ride back to Rackham Towers. Julie took a bath and went to bed. She slept badly and had a series of drab exhausting dreams; or maybe it was only one dream endlessly repeating itself. She awoke at midday with just enough strength to dress and walk downstairs. The sun was shining, the birds were singing, the flowers were florid. It was a truly lousy day.

She found a couch to lie on, and stared at the ceiling. Decorative plasterwork, very complicated, very tiring. Why did people have to make life so difficult? Luis came in, singing. It was one thing he had no talent for, his timing was sloppy, he couldn't carry a tune in a bushel basket, she wished he would shut up and go away. No, not go away: stay but change. Stay but change? Then he wouldn't be Luis. She gave up.

'I have had a very fertile morning,' he said. He pronounced 'fertile' to rhyme with 'turtle', in the American way. This was done to annoy her, so he was obviously in top form. 'Go piss in your hat,' she said, and that amused him, which made her realize that she had reacted just as he wished. Damn.

'I found a new Twenty Committee memorandum waiting on my desk,' he said. Now he was jigging around the room, fox-trotting between the furniture, his heels tap-tapping on the parquet. 'And I have already written five thousand outstandingly brilliant words. You are in the presence of the most prolific man who ever lived. Since breakfast I have created six new squadrons of heavy bombers, a division of infantry and two convoys. *And* my loyal and hardworking servant Wallpaper has discovered an amazing new invention which can double the range of an American Flying Fortress. It is called the Ski Jump. The Abwehr will love it, Eldorado will get a huge bonus, and I shall buy you a pair of French silk knickers – two pairs, I mean who deserves them more? And I too deserve a reward since I have created so much creation and yet I feel gallons of creativity still gurgling in my loins and is that couch comfortable or shall we frolic and fumble on the fireside rug? "Frolic and fumble", I got that out of a sixpenny romance. Come on, Julie, take your American knickers off.' Luis was rapidly undressing, leaving a trail of clothing around the room, until he stood by the couch, naked except for his socks.

Julie had not moved. 'You're not even a sixpenny romance, Luis,' she said. 'You think that all you need to do is wave that sawn-off frankfurter at me and I'll come running. Well, fuck you, buster.'

Luis didn't know what to do with his arms, so he folded them; but that felt as if it looked formal. He let them hang. That felt gawky. He gave up. 'I just thought that we . . .'

119

'No, you didn't. You never think "we". You think "me".'
Even as she spoke, part of her was registering the beautiful
body standing there, slim and muscular, olive-skinned and lithe.
'I don't want you,' she said. 'I don't need you. Go fuck yourself
and I hope you both enjoy it.'

She got up and walked away.

'There was a time—' Luis began.

'Several hundred years ago,' she said. She stopped at the door.
He hadn't moved. 'You look stupid in your socks.'

'The floor is cold,' he said.

She went out.

Oster and Christian flew to Brest in one of the latest Dornier 17E
reconnaissance planes. Christian was impressed by this display of
the top-level influence of the Abwehr: after they left Canaris they
drove to the nearest Luftwaffe field, Oster spent five minutes with
the station commander, and an aircraft was theirs. Two hours
and twenty minutes later they landed at an airfield outside Brest.
Brigadier Wagner was waiting on the tarmac. 'I'm starving,' Oster
told him. 'We can talk while we eat.' They went to the officers'
mess. 'You tell Wagner what it's all about while I order,' he
said to Christian. 'Have you got lots of ham and several eggs
and vast amounts of fried potatoes?' he asked the waiter. 'Also
some iced beer?'

Christian told Wagner what it was all about; all except the
supposed involvement of the SD. Wagner was surprised but not
shocked. 'Garlic,' he said. 'If it had to be anybody I would expect
it to be Garlic. Medical students are notoriously hard-up. It looks
as if Garlic got a little bit too greedy.'

'Kill him,' Oster said.

This time Wagner was slightly shocked, or perhaps hurt. A
dead Garlic meant a lessening of Wagner's authority, especially
when it was done on Oster's orders. 'Is that absolutely necessary,
sir?' he asked. 'I'm thinking of the morale of the network. How
will Eldorado feel if—'

'Listen, Wagner,' Oster said. 'We haven't come rocketing down

120

here from Berlin on a whim. Eldorado is the hottest property the Abwehr has ever had or is ever likely to have.' He stopped talking as the waiter approached with plates of food, and waited until he had left. 'Eldorado could be a turning point in this war,' he said. 'I'm not exactly sure what a turning point is or does, to tell the truth.' He took a forkful of ham.

'I think it means—' Christian began.

'I don't honestly care, thanks,' Oster said. 'It's bound to be different in the Navy anyway; everything always is. What matters is that Eldorado *works*. He works his little Spanish tail off for us. Maybe the Führer really has a secret weapon, maybe he hasn't, but until something better comes along Eldorado is the best secret weapon we have. Your turn,' he said to Christian.

'Eldorado is a weapon that works only if he is trusted and believed,' Christian told Wagner. 'It's like a witness in court; prove he lied once and the jury won't believe anything else he says. That's what makes Garlic such a threat.'

'He's got to be wiped out,' Oster said. 'Every minute he's alive Garlic is a menace to us all.'

'I think you know I'm sending four new agents into Britain tonight, sir,' Wagner said.

'That's why I'm here. Is there one of them you can trust to do the job?'

Wagner nodded. 'You ought to meet him,' he said. 'I've never known anyone with quite such an itch to kill people.'

'But is he competent?'

'Shot three in the last two weeks. Killed one.'

'Good God!' Christian said. 'Who were they?'

'Casual acquaintances. Laszlo's not fussy, he'll shoot anyone. The Spanish police were quite pleased to hear we are sending him abroad.' Christian looked alarmed. 'Egypt,' Wagner said, '*en route* to India, so the police believe.'

They drove to the seaplane base and Oster took Laszlo for a long stroll around the harbour. At first Laszlo was a bit gruff, a bit taciturn; he had never met a general before. Oster asked his opinion about Spanish wines: how did they compare with French or Italian? Which could he recommend *personally*? Oster made a

121

few notes and eased the conversation round to bullfights – how curious it was that the stupid British, always condemning the so-called cruelty, never appreciated the *courage* of the bullring? Laszlo was off and running. Later Oster asked him the story of his life and was gripped, fascinated, amazed by what he heard. Then they talked about spying, the challenge and the privilege and the glorious rewards of spying when one man, one brilliant, courageous agent, could do more than an army! They were so much in agreement, Laszlo and the General, it was quite remarkable . . . 'I think I was born for this mission,' Laszlo said. 'I have been waiting for it, and it has been waiting for me.'

Oster stopped. He clasped Laszlo by the shoulder, and looked into his eyes. 'That is exactly what I hoped you would say,' he declared. 'There is a man in Britain who is waiting for you, although he doesn't know it. Waiting for you to kill him.'

'Yes,' Laszlo said. 'Winston Churchill.'

Oster was taken aback but only a rapid blink betrayed it. 'An even greater threat to the Third Reich than Winston Churchill,' he said. 'All I can tell you is that his codename is Garlic, he is a medical student at Glasgow University in Scotland, and he is Venezuelan. Will you find him for me?'

Laszlo didn't think twice. 'There can't be many Venezuelans studying medicine at Glasgow, can there?' he said.

They shook hands. 'Of course the others must know nothing about this,' Oster said. 'Utter, total secrecy is paramount.'

'Naturally.'

'There is a simple way of communicating to me from Glasgow,' Oster said, 'which I shall now explain and you will memorize.'

They strolled back, arm in arm. An hour later, Oster and Christian flew to Berlin. 'Will he do it, d'you think?' Christian asked.

'He'll kill Garlic, Garlic's best friend, and the band of the Coldstream Guards if they get in his way,' Oster said.

Stephanie Schmidt was curious about Laszlo's long conversation with the distinguished visitor. 'It's top secret,' Laszlo said. 'I've got to bump somebody off.' Stephanie was thrilled.

Julie went to their room and packed all her clothes. Then she found the most remote bedroom in the building and moved into it. Freddy met her lugging a suitcase along a corridor. 'Oh dear,' he said.

'I quit.' She kept walking. 'Luis loves Luis. Who am I to spoil the romance of the century?'

'Is there anything I can do?'

'Sure,' she called over her shoulder. 'Kick the living shit out of him. Should keep you busy for the rest of the week.'

Freddy went downstairs and found Luis in a favourite position: upside-down in an armchair, his head on the floor, his feet hooked over the top. 'Seen my latest?' Luis asked. 'Isn't it terrific?'

Freddy hadn't read a word of Luis's report yet. 'Well up to your usual standard,' he said. It was hard to tell, but Luis looked disappointed. 'Did you like the Ski Jump?' Luis asked.

'*Loved* it, Luis. Absolutely loved it. How on earth did you get the idea?'

'I was thinking about the Petrified Bog and what a terrific difference it would make to aerodromes in the rainy season, although there's a drainage difficulty that I'm still working on . . .' Luis frowned and then quickly put it aside. 'Anyway, I suddenly realized that the real problem with bombers is take-off. You can actually fly with a far heavier load than you can take-off with, did you know that? Getting the stuff off the ground, that's the big obstacle. So I just thought, well, gravity's free, isn't it? And there are plenty of hills, aren't there?'

'Brilliant.' Freddy had no idea what Luis meant. 'Madrid Abwehr will be thrilled, and as for the Luftwaffe . . .' He shook his head in wonderment.

'Maybe they'll try it out.' Luis unhooked his heels and slid off the armchair, ending up in a heap on the floor. 'Oh well, back to the drawing-board,' he said, not moving.

'I just bumped into Julie in the corridor,' Freddy said.

'Lucky you. Did she bump into you?'

'She's packed her things, Luis. She's moved to another room.'

'Yours?'

123

'She was very upset last night. I was only trying to comfort her.'

'Don't kid yourself, Freddy. That woman is made out of armour-plating. You couldn't upset her with a blow-torch.'

Experience told Freddy to back off, not to interfere in other people's love-hate affairs. Freddy told experience to shut up. 'That can't possibly be true,' he said. 'And frankly, I'm appalled to hear you say it.'

Luis stood, and straightened his clothes. 'Are you feeling brave, Freddy?' he asked. 'Brave and strong and what's the word? Resilient. That's it. Because the terrible truth is that she doesn't love me. Isn't that dreadful? Shall I tell you why? Because I'm not lovable. Anyone who was stupid enough to love me would have to be an idiot and Julie is no idiot. You don't believe me. I can see it in your eyes. Too bad.'

'I'd sooner let Julie speak for herself,' Freddy said.

'No point in asking her. She thinks she can make something of me. All women do. They find a man and they say to themselves he's not bad, he'll be OK when I've smartened him up and changed his habits and generally knocked him into shape.' Luis began shadow-boxing around the room. 'They can't help it. All women are mothers. Well, I don't need a mother. I've managed very nicely without one all my life and I don't intend to get trapped now.' He aimed three jabs at a lampstand.

'Sounds simple,' Freddy said. 'Sounds lonely too.'

'I've got Eldorado and his gang to keep me company.'

'Fine!' Freddy said. He knew when he was beaten. 'If you're happy, I'm happy. But just bear in mind that we've all got to live together and work together, so try and be pleasant to each other. Yes?'

'What a good idea.' Luis shadow-boxed his way out of the room.

'I didn't mean *now*,' Freddy called. Too late.

Luis went striding up and down corridors, banging on doors with a heavy walking stick, until he found Julie's room and went in. 'Hullo, you miserable bitch,' he said.

She was in her slip, hanging stuff in the wardrobe. 'Get out of here or I'll kill you,' she said. Not original but she felt very tired.

'Freddy sent me.' Luis brandished the stick. 'He told me to give you a damn good walloping. He said that's what the English do to their women if—'

'I'm not your woman and you're nobody's man.'

'Boot-faced old bat.'

'You're a bag of wind, Luis. Go blow up your balloons someplace else.' A growing fury made the hangers rattle as she hooked them on the rail.

'Aren't you getting fat?' he asked. 'And a bit hairy? I'd lend you my razor but you might—'

She turned on him, wrenched the stick out of his hands and flailed but missed because he dodged. She felt stupid and helpless, glaring and panting for breath while he stood in the doorway and smiled. She swung the stick again and he jumped back. She slammed the door and turned the lock. After a while she heard him walk away, whistling.

Freddy was reading the draft Eldorado report when Luis strolled in. 'Can't find the silly woman,' he said amiably. 'I expect she's gone for a walk.'

'Um.' Freddy was in the middle of Operation GABLE, Eldorado's acronym for Gravity-Assisted Bomber Lift Experiment. 'This Ski Jump idea of yours is a real pippin. It's so simple, so obvious. I wonder whether we ought to offer it to the Air Ministry?'

Luis went over and reread it. 'Far too good for the silly bloody Abwehr,' he said. He ripped the page out, squashed it into a ball and threw it into the fire. Then he wandered round the room, shifting the chairs by an inch or so as he passed. 'Anyway,' he said, 'I left some flowers beside her bed, with a nice note.'

'Jolly good.'

'I think I'll kill Haystack,' Luis said. 'He hasn't been pulling his weight lately, has he? Time he got knocked down by a double-decker bus.'

The surf rushed ashore as if it couldn't wait to kiss the white sands of Galway Bay, and it carried the rubber dinghy with it, delivering the four new agents high up the beach. Before the next wave came creaming in to reclaim the boat, they had scrambled out and grabbed their suitcases from the crewman. Nobody spoke until they reached the coastal road, only a few minutes' walk away: the navigator of the Heinkel seaplane had done a very good job. 'I've got sand in my shoes,' Stephanie Schmidt said. She took them off and shook them.

'I can't hear you,' Ferenc Tekeli said, 'my ears haven't popped yet.'

They sat on their suitcases and looked at the night.

'It's got the smell of Ireland, all right,' Docherty said, filling his lungs and thumping his chest. 'Pigshit, potatoes, and poetry. There's nowhere like it in the world.'

'You thought France was Ireland, yesterday,' Tekeli said.

'And I feel deeply ashamed for it. France smells of armpits and arrogance. My nostrils deserve to be shot for treachery.'

Laszlo cleared his throat. 'We are the vanguard,' he announced. 'We lead the advance.'

'Not yet,' Ferenc said. 'Stephie's only got one shoe on.'

'Ours is the place of honour,' Laszlo said. 'These are the first strides of a great crusade.'

'If you say so.' Ferenc's stomach rumbled. 'Did you eat all your sandwich on the plane?'

Stephanie said, 'I'm ready.' They stood. A gentle growl sounded, deeper than the surf. 'There he goes,' Docherty said. They all stared out to sea, but of course there was nothing to be seen and quite quickly the growl faded and died. It could have been a fishing boat. 'We're really on our own now,' Docherty said. He meant it bravely but it sounded a little rueful.

'That's nothing new,' Stephanie said. 'We are born alone and we die alone.' She had meant it to be reassuring, but in the chill small hours of the morning her words fell as flat as tombstones. Docherty picked up his suitcase. They followed him.

*

If Christian slept badly there was usually a good military reason for it: too much strong cheese for supper, or an aching shoulder that twinged if he turned over. So when he found himself abruptly awake and staring into the dark he thought it must be the telephone. Or a knock at the door. 'Who's there?' he called. Silence. He found the bedside light. The time was exactly 4 a.m. He picked up the phone. It buzzed in his ear, softly and smugly: *nothing to do with me, chum.* He put it down.

No point in going back to bed. He was wide awake, his pulse was brisk, his brain was clear. Also he was wet with sweat. Christian took a shower and dressed in slacks and a sweater. All the while he puzzled over this jolt back into consciousness. A violent dream? He remembered nothing. An air raid? Berlin was silent. And yet here he was, aroused and alert with no dragon to slay. He had to do something. He would go for a walk. He took a reefer jacket and left his flat and immediately changed his mind: he would go to his office instead. Reason demanded to know why. Why go to the office? Well, there might be some new signals in from Madrid, or . . . or something. Anyway, it was his office, he didn't have to justify going to it, he could go if he wanted. But why did he want? Christian felt determined but also slightly foolish. Then he turned a corner and saw that the lights were on in General Oster's office.

Oster seemed pleased to see him. 'Come in, come in,' he said and swung his feet off his desk with a flourish that sent his revolving chair sailing round. 'Tell me what you think of this. I think it's rather good.'

A sheet of white cardboard as big as a newspaper lay on his desk. At first glance, Christian took it to be an elaborate family tree; then he recognized the names of various Army units based at the different military districts of Germany. Elsewhere, lines led to Wehrmacht headquarters in Paris, Rome, Warsaw, Brussels; in fact to every occupied country. Linked to this network were the names of many Gauleiters, Reich governors, police commissioners, Gestapo chiefs, and SS commanders. It was quite a complex set-up. At the top, the web of lines converged on three names – Thiele, Olbricht, and von Witzleben. They in turn led to one name: Beck. Above him, someone had scribbled in red crayon: *Valkyrie.*

'It's a chain of command,' Christian said.

Oster gave a little, high-pitched grunt of amusement. 'The chain would be around their necks if Himmler saw this. And Hitler would go straight through the roof, of course. Supposing he landed on his head and broke his neck, then Operation Valkyrie might possibly come into effect. It might just work, too. Don't look so constipated, Christian.'

'I'm not constipated, sir. But I hope I'm patriotic.'

'Comes to much the same thing, in this country. Nobody's bowels have moved since we all took the Oath of Loyalty in what was it? 1934? Ever since then the entire German nation has been standing to attention, blocked solid, too frightened to fart. Too frightened to think. That's all this is, you know.' Oster rapped the sheet of cardboard with his knuckles. 'Somebody did his thinking on paper. Believe it or not, it is possible to be patriotic *and* intelligent.'

Christian took a chance. 'Did you prepare this, sir?'

'Heavens, no. If I'd prepared it I'd be on it, and up near the top, too.'

'So who did?'

'An opposition group. They exist, you know. Very respectable, too, some of them. You must have heard of the Kreisau Circle? Count von Moltke's pals? They meet regularly at his country estate to discuss Alternatives, with a capital A.'

'Kreisau's in Silesia,' Christian said. 'Back of beyond. Nothing ever happens in Silesia. Besides, the Circle doesn't believe in violence, or so I'm told.'

'There are others. Schulenberg, for instance; he was our ambassador in Moscow. Ulrich von Hassell, he's another; he's the son-in-law of Admiral von Tirpitz. And Carl Goerdeler, used to be Mayor of Leipzig. Men of that stature. They can't stand the Nazis, they get plenty of sympathy from the old guard, and some of them won't mind a bit of blood on their hands if they think it's for the good of Germany.'

'Does Admiral Canaris know about them?'

'Canaris knows everything,' Oster said. 'And nothing.'

What the hell is that supposed to mean? Christian thought. He said, 'Well, I suppose it's none of my business.'

'Isn't it? You certainly look . . .' Oster chewed his lip while he picked the right word. 'Concerned,' he said.

'It just seems to me that these people are planning to overthrow the government, and they ought to be arrested.'

'No. Not a good idea.'

'High treason?'

'Yes, but there would have to be a trial – several trials – and a lot of undesirable publicity, and then they'd be hanged and they'd turn into martyrs. Besides, you'd never catch everyone. Far better to watch them and see what bright ideas they come up with.' Oster nodded at the sheet of white cardboard. 'This isn't bad, you know. Somebody's done a lot of work. Those are three key men at the top: Lieutenant-General Thiele is the Army's communications chief, General Olbricht is an experienced organizer, and Field-Marshal von Witzleben is just the chap to enforce internal security while they're about their business.'

'Meanwhile the new Führer, General Beck, proceeds to win the war,' Christian said. He felt free to use a little sarcasm; Thiele, Olbricht, and von Witzleben were nobodies; Beck was a retired nobody. If these were the biggest names the plotters could recruit, their crime was not so much high treason as low farce.

Oster wandered over to the window and pulled back a corner of the blackout curtain. 'The moon's down,' he said. 'They'll be ashore by now. That's why you couldn't sleep, wasn't it?'

'Was it, sir?' Christian didn't understand the question but he wasn't going to admit it to Oster. Oster had already scored too many points.

'We send them off to death or glory, Christian,' Oster said, 'and after that there's damn-all we can do to help them, except stay awake and worry. Tell me the truth, now: would you rather be with them?'

Christian scratched his beard.

'No,' Oster said. 'Neither would I.'

*

The suitcases were too heavy. Even Ferenc Tekeli, whose hands were hardened by prison work, began to suffer. Docherty found a broken fence and slid a rail through the handles of two suitcases. With each pair of agents carrying a rail on their shoulders, they marched on until Laszlo complained that his feet hurt. 'We can't stop now,' Stephanie told him. 'We are the vanguard, remember? We lead the advance. You don't want the advance catching up and trampling all over you, do you?'

'Go to hell,' Laszlo growled. He felt badly let down by Madrid Abwehr. After three years of war, you'd think they'd have installed someone in Ireland with a car to meet new arrivals. Elementary, that was.

'Don't you dare use that tone of voice to me,' Stephanie said. 'I'm an Englishwoman, remember? The English are always polite.'

'Go to hell, please,' Laszlo snarled. 'Thanks so very awfully, I am terribly obliged, you are fearfully dreadfully kind, what a very nice lady.'

'Who is this appalling foreigner?' Ferenc asked in an aristocratic drawl. 'I say, do piss off, you dago.'

Stephanie giggled.

'Do not take liberties with me,' Laszlo warned. 'I have been given a mission and it is no joke to me.'

'Awfully frightfully fearfully sorry,' Ferenc said.

Dawn had broken when they reached a signpost that said three miles to Galway. Docherty told the others it would be a mistake to arrive in the town too early: nothing would be open, nobody would be about, four strangers would be very conspicuous. They found a falling-down barn and rested inside it for a couple of hours, then strolled into town as casually as their nagging hunger and their leaden suitcases allowed. Docherty, by some instinct, went straight to the railway station. It was shut.

'Now isn't that just our luck,' Docherty said to a man who was unloading milk-churns from a cart.

'What train were you wanting to catch?' the man asked. He had a round face with cheeks that were apple-red.

'The Dublin train.'

'Ah, that won't be in for a long time yet, if it's on time. It's a very good train, so they say.'

'We were hoping to leave our bags in the left-luggage,' Docherty said.

'Old Mick has the key to the left-luggage,' the man said. 'But he's not here now. He'd have nothin' to do, you see.'

'To be sure,' Docherty said. 'Well, that's the way it is, then, and we'll just have to make the best of it.'

The man unloaded two more churns. 'Of course you could always carry your bags inside yourselves,' he said, 'if you don't mind payin' Old Mick when he does get here.'

Docherty pointed to the padlock on the gates.

'That thing hasn't worked in years,' the man said. 'Not since Old Mick lost the key.' He unhooked the clasp and the gates swung wide. The agents trailed after him. It was a small station, with just two platforms. The left-luggage office was shut but the man, chatting easily with Docherty about the weather and the crops, groped along the top of the doorframe until he found a key. They put their bags inside. Docherty took four numbered tickets from a roll that hung on a loop of string, the man relocked the door and put the key back where he found it.

'D'you mean we're just going to leave them there?' Stephanie asked.

'Sure. Why not?' Docherty said.

'Because there's no security! *Anyone* could just walk in and . . . I mean, think of the *risk*.' She was pink with concern. 'At least let's take the *key*.'

'Ah, the key's just for show,' the man said. 'You can easily get in without it, just give the handle a good hard twist, it's a very old lock, so it is.'

'If it worries you, Stephie,' Ferenc said, 'you stay here and keep guard while we go and get some breakfast.'

Stephanie followed them out of the station, but she was not

131

happy. 'Anyone could just walk in there and steal those radios,' she hissed at Docherty.

'No, no. It's not at all likely.'

'How can you say that? Obviously the whole of Galway knows how to get into that room.'

Docherty put a fatherly arm around her shoulders. 'So nobody would go looking to find anything worth taking, would they? Especially before breakfast. There's not a big demand for short-wave radios around here, you know. I doubt if many folk would get up this early to go and steal a suitcase, come to that.'

Galway was not a very dynamic town. Grass grew in the streets and the solitary statue (of the late Pádraic O Conaire, poet and wit) held an empty stout bottle in its outstretched hand. There was only one place that looked as if it might provide breakfast: a grey, square hotel near the harbour. The dining room was empty but in the bar a boy wearing a stained white apron reaching to his ankles was sweeping the floor. 'Me da's out gettin' in the lobster pots,' he said. 'The bar won't be open till ten.'

'To tell you the honest truth, it's a bite of breakfast we were hoping for,' Docherty said, 'and here's an English half a crown that I just found in the street, probably fell through a hole in your pocket.'

'Me mam's out the back collectin' the eggs. Will you have a drink while you're waitin'?'

'Waiting for what?' Laszlo asked suspiciously.

'Waiting for the bar to open,' Docherty explained, like a parent with a very dull child. 'Four pints of Guinness, if you please,' he told the boy. 'You're in the cradle of civilization, remember,' he told Laszlo. The boy heaved carefully on the pump handles. Laszlo watched the rich black stout rising in the glass, slowly pushing up its thick and creamy head, and he felt uneasy. This was not how he had expected to serve the Third Reich.

Breakfast turned out to be not only possible but impressive. The bacon had been sliced thick and there were new-laid eggs, black and white puddings, fried mushrooms, a bowl of boiled potatoes, grilled pork sausages, and a new loaf of soda bread with a pound of farm butter on a glass dish. Long before it arrived,

132

Ferenc Tekeli had finished his first pint of Guinness. Docherty watched with interest as Ferenc drank it in three long swallows and handed his glass to the boy for a refill.

'You want to be careful, Ferenc,' he said. 'The stuff's stronger than it seems.'

'Don't worry, chum. I won't let anybody else get hold of mine.'

'That's not what I meant.'

'The Irish are very friendly, aren't they? I'm beginning to think this was a damn good idea.'

Laszlo said, 'It would be a damn good idea if you began to think.'

'I don't like the taste,' Stephanie said. 'Can't I have a brandy?' She gave the remains of her Guinness to Ferenc. 'Of course you can, darling,' he said. 'Have a double and save on the washing-up. Put it all on the bill and have one yourself,' he told the boy.

'I'm not allowed to drink yet,' the boy said. He was no more than twelve.

'Then rub it on your chest!' Ferenc cried. 'Pour it on your hair!'

'Can I have a Mars bar instead?' the boy asked.

Laszlo tapped Docherty on the shoulder, hard. 'This is not good enough,' he said. 'This is not professional. We should not be wasting time here. When is the train?'

'You've tons of time,' the boy said. 'It never leaves until half an hour after it gets here.'

'And that is when?' Laszlo asked.

'Depends. Old Mick at the station would know, for sure. You should ask—'

'He's not there,' Stephanie said crisply.

'Well of course he's not there,' the boy said. 'Why would he be there? There's nothin' for him to do until the train comes in, is there?' He gave her a look of mild contempt.

The first customers drifted into the bar as the agents were finishing breakfast. Prison had taught Ferenc to eat quickly; he had cleared his plate twice and was now drinking Guinness and playing gin rummy with the boy when an old man with a nose

133

like a potato and a mane of white hair sat beside them. 'I'm Patrick Mooney,' he said. 'Formerly harbourmaster here.' They shook hands. 'I expect you'll be tourists?'

'Yes.'

'He's no such thing,' the boy said, busily improving his hand, 'he says he's a spy, and his name's Frank Tickley.'

'Ferenc Tekeli,' Ferenc said.

'See?' the boy said.

'You hold your peace, you little ruffian,' Mooney said. 'What sort of a spy would go about telling the likes of you that he's a spy? Have some sense, man.'

'Is there anything for a spy to spy on here?' Ferenc asked.

'There is, too. We had a German U-boat came into the bay just two months ago. And a big American bomber fell in a field not two miles from Ardnasodan the day after the races.'

'And you told me nothing ever happened here,' Ferenc accused the boy. 'Your glass looks seriously empty,' he said to Mooney. 'What was in it?'

'Guinness,' said Mooney.

'Gin,' said the boy, fanning his cards on the table. 'Now you owe me fivepence. So there!'

At the other end of the bar, Laszlo was twitching with rage. 'That Hungarian idiot is blind drunk!' he told Docherty and Stephanie. 'He will ruin everything for all of us! Have you heard what he is saying?'

Docherty nodded, and smiled. 'This is Ireland,' he said. 'Nothing is really serious in Ireland, you know. Ferenc isn't really serious.'

'Ferenc is turning into a disaster,' Stephanie said dourly.

'So what? Jesus Christ, if all the disasters in Ireland were serious the entire bloody island would have sunk under the weight of its anxieties long ago. Now for God's sake take a drink and cheer up. You both look as if you've wet your last pair of drawers.' Docherty walked away and left them.

Laszlo did not cheer up. 'This is not good enough,' he said. 'Something will have to be done.'

Julie had a longish list of comments, questions, and proposals concerning Eldorado's latest draft report. Luis and Freddy discussed them with her and Luis rewrote several passages. Most changes were in the interests of consistency: if Hambone had reported the disembarkation of a new American infantry division in Plymouth a week ago, it was time some other sub-agent noticed their arrival at a camp in Yorkshire or wherever. That sort of thing. After a couple of hours' work, Freddy took the amended sheets away to be retyped. He was very pleased.

Julie sorted out her notes, stapled them at the corner and tucked them away in a box file. Luis sat leaning forward with his elbows on his knees and watched her. When she stood he said, 'Do you want me to apologize?'

'Do you want to apologize?'

The look on her face was something he had never seen before: remote, indifferent, almost blank. Yet the face was still wonderfully attractive. She blinked, and he tried to forget the face and organize an answer. 'I was excited,' he said. 'You know how it is when I've been writing, I sort of tend to lose control a little bit. Anyway, it was all a joke, wasn't it?'

'A joke,' she said, testing the word to see how it sounded.

'Well . . .' Luis threw up his hands. 'We've got to have some fun around this dump, haven't we? Otherwise . . .'

'You didn't look too funny, standing in your socks. You looked like what you are, Luis: a typical man. You know what men want? You know what they all want from a woman? Someone to fuck, and someone to make sure they have clean clothes. Sex and socks. You don't care a damn about me. You don't even know who I am. As long as you get your sex and socks you're happy.' Luis sat as stiff as a statue. Only his eyes flickered, and a flush darkened his olive cheeks.

'What a rotten lot we are,' he said, trying to sound very casual, very English. 'I wonder why you bother with us.'

'Well, you can stop wondering,' she said. She picked up the box file and went out. Luis sat for a long time, rubbing one thumb against another until he made the skin sore, and stopped.

Brigadier Wagner summed up by saying that this is war, and Otto Krafft before he could stop himself said, 'What, another? We haven't won the first yet.'

'I can easily find you a role elsewhere if you find your work distasteful,' Wagner said, cleaning his fingernails with a spent match. 'I'm told there are thrilling opportunities for ambitious young officers on the Russian Front.'

'I spoke without thinking, sir,' Otto said.

Only Wagner and Fischer had gone to Brest to see the agents off. They flew back to Madrid immediately afterwards and Wagner called an 8 a.m. meeting in his office to discuss the startling news of Garlic's treachery. It hit the other controllers very hard. Dr Hartmann, who more than anyone had monitored Garlic's reports and had drafted notes of thanks and encouragement, was almost in tears. 'Pride, honour, trust, loyalty,' he whispered, 'are they worth nothing any more?'

Otto Krafft feared that Garlic's defection might have a contagious effect on the whole network. 'How can we be sure that Garlic hasn't gone around recruiting Knickers and Wallpaper and Nutmeg for the SD?' he asked.

'Not Nutmeg,' Franz Werth said confidently. 'Nutmeg commanded the Poona Horse in the 2nd Indian Cavalry Division. He wouldn't trust a Venezuelan student from Glasgow, not for an instant. Nutmeg's a man of honour.'

'Besides,' Richard Fischer said, 'none of the sub-agents knows each other. Only Eldorado knows them.'

'So how did the SD manage to find Garlic?' Otto asked.

'The most likely explanation,' Brigadier Wagner said, 'is that Garlic has been supplying intelligence to some *other* agency; he's been free-lancing or moonlighting or whatever you care to call it, and the SD stumbled across him and realized they had a link with Eldorado and therefore a back door through which they could chuck a bomb into the Abwehr.' Wagner eased his backside, which was bruised from being bounced about on a steel seat throughout a very turbulent flight, and made his remark about this being war, which prompted Otto's rash reply.

'Getting rid of Garlic is only half the problem,' said Richard Fischer. 'Garlic's as good as dead. The big question is: how do we stop it happening again? How do we protect the network from the SD?'

'Which means the SS, which means Himmler, which means also the Gestapo,' Dr Hartmann said. His distress had gone, evaporated by the heat of his anger. If he had taken his glasses off, his eyes would have blazed; but without his glasses the world was a blur, and he couldn't bring himself to blaze into a blur. 'I am only saying what we are all thinking,' he added briskly.

That produced a thoughtful silence. The SD held dossiers on every German of the slightest interest to Himmler, which certainly included all Abwehr personnel. Nobody in his right mind wanted an adverse note on his dossier. On the other hand, this Garlic business could put a blight on promotion prospects. It was tricky.

'Any suggestions?' Brigadier Wagner asked.

Everyone waited for everyone else. Finally, Franz Werth said, 'I honestly don't think this is our pigeon. I think it should be settled at the highest level.'

'Canaris and Himmler aren't on speaking terms,' Fischer said. 'Canaris thinks Himmler's a thug, and Himmler thinks Canaris is a damp handshake.'

'One thing we *can* do,' Wagner said. 'We can minimize the damage and maximize the gain. The SD want to sabotage Eldorado; fine, we'll make damn sure that Eldorado is twice as useful as before.'

'Himmler gives us shit and we use it as fertilizer,' Werth said.

For the first time, Wagner smiled. Everyone smiled. 'Start shovelling,' he said.

Breakfast lasted so long that they missed the first train.

This should have been the 10.05 but the train from Dublin due

137

at 9.35 was half an hour late so – as Old Mick explained to Laszlo – it left at 10.27 prompt after the driver had had his breakfast. The driver was a decent Christian man and who would deny him the right to a bacon sandwich and a pint of tea? It was a long way to drive a big heavy train from Dublin, and even further to drive it back, the way the weather was looking.

The weather looked fine and bright, with small white clouds blowing across a scrubbed-blue sky like an archbishop's laundry out to dry; but Laszlo let that pass. He had stumped out of the bar, silently furious at Ferenc (happily buying drinks for his many new friends) and Docherty (deep in conversation with a namesake who was sure they shared some cousins in Cork) and even Stephanie (half-asleep in a corner) and marched to the station. 'When is the next train to Dublin?' he asked Old Mick.

'Oh . . . midday, you know. One o'clock at the outside, God willing. That's Dublin time, of course. Some people here still set their watches by Galway time, which is forty minutes late according to Dublin, although we like to think that Dublin's forty minutes fast. Either way, you've time enough for a drink.'

Laszlo gave him an English one-pound note. 'Please inform me immediately the train arrives. *Immediately.*'

'I'll do better than that,' Old Mick said, 'I'll come with you now. I fancy a small glass meself.'

Laszlo forced himself to be calm. The morning papers had come down with the train, and as they walked his companion cheerfully reviewed the news. 'What about the Reds, eh? You wouldn't want to meet a Russian soldier down a dark alley, now would you? And did you see Hamburg got itself bombed again? The wonder is there's one brick left standing on another . . . Your man Hitler must be wondering whether he really wanted Poland in the first place . . . ' For one terrible moment Laszlo thought that Old Mick knew everything, and his guts squirmed like a bag of eels; but then the Irishman said something about *your man Churchill* and *your man Roosevelt* and Laszlo realized that it was just a figure of speech. He was so relieved that he laughed. This emerged as a strange nasal sound. He had not laughed spontaneously for months, and he was not very good at it.

138

Then they reached the bar and he felt that he might never laugh again. Ferenc Tekeli was missing.

'How the hell would I know where he is?' Docherty said.

Laszlo woke Stephanie. She complained bitterly, and when he shook her she hit him in the face. For a little girl she had a solid punch, and it gave those in the bar something to talk about for the next ten minutes. Laszlo went back to Docherty. 'How could you let him just wander off?' he complained. 'He's drunk, he's liable to say anything.'

'You're right.' Docherty sipped his Guinness and watched the mark on Laszlo's face turn a deeper, angrier red. 'Tell you what: if he's not back by lunch-time we'll send for the Garda. That's the Irish police.'

Laszlo turned away in disgust.

'The Garda will throw a dragnet over the entire town, so they will,' Docherty said. 'They'll have Ferenc back here in time for tea, you watch. Where have you been, yourself?'

'To the station. The bloody train has left. We should have been on it. If we had hurried . . .'

Old Mick, drinking near by, heard him and said, 'If you want my advice, never run after a train or a woman or an economic panacea, because another one will come along in a little while, and that's God's honest truth, so it is.'

Laszlo went outside and stood in the sunshine. Sheer desperation fuddled his brain: he couldn't decide between staying and going. If he stayed he might drift down to disaster with the rest; if he travelled alone, without Docherty's guidance, he might never reach England. The mission was collapsing almost before it had begun, and all because of the drunken irresponsible idiocy of Ferenc Tekeli, who now arrived outside the hotel with Patrick Mooney. 'We are going around the town!' Ferenc shouted. 'To see the sights! Do you want to come?'

Laszlo hesitated. If he went with Ferenc, at least he would know where Ferenc was. On the other hand Docherty and Stephanie might get hopelessly drunk. But if he stayed with them, Ferenc might disappear altogether. He couldn't win. He climbed on to the cart. 'We must be quick,' he warned sourly.

'This animal is the fastest beast west of Dublin,' Patrick Mooney said, 'so it is.' The cart set off at a great rate.

Nevertheless, they missed the midday train, which surprised everyone by leaving at twelve-thirty, a good twenty minutes ahead of time.

Laszlo was pale with fury. 'If I am not in England by tomorrow—' he began.

'Oh, shut up, you miserable pygmy,' Ferenc said. Ferenc had put away a lot of drink since breakfast and now his natural goodwill was beginning to sour into belligerence. They all trailed back to the pub and ate lunch. Laszlo refused to shut up. He nagged and nagged. This time he was successful. He got them to the station in time to catch the next Dublin train, which left at mid-afternoon.

Everyone slept on the train, except Laszlo. The words 'miserable pygmy' kept repeating themselves in his brain, in time with the chant of the track, and there was a slow rage burning like indigestion inside him. Also he was suffering from real indigestion. He should never have had pickled eggs for lunch.

Only Domenik whistled as he walked about Abwehr headquarters. Usually he whistled the catchier bits of Gershwin or Jerome Kern, which was unwise. Sometimes it was one of the Hit Parade numbers from America: 'Shoo-shoo, Baby' or 'Johnny's Got a Zero'; and that was really asking for trouble. Even listening to such music on the BBC was a crime in Germany.

Christian heard 'Deep in the Heart of Texas' coming along the corridor and got up and shut the door. None of Domenik's jokes ever struck him as funny and in any case the war was not a joke. Domenik tapped on his door and came in. Before Christian could speak, Domenik said, 'Want to read your obituary?'

It was a blurred photocopy of a two-page typed document with an old picture of himself stuck in a box on page one. Christian skimmed through it. 'God in heaven,' he muttered. 'Somebody doesn't like me, does he? Where did you get this?'

140

'A friend in the SD. I give him chocolate from Brussels, he gives me the odd plum from their files. Is any of it true?'

'About half.' Christian read through it again. This time he felt sick. 'They're trying to make me out to be some kind of traitor.'

'Not trying, old sport: succeeding. Well, allegedly succeeding. You do seem to have met rather a lot of British agents.'

'Of course I have. That's how the *Abwehr* works: by recruiting English-speaking people to go and spy in England. A lot of them turn out to be enemy agents sent to spy on *us*. If we catch them we shoot them. But you've got to meet them before you can catch them, haven't you?'

'Absolutely. Oh, absolutely.' Domenik smiled cheerfully. 'Keep it, if you like. Hang it over the fireplace.' He went out. Christian struck a match and burned the pages in an ashtray, while 'Deep in the Heart of Texas' slowly faded and died. When he thought of the SS and of what they could do, panic fluttered in his chest like a trapped bird. 'The Führer would never permit it,' he said aloud. 'The Führer needs us; the Führer needs me.' Christ Almighty, he thought, now I've started talking to myself. What the hell is going on?

Quick results in war are very rare. Warfare itself is a lumbering, cumbersome business: the aeroplane that flies so fast has taken years to design and build; the warlord who wants to strike hard, here and now, for sudden victory, finds to his chagrin that by the time he has gathered his striking force the war has moved on, and the chance of victory with it.

So the experience of the Double-Cross System over two days in the early summer of 1943 was unusual.

On the first day the latest dispatch from the Eldorado Network was flown as usual in the Spanish diplomatic bag (or so the Abwehr believed) and forwarded by express mail from Lisbon to Madrid. It arrived at about noon. By chance, this was the day on which Brigadier Wagner and Richard Fischer had hurried back from Brest with the bad news about Garlic, so the controllers seized on

141

the report with even more interest than usual. They were pleased to find that although it was thick, there was very little in it attributed to Garlic. What's more, all the rest was stuffed with goodies.

Each controller took a section and scanned it quickly.

'How d'you get diphtheria?' Otto Krafft asked. Nobody knew. 'The Hampshire Regiment's got it,' he said. 'Quarantined on Dartmoor. Bad rations, perhaps?'

'That could mean the U-boat war's been worth it after all,' Fischer said. 'Berlin will like that . . . I wonder what all this intensive low-flying training is in aid of?'

'Obvious,' Franz Werth said. 'It's in aid of a lot of intensive low-level strafing, in due course. Who's doing it?'

'Yet another American fighter wing. The 293rd.'

'Christ Almighty!' Otto said, flipping pages. 'Look at all these troop movements! *And* two new American infantry divisions, *and* one Canadian, *and*—'

'Haystack's having an affair,' Richard announced. They all looked up. 'Wife of a building contractor. She never sees him because he's always building Army camps, dozens of them, Haystack says, all over south-east England.'

'Just a hop, step, and a jump from Calais,' Franz said. 'Well, well, well.' He waved a page. 'Remember the highly secret Low-Level-Opening Parachute that Luftwaffe Intelligence were so snotty about? Eldorado's found two – no, *three* independent confirmations. It's beginning to form a pattern, isn't it? After the low-level strafing come the low-level paratroops. What d'you think, Doctor?'

'Possibly.' Dr Hartmann was staring into space. He took off his glasses and frowned so hard that his poor overworked eyes almost disappeared. 'Possibly . . .' Now he was mumbling. 'I wonder . . . Of course doubling the power won't double the bombload but they probably don't care about that . . .'

Richard went and looked over his shoulder. 'An eight-engined bomber,' he said. 'Pinetree reports that Boeing are planning a production line for an eight-engined bomber.'

Hartmann put his glasses on. 'The Brigadier must know of this immediately.'

'What's the fuss?' Otto asked. 'We had a five-engined bomber in the last war. This is nothing new. Just a bigger target for the flak to hit.'

'No, no. It's not as simple as that. Consider the variables. And then the variables of the variables. The implications are manifold, can't you see?' Dr Hartmann looked at Otto and saw a scientific caveman. He gave up and turned to Richard. 'Not merely manifold but threatening.' That was not a word they had heard him use before.

Fischer took him upstairs to Wagner's office.

'Power can be converted in many ways,' Dr Hartmann said to the Brigadier. 'It can mean speed, it can mean load, it can mean range, or any combination of these three.'

'Wait a minute,' Wagner said. 'Does doubling the engines mean doubling the power?'

'Of course not. Not the *useful* power, that is.' Dr Hartmann suppressed his impatience at having to explain the obvious. 'You need a bigger aeroplane to carry eight engines, therefore a heavier aeroplane. Engines themselves are heavy. Much of the extra power is absorbed in the work of lifting the extra weight.'

'So what you're saying, Doctor, is that one eight-engined bomber is worth two four-engined bombers because it's twice the size.' Wagner signed a letter and tossed it into a tray. 'Pardon me if I don't panic.'

'There is more,' Hartmann said softly. If the bloody Brigadier wanted to play silly games, then so be it. He pointed a finger upwards. 'Look at the ceiling.'

'Oh?' Wagner actually looked at the ceiling; looked for some secret message written overhead; before he worked it out. 'Ah,' he said. 'Ceiling. Yes.'

'Eldorado mentions pressurized cabins. The existing B-17 Flying Fortress is not pressurized, yet it has a ceiling of thirty thousand feet. Some new models even reach thirty-five thousand feet, which is an embarrassment to our fighter defences. Suppose this eight-engined model operates at forty thousand feet?'

'We won't be able to touch it,' Richard Fischer said.

Wagner gave it perhaps five seconds' thought. 'What a scoop!'

he said. 'Eldorado strikes again. I want that on the teleprinter to Berlin Abwehr within the hour.' He smiled at the ceiling. 'Thank you, God. Nice timing.'

Oster was not in the building as the telephone clacked out its message. Christian discovered this when he took the printout to Oster's office. He did not hesitate. He went straight to Admiral Canaris.

'Um,' Canaris said. 'Numbers. Are we impressed by numbers?' He was wearing a double-breasted grey flannel suit with a dark green silk tie and his hair was brushed hard until it shone like silver. He had the appearance of a banker wondering whether or not to refuse a large loan to an old friend. 'A multiplicity of engines is nothing new. I seem to remember that Dornier built a flying boat that had twelve engines, and everyone cheered, but it didn't last long.'

'Very true, sir. Dr Hartmann comments on that precise point.' Christian leaned over the desk and indicated Hartmann's words. 'The difference, he says, is that Dornier had to use lots of small engines to compensate for the fact that no really powerful engine was available and flying boats have to overcome considerable drag on take-off. Whereas . . .' Christian moved back respectfully and let Canaris see for himself.

Canaris read, and grunted, and read again.

'Whereas,' Canaris said, 'Hartmann has reason to believe, from previous Eldorado intelligence, that Rolls-Royce have discovered how to improve engine performance out of sight, the British have told the Americans what the secret is, and so this new wonder-bomber may well fly at over forty thousand feet.' Canaris scratched his head, disturbing the silver sheen until he smoothed it back. 'What if I said that this is good news, Commodore?'

Christian worked hard on the question, gave up, and shook his head, baffled.

'As often as not, from twenty thousand feet the enemy cannot guarantee to hit anything smaller than Hamburg,' Canaris said. 'From forty thousand they'd have difficulty hitting Schleswig-Holstein, wouldn't they?'

144

'Hartmann has a comment on that too, sir. Paragraph seventeen, I believe.'

Canaris found it and read it. He shook his head, rather sadly, took a firmer grip of the paper and read it again.

'Do you understand this?' he asked.

'I understand some of the words, sir,' Christian said; which at least made Canaris smile, so Christian didn't feel so bad. 'Radar-controlled, for instance,' Christian said. 'I understood that.'

'Well, if we can have radio-controlled planes, I suppose they can have radar-controlled bombs, in which case great height might even be an advantage.' Canaris was alarmed by a sudden thought. 'None of this is tainted with Garlic, is it?'

'No, sir. It's all pure Eldorado.'

'Good. Boil it down, forward the results to OKW with a copy to the Führer's own headquarters at Rastenburg. Top priority, both. And be sure they're marked "Source: Eldorado".'

Christian got the signals out by mid-afternoon. Next morning Freddy Garcia got a call from the Director asking him if he could pop into London. Freddy could, and did, and the Director showed him the translations of some intercepted German radio messages. 'Crikey,' Freddy said.

'We can't claim all the credit,' the Director said. 'If they're alarmed at the prospect of an eight-engined bomber it's because of the damage our four-engined types have done. Besides, Hitler's just as likely to revoke this directive next week.'

'Still,' Freddy said, 'it does amount to a huge switch of enemy resources, doesn't it, sir? I mean, just to develop an anti-aircraft gun that can chuck a shell forty thousand feet . . . And putting all these factories underground . . . And forming new squadrons of Junkers JU 188s. What on earth are they?'

'An advanced version of the JU 88. Mainly used for reconnaissance. They fly rather high. Perhaps the Luftwaffe believes it can turn them into fighters. It really doesn't matter, does it?'

'No, sir,' Freddy said. 'What matters is they're wasting their time and brains and aluminium and energy on the wrong priorities.'

145

'And that relieves a bit of pressure on us. The gratifying part is that it all happened within forty-eight hours.'

Freddy looked at the dates and times on the transcripts. 'Last night,' he said. 'This directive got sent only last night! How the dickens did we get it so fast? Or, come to that, at all?'

'I never ask,' the Director said, 'and nobody tells me. How is Eldorado, by the way?'

Freddy searched his mind for a diplomatic phrase and found nothing. 'Fairly bloody, sir.'

'Most spies are,' the Director said. 'I've never met a nice spy yet and I don't think I want to. It's not a nice job, is it?'

'Eldorado isn't really a spy, though, is he, sir? He's a writer.'

'Even worse. Writers are thoroughly nasty. Just because they understand the subjunctive they think they created the world. Agents are bad enough, but at least they're in it for the money. Writers . . .'

'You sound as if you speak from experience, sir,' Freddy said.

'My sister married a novelist,' the Director said bleakly. 'He's in MI6 now. In Casablanca. Says he hates it, but you never know when they're lying, do you?'

'I'd better get back,' Freddy said. 'I'm up to my ears in Bamboozle.'

By the time the complete version of the Eldorado report had been teletyped from Madrid to Berlin, Oster was back in his office. He was delighted with what he saw. In particular Eldorado's response to three queries which the Abwehr had sent, regarding previous items of intelligence, pleased him. 'That explains what became of the convoy that didn't take Churchill to India,' he said to Christian. 'Cancelled because the British Admiralty found out the U-boat packs were waiting. Doesn't say much for our naval communications, does it? And the Low-Level Parachute story is kosher, if you'll pardon the expression, so Luftwaffe Intelligence gets another black eye. And Buranda . . .' Oster laughed. 'Remember the elusive Buranda?'

'Something to do with manganese. In Peru, isn't it, sir?'

'No. No, it isn't. Buranda doesn't exist.'

'Eldorado blundered?'

'Not really. Haystack got conned. He met a man in a pub who said he was one of the Buranda Manganese Delegation. Actually, Buranda is the brand name of a patent medicine for shrinking piles.' Oster could scarcely speak the word for spluttering with laughter. 'Dear me . . . There's nobody more gullible than a spy, is there? Eldorado is profoundly apologetic.'

'So he should be,' Christian said.

'Rubbish! Don't be such a schoolmaster, Christian. No harm's been done, and Eldorado didn't try to cover up Haystack's mistake. Nobody's perfect, you know, and there is such a thing as a redeeming fault in a man. I must tell Domenik about Buranda.'

Later he did, and Domenik enjoyed it. 'It's the piles that really makes the story, isn't it?' he said. 'I mean, Buranda could have been a brand of tinned pilchards, but that wouldn't have worked nearly so well.'

Oster stretched his neck and eased his tie. 'I don't follow you,' he said. 'Eldorado didn't *choose* to make Buranda a patent medicine.'

'Didn't he?'

'Certainly not. What are you driving at?'

'Nothing at all,' Domenik said. 'It's just my wild imagination at work. Besides, you know him far better than I.' And he strolled away, whistling. Not 'Deep in the Heart of Texas', but 'Take the "A" Train'. Just as bad.

At Athlone, bang in the middle of Ireland, the train stopped and everyone woke up. Ferenc Tekeli woke up to find Laszlo Martini watching him. 'You will not get out here,' Laszlo said. Ferenc got out and drank two pints of Guinness in the station bar. He cantered across the platform and swung aboard the train as it was pulling away.

Laszlo had a face like warped wood.

'Laszlo, Laszlo, don't you recognize me?' Ferenc cried. 'It's me, your twin brother Ferenc, kidnapped by gypsies when I was two days old but now I'm back to claim my inheritance and you . . .' He grabbed Laszlo by the ears and kissed him on the forehead. 'You will get bugger-all, you miserable fart.' The compartment was full of nuns. 'I beg your pardons, ladies,' Ferenc said. 'He hates me because I was born ten minutes before him. Even then, you see, Laszlo was abysmally slow.' Ferenc enjoyed the word. 'Abysmally, abysmally, abysmally,' he said. The train clattered over points and he staggered. Docherty grabbed the back of his coat and made him sit down, with a bump. 'My manservant,' Ferenc explained to the nuns, who were fascinated. 'And that is my maidservant. The oxen and the asses are travelling in the guard's van.'

'He has the drink taken,' Docherty told the nuns.

'Also the serpents,' Ferenc said. 'I brought lots of serpents, in case anyone needed a plague of them. It's been an awful long time since we had a plague of serpents but I think we're due for a change, don't you?' Ferenc waved at the late-afternoon sunshine flooding the compartment.

'There are no serpents in Ireland,' an elderly nun said firmly. 'Saint Patrick saw to that, God bless him.'

'A fine fellow,' Ferenc agreed. 'He gave me a very fair price on the little creatures.'

'Preposterous.'

'With an option on the next plague of locusts he can get his hands on.' She shook her head, angrily. 'Listen,' Ferenc said, eyes wide with sincerity, 'make me a better offer, I'm always ready to listen. Or manna from Heaven, now there's something never goes out of fashion. I can—'

'Shut up, you fool,' Laszlo barked.

Ferenc sat back and folded his arms. 'Take my advice and you'll never buy a pig from that man,' he said to the nuns. 'He hasn't been to Mass in forty years.' They looked sideways at Laszlo. He stared at the luggage rack and tried to soothe his acidic stomach. He knew what they were thinking: *Forty years! That's almost worse than being a Protestant!* It wasn't true (Laszlo went to Mass each year on his birthday without fail) but denial would sound feeble.

148

On the other hand the silence was intolerable. 'As it happens I do not sell pigs,' he stated. 'I am not engaged in the pig trade.'

'That's true,' Ferenc said. 'He's a full-time spy. He spies for the Czar against the Emperor of Prussia. I told you he was slow.'

Laszlo stood and beckoned to Docherty. They went into the corridor and Laszlo slid the door shut. 'He has betrayed us,' he said. 'It's all a big joke to him but none of you will be laughing when the pain begins, I promise you.' He was sweating; Docherty could smell the sour odour radiating from his thin body. And there was a twist to his jaw that made Docherty think he was about to be physically sick. 'I won't give them that pleasure,' Laszlo said. He wiped some tears away with the back of his hand. 'Nobody tells me when to die.'

Docherty glanced into the compartment. Ferenc was talking earnestly to a young nun who had a hand over her mouth to conceal her giggles. 'What in hell's name's the matter with you, man?' he asked Laszlo. 'It's just Ferenc playing the fool.'

'Too much! Too often! Ever since we landed, that idiot Hungarian has attracted attention and now . . .' Laszlo sank to his haunches. 'We pay the price. The nun in there is a British secret policeman.'

'The nun? Which nun?'

'The old one, the one with a moustache.'

'Oh, that! That's nothing. Did you ever see an old nun that didn't have a moustache? Anyway, she's Irish. You heard her speak.'

'It's a man. Look at his hands. Look at the size of his feet.'

'You think that's big? I've known nuns with feet like—'

'Shut up if you don't want to listen. I know he's a secret policeman.' Laszlo was shivering. He couldn't keep his head still: he was like a man in a fever. Docherty left him and went back into the compartment.

'Of course, like all true Romanovs I am haemophiliac,' Ferenc was telling the nuns. 'The smallest cut or bruise and I bleed to death. Docherty, who is very clumsy but slightly loyal, stood on my toes last week and I nearly died, but my life was saved by my lovely maidservant Stephie who rubbed me all over with imperial

149

almond oil, didn't you, Stephie?' She blushed and tugged her skirt down. 'That's what these suitcases are full of,' Ferenc said. 'Imperial almond oil, specially blessed by the Pope.'

'Shut your ears,' the old nun told the others. 'Read your Bibles.'

'I really am a Romanov,' Ferenc said. 'Look, I have the secret Romanov birthmark.' He began unbuttoning his shirt but Docherty put a restraining hand on his arm.

'Remember what the doctors said,' Docherty warned. 'Excitement could be fatal.'

'Fatal to all of us,' Stephanie said.

Ferenc did up his buttons. 'They live only for me,' he explained, but the nuns had their eyes shut and they were telling their beads. The show was over.

The nuns got out at Mullingar. Laszlo refused to come in from the corridor. His legs were stiff and his knees ached but even when Stephanie tried to persuade him, he shook off her hand. 'Get away from me,' he muttered. 'You all think it's a terrific joke, don't you? Good, go ahead and laugh. I am serious about what I do.'

'Nobody's laughing, Laszlo.' He looked so upset that Stephanie too became upset. She was a motherly girl; she loved the Fatherland with a mother's passion and blindness. 'Have some chocolate,' she said. 'One of the nuns gave me a piece. I don't want it, honestly.' But Laszlo would not look up, would not eat, would not speak; and eventually she left him in the corridor. In truth, Laszlo was more than serious: he was miserable and frightened. This was the first time in his life that he had left Madrid, apart from a few months in prison at Valladolid when he was eighteen. He had taught himself American-English in order to swindle rich tourists all the easier but he wasn't comfortable with English-speaking people and the Irish baffled him. Now he hated Ferenc Tekeli, loathed him with a ferocity that made his skin prickle, because Tekeli kept making a fool of him. Laszlo wanted to do his duty. It had all seemed so simple when General Oster talked to him at the seaplane base near Brest. Dangerous but simple. Now he was being cheated of his destiny by the alcoholic antics of this Hungarian halfwit while bloody Docherty pretended that everything was fine and that silly cow tried to give him chocolate! Treated him like a child! His eyes leaked tears. Everyone and everything betrayed him, even his own eyes. That was another reason why he couldn't go into the compartment. His body ached. Just to sit would be luxury. All Tekeli's fault. How he hated the bastard. Hated him.

'You can't move the 114th Division *again*,' Julie said. 'I mean, a division's twenty thousand men and you chuck 'em about the country like mailbags.' They were in Liverpool, and she was sitting crosslegged on one of the twin beds in Luis's hotel room. 'Anyway, if you're going to talk about maddening habits, what about the way you stack the plates?'

'I stack the plates the way they ought to be stacked,' Luis said, 'and that's in order of size. Anyway, the 114th Division has its own transport, it's self-contained, and they dry faster when they're stacked properly.'

'Balls. You can't stand irregularity. You must have been toilet-trained by the Jesuits. And since when did the 114th have their own transport?'

'Today.' Luis, sitting on the floor, scribbled a note in the margin of his draft report. 'I just gave them five hundred new Dodge trucks. See? Happy now?'

Julie turned a page of her carbon copy. 'You've always got to damn well win, haven't you? Every time I washed the dishes and I stacked the dishes, along came Luis and restacked them.'

'Yes. Properly. Better.'

'You have no idea how mad that made me.'

'Well, you never put your clothes away.'

'So what? And I don't understand this crazy new anti-personnel mine of yours. So it's made out of wood. So what? Anyway they were my clothes. If I hang them on the floor that's my affair.'

'It's my affair when I trip over them. Why is it such a terrible burden to put your clothes away? I don't understand you, I really don't.'

'Well, I don't understand your obsession with toilet rolls.'

'The whole point is they don't show up on mine-detectors. I thought I made that clear,' Luis said. He frowned at the page. 'I must have forgotten to put it in.'

'Heavens above,' Julie said. 'God has stumbled.'

'I'll write something. Also wooden splinters can be very lethal at close range. Wood is cheap. Satisfied?'

'*Very* lethal?' Julie stuck her pencil in her hair and scratched her head. 'I'd have thought a thing was either lethal or it wasn't. Still, you should know.'

Luis crossed out *very*. 'Christ Almighty, for someone who can't hang her clothes up you can be damn touchy.'

She slid off the bed and stood staring at him. 'You sure you want to go on with this? Or d'you just want to score points? I can think of—'

'Here we go again. Same old—'

'Am I allowed to finish?'

Luis threw up his hands. 'Go ahead. Make your little speech. I've heard it a dozen times.'

'You've *never* heard it because you never listen because you don't really care about anyone except Luis.'

'See? Told you I'd heard it.'

'Go ahead: score another point. You remind me of my kid brother. You think you win everything by scoring points.'

'And your trouble is you never left home. I am nobody's kid brother!' Luis was beginning to shout. 'You would like it, wouldn't you? Someone you could boss about! Not me, baby. Not me!'

'More B-movie dialogue.' She put her shoes on.

'Life is a B-movie,' Luis said sourly.

'Yours, maybe. Not mine. And this is a lousy B-movie script.' She tossed the carbon copy on to the other bed. 'Where did you get this crap about bomber-crew losses over Frankfurt? It stinks.'

'I got it from Knickers. Can't you read?'

'Knickers is a jerk. Average nine per cent losses per raid? If you think anyone's going to believe that you're dumber than my kid brother. Still, if you want Eldorado to look stupid, go ahead. Why should I care?'

'No reason at all. It's only a world war.'

'You could have fooled me.' She went out. *Selfish self-centred immature bastard*, she was thinking when she met Freddy Garcia coming along the corridor.

'I just knocked on your door,' he said. 'There's an extra treat laid on for tomorrow. A visit to Liverpool railway station.'

'Shit-hot,' she said flatly.

'I'm told it's an architectural gem,' Freddy said.

'Listen: when you put a new toilet roll in the holder, how do you fit it? With the tail hanging down the front of the roll, or the back?'

He frowned. 'To be honest, I've never given it much thought.'

'Luis thinks of nothing else. If the tail doesn't hang down the front it's a capital offence. I discovered that in Lisbon. Can you imagine what it's like living with that sort of paranoia?'

'We all have our little quirks,' Freddy suggested.

'Tell that to the 114th Division,' she said as she walked away. 'I'm sure they'll find it a great consolation.'

'How can I?' Freddy asked. 'They don't exist.'

'Very wise decision,' she called back. 'Sometimes I wish I'd made it myself.'

Nobody can feel rotten for ever. Misery is like fear: eventually the last drop drains out of you and despite yourself you begin to feel almost half-way normal again. Laszlo maintained his misery all the way to Dublin, and even managed to stoke it up a bit on the little branch train that took them to the ferry terminal at Dun Laoghaire: speaking to nobody, taking a stoic pride in his aching hunger, loathing everyone, and courageously resigned to the utter failure of his high mission because of the selfish folly of others. *I shall make the supreme sacrifice*, he told himself over and over again, *and only God will know*. Then they were off the train and into the docks, and Docherty had bought four tickets to Liverpool, and the men in passport control didn't look at them twice, and they were on board the steam ferry *Maid of the Mersey*. A strangely unfamiliar wave of optimism swept over Laszlo before he could stop it. He was going to land in England after all. His destiny would not be denied!

The ferry fascinated him. This was the first time he had been on a ship, and it was a far more wonderful creation than the ocean liners he had seen in Hollywood movies. They had been like luxury hotels with views of the sea: spacious, bright, elegant, dotted with potted palms, and never lacking a smiling steward to adjust one's deckchair. The *Maid of the Mersey* was different. She was old and dirty and packed with servicemen returning from leave and as soon as she cleared the harbour all her outside lights went out, while the inside lights were dimmed and officers went around checking the blackout. Laszlo was impressed: the war reached right to the edge of Ireland. He could be sunk by a U-boat or strafed by the *Luftwaffe*. The thrill of risk raised his spirits. Somewhere deep in the ship there were hugely powerful engines making a rumbling thunder which (this surprised him) caused everything to vibrate. He rested his head against some hulking piece of multi-riveted steel and felt the trembling, and occasionally the shuddering, that possessed the ship as breathing possesses a great beast. No Hollywood liner had been like that. Laszlo enjoyed a quiet sense of superiority over those dumb Madrid movie audiences who thought they were watching the truth! But what impressed him most of all was the smell. It was a heady blend of ozone, burnt oil, coal smoke, and sea-salt, all laced with a whiff of fried onions. He filled and refilled his lungs until his ribs creaked.

Ten minutes on deck was enough, however. There was nothing to see but black night and white wake. Laszlo grew bored and went back to the saloon. It was packed with men: playing cards, singing, reading magazines, writing letters. Docherty was dozing; Ferenc had gone to find food. Stephanie was looking after the suitcases. 'Nothing can stop us now,' Laszlo told her. 'Remember this moment. I think history will look back and say: That was the turning point. Nothing was the same after that. Nothing.'

'Good,' she said. Laszlo was almost smiling, so she smiled back. 'I'm glad you're happy.' On impulse she gave him a quick hug. It startled him. Nobody had hugged Laszlo since he was four. 'Look, try and be nice to Ferenc,' she said. 'He

154

doesn't mean any harm, you know. He just can't resist a joke, that's all.'

'Ferenc is very funny.' Now Laszlo actually laughed, and it was Stephanie's turn to be startled. Laszlo couldn't laugh properly, he didn't know how; the best he could do was a tight *heh-heh-heh*. But she was relieved to hear it: if Laszlo could laugh, perhaps things weren't so bad after all. Ever since they boarded the ferry, and she had realized that from now on one little slip would be enough to hang her, Stephanie had known that her great mistake was in ever agreeing to come to England. She was no spy. She could never be a spy. She had been brought up to tell the truth; her family were Lutherans; her father even refused to go to the cinema because it was unreal, distorted, counterfeit. The first time she tried to tell an Englishman a lie she would blush like a beetroot, she knew it. This expedition was all a dreadful blunder. All done for love. She was here for the love of Otto Krafft. Her heart kept kicking like an angry infant in the womb and she wanted to forget the awful future she was being carried towards by this terrible squalid ship. 'We had a good time in Madrid, didn't we?' she said. 'Do you remember Ferenc at the bullfight when he bought all the peanuts?'

Docherty said, 'And the oranges, and the *chorizos*, and the sugar doughnuts.' He yawned. 'I could demolish a sugar doughnut or five myself right now.'

'That was a wonderful evening,' Stephanie said, eyes aglow. 'I really enjoyed myself.'

'So did I,' Laszlo said. 'So did I.'

'So did we all,' Docherty said. 'Maybe not the bulls, perhaps, but . . .'

'For the bulls, if they are brave bulls, it is the greatest moment of all,' Laszlo declared, and he lectured them on Brave Bulls I Have Known And Killed for five minutes, until Ferenc arrived, carrying four hot sausage sandwiches and four bottles of India Pale Ale. 'I had to fight a whole company of British grenadiers to get these,' he said.

Laszlo was salivating so strongly that he had to swallow. 'Not much of a fight,' he said, 'for a true Romanov.' The sausage sandwich tasted like prime rump steak.

155

'In fact my father was a Hungarian gypsy horse-thief,' Ferenc said. 'Killed by a tram in Budapest.' He was rapidly opening bottles and passing them around.

'That's a damn lie,' Docherty said comfortably.

'You're right, it wasn't in Budapest,' Ferenc said, 'it was in Nyiregyháza, but whoever heard of Nyiregyháza?'

'I've seen his dossier,' Docherty told the others. 'I know the truth.'

'Well, tell us, then,' Stephanie said.

Docherty took a long swig of beer. 'All right,' he said. 'Ferenc is really a woman. Ferenc is really Marlene Dietrich.'

'That's true,' Ferenc said, 'but what you don't know is that Marlene Dietrich is really Tito, the Yugoslav partisan leader.'

'Oh, yes?' Laszlo challenged. 'In that case, what were you both doing in Madrid jail?'

'Screwing the head warder,' Ferenc said. 'And his wife. On alternate nights.' Docherty laughed and Stephanie giggled but Laszlo only shrugged. He had asked a perfectly sensible question and as usual Ferenc had tried to make him look stupid. All his life, Laszlo had suffered because some worthless brainless shit had made people laugh at him. *You watch*, he thought. Now that he had some food and drink inside him he suddenly felt quite cocky, and the thought became speech. 'You'd better look out,' he said. 'All of you.'

'Myself, I intend to look out for a rich widow,' Docherty said, 'preferably a brunette. The trouble with blondes is they show the dirt. I might marry the widow of an English army officer; it would have to be a good county regiment and nothing under lieutenant-colonel, you understand.'

'Docherty's a snob,' Stephanie said.

'I never denied it.'

'I used to be a snob,' Ferenc said, 'but the doctors told me to give it up, it was sapping my strength.' He looked down his nose and flared his nostrils. 'See? I was a top snob once.'

'Where was that?' Laszlo asked.

'Barcelona penitentiary.' This amused Docherty and Stephanie, and Laszlo wished angrily that he had kept silent. 'We had the best

156

snobs in Europe in there until everyone rioted and burned the place down.' Stephanie wanted to know why. 'Oh, pride, I suppose,' Ferenc said. 'Natural arrogance. Scorn for the peasantry. Also, the food was shit.'

'I never heard of a fire at Barcelona,' Laszlo said.

'Maybe it was Valencia. I would have to consult my press cuttings.'

'You're a terrible liar, Ferenc,' Stephanie said, and kissed him.

'I was afraid you might see through me, sweetheart. It's just as well. Poor Laszlo has been memorizing all this rubbish so that he can expose me to the proper authorities.'

'Well done, Laszlo,' Docherty said. 'The act of a truly second rate snob. When I marry the widow you can be my best man. Or second-best. Would that suit you?'

Laszlo got up and walked away. He knew they were mocking him, even if he didn't understand exactly how or why. He had to go out on deck, in the fresh air, away from the crowd and the smell and the noise, but when he stepped out he found that it was raining hard. He came back inside. Only a few more hours and they would be in Liverpool. He felt a grim contempt for all the men in uniform around him. What did they know of war? They were just numbers. Numbers didn't change anything. Laszlo felt the same exciting tightness in his throat, the same rapid breathing at the top of his lungs, the same clattering, runaway pulse that he had felt from time to time during the evening of the Brigadier's farewell dinner party in Madrid. Not long now. Not long.

Only two or three die-hard card schools survived, little islands of soft talk in a sea of sleepers, when he picked his way across the saloon. All three agents were asleep, Ferenc with his head and arms resting on the stack of suitcases. Laszlo squeezed his shoulder and whispered: 'Don't make a noise.' When Ferenc straightened up and gave a soft groan, Laszlo took the top suitcase. 'Come with me,' he whispered. 'Don't wake the others.'

Ferenc caught up with him as he went through the blackout curtains and on to the deck. The rain had eased but chilling flurries of wetness came slanting out of the night from time to time. 'What's going on?' Ferenc asked. His eyes felt like boiled sweets. His tongue belonged to someone he didn't like. 'What's up?'

'I'm going to throw this case into the sea,' Laszlo said. He carried it to the rail and heaved it into the night. Any splash was absorbed by the overwhelming rumble of the ship.

Ferenc joined him at the rail. 'Well,' he said. 'So what? I don't see what it's got to do with me.' The wind chased his hair round his head.

'That's your trouble, Ferenc. You don't see what anything's got to do with you. Ever since we landed you've played the fool. I think you want us to fail.'

'And I think you're a piece of piss. No, you haven't got the strength to be a piece of piss.' For once, Ferenc lost all patience with Laszlo. 'You're a small fart in a large room, Laszlo. Why d'you think nobody talks to you?'

'I have friends. In Madrid—'

'Oh, screw Madrid.'

'*Many* friends. I am very popular in Madrid. Everyone wants to talk to me in Madrid. I am very liked and respected in—'

'There you go again. Me, me, me. Nobody cares a damn about you.'

'That is not true. And why do you always interrupt me? I am as much entitled to my opinion as—'

'Nobody's entitled to be as boring as you, Laszlo.'

'I warn you. Don't interrupt me again or you—'

'Boring, boring, boring, boring, boring, boring. Now I'm going back to sleep and you can stay and bore the seagulls.' As Ferenc turned, Laszlo raised the pistol and shot him through the ribcage, twice. Ferenc slumped against the rail as if he were about to be sick. Laszlo shot him a third time, in the back of the head, then stuffed the gun in his pocket. He made sure Ferenc's arms were hanging over the rail, grabbed hold of his ankles and heaved upwards. Laszlo was stronger than he looked. One final flourish sent the legs up in the air, and the body cartwheeled into black space.

Laszlo thought he heard the splash but he couldn't be sure.

He unscrewed the silencer and stowed the weapon in his inside pockets. The time was five to two. He felt much better now.

The whoop of the ferry's siren as it entered the Mersey estuary woke everyone up. The saloon became a tangle of moving bodies. Dawn had not yet broken, and in the dim light it was some little time before Docherty and Stephanie realized that Ferenc and Laszlo were not there. No cause for concern. They were probably in the lavatories. Twenty minutes later Laszlo turned up, freshly shaved and very perky. Where was Ferenc? He had no idea. But during the small hours, Laszlo said, Ferenc had told him he had decided not to go to England. He had said he was going to stay on board and return to Ireland. And look: he's taken his suitcase.

By now the *Maid of the Mersey* was docking. It was impossible to search the ship; indeed it was hard enough to force your way along a corridor against the mass of troops and kitbags. Docherty and Stephanie did their best, and then gave up. There were a hundred places where Ferenc might be hiding. On the dockside, Docherty said, 'Why didn't you wake me and tell me?'

'I thought he was joking,' Laszlo said. 'You know what a funny man he was.'

They stared at him. All around was loud activity; only their three figures were still. 'This isn't right,' Stephanie said. 'This is all wrong.'

'A nice cup of tea would be jolly nice,' Laszlo said. 'Don't you think, old sport?'

When Domenik produced a copy of Christian's SD dossier, he grew enormously in importance in Christian's eyes. Before, he had seemed a lightweight, even a bit of a wastrel; now he was clearly a man who had valuable contacts. Christian invented reasons to pass by Domenik's office; the door was always open and usually he was invited in. Domenik puzzled Christian because he seemed all wrong for the Abwehr: too chatty, too disrespectful, not *military* enough. He was a great gossip. Normally Christian disapproved strongly of gossip but he made an exception because Domenik's inside stories turned out to be pretty reliable. They were certainly

159

a damn sight more useful than the stuff churned out by Goebbels's Department of Propaganda to explain, for instance, the sudden death of Hans Jeschonnek, a man whom Christian had known slightly and admired enormously. Jeschonnek must have been the youngest ever officer in the German Army – he was commissioned lieutenant when he was only fifteen. That was in 1914. Three years later he became a pilot. In the twenties and thirties he worked as hard as anyone at rebuilding the German Air Force, and by 1939 he was its Chief of Staff. Then, as the war turned sour, everything went wrong for Jeschonnek. While Marshal Goering neglected his duties as head of the Luftwaffe, he also failed to give Jeschonnek the backing he needed to fight the air war. As Domenik told Christian, all the talk inside the Luftwaffe High Command was of Jeschonnek's impossible position. Day by day the Allied bombing of Germany grew worse, and week by week Hitler put the blame on Jeschonnek rather than on Goering because Hitler still liked Goering. Jeschonnek was an honourable man. In the end the pressure crushed him. He shot himself. Officially it was a stomach haemorrhage. Christian found Domenik's version far more credible, and infinitely more depressing.

Not that Domenik ever seemed depressed by anything. To him the war was one long black comedy, the source of endless jokes. He even managed to make Christian laugh at a story about von Ribbentrop, the Foreign Minister of the Third Reich. 'Old friend goes to see Ribbentrop at the Ministry,' Domenik said, 'but the building is empty! He goes from room to room, knocking on doors, until finally he knocks on the last door and Ribbentrop opens it, stark naked except for a hat. The old friend says, "Why aren't you wearing any clothes?" and Ribbentrop says, "Why should I? Hitler never wants to see me any more." And the old friend says, "Then why are you wearing a hat?" And Ribbentrop says, "Well, you never know; he *might*." '

It perfectly encapsulated Ribbentrop's vanity, stupidity, and irrelevance, and Christian enjoyed it. 'How on earth do you find them?' he asked.

'Oh, you know,' Domenik said. 'It goes with the job.'

'I can't believe that this is your whole job, collecting jokes.'

'Actually my real job is as a sort of freebooting liaison officer.'
Domenik could see that Christian was not entirely satisfied, so he
added, 'Some people need to have their imaginations stimulated;
don't you find that? Well, I'm free to go around thinking the
unthinkable.' He paused a moment to see how this went down.
'And sometimes also to speak to the unspeakable.'

'But who do you report to?'

'Posterity. Like all of us.'

Christian realized he wasn't going to discover anything more,
and he changed the subject. But he thought about what Domenik
had said, and the next time they met he asked for advice. 'We've
been having some problems with one of our agents abroad. Not
so much with that agent as with one of his sub-agents, so to
speak.'

'Eldorado and Garlic.'

'Ah.' Christian stroked his beard. 'I should have known that
you would have known.'

'I also know how to shut up about what I know.'

'Glad to hear it. Anyway, you understand the problem. We've
taken action to eliminate Garlic, which ought to be the end of
the matter. But I can't help thinking . . . ' Christian picked up
a pencil and held it at arm's length to read the lettering on it. 'I
mean, it makes you think.'

'Think aloud,' Domenik said.

'Well . . . the trouble with Garlic is he was just too bad to
be true. If *we* could see all the contradictions and anomalies
in his reports, then Eldorado should have spotted them too.
In fact, Eldorado should have noticed them *at the time*. So why
didn't he?'

'Busy man. Lots of other sub-agents to handle.'

Christian made sceptical sounds in the back of his throat. 'You
don't know how meticulous this man is. He's painstakingly
correct. If he makes a mistake he reports it. I remember he once
identified a new shoulder-flash with the letters CLB as Canadian
Low-flying Bombardiers. Later he corrected it to Church Lads'
Brigade. He doesn't care if he looks foolish as long as we get
the truth.'

'With one exception,' Domenik said.

'That's what worries me. Either Eldorado was unbelievably careless, or . . . '

'Or what?'

'Well, there are various possibilities, aren't there?'

'Are there?' Domenik was enjoying this. 'Tell me some.'

Christian hunched his shoulders defensively. 'Maybe Eldorado spotted the contradictions and actually told us he wasn't altogether happy about Garlic but his report went astray.'

'I see. And when he got no response, he said to himself, "Oh well, they don't care what rubbish they get from Garlic, so I'll send them some more." Right?'

Christian sighed and let his shoulders slump. 'Have you any thoughts, Stefan?'

'A few. I'm told that Garlic is a Venezuelan medical student, which makes him a bit wild, like all medical students, and a bit reckless, like all Venezuelans. What's more, this isn't his war, he doesn't care who wins, he's going back to Venezuela soon, and he's only doing this spying because he needs the money, like every other medical student who gets drunk seven nights a week.'

'So he's the joker in the pack.'

'Bull's-eye.'

'Still doesn't explain Eldorado.'

'Maybe Eldorado gets a kick out of playing the joker.'

Christian puzzled over that. 'Explain, please.'

'Try this on for size. I know two things about your Mr Eldorado. He works like hell, and safety bores him.'

'Absolute safety, yes. But that's true of all agents, surely.'

'The difference is that Eldorado has a sense of humour. Perhaps he's been using Garlic as his safety valve. When he gets tired of working a sixteen-hour day, running his network, he rewards himself by having a little fun. Half of everything Garlic sends him is nonsense, he knows that, but occasionally, just for a treat, he passes a little bit of nonsense on to the Abwehr, to see if he can get away with it. I used to know an actor like that. In the middle of a long run in Goethe's *Faust*, he'd be thundering out some great gloomy speech and he'd slip in a

162

couple of lines from Schiller's *Maria Stuart*, simply to see if anybody noticed.'

'And did anybody?'

'If they did, they never said so.'

'Hmm.' Christian scratched his head: occasionally the scar still itched. 'If Eldorado has been slipping wrong stuff into Garlic's reports, just for fun, that would really be something to worry about.' To Domenik's surprise he moved to an open part of the room, dropped to the floor and began doing press-ups, smoothly and easily. After twenty-three he paused, arms extended, and stared at the pattern of the carpet.

'I can hear you worrying in double-time,' Domenik said.

Christian sat on his haunches and dusted his hands. 'Even if Garlic was being used by the SD,' he said, 'and we're still assuming he was . . . even so, Eldorado must have known that Garlic was cheating, and cheating badly, so he must have known that we would find out, sooner or later. Which means that either he didn't care, or . . .'

'Or he wanted you to find out,' Domenik said. 'I told you I was here to think the unthinkable.'

'But that's preposterous.'

'The unthinkable usually is, otherwise you could have thought of it yourself. That'll be five marks. Pay the cashier, please.'

Harry Conroy had told Julie – back in the days when they were married in fact as well as by law – that Liverpool was like Hoboken with warm beer. She didn't know much about Hoboken beyond its position on the New Jersey waterfront, facing Manhattan, but what little she knew was discouraging. On the other hand Harry had gone to Liverpool to cover a story that promptly died, so he was prejudiced. Harry judged a place by the size of the story he got out of it. 'Cincinnati!' he once said. 'I love that town!' Meaning he got five thousand words describing some squalid political bribery. Julie had visited Cincinnati, and lovely it was not. So she tried to keep an open mind about Liverpool, and when she went for a walk after breakfast she found that, far from being Hoboken

163

with warm beer, it was more like Manhattan with bomb damage. There was the same jostling urgency, the same sense that tomorrow was too late, the same crackling humour. The streets were thick with uniforms, and the docks were packed with merchant ships and their escort vessels. This was the headquarters of Western Approaches, the British naval command area that was fighting the Battle of the Atlantic, and there was a constant turnaround of convoys.

Before ten o'clock Julie had been propositioned by a very young seaman in the US Navy. She smiled back when he caught her eye. 'You're American,' he said. She asked how he knew. 'Terrific teeth,' he said. 'No Britisher could have teeth like that. Also the hair and the eyes and the legs.' He was twenty, from Sioux City, Iowa, and he had never seen the sea until he joined the Navy. Now he was part of a gun crew on a destroyer. They strolled together, he asked for a date and she dumped him as gently as possible. It was nice to be asked.

She did some shopping and walked back to the hotel. Luis was in the lounge, reading *The Times*. All the other daily papers lay scattered around him. 'You're late,' he said, not looking up.

'I didn't say when I'd be back,' she said, 'so go jump in the lake.'

'Freddy's been looking for you.' He turned a page. 'You were wrong about the weather.' Rain pecked the windows.

'Look: as long as we're on this thrilling trip together, how about making a supreme effort and being slightly civil?'

Luis grunted.

'There's a spot on your nose, your flies are unbuttoned, and your socks are inside-out. Otherwise you're perfect.' She picked up her parcels. 'I hope you and your ego are very, very happy together.'

When she came down from her room, Freddy was waiting. 'I thought we might take a tram,' he said. 'Great Liverpool institution, the trams. Besides, we'll never get a taxi in this weather. Ready?'

'We've got a car,' Luis said. They had driven up from Hertfordshire.

'Being serviced.'

Freddy had two umbrellas. He and Julie shared one; Luis took the other. As they walked towards the nearest tramstop they passed a dumpy, middle-aged woman selling bunches of violets from a wicker basket. 'You dropped your 'anky, sir,' she said to Luis, and pointed behind him. He turned. There was nothing lying behind him. 'Never mind, 'ave a nice bunch of violets, dear,' she said, more softly; and he was about to hurry forward to catch up with the others when she added: 'Eldorado.' And looked him straight in the eye.

'What are you talking about?' he said, and knew at once that he had made a mistake: he should have pretended he hadn't heard her and moved on, fast. 'I'm late.' That too was a bloody silly thing to say. She had a gun in her basket, she was going to kill him. He tightened his grip on the umbrella, ready to smash it across her face.

'You're Eldorado, I've seen your picture,' she said, smiling like a proud granny. 'Tomcat showed me.'

For a long moment Luis was haunted by the memory of an ugly dream, a dream that always left him naked and wading in leaden slow-motion away from an onrushing, undefined catastrophe. Tomcat was his codename for Madrid Abwehr. Rain flicked into his face and he came awake. 'Go on, wave a few swastikas,' he said weakly. 'Let's hear it for Adolf.'

'Don't you worry, dear. We're here to help you, if you ever need help. My code name is Blossom.' She gave him a bunch of violets. 'You won't forget that, will you? Those are on the house. Off you go.'

Luis scuttled after the others and reached them as they joined a tram queue.

'Flowers. How charming,' Julie said. 'They can't possibly be for me, so they must be for you, Freddy. Give Freddy the nice flowers, Luis.' The rest of the queue watched with interest. 'It's an old Spanish custom,' she told them. 'The men give each other flowers every wet Tuesday. Pansies, usually.' The queue found that highly amusing.

When the tram came, Freddy and Julie went on the top deck.

Luis followed them and found a seat as far away as possible. What still shocked him was the confident, even casual, way that the woman had contacted him. And such a disgusting old hag, she must be every day of fifty, with dyed hair – you could see the grey roots – and that foul pink lipstick, as if she had just finished swigging some foul pink medicine. The whole memory was repellent. *Blossom*. Whoever chose that code name had a grim sense of humour. And the total implication of the meeting flooded upon Luis's mind. *We're* here to help you. Not *I'm* here to help you. The tram swayed and screeched as it took a bend, and a big man thumped into the seat beside him. 'Ah, that's better,' the man said. 'This wreck is going to Lime Street, isn't it?'

'Lime Street?' Luis remembered: the name of the station. 'Yes, I hope so.'

'Lovely place. Lovely people. Liverpool's full of lovely people and the great thing about them is they're so helpful. Take me, for instance.'

Luis looked and saw a face that was all chin, nose, and eyebrows. The haircut was short and the shoulders were broad. He seemed about thirty. 'What about you?' Luis asked. He had a great desire to get off this tram and run. Run anywhere. Run back to Rackham Towers.

'Well, me, I'm very helpful and I don't even come from Liverpool! I knew that would surprise you.' He had a genial grin. Luis returned a smile that felt as natural as an operation scar. 'I'm so helpful, d'you know what people call me?' Luis shook his head. 'They call me Gardener.' When Luis failed to respond, the big man said, 'Well, you know what gardeners do, don't you? They carry out underground work amongst the plants.' He sat back, looking well pleased with himself.

Oh Christ, not another one, Luis thought. Please Christ make this a normal everyday lunatic. 'I have no garden,' he said.

'But you like flowers.' A large hand reached across and plucked the violets from Luis's fist. 'They make perfume from these. Eau de Tomcat, very exclusive. I'm sole agent in these parts, you know.'

166

'I didn't,' Luis said, 'but I do now.' He was beginning to feel a little rebellious. 'How is business?'

'Business is very good. If you—'

'Mainly export, I suppose.'

'Oh, yes, because—'

'What about the competition? Is there much competition?'

'Nothing to worry about. There's a very good firm called Eldorado that I'd like to form a partnership with.'

'Oh, him.' Luis wiped the misted window and looked at a row of gutted houses sailing by. 'Nobody likes him.'

'Think it over. This is my stop.' The big man got up. 'We're all in this together.' Then he was gone.

Luis slowly unclenched his fists. He looked at his palms and saw the marks left by his fingernails, and watched them fade. He licked his upper lip and tasted the salt of sweat. Then he noticed that his right thigh muscle was still jumping. No matter what his mind said, his body knew best and his body was telling him that he had just been thoroughly frightened.

Go and tell Freddy. That was his first thought, and he glanced back. They were talking and smiling. They were getting along very well. Just like old pals. *Fuck you, Freddy,* he thought and turned away. Besides . . . it felt good to have a secret again, a big secret. All those wonderful months in Lisbon had been one long intoxication of secrecy – double secrecy, triple secrecy, layer upon layer of the delightful stuff, when only he knew that Eldorado was a sham who created ghosts which invented dreams. That was heaven. Now he had a secret again, and when he tasted the pleasure he realized how much he had missed it. Bugger Freddy. Bugger MI5. Let them wait. Besides, there might be more. Who could tell? Quite obviously the British security services didn't know everything. They thought they had every German agent in the bag! Bloody fools. The tram swayed and ground to a halt. Luis looked down. The man code named Gardener gave him a wave that was almost a salute, and strode off.

The tram emptied at Lime Street. Luis stood in the rain and inspected the soot-blackened portico of the station. 'Here we are at the municipal abattoir,' he said.

Julie agreed, but silently. German bombing and British weather did nothing to lighten the building. It looked strong enough to last a thousand years. A gloomy thought.

'It's more interesting inside,' Freddy said.

'They sell tickets inside,' Luis explained. 'Buy a ticket and you can kill a pig.'

'That's way beyond your mental range,' she warned. 'Don't even attempt it.'

'Her mental range is the one where the deer and the antelope play,' Luis told Freddy. 'It's knee-deep in antelope turds.'

'Do stop it, both of you.' Freddy urged them up the steps. 'Who was that large chap you were talking to on the tram, Luis?'

'Crown Prince Rupert of Albania.' Freddy gave a startled glance, so Luis said, 'Well, that's who he said he was. Wanted to borrow a fiver. D'you think he was genuine?'

The interior of the station was much grimier than the outside, despite the rain that fell through great gaps in the glass roof. The place was huge and filled with noise: the tramp of boots; the shriek of whistles; distant shouts; the squeal and rumble of platform trolleys; and above everything the dominant hiss and thunder of steam locomotives. Filling all corners was the echo and re-echo of the Tannoy, eternally announcing the incomprehensible. 'You told us this was an architectural gem,' Julie accused Freddy.

'That's what the guide-book said. There's one thing that's definitely worth seeing. Follow me.' They zigzagged between clumps of servicemen and piles of luggage, and reached platform one. Freddy stopped under the clock, a huge affair that hung from the girders as if waiting to have a church tower built around it. 'Classic, isn't it?' he said. 'Wait here while I get our tickets.'

'Where are we going?' Luis demanded; but Freddy had gone.

They found a relatively dry spot on a bench and watched the steady surge in and out of the station buffet. 'I'm not going anywhere without something to eat,' Luis said. It was five minutes to twelve. He thought he could smell bacon but that must be an illusion. Putting his arm around her would be easy and she might respond, which would be delightful. So why, he wondered, didn't he do it? Life without Julie was unimaginable, she made it all worthwhile, gave it meaning and purpose.

'Why d'you always have to be such a shit, Luis?' she asked. His arm was immediately paralysed. 'There is no Prince Anything of Albania. I mean to say, it was a reasonable question. Why can't you just tell the truth for once in your lousy life?'

'All right. If you want to know, he was a German spy, sent by the Abwehr to make contact.'

She licked a finger and touched her stockinged leg. 'You can be kind of pathetic sometimes,' she said. And that killed all conversation stone dead.

Docherty came into Lime Street station at a brisk run, his suitcase clutched to his chest and his legs stabbing outwards because his arms weren't free to balance him, and stuttered to a halt as he searched for platform one, saw it on the other side, as far away as it could be, groaned, changed direction and ran again but only for a few yards. He turned and stared at the entrance to the station. No sign of Stephanie or Laszlo. He cursed, and his head swivelled indecisively between the entrance and platform one, and finally he cursed some more and walked back.

He found them arguing with a railway porter who was trying to tell Laszlo that he couldn't park his taxi there. He heard Laszlo say, 'I tell you for the tenth time I am on urgent official business, and unless—'

'Can't leave it there, matey. More than my job's worth. If I let you—'

'Idiot! Imbecile!' Laszlo was twitching with rage. 'Take the car! Have it!' He thrust the keys at the man.

'No fear.' Suspicion crowded his face. 'What you up to, matey?'

'Sir, I can explain.' Docherty eased himself between them. 'It's by way of being an emergency, you see, a very sick lady, every second counts, sir, if you could see your way clear . . .' A five-pound note, as big and white as a handkerchief, snapped and rustled in his fingers. The porter saw a week's pay before him and saluted with his right hand while he took it with his left. 'Good man,' Docherty said. 'Come on, let's go, you two.'

It had been an increasingly terrible morning. When they got off the ferry they had hours to kill, hours that died slowly over cups of tepid tea and plates of cold toast in seedy cafés, while the rain came and went. Laszlo had wanted to go to the station but Docherty refused. Railway stations were always well policed, he said. Laszlo sulked. Stephanie wanted to know what they would do if Eldorado didn't turn up at noon; indeed she became quite jumpy and Docherty had to take her for a walk around the block. When they got back, Laszlo was missing. They found him in a tram queue and dragged him away. He said he was going to Scotland and no one could stop him. Stephanie took his arm and squeezed his hand and persuaded him that Eldorado might have some new orders for him, and look, it wasn't long now to the rendezvous. Laszlo, furious at having been made to look a fool in front of the queue, told Docherty that if his Scottish mission failed, he would recommend to General Oster personally that Docherty be court-martialled and shot; but in the end he agreed, sulkily, with Stephanie. So they set off for the station, walking in the wrong direction, each one assuming that the others knew the way. They got utterly lost. A deaf old man sent them back the way they had come but it was still not the right way, at least not according to three snotty-nosed kids who argued amongst themselves while the rain drenched the dismal interchangeable streets. In the end the agents took a tram, any tram, just to be on the move and in the dry. They changed trams twice. Time was running out. The third tram they got on was the right number service but travelling in the wrong direction: it was going *away* from Lime Street. They jumped off at a red light, splashing through puddles towards the kerb. That was when Laszlo stole the taxi. He thrust his pistol under the driver's nose and ordered him out. The passenger saw the gun and fled. Docherty and Stephanie jumped in. Laszlo had a little trouble with the gears and even more trouble with driving on the wrong (for him) side of the road; but he compensated by driving very fast and he was in good spirits when they parked in a prohibited place at the station.

Once Docherty had returned and solved that little problem, he hurried Laszlo and Stephanie into the station at a brisk trot. 'Over there,' he said, pointing.

'No. I am going to Scotland,' Laszlo said, and headed in a very different direction.

'Bastard,' Docherty said.

'I'll get him,' Stephanie promised. 'You go to Eldorado. I'll bring Laszlo as soon as I can.'

A train arrived at platform one and Luis stood up to watch it. On Spanish stations the train towered over you, and you climbed up to the coaches; here, the English built their stations so that you stood almost half-way up the side of the train, level with the doors; very quaint; more like a dockside than a station. Luis watched the locomotive wheeze and rumble by, and was intrigued by this novel view of its wheels and driving-shafts. Someone touched his elbow, and he moved to let them pass. Nobody passed.

It was an RAF chaplain, a tubby, cheery little man with a zip-top bag banging from one arm and an ash blonde from the other. He put his mouth close to Luis's ear, evidently to counter the noise of the train, and said, 'Are you by any chance Eldorado?'

'I wouldn't be the least surprised,' Luis said; but in truth he was quite shocked. The woman was lovely, in a fragile sort of way. How did a dumpy dog-collar get a winner like that? Then he realized he wasn't a real RAF chaplain. So she wasn't a real chaplain's wife. *Wake up, wake up*, he snarled at himself. 'Who might you be?'

'Is the lady . . . safe?' The chaplain blinked towards Julie.

'Oh yes,' Luis said and instantly regretted it. Madrid Abwehr had disapproved of Julie in Madrid and had been pleased to see her depart (as they thought) for America. If they learned she was actually in England, working alongside Luis, they would smell a whole colony of rats. Too late now. The chaplain was sitting next to Julie and inviting Luis to sit on his other side. The zip-top bag was balanced on his knees. Arriving passengers streamed by in a human flood, parted by the benches.

171

'In here I have a pair of tennis shoes, a towel stolen from the Hurlingham Club, and five pounds of explosive, primed and ready to be detonated. Our code names – please remember this – are Hammer and Anvil. I am Hammer. In about five minutes from now we shall assassinate three British Army generals in a first-class carriage of this train. The mission – and remember this too – is called Operation Tombstone.' Hammer spoke the two words with especial clarity, and glanced from face to face to be sure that he was understood.

'Tombstone,' Luis said. He was completely thrown by the appalling declaration; his reason rejected it; what this smiling villain proposed was impossible. 'Why Tombstone?'

'Why not?' Julie said.

'I don't choose the names,' Hammer said.

'I expect it was the next on the list,' Julie suggested, and smiled when Hammer smiled his agreement. She could see that Luis was struggling to catch up with events and she was afraid he might start discussing Operation Tombstone, analysing it, getting involved in it. That would be his instinct. It wasn't hers. Her instinct was to say goodbye to Hammer and Anvil damn fast, and call the cops. 'Anything else we should know?' she asked.

'Five pounds, did you say?' Luis was waking up. 'Five pounds of TNT makes a hell of a bang. *Hell* of a bang. I've seen it. Heard it.'

'Three generals take some killing,' Hammer said. 'We may not survive, of course. If we do survive, we may get caught. So it's up to you to make sure that—'

'Eldorado! Saints preserve us!' Docherty overshot the bench and had to turn and come back. 'What a journey! And what stinking weather! Tomcat sends his love and this item is for you to keep.' He slung the suitcase between Luis's legs and slumped beside him. 'God save us, but this is a terrible town.'

High above platform one, sitting at the window of the station-master's office, Freddy Garcia and the man code-named Gardener watched the scene through binoculars. 'Now what's happening?' Freddy asked.

'Beats me, sir,' Gardener said. 'The chap with the suitcase isn't part of Bamboozle.'

'Well, I've certainly never seen him before. Look: he's giving Eldorado that suitcase. What the *devil* is going on?'

Docherty was apologizing for being a minute or two late. 'This awful weather, you know. And then we had a little trouble parking . . . The others will be along in a second.'

'Do I know you?' Luis asked.

'Weren't you expecting me? I'm Teacup.'

'Of course.' Luis told Hammer, with the casual confidence of the beginner: 'Teacup is with Gardener and Blossom.'

'Am I?' Docherty looked blankly from face to face. Maybe Gardener and Blossom was a new password that Madrid had forgotten to give him. When Julie winked and nodded he said, 'And why shouldn't I be, after all?'

Anvil, who had been strolling about in the background, came over to Hammer and said quietly, 'You haven't finished briefing Eldorado, dear.'

'Quite right.' Hammer was no longer looking chubby and cheery; suddenly he seemed haggard and anxious. 'Could we have a word in private?' He took Luis and Julie to one side. 'Is that man really safe?' he asked.

'Well, he's from Tomcat,' Luis said.

'Which speaks for itself,' Julie added.

Luis gestured towards her. 'All my code work is handled for me by . . . um . . . by Paperclip here.' Julie's eyes widened. He edged away from her.

'Well,' Hammer said. 'If you're sure he's safe.' But he did not sound convinced. They rejoined Docherty, who was chatting easily with Anvil. 'As I was saying, we can't be sure of coming through Operation Tombstone intact,' Hammer said. 'That's why I set up this meeting. We depend on you to get a signal off to Tomcat, telling him we've brought it off. Right?'

'Right,' Julie said crisply. 'Well, good luck.'

'We can't go yet,' Anvil said. She had a curiously attractive voice, deep and husky. 'The targets haven't arrived. We don't know which carriage they'll be in.'

173

'What targets?' Docherty asked.

For a moment nobody answered. The platform had almost emptied; the Tannoy was silent; this end of the station was, briefly, quite calm. The members of the party stood apart from one another, as if any hint of intimacy was a confession of bad taste. They resembled (Freddy Garcia thought) an oil painting from the Great War: *Waiting for the Train to France, Victoria Station, 1916.* 'Eldorado looks worried,' he said. 'I suppose that's good.'

'Up to a point, sir,' Gardener said. 'They all appear a bit dumbstruck, don't they?'

'Where are your blessed generals?'

'On their way. There's still a good minute to go, sir. Hullo, our man Hammer's found his voice.'

It was a cautious voice. 'This network operates on a policy of need-to-know,' Hammer said. 'I know that Eldorado is a need-to-know, for signals purposes. On the other hand, I don't see why Teacup is a need-to-know.'

'You shouldn't have told me,' Docherty said. 'Now I know I'm not a need-to-know. I had no need to know that, you know.'

'Know what?' Julie asked.

'You're right, I've forgotten already,' Docherty said. 'What was the question again?'

'You might as well tell Teacup,' Luis told Hammer. He had an urgent wish to spread the bad news far and wide, in the hope that this might somehow dilute its horror. 'After all, everyone's going to hear it pretty soon when the bomb goes off.'

Hammer clenched his teeth and turned away.

'I didn't hear that,' Docherty called to him. 'Honest I didn't.'

'The targets are coming,' Anvil announced softly.

'Enter three generals, sir,' said Gardener. 'Spot on cue at exactly twelve-oh-three.'

Freddy swung his binoculars and found the three Army officers in line abreast, all in British warms, all gloved and booted and spurred, chatting as they strolled on to the platform. 'Actors, are they?' he asked.

174

'No, no. Three genuine brasshats, sir. Bored stiff, all await-
ing new appointments, they jumped at the chance of a bit of
fun . . . Hullo, hullo . . .'

'What is that extraordinary woman playing at?' Freddy asked.

It was Stephanie Schmidt, running flat out along the platform,
or as flat out as her suitcase allowed. She dodged between the
generals, who momentarily checked their stride and thereby got
in the way of Laszlo Martini, chasing Stephanie with the clear
intention of bashing her with his suitcase as soon as he got within
striking range. 'And who is that peculiar man?'

'Definitely not Bamboozle, sir,' Gardener said. 'Must be civil-
ians. Drunk, maybe.'

Freddy tightened the focus and worried, and suddenly found
the explanation. 'No they're not!' he said. 'I mean, yes they
are . . . They're everything to do with us. Madrid Abwehr set
up this rendezvous, to test Eldorado. That meant having someone
here to see whether or not he turned up. Right? Well, there they
are. Three of them.'

'So why are they running?' Gardener asked. 'And why are they
trying to hit each other with identical suitcases?'

'Beats me.'

Stephanie had put on a spurt and reached the safety of
Docherty's group. She recognized Eldorado at once, and felt a
huge surge of relief: the first part of their mission was accomplished. 'Laszlo was trying to buy a ticket,' she told Docherty,
and had to pause for breath. 'But I stole his wallet.' She waved
it as proof.

'Well done. This is Matchbox,' Docherty told Eldorado. They
shook hands. 'I'd like you to meet Paperclip,' Luis said. The two
women exchanged bright little smiles. 'I'd also like to introduce
you to Hammer and Tongs,' Luis said, 'but I'm not sure whether
it's allowed.' He heard his own voice but disbelieved what it was
saying. He seemed to have wandered into the middle of a gentle,
soft-edged nightmare. People walked in and said insane things in
polite tones; others arrived in a rush and then seemed to forget
their lines; here was this tubby young woman, now presenting
him with yet another suitcase as if it were a prize he had won in

175

a raffle. He took it and was startled when its weight dragged his arm down. Everything was strange. Nothing was right.

'Not Hammer and Tongs,' Hammer growled. 'That's a mistake.'

'Oh dear,' Luis said sadly. 'I'm not doing very well, am I?'

'Hush, now,' Anvil said. They stood in silence until the three generals had walked past. Then Laszlo trailed in, dragging his suitcase by its broken handle. He let it drop and gave it a good hard kick. 'You fat little bitch,' he said. 'You cross-eyed little tart.' He was too tired and too bitter to swear any harder or any better. Only violence could satisfy him now.

'This is Lampstand,' Docherty told everyone.

'Please,' Hammer said to Luis, 'you must get the signal right. It's Hammer and *Anvil*, not Hammer and Tongs.' He no longer looked like an RAF chaplain; he looked like a desperado in disguise. Julie, seeing him in profile, noticed the sweat in his hairline and the heavy throb of a pulse in his throat, and for the first time she began to fear that this couple might really be dangerous; might be more than fancy-dress saboteurs who could easily be turned over to the police. And what the hell was keeping Freddy? Hammer picked up his zip-top bag. 'Operation Tombstone is of crucial importance,' he said, 'but our success will be meaningless unless you signal Tomcat at once. Don't waste a minute.'

'That could be difficult,' Luis said.

'Why?'

'Hard to explain.' Luis was thoroughly miserable.

Julie said, 'I think I have a solution. Excuse us for a moment.'

'You must be quick,' Anvil said. 'We have a job to do.'

'What sort of job?' Stephanie asked.

Julie took Luis aside. 'What the blue blazes is the matter with you?' she whispered. 'They want you to send a signal, tell them you'll send a signal! Send a dozen goddam signals. Just let's get out of here.'

'They don't understand how the Eldorado set-up works,' Luis mumbled.

'Who gives a shit? Lie to them.'

176

'Lie?' He was startled. 'I'm not much good at that.'

'Oh, Jesus . . .' Julie took a pace back and looked him straight in the eyes. 'Luis, you're the best. You do it all day, every day, remember?'

'That's different.' He really meant it. 'I believe in Eldorado. It's a matter of integrity.'

For a second, Julie was baffled. Then she said: 'So cheat yourself too. Betray Eldorado. Cross your fingers and it's not a real lie, OK? Just tell them you'll send their precious signal today, now, toot sweet. Yes?'

They went back to the others. 'We can do it,' Julie said confidently. 'No problem.'

'It's just that I usually operate from London,' Luis said. 'That's the trouble, you see.' Julie groaned and tried to turn it into a cough, and failed. Hammer looked alarmed. He said, 'Our orders are—'

'You want to send a signal, is that it?' Docherty said. He nudged his suitcase with his foot. 'Use this radio, why don't you?'

'There is a radio in your suitcase?' Luis was tremendously impressed.

'Don't go any further along this platform,' Hammer warned. 'There will be danger from flying glass.' Anvil took his arm.

'You came all the way here just to give me a radio?' Luis asked.

'Three radios,' Stephanie said proudly. 'Nearly four.'

'Awfully nice to have met you,' Anvil said. They walked away.

'Four radios!' Luis said. 'I could send four signals.' That didn't sound right. 'Or one signal four times.' That was even worse. 'It's the honest truth,' he said to Julie, and then remembered that he should be lying. 'Anyway, it's not my fault,' he mumbled.

'Praise be!' Freddy Garcia said. 'Action at last. Now for the fireworks.' He lowered his binoculars and rubbed his eyes.

'Eldorado and his gang are on the move too, sir,' Gardener said. 'Off to look for you, I expect.'

In fact Luis was walking backwards, relying on others to get out of his way, while he watched Hammer and Anvil approach a first-class carriage and open the door.

'You are expecting something important to happen?' Laszlo inquired softly.

'Don't tell him, he has no need-to-know,' Docherty said.

'Oh, rubbish. We all know,' Stephanie scoffed. 'I know because Anvil just told me. They've gone to assassinate three British generals. With a bomb.' It gave her an unexpected thrill to announce such rich violence. She hadn't realized she could be so callous, and it made her feel strong. 'They'll be blown to bits any moment now. All of them. It's a suicide mission. I think they're splendid, don't you?'

'It's quite routine,' Luis said. 'This sort of thing goes on all the time.' *That's better*, he thought, and glanced at Julie, who rolled her eyes.

'No need for suicide,' Laszlo said. 'I could have shot them and walked away, if you had only asked me.'

'Next time . . .' Luis began, and jumped at the crack-boom of an explosion that blew out the window of a compartment and sent red and yellow flames chasing into the grey of the day. The bang echoed three times around the station until it seemed to have flattened all other noise. Then the normal noises came slowly to life again. The Tannoy shouted. Whistles were blown. The clang of an ambulance bell began to hammer out. Men in uniform came surging down the platform. Most were military police. Laszlo saw the red caps and the white belts and did not stop to think. He flung open a door and leaped into the train and ran.

'Smashing!' Freddy said. 'Did you see Luis's face? And Julie too . . . That'll give them something to think about.'

'I think they're thinking about making a party of it, sir,' Gardener said. 'Our pair is going off with their pair.'

'Crikey. So they are.' Freddy's satisfaction suddenly faded. 'I hadn't planned on that.'

'They won't get far, sir. Our security people will scoop them up. It's all part of Bamboozle.'

'Forget Bamboozle. I want those Abwehr agents to send their report to Madrid. And I'd like to know where they're living, too.

Go and tell security to scoop them up and let them all go. Then we'll follow them.'

As he left, Gardener said, 'Don't forget one got on the train, sir.'

'That won't do him any good. The bally train isn't going anywhere, is it?'

Laszlo had had very little sleep in the past two days and his nervous system had taken a beating from the strain of the landing in Ireland, the frustrations of the journey to Dublin, the high excitement of Ferenc's murder, the anticlimax of hanging about in a rainy Liverpool. So his brain was not working well. If he wanted to hide in the train he should have gone *towards* the oncoming redcaps, in the hope of jumping out when they had passed. But he ran the other way, through the first open door he saw, ran away from the redcaps, and knew they were behind him, and so had to keep on running. This made no sense: he wasn't going anywhere, he was just going; he pounded along the corridors and wrenched open doors that led to more corridors. Once he collided with a soldier who had been asleep when the train reached Lime Street and had been woken up by the blast. 'Is it an air raid?' the soldier asked. Laszlo cursed him and kicked him and hammered his ribs with his elbow until the man staggered aside, and Laszlo ran on. But the shock had jolted him into realizing that he was running into danger: he was heading for the carriage where the bomb had gone off. So he dragged the pistol from its holster. Impossible to stop and fit the silencer; anyway, who needed silence after a bang like that?

He smelled the bombed carriage before he reached it: a harsh stink, sucked into his throat and nostrils as he gasped for air. The last door was half-open. He kicked it wide. Three generals turned and stared at him. Behind them stood the RAF chaplain and his lady. From their various attitudes, Laszlo knew they had been examining the bombed-out compartment. The air was steel-grey with hanging smoke. Laszlo saw the compartment and it was not bombed-out at all; except for the shattered window it was scarcely damaged. In the instant that this took to explain itself to him he felt sick with betrayal and then frenzied with a lust for revenge. He

179

shot the nearest general in the chest. The crash was stupendous, deafening. By a fluke the bullet hit a tunic button and punched it deep into the man's body, smashing open a hole which bled so fast that his khaki tunic was a drenched and spreading red. The impact flung him against the other two officers. One stumbled and fell to his knees. The chaplain shouted and threw his zip-top bag: it struck Laszlo full in the face. The dying general slid to the floor. Now the corridor was blocked. Laszlo could not shoot them all and even if he did they would still be in his way. He heard the pounding clash of boots on the platform: no escape there. For a fraction of a second he wondered about suicide and rejected it. If he had to die it wasn't going to be in a squalid railway carriage. He dodged back and ran until he found a door that gave on to the empty tracks. He swung it open.

At once someone began shouting at him. Laszlo saw a railway official standing on the next platform, waving violently, and he jumped. It was only six feet but Laszlo had not fallen six feet since he was a boy and he landed badly, sprawling on his hands and knees on the oily stones and cinders. He was shaken, and shaking. He had dropped the pistol but it could not be far away so he stayed down, searching for it, and the shaking got worse. He could not keep his body still: the very ground seemed to be trembling. Laszlo looked up and saw a train bearing down on him, black and huge, with monstrous white sidewhiskers of steam jetting from the churning wheels. It was in no hurry and this grinding deliberation frightened him more than any speed: the monster was taking its time about killing him because it knew he could not escape. He dropped flat and pressed his face into the greasy rubble and shut his eyes. The trembling developed into a vibrant, shuddering rumble that became a lusty, clanking roar. It passed and faded, and Laszlo dared to look up. He was lying between the two trains. There was ample room. He saw his pistol, crawled towards it and stuffed it in a pocket. Brakes squealed. While the train was drifting to a halt he got up and ran. As he went past the carriage that contained the dead general a door opened and the RAF chaplain aimed a kick at his head, but Laszlo was too short and he ducked under it. Ahead, only thirty

180

or forty yards away, the trains ended. Then he could cut across the tracks, get away, lose himself in the wet anonymous crowds of Liverpool.

It nearly worked. He could see broad, rain-soaked daylight ahead, widening with every stride, when angry shouts broke out behind him. Why are they shouting? he wondered. Why aren't they shooting? It made little difference: they would catch him, they must be younger and taller and stronger. He ran on, determined to make them work for their grubby little triumph, and out of the slanting drifts of rain came salvation.

It was a locomotive – isolated and solitary – reversing cautiously towards the train standing at platform one, ready to hook up and haul it away. Laszlo sprinted hard and then checked as he got a grip of the grab-rails and went up the steps to the cab like a monkey in a double-breasted suit. The fireman was hanging out of the other side, guiding the driver. 'Stop!' Laszlo shouted. He was black with the filth of the track.

'Stop what?' the driver asked, disgruntled.

Laszlo fired a shot wide of the driver. The bullet ricocheted three times and nicked the fireman's arm. He yelped and fell out of the cab. The driver slammed the controls. Laszlo stumbled and nearly fell as the brakes bit and the wheels locked solid. 'Go!' he bawled, pointing with the gun. 'Go, go, go!' The brakes got thrown off, the wheels spun and gripped and the locomotive began to lumber forward. Laszlo glimpsed a face below and brandished his pistol at a military policeman who was trying to climb on board. The man gave up and vanished. 'Faster, faster, faster!' Laszlo screamed. The driver did things. They accelerated. There was shouting alongside but they soon left it behind. The driver dragged down a chain and the steam whistle whooped with gusty joy. Laszlo grinned. He seized the chain and blew and blew until he remembered that he was on the run, and he stopped. By then they were well away from Lime Street and travelling at a fine clip. Everything was perfect.

*

181

'You've got your wheels on the kerb again, honey,' Julie said.

'Have I? Sorry.' Stephanie Schmidt steered to the right. The taxi suffered a couple of bad jolts and then ran smoothly.

'Couldn't you tell the difference?' Julie asked.

'I thought the tyres were flat. Put my hand on the gear-lever, please.' Stephanie hated taking her eyes off the road in order to look for anything. She was always using the wrong hand, on the wrong side. Everything in this country was on the wrong side. She had a noisy fight with the gear-box, and won. 'Which gear is that, please?' she asked.

'It sounds like two but it feels like three,' Julie said. 'Have you thought of using the wipers?' The windscreen was pebbled with rain.

'I lost the switch. I turned it off when I used the horn and now I can't find it.' Stephanie sat on the edge of the seat and squeezed the wheel until her fingers hurt. There was too much traffic and the road was narrow and full of bends, that was the trouble. It had been the trouble ever since they recovered the taxi from the railway porter (another fiver from Docherty) and left Lime Street station. She was very brave to drive the taxi. They all said so. None of them had ever driven on the left, not even Docherty, so Stephanie had volunteered to drive to London. It was a time for courage: look at what Hammer and Anvil had done. Even Laszlo, in his way, was daring. 'Where are we?' she asked.

'Hard to tell, but I think this place is called Ormskirk,' Julie said. There were no signposts. All the signposts in England had been taken down to help frustrate German invaders in 1940. 'There's a pub called the Ormskirk Arms, anyway.'

'Where the dickens do they think they're going?' Freddy Garcia asked.

'Could be Scotland,' Gardener said, wiping condensation off the windscreen. 'Could be anywhere . . . By the way, sir, the police say they stole that taxi.'

'Curiouser and curiouser. Maybe they'll stop for lunch. I'm starving.'

182

'Ormskirk doesn't sound right,' Docherty said. 'Hasn't anybody got a map? We need a road map.'

'I can't stop,' Stephanie said. 'There's a bus behind me.'

'Where is it going?' Julie asked.

Docherty wiped the mist from the rear window. 'Skelmersdale,' he reported. 'Is that near London?'

'Just outside,' Luis said.

'Follow that bus behind you,' Docherty told Stephanie. 'Don't let it get away.'

But the bus soon disappeared and Stephanie got lost at a crooked five-way crossroads. By now Julie had found the wiper switch, and the way ahead was clear, and clearly wrong: they were splashing along a narrowing farm lane. Soon they had to slow to a crawl behind a herd of sodden cows. Docherty got out and walked with the small boy who was in charge of them. When he came back he said, 'His advice is to go back to Liverpool and start again. He says there's nothing at the end of this road but the biggest heap of cow-shite you ever did see.'

'I can't stop here,' Stephanie said. 'There's a tractor behind me.'

She went on and turned in the farmyard and came back. They drove for an hour, seeking the London road but never finding it. Julie managed to buy a loaf of bread in a village. 'They told me that if we stay on this road we'll get to Wigan,' she said. 'Eventually.'

'Is Wigan near London?' Stephanie asked.

'On the outskirts,' Luis said, stuffing bread into his mouth. He had given up trying to alter events, and he guessed that Julie felt the same. The bomb blast – even after Hammer's warning – had come as such a shock, and the consequences had been so swift and overwhelming – squads of military police, three ambulances, two fire engines, barriers thrown up, nobody allowed to leave, the station Tannoy barking order after order – that he had simply done what he was ordered and allowed authority to control him. Authority put the four of them (nobody knew where Laszlo had gone) into a small office, scrutinized their identity cards and asked what they were doing on platform one. Docherty said he and Stephanie had come to see the other two off. Everyone else agreed that that was so, and amazingly, after ten minutes, authority let them go, and they walked away. That was the good part. The bad part was that these two Abwehr agents still clung to them. 'I expect you've got a train to catch,' Julie said brightly.

'We might, if we had anywhere to go,' Docherty said. 'As it is, we're in your hands.'

'You must have a safe house we can use,' Stephanie said. 'I need a hot bath and a change of clothes. Can't we go to your safe house?'

'Of course,' Julie said. She knew nothing about these Abwehr agents except that they were reckless and probably ruthless, which meant they might be murderous if crossed. Two Abwehr agents had just killed three generals. This was no time to be awkward. 'We can go to Freddy's place,' she said quickly. 'Freddy will know what to do.' That was when they learned about the taxi. 'What a perfect solution!' Julie said. 'Aren't we lucky, darling?' She put her arms around Luis's neck and kissed him. 'Act tough, for Christ's sake,' she whispered. 'Or they'll shoot us both.'

The taxi ran out of fuel at the worst possible place: in the middle of a stretch of moor, with nothing but gorse and rain in sight. By now Stephanie felt that she had done her bit. 'One of us should go for help,' she said, looking at the men.

'What help?' Docherty said. 'We've no petrol coupons. I doubt there's a tow truck within ten miles. I vote we all go or nobody goes.'

A gust of wind rocked the car on its springs and the rain began a long drumroll on the roof. For a while they sat in silence.

'Couldn't you go and telephone someone?' Stephanie said to Luis. 'Someone in your network, I mean.'

'That's exactly what I intend to do,' Luis said. 'As soon as it stops raining.'

'Is it a big network?'

'Not bad. Two hundred and sixty-three agents, last time I counted.'

184

She sucked her breath in admiration. 'All working towards the triumph of the Third Reich.'

'Mind you,' Julie said, 'we lose one or two from time to time. The British are not complete fools.'

'What happens to them?' Stephanie asked.

'The usual,' Luis said curtly. 'They know the risks.'

'Of course they do,' Docherty agreed. 'We all do. It's like climbing mountains. Nobody would do it if it wasn't bloody dangerous, now would they? We know the odds.'

'They are heroes,' Stephanie said. 'Their names will be on the roll of honour. The Reich will always remember them.'

'I wonder what the odds are,' Julie said.

'Fifty-fifty,' Docherty said promptly. 'Mind you, it's far worse in Germany. The typical British spy has a ten-to-one chance of being caught. That's why so many of them give up.'

Brief pause.

'No, you lost me there,' Julie said.

'Well, it's obvious. If they give up and agree to work for the Abwehr they don't get shot. They keep on reporting to the British Secret Service, of course, only what they report is what the Abwehr tells them to report.'

'Traitors,' Stephanie said.

Docherty clicked his fingers. 'That's the word I was trying to think of,' he said. 'I don't suppose you have any trouble with that sort of nonsense in your network.'

'None,' Luis said.

'Our guys are like crusader knights,' Julie said. 'You know, incorruptible.'

'I met the Führer once,' Stephanie said. Her head was back, her eyes were looking at the roof but her mind was seeing Nuremberg. 'At a rally. He touched my arm. I thought my heart would burst.'

'If I so much as suspected a man's loyalty,' Luis said, 'I would strangle him with my own hands.' He held them up for display. Stephanie reached back and took one in her own hands and kissed it. 'We are all pledged to the cause of the Fatherland,' she said.

'Fifty-fifty,' Docherty said. 'That's not so bad, is it?'

185

'Who wants to live for ever?' Julie asked.

'Well, exactly,' Luis said. 'That's the key question.'

'On the other hand . . .' Docherty sniffed, and kept them waiting. 'Who really truly wants to die tomorrow?' There were no immediate takers. 'Or even later this afternoon?'

'For the Cause—' Stephanie began.

'Indeed, indeed. That's our great advantage over the poor, treacherous British agents who give up so easily. We have the Cause to fortify our souls, whereas they're just spying for a ramshackle Imperialist-Capitalist-Communist alliance. No wonder they swap sides!' Docherty chuckled at the thought.

'It couldn't happen here,' Luis said. 'MI5 are too stupid.'

Someone knocked on a window. Luis wound it down. 'Are you all right?' Freddy Garcia asked. 'You look abandoned or marooned or something.'

'About bloody time,' Luis said. Suddenly all the doors were being opened by armed policemen in streaming oil-capes. 'Those two are spies,' he said. 'He's Teacup and she's Matchbox.'

The policemen took them out and searched them. Standing in the rain, with her arms out sideways like a scarecrow and the wind making a mess of her hair, Stephanie Schmidt was crying like a child being bullied on her first day at school. 'Here, here, it's not as bad as all that,' Docherty comforted her. 'One door closes and another opens. Now you can turn your coat and work for the British. That's what I'm going to do.' She tried to kick him and lost her balance. The policemen helped her up. 'I hear the food's OK,' Docherty said. 'And nobody's going to thank you for dying, you know. There's no future in death. As a goal in life it's highly overrated.'

Freddy was looking inside the three suitcases. 'You never sent any messages,' he said. 'I was waiting for you to send messages.'

'Forgot,' Luis said. 'Sorry.'

'Lovely to see you again,' Julie said. 'It seems like only yesterday you went off to buy some rail tickets.'

'Long queue,' Freddy said.

'Those radio valves are all bust,' Docherty told him. 'Bloody Abwehr rubbish. It's an absolute scandal, so it is.' They watched

186

Stephanie being put in the back of a police car and driven away. 'She's in love with a man in Madrid called Otto Krafft,' Docherty said. 'That's another scandal, in my opinion. War is bad enough without love to make it worse, wouldn't you say?' Julie's eyes flickered towards Luis, who was staring down at a puddle, and she gave a small and sceptical smile. 'My apologies,' Docherty said. 'Sometimes I think my own valves are all bust too.' Another police car pulled up and he got in.

Operation Tombstone pleased almost everybody.

It pleased Madrid Abwehr when they got a signal indicating that their agents had successfully infiltrated and made contact with Eldorado. The report of the Lime Street bombing was an unexpected bonus, and led to much speculation. Evidently there was a sabotage and assassination unit operating over there. 'Ask Eldorado to find out who they are,' Brigadier Wagner told Richard Fischer.

'I expect they were really after Winston Churchill. After all, that's why Eldorado was in that part of the station at that particular time, wasn't it?'

'Try not to be a complete buffoon, Fischer. I invented Churchill's visit to Liverpool, remember?'

'Eldorado might have leaked it to someone, sir. Rumour can be as powerful as fact.'

'Ah.' Wagner hadn't thought of that. 'You may be right.' It pleased Wagner to think that his imagination was strong enough to prompt death and destruction in a distant country.

Berlin Abwehr was pleased because Eldorado could now communicate by radio and because Garlic would soon be dead. MI5's radio section had repaired (and improved) the suitcase transmitters, and Docherty's brief message stated that Lampstand, Matchbox, and Teacup were operational. Ferenc Tekeli's code name was 'Deckchair', so Docherty added 'Deckchair broken', which could mean anything.

The Director was pleased because Tombstone had made Bamboozle a success: Julie Conroy and Luis Cabrillo now believed that Abwehr agents were operating undiscovered in Britain.

Freddy was pleased because the Director was pleased.

Luis, once he recovered from the shock of it all, enjoyed knowing that he had captured two spies. For Julie, the whole episode had been so bizarre – a cocktail of tedium and violence, laced with farce – that she soon quit trying to understand it and was simply glad to have survived. When she asked Freddy why he had vanished in the station, he said he'd been caught up and held in a sudden security check – police looking for deserters, so they said, but personally he thought they had probably got wind of Matchbox, Teacup, and Lampstand.

'So why didn't they nab them?' she demanded. 'They were running around like the Three Stooges in the high hurdles.'

Freddy sighed. 'No excuses, I'm afraid,' he said. 'Still, you did jolly well, old girl. Very good show.'

She raised one eyebrow. 'Uh-huh,' she said. 'Pity about the generals.'

Almost certainly the dead general was not pleased. But then, as the Director suggested to Freddy, how could one be sure? The chap had a game leg and a glass eye and no great prospects of a decent appointment; at least he was able to die in action, doing service for his country.

'Any trace of Lampstand, sir?' Freddy asked.

'Teacup thinks he's making for Scotland. We're on the lookout but it's a big country. Teacup says Matchbox knows more, but the silly woman is being noble and brave and silent. Still . . . No money, nowhere to live, Lampstand can't last long, can he?'

Knightsbridge was a huge improvement over Rackham Towers. As soon as they got back from Liverpool, Luis and Julie were moved into a big three-bedroom apartment with a fine view over Hyde Park. It was serviced by MI5 and it was just around the corner from the office block where the Double-Cross department had its headquarters (and where Docherty and Stephanie Schmidt were being very thoroughly interrogated). Freddy Garcia helped them move in. 'Take a couple of days off,' he said. 'Do the town, see some shows. Have fun.'

'Where are you sleeping?' Julie asked Luis.

'Anywhere!' he said. He was slightly manic: the after-effects of excitement. 'You choose.'

'You're in here.' She threw his hat on to the bed. 'I'm in there.' She went into the next room.

He bounced on the bed. 'You don't know what you're missing!' he called.

'Wrong both ways. I do know, and I don't miss it.'

'I save her from those Nazi thugs,' Luis told Freddy, 'and this is how she thanks me.'

Freddy said goodnight and left. Luis was still sitting on the bed, swinging his legs, when Julie came in and sat on the other side. 'You didn't save anyone from anything,' she said. It was a comment, not an accusation. 'Whenever I looked, you had eyes like my old teddy bear. Solid glass and out of focus.'

He reached behind him and found her hands on the bedspread and linked fingers. 'I was playing a part,' he said. 'It was a masterly performance.'

'You were scared shitless.'

'What rubbish. I was in total command.'

'Oh, Luis.' She pressed hard with her thumbs. 'Don't you think I know you? I've seen you scared before. You were scared today, I was there, remember? I was scared, too.'

'Well, then.'

'So why not admit it? Why try to hide it from me? I mean, what have you got to lose, for God's sake?' She sighed, and relaxed, and leaned back against him so that he had to lean against her. 'You can be such a phoney,' she said.

'Well, that's what I am, isn't it? A professional cheat.'

'Do you have to cheat me? Sometimes I think there's something wrong with me, some deficiency, it's the reason he can't trust me, so he's never honest with me. But it isn't me, is it? It's you. And I get sick of always having to be the interpreter. You can cheat and chisel the rest of the world, that's your business—'

189

'Yes it is.'

'—but if you can't be honest with me then the hell with you, I'm not going to waste my time figuring out what's going on between your ears.'

They sat staring at the walls, looking like a couple of bookends with no books. Luis thought: I really must do something about that Petrified Bog idea, it's been hanging about far too long. 'Why can't we be like we were?' he asked.

'Because we're not like we were any more!' She got up so suddenly that he toppled over. 'Forget *then*. This is *now*. What are you going to do about it?' She went over, came back, and kissed him on the forehead. 'Creep,' she said, and went out.

Next morning the sun shone. They walked in the park, walked all the way up Piccadilly, and did the tourist trail: Trafalgar Square, Whitehall, Houses of Parliament. The streets were awash with uniforms, the sky bubbled with barrage balloons, there were always aircraft high above the balloons speeding on some urgent mission. London had been badly knocked about, but the unexpected gaps and the fire-gutted shells of buildings were collecting fringes of grass and odd tufts of purple buddleia, which gave them a sort of raffish charm. Luis was delighted with the place. He was still full of fizz, and he let Julie – who knew London – guide him while he chattered cheerfully about nothing special. He was very taken with the appearance of American Army officers in pink trousers and maroon tunics. 'Poor devils,' he said. 'Can't they afford a top and bottom to match? It's a scandal. We're not going to invade Europe looking like a chorus line from *The Gay Hussar*, are we?'

'Not us,' she said. 'We're going to eat. Now.'

After lunch they walked back to Trafalgar Square. 'I want a picture of you feeding the pigeons,' Luis said. He took a bread roll from his pocket. 'Stole it while the waiter wasn't looking,' he said.

'We haven't got a camera.'

'Isn't there always a photographer hanging around?' He looked, and failed to find one. 'Go ahead anyway. I'll just have to remember you.'

He tried to give her the bread roll but she would not take it. 'That's not such a smart idea, Luis. You know, wasting food in wartime. There's probably some regulation.'

'You mean they'll arrest us? I can't see a British bobby. Can you?'

She turned and walked away. 'I don't care. Pigeons give me the heebie-jeebies. I don't like them. In fact I hate them.'

Luis followed her, tossing the bread roll from hand to hand. A few pigeons followed him. 'You hate *pigeons*?' he said. 'That's ridiculous. How can anyone hate pigeons?'

'Because they terrify me. They're stupid and they stink and they're all feathers and they panic and fly up in your face. I really loathe the little bastards.'

Luis took her arm. 'That's crazy,' he said. 'They're just pigeons. How can they hurt you? Look.' He stamped his foot. The nearest birds took off in a rush of wings. Julie broke free and ran.

Luis had plenty of time to work out where he went wrong. She ran a long way. By the time he found her she was sitting on the steps of the National Gallery. 'My fault entirely,' he said.

She looked at him as if he were a pigeon. 'That was a really shitty thing to do,' she said. 'Don't you ever think of anyone but yourself?'

He sat beside her and watched the crowds go by. Part of him was sorry and ashamed; another, rebellious part was saying: *What a fuss over a few scruffy pigeons. I was only trying to help. If she didn't want me to help, she shouldn't have . . .* He couldn't finish the sentence.

'Now I know you can't stand pigeons,' he said.

'Don't sound so goddam smug. Everybody has something. Even you.'

Cracked glass, Luis thought. He couldn't bring himself to touch a piece of glass that was cracked, a windowpane, for instance, in case it shattered and cut him. He hated to see it. Just thinking of it made him shiver. He shook his head to chase the awful thought away.

'OK,' she said flatly, 'so don't tell me.'

'I didn't mean that.'

191

'So what did you mean?' It was supposed to be a simple request for information. Somehow it came out coated with sandpaper. She knew from the way he hunched his shoulders and ducked his head that he wasn't going to answer.

They walked up St Martin's Lane, for no particular reason, not saying much, looking in secondhand book shops, each silently juggling with blame and fault, guilt and regret. The sunshine had exhausted itself already; the sky was grey and odd freckles of rain appeared unexpectedly on the flagstones. They took cover beneath the canvas awning of a shop. Each knew that neither wanted to go back to the apartment; not like this. The owner of the shop came out and closed the awning.

'So what's the point?' Julie asked him.

'Keeps the sun off the books,' he said. 'You wouldn't want to buy a bleached book, would you?'

'I might,' she said. 'What's it about?' He went back inside.

Luis pointed. Across the road was a theatre. The play was called *So Much For Love*; the *Telegraph* said it was beguiling, enchanting, delightful, and there was a matinée. They bought tickets and saw it. The *Telegraph* must have seen a different play but at least it killed the afternoon, and it made them hungry. As they ate they talked about the one subject they both knew was quite safe: their childhoods. Then they were standing in the street again. It was night; the blackout was total except for the soft glow from heavily shielded headlights. Buses rumbled past and the passengers were lost in shadow. Luis felt suddenly helpless. He had no idea how to get home – which way to go, where the Tube stations were, how to get a taxi when you couldn't tell a taxi from an army truck. 'What now?' he said brightly.

'I want to see *Casablanca*,' she said.

'I thought you'd seen it.'

'That's why I want to see it again.'

'Is it on?'

'*Casablanca* is always on, somewhere.'

She bought an evening paper and checked the listings. She took him by Tube to a part of London he had never heard of, Notting

Hill Gate, and they saw half a western, a gung-ho newsreel, and *Casablanca*.

They took a bus back to Knightsbridge. Luis was still caught up in the film; he had never seen it before; it left him both limp and elated. He wanted to share his feelings but Julie was so silent that he decided to wait until they got home. Then he said: 'That was a good idea of yours.'

'Glad you liked it. I used to like it.' She was looking in a mirror, taking off her ear-rings. 'Now it does nothing for me any more.'

He went to the kitchen and got a bottle of beer from the fridge. 'Want some?' She shook her head. 'I can't see what more you could ask for,' he said. 'Good story, good acting. Terrific song.'

'Sure.' She was moving about the room, straightening the blackout curtains. 'It's box-office, no two ways about it. I guess I've got tired of watching people run away all the time. *Casablanca*'s full of running away, isn't it? It's set in Casablanca, for a start. Ever been there? I spent my honeymoon in Casablanca. The Atlantic City of North Africa. I know the cinema's about escapism, but what a place for a war movie.' There was a touch of sandpaper in her voice again and she could see he didn't like it. Too bad.

'It's not a war movie, it's a love movie,' he said.

'Yeah, I heard the lyrics. "Woman loves man and man must have his mate", on account of it rhymes with "fate". D'you believe that?'

'It worked for Bogart and Bergman.'

'No, it didn't. He lost her, then she found him and what do you know? He lost her again. Which makes me think he didn't really want her in the first place.'

Luis drank more beer, and belched like a baby. 'I have a nasty feeling this is getting painfully close to home,' he said.

'Then run away from it. You're good at that. You don't love me, Luis. You don't love anyone except Eldorado and he doesn't exist, so you're safe there.'

Luis swigged his beer. He was bored with it. 'Does that mean we're finished?' he asked.

'What do you think?'

Luis had had enough. It was late, he was tired, he had a great desire to escape, to fly to Casablanca, to spend the rest of his life in a corner of Rick's Bar. 'I'll tell you in the morning,' he said.

But in the morning he told her nothing, and in the afternoon she talked to Freddy Garcia and moved into a flat on another floor. Luis knew it was happening but he didn't see her go. He was shut in his room, writing.

The corridor was crowded, but Domenik saw Christian coming and pitched his voice to reach him. 'What's a hundred yards long and lives on cabbage?' he asked.

'Don't know. What?'

'A German meat-queue,' Domenik said as they passed. Christian winced. He wished Domenik wouldn't do that to him. Even if it was true.

Laszlo saw three street-fights in his first half-hour in Glasgow. It was dusk, and he was somewhere between the docks and the red-light district, with plenty of drunks lurching out of plenty of bars, but even so he was impressed. The tenements were tall, gaunt, and smoke-blackened, and the air tasted of sulphur; people shouted and swore; the trams lurched like drunks and screeched like whores. Laszlo had spent the last two-and-a-half days trundling along quiet country lanes and the raucous vigour of Glasgow nearly overwhelmed him. Here was a big, bleak, hard, ugly port-city with money in its pocket and fire in its belly, working flat-out twenty-four hours a day to handle all the trade the war kept sending it. Laszlo inwardly rejoiced.

A couple of miles outside Lime Street he had made the engine-driver stop the locomotive on a bridge over a main road. He had taken the man's money and his identification papers, and told him to shut up or he'd shoot him. The driver had thrown lumps of coal at Laszlo as he scrambled down the embankment, and missed. It was raining hard; nobody looked up at a lonely locomotive. Laszlo took a bus. He kept taking buses until he got into the country. He slept in a barn, and took more buses next day, and the day after, always heading north, feeling sure that the police and the Army would be watching for him at railway stations and long-distance coach depots and gambling on their inability to check out every scruffy little country bus. It was a long journey. Thirty miles at a stretch was good going. He sat and waited in many little towns and villages, all the way up through Lancashire, Westmorland, and Cumberland, over the border into Dumfries and Lanark. He was asleep when the last bus carried him into Glasgow. The driver came back and shook him awake, saying something cheerfully guttural and totally incomprehensible, and Laszlo got out. Language was a problem he had not expected. He could get by in English but up here they talked a strange, swooping dialect, marked by harsh use of the back of the throat, which explained (he thought) why they spat so much. He understood occasional words, such as 'bus' or 'street', but the rest could just as well have been Cherokee or Polish. Here was another obstacle to be overcome.

But first he needed money.

The bars were full of money. Laszlo found a big bar, bought a drink – they understood 'beer' – and eased through the din of customers to a place by the door where he could rest his back and blend with the stained pub wallpaper. Laszlo was not so squalid as to be refused service in a Glasgow bar but he was fairly dirty (washing in horse-troughs only diluted the dirt), he hadn't shaved for three days, his clothes were stained and his body was rank; he knew that, because he could smell it. So could others. Nobody had sat beside him on the buses for long. Well, he didn't care if he was unattractive but he couldn't risk being noticeably repugnant.

It took him the worst part of an hour but eventually he saw the man he was looking for: a merchant seaman, about Laszlo's age and build, perhaps a Lascar, probably fresh off his boat and glad to be alive after another Atlantic convoy. What mattered was that he was alone. He took his drink for a stroll about the bar, didn't find what he wanted and left. Laszlo followed.

He had no clear-cut plan; he didn't like plans, they went wrong, it was better to let his gun arrange things. When he saw the Lascar pause at a street corner he ran and caught up with him. 'Do you know what this is?' he said. There was just enough light in the sky for the Lascar to see the pistol. 'I do,' he said and Laszlo was amused by his familiarity. He put the gun in his coat pocket but still held it. The man was quite still. They waited until some people had strolled by.

'*Vamos*,' Laszlo said. They walked down a sidestreet, Laszlo beside him, their shoulders touching. On a foolish impulse Laszlo put his arm around him and kissed his neck, just above the collar. No response. Using his other hand, still in his coat pocket, Laszlo reached across and rubbed the gun-muzzle against the man's ribs. 'You're mine now,' he said. Again, no response. He raised his arm, knocked off the man's hat and leaning close, nuzzled his ear, even biting lightly on the lobe. Absolutely no reaction: the fellow just kept pace with him, not looking, not speaking; so that Laszlo felt childish and angry, and released him.

I don't care, he said to himself furiously, I can do what I like. I can kill him if I want to. I don't care.

The street petered out into a waste of bombed sites. Laszlo used the gunpoint to steer the Lascar through piles of rubble. 'Now stop,' he said. 'Give me your money and your papers.' He got the man's wallet. 'Now go,' he said, and tripped him as he turned away. The man sprawled. Laszlo bent and whacked his head with the pistol-butt. 'Stay silent,' he said. 'Tell no one, or I shall find you and kill you.'

Fifty yards away, Laszlo stopped and wondered whether he shouldn't go back and finish him off. He took out the silencer and softly blew down it. The hard cool metallic taste was far better than that seaman's soft disgusting ear.

No. Better not. A murder would provoke the police far more than an everyday backstreet robbery. He put it away.

Thirty-two pounds in the wallet, and the identity papers of A. J. Lakram. Laszlo signed the name with ease and familiarity when he registered at a doss-house that masqueraded as a hotel, and got a good night's sleep. Tomorrow was going to be a hard day.

*

'You can't give Eisenhower the pox, Luis,' Freddy Garcia said. 'Honestly you can't. I mean, there are limits.'

'General Patton, then.' Luis was lying on his bed, reading a boys' comic weekly called *The Rover*. 'Poxy Patton.'

Freddy grunted, and turned the pages of the draft report. 'Is it absolutely essential to drown an entire American infantry division?' he asked. 'Not a single survivor?'

'Troopship hits an ammunition boat at full speed. Krakatoa! What else d'you expect?'

'I don't expect the convoy commander to commit suicide. It's not the British way, old chap.'

'He was American. Didn't I say so? Admiral Orson O. Sixshooter III. Couldn't take the disgrace so he tried to cut his throat but he missed because he was pissed, so he beat his brains out with an old cucumber instead.' Luis gave Freddy a blank stare. 'Write it in the margin, there's a good chap.'

'Old cucumbers go soggy, I believe,' Freddy said.

'Not as soggy as American brains. Look,' Luis said, 'I've given you all your boring troop movements and training exercises and aircraft production schedules, so what are you complaining about?'

'I'm not complaining. I'm just wondering how cholera got into the American embassy.'

'The Abwehr will love it.' Luis went back to *The Rover*.

Freddy reread the draft, and sighed. 'Let's discuss it tomorrow,' he said. Luis nodded, deep in his story. Freddy paused at the door. 'I know it's none of my business, but I do feel sorry,' he said. 'For you both.'

'I told her to go,' Luis said. 'I've got to have peace and quiet or I can't work. You know what women are like.'

Washed, shaved, and brushed, Laszlo Martini went out into the great city of Glasgow and found his way to the university medical school in less than an hour, and it was empty. Summer vacation, a porter told him. 'They've a' ganged hame,' he explained.

'Hame?' Laszlo said. 'Where is Hame?'

'Hame is where it's aye bin, ye daft bugger. Hame is where ye hang yer hat.'

'I see.' Laszlo nodded. 'And is Hame easy to find?'

'Dinny pull ma chain, Jimmy,' the porter warned him. 'Ah done twenny-two year in the Black Watch.' His door slammed.

Laszlo bought a cup of tea at a small café around the corner. 'Not many medical students to be seen,' he remarked.

'Ah'm nay greetin',' the man who served him said. 'Next?'

Laszlo took his cup and went away and thought. So far there were two words he was confident of: *vacation* and *Hame*, although *Hame* meant nothing to him. He remembered his training in Madrid and decided to try a new tack. When a girl came round collecting used cups he smiled and said, 'The medical students – when will they be back?'

She stared. 'Dinny ken,' she said.

'I see. All of them?'

'Dinny ken.'

'Many thanks.' He gave her sixpence and left. At least he had got a straight answer, even if he didn't fully understand it. 'Dinnyken' sounded vaguely familiar, he'd heard it in the bar last night, he was almost sure of that. Maybe it was a local name for a religious feast-day, like Christmas or Easter. That made sense. Vacation ends at Dinnyken. Laszlo felt a bristling of annoyance: the Abwehr should have briefed him on these things, instead of fussing over ounces and farthings. But he quashed the feeling and shaped his face to look pleasant as he stopped a passer-by. 'Excuse me,' he said. 'When exactly is Dinnyken?'

The dirty blue overalls were patched, the left leg limped, and the eyes had just finished a long, weary shift. 'Go bile yer heed,' he said blackly.

Next Laszlo stopped two women and asked the same question. They looked at each other. 'We're baith Presbyterian,' one told him. They hurried on.

He made one more attempt, and chose a tall, elderly man in sweater and corduroy trousers who – although Laszlo couldn't have known it – was both an Englishman and a lecturer in philosophy at the university. 'When is Dinnyken?' Laszlo asked him.

'I often ask myself that very question,' he said. 'Also, where is time? And how is life? Good-day to you.' He raised his hat and went on his way.

For Laszlo all this was infuriating. He knew he must be only a mile or two from his target, yet he kept stumbling over these tripwires of ignorance and idiocy. He sat on a wall and forced himself to think. One fact was clear: anything involving the working classes was a waste of time. They spoke a kind of gibberish and even for peasantry they seemed very dense. Someone in the university must know where he could find Garlic if only he could get past these clods. Why hadn't Madrid prepared him for this sort of emergency? Gradually he sank into apathy. The people of Glasgow wandered about in front of him and he found them a sorry sight. They all dressed so sombrely, in blacks and greys and dark blues. God knew, the place itself was grim enough, nothing but blackened granite, every house pimpled with a dozen chimneypots all smudging and staining the sky. No wonder the children looked stunted, with heads close-cropped like pygmy convicts and short trousers that covered their knees as if they were made of sacks, and often no shoes or boots. The whole place was like a slum. How could a good spy operate in a slum? It was an insult. Laszlo's head turned as he watched a typical product of the slums go by, kicking a dented tin can, until he saw a policeman standing watching him, and a bag of ice dropped into his guts and froze everything hard.

That was when his Abwehr training saved him. *Look bored*, they had said again and again. *Don't whistle, don't grin, don't scratch your private parts, you're not a trained actor and you won't look innocent, you'll look peculiar. Do nothing. And do it slowly.* So Laszlo forgot the boy and counted up to a hundred. *The bastard cop probably reckons I'm some sort of pervert*, he thought when he got into the twenties. At forty his heart was thudding as if someone was attacking it with mallets. At sixty he could see his left hand shaking. He gave up counting, slid off the wall, dusted the seat of his pants to give his left hand a job, and astounded himself by walking towards the policeman. *No eye-contact. Never look him in the face. You're not interested, you're bored.* But the man was still watching Laszlo, he could sense it, and very soon Laszlo knew he had to do something, anything, or he would trip over his own feet. He took out his small change and sorted the coins as he walked. Why? What if the cop said *Where are you going?* Going to make a phone call, obviously.

He sauntered past the policeman and saw, of all things, a telephone booth just twenty yards ahead. So he went into it. There was even a phone book, looking as if it had been chewed by rats.

Laszlo telephoned the school of medicine. He knew how to do that: Dr Hartmann had coached them in British telephones. You inserted two pennies, waited for the tone to change, dialled the number and when someone answered, you pressed the button marked A.

Nobody answered. The line was engaged.

And just as bloody well, Laszlo told himself, because you haven't worked out what you're going to say, have you? Still listening to the continuous buzz he said into the telephone. 'Excuse me, I am a visiting Spaniard and I am desperate for garlic, could you possibly recommend a reliable agent somewhere in Glasgow? Give me his address and—'

Knuckles rapped on the door. It was the policeman. Laszlo felt his knees buckle under the burden of fright, as if he had come down in a lift that stopped too suddenly.

He tugged at the door. It was jammed tight. The policeman slowly shook his head, a gesture full of reproach, and pulled the door. It opened *outwards*. Everyone knew that. Bad mistake.

'Dinna waste yer breath,' the policeman said. 'They canna hear ye.'

'Ah.' The telephone was slippery in Laszlo's sweaty hand. 'I was only . . . um . . .'

'Ye didny press button A. I seen ye havin' a good blether on the phone, but ye hadny pressed button A.' The policeman's forefinger punched button B and Laszlo's twopence clattered into the return box. He took the coins out and rubbed them between his meaty fingers. 'What's your game, then, Jimmy?' he asked. 'Black magic, is it?'

200

'I am trying to call my bank,' Laszlo said. (If you must lie, Richard Fischer had stressed, keep it simple.) 'To borrow some money. The number was busy, so I practised what I was going to say.' Laszlo replaced the phone. 'Banks make me nervous,' he said. This was true. Laszlo had never been inside a bank in his life.

The policeman had let his eyelids droop until they were almost closed. 'Practice, is it?' he said. 'Tell us what you were gonny say.'

'I was going to say . . .' *Keep it simple.* 'I was going to say that I need more money because the police take what little I have.'

Neither of them smiled. The policeman seemed to find Laszlo's left ear slightly interesting. Then he got tired of looking at it. He gave him his twopence. 'Rich again,' he said, and walked away.

This time Laszlo went in the opposite direction. His next stop should have been a public lavatory but it was too far away by about ten feet and he threw up his breakfast in the gutter. 'Some party, eh?' said a passer-by, with a genial laugh. Laszlo hated him. Losing your breakfast was no joke when you were engaged in work of national importance.

An hour later he tried again. This time he got through to the medical school, and he actually spoke to the bursar. It was the wrong time of day. The bursar wanted his dinner. He didn't want to get involved in a telephone discussion with some twerp at the Venezuelan consulate when they telephoned about a student who might be the next-of-kin of someone who'd just died in Venezuela but the cable hadn't given his name, so the consulate wondered if . . . No, no. The bursar's instincts told him to stay well clear of stuff as complex as that, it always got worse. Unfortunately (he said) his secretary was on holiday, and in any case it sounded more like the sort of thing they'd know about in the Student Registration office, extension 4242, sorry he couldn't help, ask for Mrs Ogilvy, she knows everything, goodbye.

Long before Laszlo hung up, he knew that the next-of-kin story was no good. Too long-winded, too complicated, too peculiar. He must keep it simple. What he needed was some utterly straightforward reason why the university should give

201

him Garlic's name and address. Something ordinary and boring.

He walked about Glasgow for an hour, stood in a queue and bought some fish and chips wrapped in newspaper and ate them as he walked some more. In the end he was looking at a bunch of young soldiers, wondering just how young they were, and the idea came to him as easily as picking a flower. It pleased him so much that he went straight to a phone and called extension 4242.

To Laszlo's tin ear, Mrs Ogilvy sounded like Docherty in drag, but at least she was understandable and she was willing to help the Venezuelan consul.

'It's about these new forms, Mrs Ogilvy,' Laszlo said. 'The Ministry of Labour has sent us Form 8000B, "Exemption of Foreign Students from Military Service". I believe the university has one Venezuelan student? In your school of medicine? Is that right?'

Mrs Ogilvy went to get the files. She kept special files on overseas students; it was easier; the Home Office was forever fussing and fretting itself about them . . .

'Yes. Here we are,' she said. Laszlo's head jerked with joy. 'No South American undergraduates, but that's hardly surprising, is it? Not in wartime. Not many graduates, either. Our school of medicine has just the one. Is your pencil ready? It's Dr Cabezas. Initials R. M. Dr R. M. Cabezas.'

'Excellent.' Only one hurdle to jump. 'If you have an address . . .'

'La Paz, Bolivia. I can't pronounce the street, but I'll spell it out for you and you can—'

'Not Bolivia. Venezuela.'

That stopped her short. 'It says Bolivia here,' she said. 'Sometimes they move and they don't tell us, but Dr Cabezas has been at the university for some years, so I don't see how . . .'

'What I mean is I asked you for names of Venezuelan students.' The telephone started sounding urgent pips. Laszlo stuffed more pennies in the slot and punched the button and the pips stopped. 'Venezuelan medical students,' he said. 'There must be one. Are you sure there isn't one?'

Much rustling of paper. 'Are you positive you didn't say Bolivia?' she asked. 'Why did I give you Dr Cabezas's name if you didn't say Bolivia? That's what I don't understand.' She was beginning to sound tetchy. 'La Paz isn't in Venezuela, is it?' Foreigners, she was thinking, why don't they stay at home instead of coming bothering us? That was when she remembered the pips. 'Are you using a public phone?' she asked. 'Who did you say you were?'

'Mr Lakram, Venezuelan consul. My office telephone is being repaired, a great nuisance, just like these government forms, this one is, let me see, eight pages long, I suppose I could send it to you, Mrs Ogilvy, after all it concerns students, but I thought perhaps a simple phone call, I know how busy you are, and all I need is the names and addresses of your students from South America, Glasgow addresses that is, and I could do all the rest. The students have to sign their forms, you see, which means that one of us must visit them. To witness the signature,' Laszlo went on, improvising furiously.

A heavy sigh came down the line. 'So which is it you want?' Mrs Ogilvy asked. 'Is it Venezuela, or is it Bolivia?'

I want to strangle you. 'Suppose we take them one at a time,' Laszlo suggested. 'Bolivia first? Dr Cabezas? Have you his address?' He had the feeling that she wasn't listening. 'Hullo?' he said. He could hear files being thumped about and pages being slapped back and forth.

'It's as I thought,' she said. 'We've nobody from Venezuela.'

'I'll take Bolivia,' Laszlo said quickly. 'Also anyone else you can give me.'

In the end he got an address for Dr Cabezas. It was Flat 17, Renfrew House, North Hanover Street. It seemed that Dr Cabezas was a junior doctor at a teaching hospital called Glasgow Central. He also got someone from Brazil called José-Carlos Coelho, who was, or wanted to be, a forensic pathologist – Mrs Ogilvy wasn't completely sure of her own handwriting here – and might well be attached to the medical school, although a professor of law was listed as his senior tutor. Coelho lived in 22A Buccleuch Avenue. Laszlo didn't much want Coelho but Mrs Ogilvy was determined that he took him.

203

'What was all that about, Mary?' a colleague asked.

'Oh . . . just some eedjit at the Venezuelan consulate.'

'Fancy. I never knew we had a Venezuelan consulate.'

Mrs Ogilvy went back to her work. After a minute she reached for the Glasgow phone book. There was no listing for a Venezuelan consulate. She felt unhappy about that for the rest of the afternoon, but she did nothing, because anything she might have done would have made her look foolish. And they didn't pay her enough to look foolish.

The Junkers Tri-Motor was, in its heyday, a giant of the skies – maximum load, eighteen men – but it bumped and bucketed over Hamburg like a fairground ride.

The Ministry of Propaganda had arranged the flight. The passengers were senior officials of the ministry, a few favoured journalists, the odd military attaché from the neutral embassies, some high-ranking air-raid-protection people, and Admiral Canaris, who had used his influence to get the aeroplane for the Propaganda Ministry. Alongside him sat General Oster and Commodore Meyer, alias Brigadier Christian.

Oster had a typed hand-out from Propaganda. 'Apparently they concentrated on the centre of Hamburg in the first raid.' He looked out. 'Which part was the centre, do you think?'

Canaris glanced over Oster's shoulder, and then shifted to the other side of the plane and looked. 'Hard to say. The rubble seems to be piled higher on your side, don't you think?'

'The smoke makes it difficult . . .' Christian began, and grabbed a strap as the plane bucked in a hot up-draught.

A civilian heard them, and called, 'This is east Hamburg. The centre is over there. See? Beyond the Elbe.'

'Many thanks,' Canaris said.

They were flying low, only three or four hundred feet, and they could smell the burned and burning city. A few of the more queasy passengers held handkerchiefs to their mouths and noses. 'Working-class districts,' Oster said, reading the hand-out. 'Hot night, no rain for a long time, the Hamburg fire brigade couldn't get through because the streets were blocked by the bombing.'

'They say it was like a furnace, literally like a furnace,' the helpful civilian told them. 'They say the temperature reached one thousand degrees centigrade. People tried to run but the wind was like a hurricane. Everyone died, everyone.'

'They all died?' Christian said. The man nodded. 'Then who measured the temperature?' Christian asked curtly. The man looked shocked, and turned away.

Christian was surprised at his own anger. The aeroplane banked and he was looking at a different area of devastation. Here the buildings were not gutted: they were flattened, erased. It was not possible to make out a pattern of streets, and it was scarcely possible to believe that men had caused this obliteration. Christian's mind dreamed a fantasy: some careless, thoughtless giant had swept Hamburg away with the back of his hand. But this silliness made him even angrier. The giant was the Royal Air Force, sending five, six, seven hundred heavy bombers, not to hit docks or factories but to burn a city, the second biggest city in Germany. He blinked to clear tears from his eyes. If only they knew, he thought: the harder they hit us, the stronger they make us. Soon, London will look like this.

The Junkers made a pass over the undamaged suburbs, just for journalistic balance, and flew back to Berlin, where they got out and listened to a spokesman from Propaganda reading a statement: 'Deliberate terror raids . . . martyred for the Reich . . . negligible effect on war production . . . morale higher than ever . . . God will surely punish . . . a new Hamburg will arise . . .'

When they walked to the car, Canaris said, 'As ever, the communiqué is interesting for what it does not reveal. No mention, for instance, of the fact that nobody is living in the parts of Hamburg that were *not* bombed.'

Christian was puzzled. 'Nobody, sir? You mean they've been evacuated?'

'I mean they've run away. Wouldn't you? In the space of ten days their city has been massively bombed on four nights by the

British and on two days by the Americans. I ask you: why wait to be blown to pieces?'

'My information is that one million have left Hamburg,' Oster said. 'It's virtually empty. Did you see anyone on the streets? I didn't.'

'I think I saw one policeman,' Canaris said. 'I think he waved. Perhaps he was telling us to go away. I don't suppose they like having aeroplanes over their city . . . Did we get any warning from Eldorado about those raids?'

'No, sir,' Oster said.

'That's disappointing. We really need to know these things. Shake him up, will you?' Canaris said to Christian. 'Tell him it's our number-one top-priority area of intelligence. Hamburg wasn't the first and it won't be the last, will it?'

They got into the car. It made good time into the city: Berlin was far less crowded nowadays. 'Speer reckons that if five or six more cities get the Hamburg treatment, the war will go out of business,' Oster said.

'Speer should go and work for the Allies,' Canaris said, and smiled. The others chuckled, although Christian couldn't see what was funny. Not that there was anything new about that.

The Abwehr had offices all over Europe, and each had its allotted task. Oslo, for instance, was interested in weather over Britain. Brest concentrated on reports of sabotage. Paris collected information about general living conditions. Madrid's concern was the supply of arms and other war *matériel* from America, convoy intelligence, and food stocks. Hamburg took care of anything involving the Allied Air Forces. Agents directly controlled by Abwehr headquarters in Berlin usually supplied political intelligence. It was all very decentralized. Each office guarded its own sphere of operations and had little to say to any other office. When a goldmine like Eldorado came along, of course, Madrid Abwehr didn't hesitate to take everything he sent and ask for more, even if it fell outside their brief. Nevertheless, Hamburg was supposed to be the primary channel for Air Force intelligence, and Christian was uneasy about bypassing Hamburg in favour of Madrid. 'They'll raise holy hell if they hear about it,' he told General Oster. 'They've become very touchy since the raids.'

'Screw them. The Admiral wants Eldorado to do Hamburg's job, and that's what the Admiral gets.'

'I've drafted this signal. It's quite short, because now we have a radio link with Eldorado I didn't want to risk anything long.'

Oster read it. 'Better show it to the old man,' he said.

Canaris read it. 'Too polite,' he said. 'It sounds like an order for a dozen linen table-napkins. Kick the fellow's backside a bit. The Allies think they can win the war with their bombers. We need to know all about that campaign: when, where, how many, what type, which target. Forget the rest of the war. Make him focus on that. It's crucial.'

Christian went away and rewrote the signal. 'Better,' Oster said. 'Now you've tied a rocket to his tail. Now we'll see what he's worth.'

Dr Cabezas had had six hours' sleep in forty-eight, which was about average for a houseman at Glasgow Central Hospital. The houseman system had two things going for it: firstly, all the consultants had had to do it in their day and so they couldn't see why the youngsters should escape it now; and secondly, it was cheap. Instead of relays of doctors coming and going you only paid this one battered specimen whose eyes, towards the end, looked like old inkwells. The fact that fatigue might damage judgement was well known but ignored. Anyway, you might be lucky. You might have a quiet time.

Dr Cabezas was on duty in Casualty and the time was not quiet. Glasgow generated a stream of damaged humanity: everything from children who had fallen off walls to welders who had fallen off ships, and from heart attacks in the street to brawls in the bedroom. Appendicitis, electrocution, food poisoning, fits, scaldings, dog-bites, boils on the backside, unsuspected pregnancies, fingers hacked by breadknives, dislocations on football fields – the victims of these and many other misfortunes arrived at Casualty in a stream that occasionally, unpredictably, built to a sudden flood of pain.

Dr Cabezas came off duty at 6 p.m., too tired to eat and almost too tired to walk to the tram that went up North Hanover Street. Renfrew House was an ugly thing made of red sandstone long since gone black but it was home and Flat 17 contained a wonderful bed. As Dr Cabezas trudged up the stairs all she could think of was falling into it and sleeping for ever.

Laszlo was standing by the fireplace when she switched on the light. He was startled to see a young woman; a slim, pretty, black-haired young woman, brown eyes slowly widening with shock. Nobody had said Dr Cabezas was a woman. But nobody had said she wasn't, either. His arms were folded, hands under his jacket.

'You are Garlic,' he said firmly and clearly. Two days and two nights of doctoring the sick had left her brain dull and her reactions slow. 'I am garlic?' she said. The words were nonsense. They were enough for Laszlo. He unfolded his arms. The pistol swung out and up as if his arm were on a spring and he shot her, aiming at the breastbone and missing and hitting the throat. She was holding the doorknob with her left hand and the impact made her seem to fling herself away from Laszlo in revulsion. He did not like that. But at least it slowed her fall and she collapsed with no more noise than someone dropping a pair of boots, which was lucky because the silencer had been much louder than usual, like someone slamming a heavy book. Maybe it was wearing out. Laszlo held it up and looked at it. Nobody in Madrid had said anything about silencers wearing out. And nobody had said anything about Garlic being a woman. Madrid Abwehr wasn't half as clever as it thought it was. It had been all wrong about Venezuela. Venezuela was really Bolivia. That's what Laszlo called really sloppy, making a simple blunder like that, and when he remembered how much extra work it had caused him he got quite annoyed. He had thought hard about the problem all afternoon and finally reached the only possible solution. Garlic had to be a medical student at Glasgow University from South America, allegedly Venezuela. The only South American medical

208

student was Bolivian. Therefore the Venezuelan connection must be wrong, which left the Bolivian medical student, who must be Laszlo's man. Or, as it turned out, woman. He went over and looked at her.

Dr Cabezas lay in an awkward sprawl, not at all like the tidy postures of death that Laszlo had learned from the movies. There was a tremendous amount of blood; it did not seem possible that such a slender creature could flood the floor with redness. He supposed she must be dead; he didn't want to tread in the blood in order to find out. The pistol felt heavy and he let his arm fall to his side. A kind of wistfulness crept over him, a feeling of flatness, of anticlimax. He had come such a long way to do this and now it was over too quickly. Perhaps she wasn't dead, not completely dead. Perhaps he ought to shoot her again. The more he thought about it, the more it revived him and he stooped to see if he could figure out where her heart was. In the end he decided it was hidden behind her left breast. He couldn't bring himself to damage a woman's breast. It was a sacred object: the thought of injuring it made him feel ill. So he shot her in the head. Another big book slammed. That was enough.

He was satisfied, but he was also bored. He used the poker to lift her purse out of the blood, and he searched to see whom he had killed. Dr Rosa Maria Cabezas, so her papers said. He took them, and the money; had a look through the clothes in the bedroom, to convince himself that she really was a woman; and stretched out on the bed, just to see if it was as comfortable as it looked.

When he awoke it was past midnight. He took a bath, ate all the tinned food in the kitchen (there was very little), and went back to bed. He had even found a pair of her pyjamas that fitted him quite well.

'In case you're thinking it's black market, it's not,' said the Director.

'Never entered my head, sir,' Freddy Garcia lied. They were sitting down to lunch in the Director's flat and he was looking at a dish of poached salmon, something he had not seen in two years.

209

'I have an old friend who fishes the Tweed,' the Director said, 'and he caught this fish on a Jock Scott, just below Norham Castle, yesterday tea-time, and he had it sent down by the fast London train for me, so you can relax and enjoy it, for you're not breaking the law. Bread and salad and bottled Bass are all off-ration, are they not?'

'Indeed they are.' Freddy tucked in. He had never before been invited up here and he felt a bit nervous.

'I have something of an apology to make,' the Director said. 'I must admit the legality of the mayonnaise is slightly suspect, it came from an American PX; however that is not what I wish to apologize about. I made an error of judgement concerning Matchbox, Teacup, and Lampstand. It was obvious at a very early stage that they were making for Liverpool, and the implication had to be that they aimed to meet Eldorado.' He concentrated on pouring the Bass correctly.

'Where did they land, sir?' Freddy asked.

'Galway Bay. It's an obvious place. We have a man in Galway. He says they came into town like a three-ring circus. They even bought him drinks. I made sure they got waved through at Dublin and Liverpool – excellent passports, by the way, well up to the Abwehr's high standards – and I thought it would be a clever idea to let them reinforce Bamboozle.'

'Ah,' Freddy said. 'Eldorado meets Abwehr agents at every turn.'

'Exactly. Or perhaps I mean inexactly. I wanted the arrival of Matchbox, Teacup, and Lampstand to be a genuine surprise to your people . . . What were they called?'

'Hammer and Anvil, sir.'

'Yes. Nicely Teutonic. The general effect I was hoping to achieve was of a railway station awash with German agents, all strangers to each other, thus generating a high pitch of tension all around and especially in Eldorado and his lady.'

'I think you achieved that, sir.'

The Director ate some salad. 'Nevertheless, it was foolish of me not to inform you of those Abwehr agents. The danger in this racket is that one is tempted to play the stage-director a little too much.'

Freddy busied himself with his napkin and let the apology quietly fade away.

'What about the fourth agent, sir?' he asked.

'All I can tell you is he didn't get off the ship at either end. We've searched it three times. I don't think he's on board.'

'Curious.'

'Yes. However, the enemy don't seem particularly concerned, so I assume that Deckchair was expendable. I'll tell you what they *are* concerned about, highly concerned. They want to know where Bomber Command goes from here. We've just decoded a very urgent signal for Eldorado. You can almost smell the panic.'

'This is because of Hamburg?'

'Probably.'

'It's rather flattering that they should turn to Eldorado.'

'Flattering and worrying,' the Director said. 'They want to know the names of the next six cities on Bomber Command's list.'

'But that's absurd.' Freddy mopped a little mayonnaise with a bit of bread and examined the pattern revealed on the plate, as if it held an answer. 'They can't seriously expect Eldorado to find that sort of information.' He chewed the bread slowly. 'On the other hand, we can't afford to damage Eldorado's reputation, can we?'

'Have some more salmon.' The Director nudged the dish towards him. 'They say that fish is good for the brain.'

Christian woke up with a wild snort and the flies on his face took off in all directions as if they'd been scrambled to meet an incoming raid. His face felt strange: stiff and sticky. He raised a hand to touch it and at once his body began to slip. This frightened him and he grabbed something to stop the slide. It was wood; flat wood. He was lying on the open-step staircase that led to his flat at the top of Abwehr headquarters.

For several seconds he clung to the staircase while he worked out the difference between horizontal and vertical and just where he lay between the two. That was when he noticed the blood, a lot of blood, right in front of his face. Explains the flies, he said

211

to himself, and felt quite proud of his quick thinking. But the flies don't explain the blood. There was something wrong with that. He worried at it for a short while and gave up. The stairs were hard and uncomfortable. He could either go down or go up. He was pointing up. He climbed on his hands and knees to the top of the stairs, got cautiously to his feet, wobbled into his flat and went to the bathroom mirror. He looked dreadful. Nose, lips and chin were thick with congealed blood and a bruise like a small plum was coming up on his forehead. The eyes that gazed back at him were dull as old pennies.

That was at 7 p.m. Next morning he called in at Domenik's office. 'Know any good medical jokes?' he asked.

'Medical,' Domenik said. 'Well, there's quite a ripe one about Goering and enemas that's going about, but it's a bit early in the day for that sort of thing. Why?'

'Funny thing happened to me last night. I was going up to my rooms, using the stairs, when I must have had a blackout. Fell flat on my face, banged my nose, severe nosebleed. Blood everywhere. Or so I assume. I mean, how do I know what happened? I was unconscious at the time.' Christian dropped into an armchair and put his feet on Domenik's desk. 'What d'you make of all that?' He sounded jaunty. He wished he felt jaunty.

'How long before you came to?' Domenik asked.

'Oh . . . judging by the volume of blood, about a day and a half . . . I don't know. Two or three minutes, probably.'

'And is there any history of this sort of thing in your family?'

'Not that I know of.' Christian's fingertips were sending Morse on the armrest.

'Don't tell me if you don't want to,' Domenik said, 'but did you bite your tongue? Or wet yourself?'

'Good God, no. No to both.' Christian swung his feet off the desk and stood up. 'I fainted, that's all. I didn't disintegrate. I'm a fully house-trained adult, remember?'

'It crossed my mind that you might be epileptic, and don't look so damned offended. It happens in the best of households. Julius Caesar, Alexander the Great, Napoleon, not to mention some of my smartest friends . . . Anyway, you're probably not clever enough to be epileptic. Are you worried?'

'Why should I be worried?'

'It might happen again.'

'Yes, of course I'm worried. Last night I woke up every hour on the hour, just to make sure I wasn't dead, I suppose. Mind you, I might as well be dead for all the good I'm doing here.' Christian prowled around the room, whacking the tops of filing cabinets with the flat of his hand.

'Don't do that,' Domenik said. 'There are people trying to sleep in there.'

Christian stopped doing it, and looked out of a window. 'It's not a joke to me,' he said.

'That wasn't a joke,' Domenik said a little wearily. 'My files are full of insomniacs.'

Christian wasn't listening. 'Last night, when I couldn't sleep, I kept thinking: maybe this is my last chance to do something for my country while I've still got a body to give. I'm forty-seven. Bits of my system are beginning to wear out. I'm not interested in medals or promotion, I simply want . . .' He sighed, and clenched his jaw, and fell silent.

'Would you do anything for Germany?' Domenik asked.

'I'm ready to give my life.'

'Would you commit treason? For Germany?'

Christian stared. 'Is that another of your jokes?'

'Ah. So there are limits to your patriotism.'

Christian gave a brief, displeased grunt. 'I'm afraid I'm not in the mood for your comedy today.'

'Look at it this way,' Domenik said. 'Sometimes you have to turn things upside-down in order to stand them on their feet.'

'That's not funny either.'

'I know,' Domenik said sadly. 'It's the way I tell them.'

Each flat had its own letter-slot and the postman delivered Dr Rosa Maria Cabezas's mail while Laszlo was in the kitchen, eating a breakfast of toast with marmalade and sweet tea.

He opened her letters. Not much: a bill, a medical journal, and a letter in Spanish from a passionate boyfriend in Edinburgh. Too passionate for Laszlo's liking. So much yearning for intimate physical contact with a stiff corpse struck him as improper, and he burned the letter in the sink.

The bill was from the gas company, and it gave him an idea. He found her chequebook in a little writing-desk and forged her signature, copying it from a hospital identity card, and put the bill and the cheque into an envelope, which he addressed and stamped, to be mailed later. Dead woman pays gas bill! Let the police pick the bones out of that.

He washed up the breakfast things and spent an hour searching the flat from end to end. Nothing hinted that Dr Cabezas was a spy, let alone a disloyal spy, and of course that was exactly what Laszlo expected. He was dealing with professionals here. No doubt she had another place where she was Garlic. This flat was merely her cover. He knew the form; he had read about it a hundred times.

The body was beginning to smell. It was time to go. The lock he had picked yesterday in twenty seconds (that was one skill Madrid Abwehr had had no need to teach him) slammed solidly behind him, and he sauntered down to the street full of secret pride in a job well done, a nation well served. He even touched his hat to a lady he passed on the stairs. Why not? Courtesy costs nothing.

This was his third day and Laszlo was an old Glasgow hand. He jumped on the first tram he saw and told the conductress he wanted to go to the offices of the *Glasgow Herald* newspaper. She mothered him, put him off at the right stop, told him which street to go down. At the *Herald* offices he stood in line and placed an advertisement to appear in the personal column for three days. It read: *King – Happy days are here again – Ace.* General Oster would know what that meant.

'Anyway, somebody's got to die,' Luis said bleakly. 'I don't care who. I'm sick of the whole rotten gang, they're all creeps, let's dump the lot.'

214

'No, no. Certainly not,' Freddy said. 'They're all quite splendid. I mean, Madrid loves them, doesn't it?'

'Madrid's dumb. Madrid's full of creeps, too.'

'But they pay well.' That was Freddy's ace. Luis had no answer to that.

It was a fine summer's day, and they were walking along Chelsea Embankment. The Thames was briskly going about its cocoa-coloured business, the plane trees were greenly doing their stuff, and nobody in sight was being bombed, shelled, fried with flamethrowers, or raked with machine-gun fire. For 1943, it could have been a lot worse, and Freddy wished that Luis would stop complaining; but they had a major problem to solve and he needed all of Luis's help, so he buttered him up yet again. That was part of Freddy's job and he did it skilfully. 'And you know why they pay so well, of course,' he said. 'It's because the Eldorado Network which you created, and which you conduct like a Paganini of the intelligence world, is simply the best there is. And the Abwehr knows it.' Freddy let that sink in for a moment. 'OKW never takes a step until it has checked its plans against the latest Eldorado appreciation.'

'More fools they,' Luis muttered, but he had a slight smirk of gratification.

'That's not fair, Luis. They conquered Europe, remember. Nothing foolish about that.'

'True.'

They strolled in silence as far as a niche in the Embankment wall, where they leaned and watched the river traffic.

'Oh, by the way,' Freddy said, 'Graham Greene asked me to give you his fond regards. He says he still recalls the literary style of your early reports from Lisbon with great pleasure.'

'*Really?*' Luis squared his shoulders. 'Does he *really?*'

'He was on the phone from Sierra Leone. Graham runs an office for the Secret Service in Freetown.' This last statement was true. The rest was not. 'He's fascinated by our latest signal from the Abwehr. He made me promise to tell him how you solved the problem. Eventually.'

Luis took a half-crown from his pocket and scratched a series

215

of crosses on the masonry. 'The Abwehr's mad. It can't be done. They want the next six target cities, and you tell me they mustn't know. Mustn't even begin to suspect. So that's that. Nothing left for Eldorado to do, is there?'

'Let's say there's no easy solution.' Freddy took the coin from him and tossed it in the river.

Luis stared. 'Why did you do that?' he demanded in a high voice.

'Pure blind impulse,' Freddy said. He sniffed, and jerked his chin out defiantly. 'No, it wasn't,' he said, 'I wanted you to remember what life was like when you had no money. Back in Lisbon, setting up your system. You'd have worked all day and all night then to make the Abwehr happy, wouldn't you? Well, do it again, Luis. Make them happy.'

Luis looked from Freddy to the row of scratches, to the river where the coin had splashed, to the sky. 'That was mine,' he said. 'That was a really rotten thing to do.'

Oh, don't be so blasted stuffy, Freddy thought. But he said, 'I'll buy you lunch. Anyway, it was only half a crown.'

'Only. Only. D'you know how long it takes me to earn half a crown?'

'About . . . sixteen seconds.'

'I see. Sixteen seconds. Well, it doesn't matter, then, does it? Nothing matters.' Luis dragged the rest of his change from his pocket and flung it at the river, slashing the surface with a spatter of tiny cuts which healed immediately. 'It's only money. It's only sweat, blood, and tears. Plenty more where that came from.'

They turned back. Freddy was not especially worried: he had been through this sort of scene before. Luis responded to flattery and reassurance but every now and then it was necessary to put salt on his tail, or he stopped listening.

Luis strode in a scowling silence, purposely treading on the cracks between the paving stones at every pace. They all think they're so fucking clever, he told himself savagely. If they're so fucking clever how come I was the one who got the Iron fucking Cross?

'Listen,' Freddy said, and stopped.

A rich and vibrant rumble had undercut the roar of the traffic. The clear blue sky itself seemed to tremble with the distant arrival of mighty machinery. Formation after formation of high-flying bombers, shining like a collection of tiny silverware, followed each other, impeccably aligned, apparently unhurried, as if they owned all of space.

'Fortresses,' Freddy said. 'Off to bomb France, by the look of it. Or Belgium.'

Luis grunted.

'Better than raiding Germany, anyway,' Freddy said. 'The Americans have been taking heavy losses over Germany. Imagine one in ten of those planes getting shot down. One in five, even. Pretty grim.'

'Come on,' Luis said. 'I'm hungry.'

At five-twenty he telephoned Freddy on the direct line from the flat to Double-Cross headquarters. 'Come and get it,' he said, and hung up.

Julie, working at the same desk, recognized the voice. 'Remember to touch the hem of his garment,' she said.

Luis was drinking neat gin out of a cup. A small pile of handwritten yellow pages lay on a coffee table but Freddy knew better than to touch them. 'One problem,' Luis said, 'two solutions. That's the answer. They can't have what they want so we gently fend them off with one hand while we give them something they didn't know they wanted with the other hand.' He walked away and stretched out on the sofa.

Freddy read the pages. They began with a long, tedious, convincing analysis of the extraordinary difficulty of predicting Bomber Command's targets. Security was labyrinthine: at each stage – from squadron, to wing, to group, to Command – there were double-checks and triple-checks on all personnel. Nothing went by radio or land-line. Everything went by dispatch rider. And so on and so on. The Abwehr should not think their signal came as a surprise to Eldorado. Eldorado had been labouring at the problem for months. At least one potential sub-agent had been lost in the process, arrested, almost certainly executed. That was the security aspect. Then there was the weather. Targets were altered at the last minute, sometimes when the bombers were actually airborne. Furthermore . . .

And after furthermore, nevertheless. Nevertheless, the Abwehr could rest assured that Eldorado had now redoubled his efforts to get this most vital military intelligence. This reassurance occupied a very earnest, very tedious page.

Then came the giant lollipop.

Freddy read:

> US 8th Air Force has formed a separate unit called OWCH (which stands for One-Way Cargo of High-explosive) to use B-17 Flying Fortress bombers which have become non-operational from damage received (either from enemy defences or from landing accidents, collisions, etc.) as unmanned, radio-controlled 'suicide' bombers.
>
> OWCH aircraft are repaired sufficiently to allow them to fly with what American bombardiers call 'wall-to-wall bombloads' plus enough fuel to reach the target. Each bomber is flown off the airfield by an expert pilot who climbs to five thousand feet and bales out. A master aircraft then controls the OWCH bomber by VHF radio, steers it to the target city, and directs it to crash on the target site.
>
> With no crew, no guns, in fact no equipment except its radio, and a light fuel-load, the OWCH machine can carry a great weight of explosive. Some sources claim a maximum of 20 tons of high explosive.
>
> First reports of this development were discounted because it appeared that any OWCH bomber must be highly vulnerable to attack by virtue of its slow speed and inability to manoeuvre or defend itself. However, this is to overlook three factors:
>
> (1) The OWCH raid may be by night.
> (2) By night or day, the OWCH bomber can be steered through thick cloud by the master aircraft flying high above the cloud (probably an RAF Mosquito).
> (3) Any German fighter close enough to destroy an OWCH raider would almost certainly destroy itself in the consequent explosion.

There was another page of extra details about the use of rockets or tows to assist take-off, the tactics of putting the OWCH bomber into a vertical dive over the target, and so on. Freddy took them in at a glance and said: 'Splendid. First-rate. Top marks.'

'You see, it occurred to me . . .' Luis turned on to his side and propped his head. He might have been a tutor reviewing an undergraduate's essay, if their ages had been reversed. 'The Americans are losing ten or twenty Fortresses per raid anyway. They lose new planes with small bomb-loads because the thing has to carry a crew and the crew wants to come home. My way, the Americans lose the same number of tired old wrecks and they hit the target very accurately with five or six times the weight of bombs.'

'And nobody gets killed.'

'Nobody on our side, certainly.'

'Should give the Abwehr something to occupy their minds.' Freddy tucked the pages in an inside pocket and wandered over to the window. 'Very well done. You must be jolly pleased . . . My goodness, doesn't the park look lovely from up here?' Luis said nothing. After a while Freddy came back. 'You seem to be pretty well settled in. If there's ever anything you need . . .' He looked at his watch. 'My goodness,' he muttered.

Luis had not moved. He seemed to be looking into the next room, or perhaps the next street. 'I don't miss her, you know,' he said. 'Not in the slightest.'

'Oh well.' That sounded inadequate. 'These things happen,' Freddy said. That wasn't much better. 'I suppose I'd better be going.'

'The whole thing was a colossal mistake,' Luis said. 'It's much better to be completely free.' But when Freddy let himself out, and glanced back, Luis still hadn't moved. So much for freedom.

The Allies' intelligence agencies read all the German newspapers they could get, and the German intelligence agencies read all the British newspapers they could get. Both sides used neutral countries as go-betweens. In the case of the *Glasgow Herald* it was Sweden, and the system worked so smoothly that General Oster was reading Laszlo's message in the personal column of the classified advertising only two days after the paper was printed.

Admiral Canaris was at Rastenburg along with the Heads of

Staff, waiting to be called into a conference with the Führer. Oster got him on the phone. 'Garlic is off the menu, sir,' he reported. 'Permanently.'

'Well, I always thought it was over-rated. Thank you for calling.'

Oster sent for Christian and showed him the message. ' "King" is me and "Ace" is our little Spanish thug,' he explained, 'and that's the signal for success. It's the only signal I gave him, so he couldn't get it wrong. He was hopeless with the radio; quite useless. He has a tiny, tiny brain. Well, you've seen him; you know. He's like a dung-beetle. Give him a ball of shit and tell him to keep rolling it and he's happy but don't confuse him with alternatives. Frankly I never thought he'd roll his ball all the way to Glasgow.'

'He didn't cut a very impressive figure at Brest, did he, sir? But then . . . I suppose we don't want our agents to look impressive.'

Oster wasn't listening. 'Tell Madrid,' he ordered. 'He was their man, they've a right to know. I bet it makes their day.' Christian turned to go but Oster hadn't finished. 'Don't bother to tell the SD, let the bastards find out for themselves. No more garlic in their goulash!' He rubbed his hands and laughed; he was like a racehorse owner with a winner at long odds. 'Come on, this deserves a drink,' he said. 'Champagne!' he shouted at his secretary. 'And ask Domenik to come and join us!'

While the bottles were being opened Christian slipped out to send the signal to Madrid. When he came back a real party was developing: Oster had invited his colleagues from nearby offices plus all the bright young assistants and pretty secretaries who could be spared. Corks bounced off the ceiling. 'D'you know,' Oster confided in Christian, 'I didn't appreciate just how worried I was until I stopped worrying half an hour ago. Garlic could have destroyed Eldorado, d'you realize that?'

'Indeed I do, sir. I was the one who exposed Garlic.'

'Course you did. Brilliant work, brilliant.'

'I launched Eldorado, too, sir, so I'm more than happy he's still our top agent.' Christian felt a twinge of unease and rapidly drowned it in champagne.

'Worth two Panzer divisions,' Oster said. 'Maybe three. Now you see why we can't let you go, Christian? You're invaluable. Indispensable!' He moved away.

Christian found a bottle and refilled his glass. Somebody's secretary bobbed up, giggling, beside him and he topped up her glass. 'Thank you, kind sir,' she said. 'Is this your party? What are we celebrating?'

'Hitler's birthday.'

'Oh.' She sipped and thought. 'Didn't we do that in April?'

'Then we're celebrating the fact that it's not Hitler's birthday.'

She gave him a startled glance and sidled away. That was a damned unpatriotic thing to say, he thought angrily. Why in God's name did you say that? He looked around and saw Domenik watching him.

They met in a quiet corner. 'Why aren't you cheering like everyone else?' Domenik asked.

'I don't know. I suppose it's because now we've eliminated Garlic there's even less for me to do here.'

'I wouldn't agree. It could be that there is a great deal for you to do.' Domenik tested a balcony door and found that it opened. 'D'you mind? It's getting a bit stuffy.' They went outside and leaned on the railing. Five flights below, a trolley-car went grinding by, dragging long sparks from its overhead cable. The light was murky; the air smelt of overdue thunder. A gusty breeze kept tossing a bit of litter like a boy in a blanket, until eventually the scrap of paper whirled higher and higher and went above the two men.

'You said the other day that you were ready to give your life,' Domenik said.

'Yes. I'm not ready to throw it away, but . . .'

'But if it . . . what shall we say? . . . pays a big enough dividend, then you'd contemplate pretty well anything.'

'Certainly.' Christian flinched at a flicker of headache.

'To take an extreme example, there wouldn't be much point in getting yourself killed on the Russian Front. All loss, no profit.'

'That depends.'

'Anyway, you said you're not interested in honours or fame.'

221

'That's true. I don't give a damn, as long . . .' Christian made himself look up. If he looked down at the street his senses began, very slowly, to riot.

'As long as you have a chance to serve the German people,' Domenik suggested.

'Yes.' Christian felt the sting of salt in his eyes, and touched his brow, and found it wet with sweat. Something was going very wrong with him. 'Look here,' he said, 'I don't know . . .' But now his brain refused to finish the sentence. He didn't know what it was he didn't know.

'Let me explain,' Domenik said. 'One man started this war. Am I right?' Christian nodded, too dazed to argue. 'Well, one man can end it too,' Domenik said, 'if he's prepared to end himself at the same time. The question is, are you the man?'

Christian struggled with the question. 'Why me?' he asked.

Domenik answered but his words were just noise. Christian knew he was going to fall down. His whole brain seemed to be packed with pressures and vacuums which were spinning against and through each other like some phantom gyroscope.

'Look,' he said. He pointed over Domenik's shoulder at the blackened sky where a slash of lightning had scribbled the eternal answer to all questions, if only he could read the writing.

Domenik turned, but the flash had died. He turned back just in time to catch Christian as he fell. 'Oh, shit,' Domenik said. The thunder arrived with a self-satisfied crump, too late as usual.

Julie Conroy was listening to Glenn Miller on the radio and eating baked beans out of the tin when Freddy tapped on her door and she shouted for him to come in. He had that gentle let's-all-be-friends smile she had come to know so well. 'You'll never guess who wants to talk to you,' he said, and knew at once he had made a bad mistake.

'Funny you should say that,' she said. Miller died, smiling. 'I've been wondering what great quality men have besides selfishness. Now I know. It's clumsiness, isn't it? There was a time when I used to find it, I don't know, charming I suppose. Touching, in a gauche and masculine way. Not any more.'

'Look . . .' Freddy began.

'Luis's idea of affection is to trip over his own emotional feet and just accidentally rip your dress off as he falls. That is, if he's feeling horny. Why has it taken me so long to see through him? He's a selfish, clumsy bum, period. I may be a dumb broad but I'm not that dumb, not any longer.'

'My fault,' Freddy said quickly. 'This has nothing at all to do with Luis. I do apologize. It's about agent Matchbox, the girl called Stephanie Schmidt. She wants to talk to you.'

'Oh, for God's sake . . .' Julie ate the last bean, went into the kitchen, threw the tin into the bin. 'Why me?' she called.

Freddy looked amiably baffled. 'Beats me. But she won't talk to anyone else, so . . . Would you mind awfully?'

Stephanie Schmidt was locked in a simple, almost spartan room with beige walls and no windows and every piece of furniture bolted to the floor. She was wearing a grey boilersuit that zipped up the front. It was far too big for her, and the sleeves and trouser-legs were doubled back; this made her look more girlish than she was. The first thing she wanted to know was whether or not Julie was married to Luis.

'Not on your life.'

'Ah.' Stephanie was disappointed. 'So you are friends?'

'We work together, that's all. No we don't. We work as far apart as possible.' Julie saw Stephanie looking wistfully at her wedding ring. 'I've got a legal husband somewhere,' she said. 'You can have him if you can find him. I wear this to keep the wolves at bay.' Stephanie didn't understand that. 'You know: the gropers and pinchers,' Julie said. Stephanie frowned. 'Jeez,' Julie sighed. 'You don't know anything, do you? How long have you been out of the convent?'

That touched a nerve. 'I am not a Catholic,' Stephanie said stiffly. 'I am a good Lutheran.'

'Slice it where you like, it's still baloney.' Julie looked at the room, at its bareness, and finally at the sad German girl with her greasy hair and slumped shoulders and hands hidden inside the opposite sleeves of the drab boilersuit. 'So tell me,' she said. 'What's a dump like you doing in a nice place like this?'

'I met a man. His name is Otto Krafft and I love him.'

'Oh boy. Tears before bedtime. I can see it coming.'

'But I *do* love him.' She started to cry. Julie let her get on with it while she found a towel. This looked like turning into a major weep.

Stephanie cried for ten minutes. Julie knew what to do (others had done it for her) and she merely held her hand until she had exhausted her tears. 'Blow your nose,' Julie said. Stephanie snorted into the towel. 'Wash your face,' Julie said. Stephanie obeyed. 'Now tell me about this *schmuck* Otto,' Julie said, and Stephanie laughed at the lovely rude word which her father had always forbidden.

'He has beautiful blond hair,' she began.

Forty minutes later, Julie left. Freddy was waiting. 'Now we know all about Otto Krafft,' he said. 'Except the size of his whatsit.'

'Assume it's on the heroic scale. Everything else is.'

'Sorry to be so crude. It's been a long day.'

'That's OK, Freddy. After all, love is a pretty crude arrangement, wouldn't you say? What's all this talk about affairs of the heart? Affairs of the whatsit would be a lot closer the truth. Not so nice, maybe, but a damn sight more accurate.'

'Not in this case.' By now they were in his office, and he was pouring whisky. 'From what she said they were never lovers. Krafft never even kissed her.'

'Sure. He got her for nothing. So what's new? The world is full of women like that. Gave everything, got nothing. I should know, I've done it twice. We never learn.'

'Perhaps you might mention that to Matchbox next time,' Freddy said.

Her left eye felt scratchy. She pulled down the lid and looked at him with the right eye. 'I'm not one of your interrogators. Give me one good reason why I should go back.'

'We really ought to know what's become of those other two agents. Deckchair and Lampstand.'

'Not a good enough reason.'

'And if she doesn't co-operate soon we shall have to hang her,' Freddy said. 'The public expects it, you see.'

It took twenty-four hours for the Double-Cross Committee to consult its various representatives from the intelligence bodies and give Eldorado's draft report its approval. Luis had a second look at it, tightened it and polished it, and Julie cross-checked it with other reports to make sure there were no anomalies or contradictions. Then it was encoded and radioed to Madrid Abwehr, nominally by Docherty. (The story was that Eldorado, who Madrid knew to have poor radio skills, was still trying to recruit an operator for his sets, so Teacup – Docherty – was sending his messages. In reality an MI5 man operated the set.)

There were only two changes of any significance in the report. Air Ministry suggested using B-24 Liberators instead of B-17 Fortresses in the OWCH item, since the Liberator had a long square fuselage which could transport more explosive. The other change was prompted by Freddy. 'OWCH is a very big secret,' he said. 'Who found it?'

'I did,' Luis said. 'Says so here. Eldorado's many contacts in the ministries and embassies and so on.'

'It might be even more convincing if you shared the credit, made it a team effort. Don't you think? OWCH is really big. It needs support.'

'Maybe.' Luis thought it over. 'How about this?' he said. 'Eldorado picks up rumours of OWCH. He tells Pinetree, and Pinetree gets half the story from someone in the American embassy. He also tells Nutmeg, who picks up the other half by chatting to American aircrew in pubs around Cambridge. Then Eldorado puts the whole story together. That way, there's no total breach of security, which is as it should be for a big secret.'

Freddy wrinkled his nose. 'Not happy about Nutmeg, to be perfectly frank. Nutmeg loathes Americans, doesn't he? Ex-Indian

Army and all that. Thinks they're a lot of cowboys. We've said as much.'

'OK. Somebody else can go to Cambridge. Garlic can go to Cambridge. Garlic goes to Cambridge to be interviewed, he wants to study his medicine at Cambridge, he is sick of Glasgow, and he meets lots of Americans in lots of pubs. Why not? He is American himself. South American. Garlic *likes* Americans.'

The report caused a small sensation in Madrid. Wagner had everybody in his office on the double. 'Berlin tells me that Garlic is dead,' he said. 'Now Eldorado tells me that Garlic is not only alive but supremely active. Somebody's lying, which means somebody's made a cock-up, which means somebody's ass is going to get kicked from here to Smolensk. It is not going to be mine but it could be yours. So – any bright ideas?'

The controllers had plenty to say but none of it was comforting. The trouble was that Eldorado was precise about the timing of Garlic's trip to Cambridge. The visit spanned the date of his reported death. No amount of discussion could alter that. In the end Richard Fischer suggested forcing the issue by sending Eldorado a signal asking if Garlic was dead or alive.

'Why not ask about the state of his health?' Dr Hartmann said. 'It's a little more subtle. If he's dead, let Eldorado say so.'

'No. Ask about them all,' Wagner said. 'Send a signal now, asking Eldorado for a health check on *all* of his sub-agents. Let's not give anything away at this stage.'

Freddy and the Director discussed this curious signal and could make nothing of it. 'Luis was thinking of pushing Haystack under a bus,' Freddy said, 'but we never did it. Everyone is perfectly fit.'

'Then I suppose we might as well say so,' the Director said.

That reply brought a further signal from Madrid. It referred to the recent OWCH report and asked whether Garlic merited a bonus payment for his work. It seemed a harmless question. The answer had to be yes.

'That clinches it,' Wagner said. He took all the documents and flew to Berlin. He went straight into a meeting with Canaris, Oster, and Christian. There was little to discuss: the facts were

226

clear, the implications were obvious, the possible consequences serious.

'A preposterous thought occurs to me,' the Admiral said, 'but then the preposterous seems to happen all the time nowadays . . . Our man Ace has killed a Venezuelan medical student at Glasgow University. Just suppose there are *two* such students?'

'I briefed Ace on that possibility,' Oster said. 'If there were two he would have shot them both.'

'Just a thought.' Canaris glanced at the others. Nobody had anything further to say. 'There's only one thing for it, then. I'd better meet Eldorado. I'm certainly not going over there, so he'll come to me, won't he?'

After his first blackout Christian had not gone to the Abwehr HQ doctor. When he suffered the second he had no choice: the doctor came to him. The first thing Christian saw as he woke up was the man's smooth, pointed face framed by his stethoscope. 'Welcome back,' the doctor said. 'Can you feel that?'

The steel of the stethoscope slid across his chest. 'Yes,' he said. His fingers moved and touched carpet. He was stretched out on the floor.

'Can you see my moustache?' the doctor asked.

Christian searched his face. 'No,' he said.

'That's good. I shaved it off last year. All your senses seem to be working satisfactorily. How do you feel?'

'All right. Hearing's a bit funny. Everything sounds sort of fuzzy. Trashy.' It was the wrong word but Christian couldn't find the right one.

'It's the rain, old chap. It's pelting down.'

Christian raised his head and saw Domenik standing in the doorway to the balcony. The sky was charcoal. Now he could hear grunts of thunder behind the rush of rain. 'What happened?' he asked.

'You tell me,' the doctor said. He was busy reading a pulse. Christian's memory cleared, slowly, like solids settling in a liquid. Another blackout. Another bloody blackout. What a curse.

Domenik came over. For the first time, Christian realized that the room was empty: he had ended the party. 'No prospect of the Russian Front for you,' Domenik said.

'Was I going there?'

'Probably not. It was just talk. I'm afraid my tedious conversation was too much for you.'

Christian felt his nose. No blood. Well that was an improvement, anyway. 'I can't remember a single word you said,' he told Domenik. 'Not one.'

'Just as well, I expect.'

'Can you sit up?' the doctor said. His fingers worked their way over Christian's skull. 'Hullo, hullo,' he said. 'When did that happen?'

'Months ago. Someone hit me with a bottle. You weren't here then. Another doctor took the stitches out.'

'Must have been a nasty bang,' the doctor said. 'Very nasty indeed.'

For a couple of days Glasgow was enjoyable. The weather was mild and dry, the city was crowded and bustling, Laszlo liked hanging about and watching others work. He had earned a holiday. It was pleasant to be near the docks when a big American troopship was unloading and to watch the big Army trucks with their massive engines and air brakes come growling and gasping on to the cobbled streets. Many of the trucks were full of troops, and they always cheered and waved when they came through the dock gates. Often they were still cheering as they went out of sight. The Glasgow people waved back, or some did; they had seen and heard it all a hundred times before. 'Why do they cheer so?' Laszlo asked an old man sitting on an empty fish-crate stencilled STOLEN FROM JOE CROAN.

'They didny get torpedoed,' the old man said, 'an' for that they each got a wee medal.'

'Thatafack?' Laszlo said. He was picking up the lingo.

'Och, aye. The Yanks gi'e their sodgers dozens a medals. Fire

228

yer rifle, ye get a medal. Go to the lavvy, ye get a medal. Wipe yer bum, ye get a bar.'

Laszlo strolled on, secretly counting the trucks. When he reached a hundred it seemed pointless to go on. He had some vague thought of informing Madrid, but how? He could do nothing until General Oster arranged for someone to contact him. Each day he bought the *Herald* and searched the personal column. So far nobody had inserted any message for Ace. Laszlo was beginning to feel a tiny bit impatient.

On the other hand he had mastered bits of the local dialect. He could order simple food and drink, although he slipped up once by asking for a fried egg, which brought a startled glance. 'Fried bread, ye mean?' the woman said sharply and Laszlo agreed at once. He could get a bed for the night. Sometimes they looked at his identity papers; sometimes they didn't. He had wrinkled the Lascar's photograph and rubbed it with an oily thumb but he couldn't change the name. What if the police had told hotel-keepers and the like to look out for A. J. Lakram? Whenever he registered he kept his hand on his gun in his pocket, ready to fire through the cloth if necessary. It always worked for James Cagney. It meant writing with his left hand, so the signature was a mess. Nobody cared. Everybody's signature was a mess.

He never stayed more than one night in the same place. He now owned a second-hand suitcase, very old, very empty, to lend a touch of respectability when he was asking for a room. All the case contained were several copies of the *Herald*, a piece of soap and a razor. He needed clothes – his socks were ragged – but his clothing coupons were in his wallet and Stephanie had that, the little shit.

Laszlo settled into an easy routine. In the morning he took his suitcase for a walk and saw the sights. When the pubs opened he had a pint or two. In the afternoon he bought a *Herald* and went to the cinema: *Bombs Over Burma*, followed by *Random Harvest*, with Ronald Colman and Greer Garson. Fish and chips came next, and another pint, and another film. He liked lots of action. Randolph Scott was good in *The Desperadoes* but James Cagney was wasted in *Yankee Doodle Dandy*, which turned out not to be

229

about gangsters. Alan Ladd wasn't bad in *Lucky Jordan* but best of all was John Wayne in *Flying Tigers*. Then it was time to find a bed. The daily routine was pleasant and undemanding. There was only one problem. He was running out of money. An awful thought occurred: maybe Oster had missed the message, God knew how or why, but maybe it had never reached him? Laszlo went to the *Herald* office and ordered another insertion. This time he made it more urgent: *Happy days are really here again*. That cost money too.

'Dear me, no. What? No, no, no. It's a ludicrous suggestion, quite absurd. What has got into their little heads? I'm amazed.' The Director handed the piece of paper to Freddy Garcia. 'They can't be serious.' He took the paper back. 'It's mistranslated. Not properly decoded. Garbled in transmission. All three.' He screwed it into a ball, tossed it in the air and tried to head it, soccer-style, and missed. His glasses fell off. 'Buggeration,' he said.

Freddy picked up his glasses and found the paper and flattened it. The Director put his glasses on and read it again. '*Double* buggeration,' he said brusquely. 'Just when things were going so well . . . I assume you've double-checked the decoding and everything?'

Freddy nodded. He said, 'It's so short, sir, that there's not much room for error, is there?'

'No, I suppose not. "Eldorado to proceed to Berlin earliest opportunity. Authority: highest." That has to be Canaris.'

'He's as high as you can go.'

The Director cleaned his glasses, and brooded. Freddy stood on the fireplace fender and made it rock, until the Director frowned. 'Don't fidget,' he said. 'I was never allowed to fidget when I was a boy. Did your parents let you fidget?'

'All the time, sir. My mother positively encouraged it.'

'Lucky devil. Mine gave me a good skelp around the lugs. The result is what you see before you. A man in a virtual catatonic trance.' The Director stopped gesticulating. 'What d'you think is going on over there, Freddy?'

'Possibly another medal. He only got the Iron Cross second class last time, sir, so there's scope for advancement. Or . . . I can't imagine why, but we shouldn't exclude it . . . they might want to give him the chop. Kill him.'

'That was my thought. But they've just awarded Garlic a fat bonus.' The Director sat on the end of a sofa and fidgeted, tapping his feet, plucking at the upholstery. 'It's such a frivolous request. Fancy wanting to take your chief agent out of the field at a crucial stage in the war! It's irresponsible. I'm most surprised at Canaris, I really am. Berlin, of all places. Eldorado could get hit by a bomb. What then?'

'So I take it the answer's no, sir.'

'Deep regrets, of course. Pressure of work. Pile it on. If we fob him off maybe Canaris will forget all about it.'

After a day and a half of isolation, Stephanie Schmidt was ready to run off at the mouth when Julie came through the door.

She was painfully homesick: for Bavaria, for Wasserburg, for her family, for Emil the spaniel and Coco the cat, who might or might not have had her kittens by now. In Madrid she had preserved a comfortable selection of warm memories of home and had tinted them with all the sentimentality of the exile. Now she turned them out again: the beautiful garden, all roses and honeysuckle; the romping pets; her mother's delicious cooking; trusty schoolfriends with swinging plaits; favourite cousins in uniform; the awful night when the big beech tree got blown down and just missed Emil but all the neighbours came around with saws and . . .

Julie lay on the bed and grunted occasionally. Two things became obvious. Not much about the father, and zero about boyfriends. Otto Krafft was probably the first love.

Stephanie was trying to remember the words of a pokerwork poem that hung above the kitchen sink when Julie interrupted. 'What d'you think about men, honey?' she asked.

Stephanie was flustered. 'I think . . . I think that God, He created men and . . . and so we—'

'Forget God. You can't take His word for anything, can you?

231

He's another man, for Christ's sake. They're all out for what they can get.'

'Not all. My father—'

'You hate your father. He's a miserable son of a bitch.' For a second their eyes met, and then Stephanie turned away, defeated. 'And if God made men, He did a bum job. Have you seen a man with his clothes off? Gross. Not a bit like those Greek statues. Fat and flabby and covered in hair.'

'I don't know about that,' Stephanie mumbled.

'Come off it, kid. Don't tell me you never think about your hero Otto all naked and shining. Let me put you straight. His private parts look like they just fell off the cold cuts counter at your local deli. Sad but true.'

Stephanie shuffled up and down. She had been given school gym shoes, black and laceless, a size too large. The boilersuit had no pockets. She needed a bath and a shampoo. There was no mirror. She cried out, plaintively, 'Why do they keep me here?'

'Why did you come here?' Julie asked. She made room on the bed. 'Come and sit here. Look, I know how you feel. I'm a long way from home too, all on account of a guy who swore he loved me.' Briefly, she wondered who she was talking about: Harry or Luis? It wasn't the whole truth, either way. 'They'll say anything. Absolutely anything.' Stephanie sat beside her. 'Tell me about these three clowns you came with. Which did you like best?'

'I cannot tell. That is all secret.'

'Oh, horsefeathers. Docherty's three doors along the corridor, talking his Irish head off. I had lunch with him. We're going to the cinema tomorrow.' Julie impressed herself with the fluency of her lies. The first prompted the next. 'He likes you, you know that? He says you were the best at putting Laszlo in his place. That time in the pub, in Galway. What exactly did you hit him with? Docherty says Laszlo landed on his butt in the sawdust.'

Stephanie laughed. That couldn't possibly be a secret. Not what the Abwehr meant by a secret. 'I hit him with this,' she said, showing her right fist.

'Wow!' Julie said. She felt her biceps. 'Attagirl! I bet he understood *that* message.'

Stephanie talked about the pub. After that she couldn't resist telling the story about Ferenc Tekeli and the nuns in the Dublin train, and was proud of herself when Julie laughed so much she nearly slid off the bed. In the end she talked about nearly everything. But when Julie asked, 'What happened to Laszlo?' she fell silent. The past was past; she was ready to be indiscreet about it; but Laszlo was on a mission of crucial importance to the war and to the German people. She had a sacred duty to the Führer not to betray that mission.

'Docherty says Laszlo kills people for fun,' Julie said. 'Otto Kräfft told him so. Think about it.' She left.

Luis stood in front of a wall-map of the world, colourfully studded with pins, and searched for some good news; some *really* good news. North Africa – nothing there; all gone beyond reclaim. Malta was a lost cause now that Sicily had fallen, which meant that Italy would be next, and that was a gloomy prospect. You couldn't expect the Italians to fight to the last man to keep the Allies out of Germany. No, there was trouble brewing there. Yugoslavia? He shuddered. More and more partisans sucking in more and more German divisions. And Greece? You couldn't trust the Greeks. The whole of the Eastern Front was bad news, of course. The Americans had started bombing Romania and the appalling, ferocious, unstoppable Russians were . . . Luis looked for Stalingrad, and found it hundreds of miles behind the Russian front line. What a disaster! By contrast the Allied capture of Sicily was a lost sixpence. That left Britain. Well, there was still some juice to be squeezed out of the U-boat war in the Atlantic but to be honest the Abwehr had gone off the boil when it came to convoys. Madrid's questionnaires were often quite tepid on the subject. What agitated Berlin was strategic bombing. Luis looked at the black flatheaded pins marking German cities that had been regularly bombed. What a lot! A moderately athletic caterpillar could have crawled over most of Germany without touching the map.

'It's a dismal picture,' he said.

Freddy looked at his watch. 'An hour to transmission time. I really would like to get this signal off to Madrid today. It would show them that we take their request seriously.'

Luis nodded. 'What would the Germans most like to happen?' he murmured. 'Given this awful map, what would cheer them up?'

He stood still, apart from an occasional blink, for several minutes, until Freddy could stand it no longer. 'Suppose the OWCH unit has a catastrophe?' he suggested. 'Test flight goes wrong, bomber crashes on American Army camp, huge bang, ten thousand killed.'

Luis made a short, thoughtful noise in his throat.

'Better yet,' Freddy said, 'crash it on a British Army camp. Fifteen thousand dead. Think of the uproar.'

'Do shut up, Freddy. Crashed bombers! Who cares about crashed bombers?' Luis went to his desk and took the cap off his fountain pen. 'That's a mere trifle compared to Winston Churchill's heart attack. *Alleged* heart attack. It's being kept secret, of course. Eldorado got wind of it from sub-agent Garlic, who is now at Cambridge University studying under one of the world's greatest heart specialists. Eldorado and Garlic are working around the clock on this sensational scoop.'

'Nice touch,' Freddy said. 'Since they like Garlic, let's give them more of him.'

'Now we've sugared the pill. I hate to say no without giving a damn good reason.' Luis finished writing. 'You know, I'd quite like to see Berlin,' he said. 'I've never been there.'

'You wouldn't like it with seven hundred Lancasters overhead,' Freddy said. Luis blotted the page and conceded the point silently.

Two days bed-rest.

Well, it could have been worse; it could have been the sack, discharged as medically unfit, end of a career. Christian was too restless to stay in bed but he compromised by lying on a couch or sprawling in an armchair. Domenik visited, bringing

234

the newspapers. 'Hold the headlines up to a mirror,' he said, 'and you'll get somewhere near the truth. But then maybe you don't want the truth.'

'It's the only thing the doctors haven't forbidden,' Christian said. 'I'm not allowed to drive a car, ride a horse, ski, swim, shoot, fish, take part in athletics or strenuous sports especially boxing, or have a bath.'

'Why no baths?'

'Might fall down and drown myself. Showers are permitted, thank God, or I'd end up choking on my own stench. Got any new jokes?'

That was when General Oster walked in. 'Don't let me stop you,' he said.

'Bit simpleminded, this one,' Domenik said. 'An Englishman, an American and a German.'

'Why do your jokes always go in threes?' Oster wondered.

'It's so they'll always have a leg to stand on,' Christian said without thinking. Oster was amused.

Domenik began: 'The Englishman boasts: "Churchill can stand on the top of St Paul's Cathedral and see all of London." '

'Technically untrue, but continue,' Oster said.

'The American says: "So what? President Roosevelt can stand on top of the Capitol and see all of Washington." '

'Rubbish,' Christian said. 'Roosevelt's in a wheelchair.'

'The German says—'

'Hang on to your hats, here it comes,' Oster announced.

'The German says, "That's nothing – the Führer can stand on a kitchen chair and see all of Berlin!" '

'Not worth waiting for,' Oster said. 'A subtly satirical allusion to the effects of bombing, I take it? Feeble.'

'Anyway,' Christian said, 'just look out of the window.'

'Jokes aren't about reality, they're about fears,' Domenik said. 'Jokes are hostages to ill-fortune. Make a joke and it won't happen. Of course it always does happen, but at least you get a chance to laugh at the bomb before it kills you.'

'I have a much better joke,' Oster said. He tossed some cushions on to the floor and lay on them. 'Our gallant allies the Hungarians

235

have made a secret treaty with the British and American Air Forces. Hungary promises not to fire on any of their bombers and they promise not to bomb Hungary. Sweet, isn't it?'

'Is that definite?' Domenik asked. 'I mean, there are so many rumours . . .'

'Stefan, old fellow, there is nothing so loud as the sound of bombs not being dropped. Believe me, Hungary is echoing to the racket.'

'Didn't we send a Hungarian to England?' Christian asked. He disliked talking about the disloyalty of Germany's allies; even hearing about it built a swirling tension in his head. 'What happened to him? What became of Ace, come to that?'

'Oh, well, you know,' Oster said. 'You reckon on losing one or two.' He rearranged the pillows behind his head.

'But surely, sir . . .' Christian hesitated; he could sense failure ahead; but it was too late now. He might as well put the unasked question into words. 'Surely Ace wasn't lost? Didn't we get his message? From Glasgow?' Oster nodded. 'So where does he go from there?' Christian asked.

'Good question.' Oster heaved himself up and threw the cushions at Domenik. 'Come along, Stefan. We're interrupting the convalescence.' As they went out, he said: 'Since you're so concerned, Meyer, maybe Eldorado can take him on. Remind me to suggest it when he comes.' Christian nodded. That 'Meyer' really hurt.

The moustache he was trying to grow was so far just a smear but Laszlo liked the feel of it, and he was brushing what little there was with his fingertips as he came away from breakfast when the man who ran the hotel said, 'Good morning, Mr Lakram.'

That wasn't good. That wasn't right. The people who ran the sort of hotel Laszlo could afford didn't acknowledge the guests; certainly didn't speak to them by name. They fined them five shillings for burning cigarette holes in the sheets and kicked them out in the rain. If they had to address a guest they called him 'Muster' or 'Jummy' but usually they said nothing at all. Laszlo took fright. He replied politely and hurried upstairs to his room, grabbed his suitcase and went out through the back window. It was a six-foot drop to a shed with a corrugated iron roof. He hit it with a crash and a tinkle and bounded along the roof, stamping out a concerto for cymbals, then dropped again into the back alley and ran until he found streets and crowds and safety.

It was a bad start to a worse day. The tinkle that followed his crash on to the roof had been the coins jolted out of his pockets. Laszlo counted his money and found he was left with less than two pounds. Well, you could live for a few days on a couple of quid in 1943 if you slept in the open, but it was raining by noon and that wasn't the worst of it. He had no identity papers. A. J. Lakram's documents were in the hotel-keeper's possession.

Laszlo wasted a couple of pennies on the *Glasgow Herald*. RUSSIANS RETAKE KHARKOV, the front page shouted. *Nobody cares about Laszlo* was the news in the personal columns. His own message, now making its last appearance, was starting to look pathetic. If these are the really happy days, he thought, God help us when they run out.

There was nothing to do but drink while the pubs were open and hide in the cinema when they weren't. That evening, when he came out of *Edge of Darkness* (Errol Flynn and Ann Sheridan) the weather was worse. Dusk had come early; people were hurrying home, heads down against the gusting rain. Laszlo had no home. He got very wet trudging to the pub where he had first seen A. J. Lakram, and he drank too much beer, too fast, while he was waiting for another likely-looking merchant seaman to come in. None did.

At chucking-out time the rain was heavier than ever, and bitingly cold. He had eaten nothing since breakfast. His head and his legs were not working very well as he stumbled uncertainly in the blackness. He kept bumping into people but they were gone before he could grab them and show them his pistol and say the words.

Fool, he told himself, they can't see the pistol in the blackout. That was a bad moment, one of the worst. No gun, no hope. Then he thought of a solution. Ask for a light. Ask for a match.

Strike the match and say, 'See this?' Brilliant solution. Laszlo was grinning as he lurched off the kerb and got lightly clipped by the wing of a car.

The driver pulled over, walked back and found Laszlo leaning against a tree, laughing like a schoolgirl. 'Are you hurt?' he asked.

Laszlo clutched the man's sleeve. 'Have you got a light?' he said. 'A light is what I need. Have you got a light?'

'There may be some matches in the car. Can you walk?'

While he was searching for matches Laszlo got into the car and waved his pistol. 'Can you see this?' he asked. The man, stocky and curly-haired, was unsurprised. 'I see it,' he said. 'Is it loaded?'

Laszlo aimed it at him while he screwed on the silencer. 'Look carefully,' he said, 'because you won't hear anything.' He fired a shot through the roof. It made a bang like a tractor backfiring. 'Sorry,' he said. 'Now give me all your money. Identity card too.'

Later, scuttling off in the wet dark, he realized that he could have stolen the car. Still, seventeen pounds wasn't a bad haul. He stood in the doorway of a late-night chip-shop to see who he was now. William Kenny, farmer. Good enough.

'The OWCH report is excellent, sir,' Christian said.

'Oh, invaluable,' Canaris agreed.

'Luftwaffe Intelligence are fascinated, quite fascinated.' Oster said. 'They have a hundred new questions for Eldorado.'

'And that's on top of the eight-engined bomber report, sir,' Christian said.

'We're spoiling them,' Oster remarked.

'But nothing so far on RAF Bomber Command's next big target cities,' Canaris pointed out. 'And that's what we specifically asked for.'

'In all fairness, sir, I do think you're pressing a little hard, bearing in mind the obstacles. I mean, we're asking Eldorado to

238

break through a whole army of security systems. It's bound to take time.' Christian shuffled his bundle of folders. 'Meanwhile there's this truly startling development regarding Churchill's health. I know it involves Garlic again, but . . . Is it really wise to pull Eldorado out of England at this precise stage?'

Canaris turned to Oster. 'D'you think he's afraid of Berlin? The bombing?'

Oster shrugged. 'It's certainly a lot noisier than London. Perhaps that's it.'

'Then make it Switzerland,' Canaris told Christian. 'Tell him I want to meet him in Zurich. No excuses. Do it now.'

Julie brought Stephanie Schmidt a potted geranium, vivid scarlet, and a small bottle of shampoo. The plant pleased her and the shampoo delighted her: a tear of thanks ran down her cheek. 'As soon as you have gone . . .' she began.

'Why not use it now?'

More tears, which were soon washed away with the grease and dandruff when Stephanie bent her head into the wash-basin. Julie dried her hair, scrubbing it with the towel until the scalp felt purified, and then combed it, and tied it with a yellow ribbon from her own hair. 'You look like a million dollars,' she said. 'Or two million Deutschmarks.'

Stephanie glowed with gratitude. 'You are a wonderful person,' she said.

'I'll drink to that.' Julie took a small silver flask from her pocket. 'Where d'you keep the crystal goblets?'

'Oh . . .' Stephanie shook her head and made the ribbon fly. 'In my family, you see, we never—'

'That's not what Docherty says. He says that when you were in that bar in Galway even Ferenc was taking lessons from you.' Stephanie protested prettily but surrendered speedily and they were soon sharing brandy from the cap of the flask. 'You liked Ferenc, didn't you?' Julie said.

'He was lovely. Never before have I met a man who finds everything interesting. Everyone liked Ferenc.'

'Laszlo didn't.'

'Oh well, Laszlo was always in a hurry, no time to enjoy . . . Ferenc always had time to enjoy.' Stephanie didn't want even to think about Laszlo: it spoiled the nice warm atmosphere. 'And you should have seen Ferenc eat! Did I tell you about the time we all went to the bullfight?' She was off and running.

Julie sat and listened to her cheerful gossip, and kept the little silver cup of brandy going back and forth. When there was a pause she said: 'I wish I'd known him. I don't suppose I ever will. Would he have made a very good spy, d'you think?'

Recklessly indiscreet, Stephanie said, 'World's worst. He told me so. He only joined the Abwehr to get out of prison.'

Julie smiled. 'Sounds very, very sensible. I'd do the same.' She let the smile fade, very slowly. 'I wonder . . .' She touched Stephanie on the knee with the tip of her forefinger; just a tiny touch, but it made the girl's head twitch. 'Do you think he knows he's in danger?'

Stephanie tried to shrug it off. 'In war, we are all in danger.'

'From Laszlo. Docherty says he thinks Ferenc is in great danger from Laszlo.' She looked Stephanie straight in the eyes. 'Where is Laszlo, Stephanie? Tell me.'

But she would not. Julie got a long speech about trust and honour and the sacred duty of the warrior; the longer it lasted the more scrambled the grammar became and the less sense it all made; until finally Stephanie was in tears. Julie capped the brandy and gave her a towel and told her not to upset herself. Another session over.

The Director found Zurich on the map. 'Twenty-odd miles from the German border,' he said. 'Even worse than I thought.'

'You suspect kidnap, sir?' Freddy said.

'Don't you?'

'I don't know what I suspect, sir. I just wonder what Canaris is going to think if Eldorado says no again.'

'He'll think Eldorado's got flu.'

'Has he?'

'Summer flu. There's a lot of it about, you know.'

The news did not please Luis. 'I never get colds,' he said. 'I am extremely fit. Besides, how can I afford time off to lie in bed? Look at all the work I've got piling up!'

Julie was present. 'I think he ought to go to Zurich,' she told Freddy. 'I think he ought to be flown there in an ambulance plane and carried on a stretcher to the Admiral's presence. I think that would impress the Abwehr enormously. I see him with the right leg in plaster and bloody bandages wrapped around the head. Feverish, of course, and talking nonsense. And just as they award him the Blue Max for conspicuous bullshit in the face of overwhelming odds, he drops dead. What a movie it would make.'

'Can't drop dead,' Luis said gloomily. 'You've got me lying down already.'

'Anyway, it's too late for all that,' Freddy said. 'The signal's already gone to Madrid. You've got the flu. Now relax and enjoy it.'

Christian began to get giddy at the top of the bunker. It was four storeys high, and the labourers were pouring concrete to make a fifth storey. He clung to some wooden scaffolding and looked across the street at the roof of an apartment block, while behind him the site engineer explained the design of the bunker to Oster. A crane delivering buckets of fresh concrete swayed alarmingly. Christian had to look away. He found himself watching men with wheelbarrows running, actually running, along the scaffolding planks. He shut his eyes.

'Have you seen enough?' Oster asked. Christian nodded. They began the long descent, one vertical ladder after another into deepening darkness until Christian had lost count of the stages. When at last he stepped off a ladder and saw blessed ground level through a doorway, Oster said: 'Want to take a look at the basements? There are three levels. Or is it four?' Christian shook his head. 'I want a drink,' he said.

Oster's driver took them to an officers' club. It was not yet noon and the place was almost empty. Christian slumped into a deep leather armchair and let his eyes close. Oster ordered beer. The waiter's shoes clicked away across the parquet floor. 'Well,' Oster said. 'Feel better now?'

'I feel as if I just climbed the Matterhorn without ropes.' Christian squinted sideways at Oster. 'Was that really necessary, sir? The doctor ordered bed-rest, not vertigo.'

'You needed fresh air. Besides, I thought you ought to see what we're building. Some bunker, eh? It fills a whole city block. The external walls are two metres thick. No windows, did you notice that? It's designed to take five or six thousand people but I bet they pack in twice as many when Berlin gets what Hamburg got. Don't you?'

'Perhaps. Probably. I don't know.' Christian was still trying to forget the slosh and surge of cement, and the uncertain lurch of the crane. 'It's none of my business anyway.'

'Oh, I wouldn't say that.' The beer came, and Oster raised his glass. 'Here's to crime.' They drank. 'Bunkers like that are going up all over Germany, you know. Indestructible, so that engineer told me. Apparently we learned a great deal about reinforced concrete from building submarine pens at Brest and St Nazaire. The RAF bounced a lot of very big bombs off them and they never even cracked.'

'Good.'

'Yes, it's reassuring to know that something will be left standing.'

Christian thought about that, began assembling a remark about the enduring spirit of the German people, and gave it up before it was complete.

Oster waved his tankard at the room. 'I don't suppose this place will survive. A single thousand-kilogram bomb down the chimney and half the street will be in the gutter.'

'It may not be as bad as that.'

'The bunker-builders seem to think it will.'

They drove back to Abwehr headquarters. Christian was glad to get inside; he found being out with Oster vaguely alarming. The familiar buff walls and the polished mahogany, and the steady chatter of invisible typewriters, put him at his ease. Passing secretaries smiled as they walked along a corridor. Oster was repeating something he had been told by the engineer, something about the setting time of really hard concrete, but Christian was hardly listening; he was wondering if he ought to see a specialist about his head and also how it was that the Abwehr always got such very attractive secretaries. Domenik came round a corner. Christian slowed his pace; he wanted to hear today's joke. Then Domenik did a curious thing: he stopped abruptly, so abruptly that the two men walking behind him stumbled. He knelt to re-tie his shoelace and they stood flanking him: medium build, average height, interchangeable apart from their suits, one dark blue and one dark brown. When he stood up, Domenik's face was as blank as a board and he walked past Christian without a sideways glance. The blue and brown suits kept pace with him. Christian looked to Oster for an explanation and Oster was nowhere to be seen.

For a few seconds he stood in the empty corridor, feeling slightly offended by these rebuffs, until four men in SS uniform appeared, carrying cardboard boxes full of files, and marched past him. The only sensible thing to do was to follow them, get out of the building, go for a long walk, and have a quiet lunch. Christian went the other way. He went to Domenik's office. More SS men were emptying the filing cabinets, collecting every scrap of paper from the desk.

Christian tried to find Oster. His secretary, looking pale, said he was in a meeting with Admiral Canaris. 'Domenik's been arrested,' Christian told her. She knew already. 'Why? What's he done?' he asked. She didn't know. 'You mean they just walked in here and arrested him?' he said. 'How can they do such a thing?' She looked at him. *They can do anything,* her look said. *You know that.*

Laszlo thought too much and ate too little. The less he ate, the more he thought. One of the things he had too much time to think about was why General Oster did not respond to his signals in the *Glasgow Herald*. Oster must know he needed money. If he needed money he needed food. So Oster knew he was hungry.

243

Laszlo brooded over this in the long bleak hours when he sat on a variety of park benches and watched the same grimy clouds drifting in from the Atlantic and tried to ignore his complaining stomach. Garlic was dead. The Abwehr must know that. How could they not know it? Six messages, six days, they *must* know. So why didn't they answer? Tell him where to go, who to meet? They had agents, the agents had money, it was wrong to leave him waiting like this. Exposed. Isolated. In danger. Hungry. Poor.

Laszlo couldn't afford the cinema any more. He had even given up buying the *Herald*; now he read the free copy in the public library. The seventeen pounds he stole from the farmer ran through his hands with frightening speed. Black-market clothing coupons bought in a pub cost him five pounds: far too much, Laszlo realized when it was too late to argue, the man had cheated him, had conned him blind; but he desperately needed these coupons, his socks were ruined and his underwear was foul. Then he went and spent too much on new socks and underwear and a shirt. His suitcase fell to bits in the rain and he had to get another. William Kenny's identity card was good for two nights, maximum; after that the police were bound to be waiting for him to use it. Another man in another pub sold Laszlo a blank identity card for two pounds but it turned out to be useless because it had to be stamped with an official stamp, so he moved on and swapped it (plus a pound) for a very tattered RAF identity card that had once belonged to LAC Wallis, Peter John. It all cost money. Everything cost money. Even doing nothing cost money. Laszlo tried to save by not eating. He had the gun, he could always rob somebody. Trouble was, he felt too depressed to be violent. He kept wondering where he had gone wrong. Maybe he hadn't killed Garlic after all. The Abwehr had screwed up once already. They'd said Venezuela when it wasn't Venezuela. How could it be Venezuela when there wasn't anyone from Venezuela at the university? So maybe it wasn't Bolivia either. Maybe it was really Brazil. Laszlo took out his scrap of paper. *José-Carlos Coelho, 22A Buccleuch Avenue.* Maybe this was Garlic. Laszlo thought about it all day every day until his poor brain didn't know what to think.

*

'Watch your step,' Oster warned. 'He's as jumpy as a cat.'

It was mid-afternoon. Christian had lunched alone in the Abwehr restaurant; nobody seemed to want to share his table. Hardly anybody looked his way. Was it, he wondered, because he was known to be a friend of Domenik's? He sat too long, not drinking the cup of ersatz coffee, while the room emptied. The same furious question kept presenting itself: *Why Domenik?* It was like a bereavement. Christian had always been successful in keeping his personal emotions separate from his professional life. As an Abwehr officer he knew that agents were expendable and their loss never saddened him as, for instance, he had been saddened by the death of a cousin, a tank commander killed during the 1940 blitzkrieg. That loss had caused him great hurt. Karl was too full of life to die; it seemed all wrong. Now Christian felt much the same about Domenik: they had taken the wrong man. But he's not dead, Christian told himself, and got the answer: He looked pretty dead, didn't he? He looked finished. Done for.

Oster's secretary found him in the restaurant and hustled him upstairs. Oster was waiting in the Admiral's ante-room. 'I know, I know,' he said before Christian could open his mouth. 'He was my friend too. But we've got more urgent problems to solve. Eldorado says he's got flu. Zurich's off.'

They went in. Canaris was sitting on a corner of his desk, tossing a paperweight from hand to hand. It was the nosecone of a small shell and every time it thwacked into his palm his fingers squeezed it. Christian had the impression that Canaris might at any moment fling the thing, just to release some tension.

'Those were not invitations to a garden-party,' Canaris said. 'Those were orders to attend a meeting. Why is this man playing games?'

'Travel shouldn't be a problem,' Oster said. 'He's a neutral. Money's no problem, heaven knows.'

Christian felt it was his turn to say something. 'There may be reasons why Berlin and Zurich are unattractive, sir. Reasons we don't know.'

245

'Unattractive,' Canaris said. 'Unattractive.' He plainly disliked the word. 'Where next? Monte Carlo? Biarritz? Do you think he might fancy a weekend in Venice?'

An idea came to Christian like a trained hawk to the glove. 'I think he might find it very difficult to refuse to go to Spain, sir,' he said.

Canaris tipped his head back and examined the light fitting. 'Yes,' he said. 'Spain. If he won't go to his own damned country there's certainly something very wrong. Spain. Good. We'll do it.'

Christian left. Canaris tossed the nosecone to Oster and got off the desk. 'Have you found out what it is yet?' he asked.

'Treason. Plotting to overthrow the state.'

Canaris winced. 'What a fool.'

'A holy fool.'

'I didn't hear that,' Canaris said, 'because you didn't say it.'

For Docherty it was a day out, the first time he had been released from detention in Knightsbridge. For Luis it was a day out and a day off, a holiday from the endless grind of ghost-writing for a dozen ghosts. It was also a chance to escape another ghost. Julie was always at the back of his mind, always a silent listener to his thoughts as he got on with his life. They had separated without parting. Or maybe parted without separating. Either way it was an absurd and unsatisfactory outcome and it often infuriated him that she would not go away and leave him alone, and he told her so. 'Get out!' he shouted at the silence. 'Buzz off! Beat it!' Sometimes that did the trick and he felt so much better that he wished she were there so that he could tell her that he didn't need her.

An MI5 officer called Fletcher took Docherty and Luis to Paddington station. They had a reserved first-class compartment on the South Wales express. The day was fine and hot and the long dash across southern England was a succession of idyllic calendar pictures: men harvesting with horse-drawn reaping machines; women and children stacking the sheaves; fat herds of milk-cows

246

eternally converting green into white; even some early autumn ploughing, looking fresher than brown corduroy ever could. And always there were glimpses of airfields, Army camps, mile after mile of military convoy on the roads.

Docherty was good company, full of chat, and Fletcher had bought a basket of food and drink. They lunched as the train sped between the coal and the steel of South Wales – coal coming down from the high valleys, steel being forged in the coastal mills – and changed trains at Swansea, then again at Carmarthen for a brisk final clatter through the valleys of Pembrokeshire to a place Luis had never heard of: Milford Haven. The air was brisk with the tang of the sea, lightly spiced with the stink of petrol. An RAF car drove them around a bay that was busy with oil tankers and put them on board an RAF launch which immediately went out and carved up the sea like an avenging knife through silk. Luis was enormously impressed. The boat sped past some towering cliffs and then strolled between rocks to the stone landing-stage built on to an island the size of a golf course if you didn't mind losing a bucket of balls. 'Skomer Island,' Fletcher said. 'Bit of a walk, I'm afraid.'

The ground was springy with purple heather and the air was alive with seabirds. 'What are those?' Luis asked.

'They might be puffins,' Docherty said. 'Then again, they might not. What do you think, Fletcher?'

'They're either shearwaters or kittiwakes,' Fletcher said. 'If they're neither of those they must be something else. Owls, perhaps, or buzzards. I haven't got my distance glasses on.'

'So much for British Intelligence,' Docherty said. 'If you go on like this you'll lose India and never find it again.'

A man was waiting for them at the north of the island, a local fisherman. He led them across the rocks to where a yellow oilskin was held down at the edges with stones. 'It's been in the water a long time,' he said, 'and then the rocks knocked it about when it got washed up and the birds had a go at it too. Don't expect too much.' He peeled the oilskin back.

The warm stench of putrefaction arose and a dozen flies got sluggishly blown away by the breeze. The body looked broken and painful because the sea had jammed it between the rocks without consulting the joints and so everything was bent the wrong way. Half the face was missing. An ear had gone, and both eyes. The lower jawbone had become dislocated and this gave the mouth a yawning gape. Luis took one look and walked away.

'I think it's him,' Docherty said.

'Not much to go on,' Fletcher warned.

'The clothes are the same, the build, the hair. He had a funny little birthmark on his chest, just above the right nipple. Like an inkblot, it was.'

Fletcher got a piece of wood and used it to lift the remains of the shirt. 'Just like an inkblot,' he agreed. 'I'll take some photographs and then the medics can have him, and good luck to them.'

'Take a snap of the back of his head, why don't you?' Docherty suggested.

As they returned to the launch, Luis asked Fletcher: 'Was that absolutely necessary? I mean, did we have to come all this way for that?'

'Yes, we did. The body might have fallen apart if we had tried to move it.'

Luis had little to say during the long journey back to London. As soon as he was in his flat he telephoned Freddy Garcia. 'Very funny joke,' he said. 'You told me we were going to see an old friend of Docherty's. You didn't say how old.'

'Ah. A bit the worse for wear?'

'How should I know? Half the bits were missing. I can still smell the other half. Any more jokes like that, you bastard, and I quit.' Luis was so angry his voice was shaking. 'You don't pay me enough to be pissed on like that.'

'It wasn't a joke, Luis. I thought it was time you had a reminder of how seriously the other side takes this business. You are accustomed to working with fictions. But the war is real, isn't it? Sometimes it pays to remember that death is a hard imperative and not just a collection of words on a page.'

Luis had been standing. Now he sat. 'OK,' he said. 'What's happened?'

248

'Another signal from Admiral Canaris. This time he wants you to meet him in Spain. Think about it. We'll talk tomorrow. Good-night.'

Standing on a box in the narrow alley at the side of the shop, Laszlo slipped the blade of his knife under the window, found the catch, levered hard, and snapped the blade. He could have wept. It didn't happen like this in the movies. That knife had cost him a shilling in Woolworths. They didn't buy their knives at Woolworths in the movies but he had been down to his last shilling and now even that was wasted.

Think, think, he told himself. There's always another way. The shop was right (a dingy little grocer's on a quiet street) and the time was right (early-closing day) and even the weather was helpful (grey and drizzling). The big problem was that his brain was fogged with hunger. Think, think. Forget this window. Look for another.

There wasn't another, but there was a door at the back and it swung open. Laszlo smelt food. He tiptoed in, holding his empty suitcase with both hands to avoid bumping into things. Brown linoleum flowed silently past a small stock-room and around a gloomy staircase, and took him into the shop. Food everywhere: beans, cheese, macaroni, marmalade, Spam, dried eggs . . . He took a tin of Spam off a shelf and the picture on the wrapper made his stomach leap like a puppy on a leash. Three tins of Spam went into the suitcase, four tins of Heinz beans, two jars of Keillers marmalade, six tins of Skipper sardines, two packets of dried eggs, a jar of plum jam, a tin of pineapple chunks. A man cleared his throat. Laszlo slammed the suitcase shut and caught a glimpse of a tall, grey-haired figure on the stairs, lifting an air rifle. It made a pop like a burst balloon as Laszlo dived behind a stack of packets of porridge oats, and the slug sang past his head. The man gave a harsh, guttural shout; the words were meaningless but the sense was obvious: *Surrender!* Laszlo couldn't get the pistol out of his pocket. The lining was ripped, the gun was trapped in the fabric. A second balloon popped and a packet fell on his head, leaking oats.

Laszlo was suddenly enraged. The world was a conspiracy against him – Woolworths, his pocket-lining, this packet of porridge. He jumped to his feet and began hurling things at the man: tins, jars, bottles, more tins, whatever he could reach, a barrage of groceries so furious that his target cowered away. A tin of corned beef whacked the man's head and he went down in a heap. Laszlo discovered a row of bottles of tomato ketchup and flung them like stick grenades. The walls bled like a slaughterhouse.

Enough was enough. Laszlo took his suitcase, unlocked the front door and locked it again from the outside. Even then the shopkeeper came staggering towards him, one hand to his streaming head. A passer-by stopped and gaped. 'Get the police,' Laszlo said. 'I've caught a burglar.' The passer-by ran one way. Laszlo walked the other.

He walked for a mile and took shelter in a derelict bandstand in an empty municipal park. The food looked splendid but he had no tin-opener, and today was early-closing day so he couldn't even steal one. The sardine tins had little keys attached to open them. He ate six tins of sardines and half a jar of plum jam. The rain got worse. That night he slept on the bandstand, very badly.

The third summons from Admiral Canaris worried the Director more than anything that he had faced since he took on the Double-Cross job. It worried him because the three signals had arrived in quick succession, each phrased more curtly than the last. Far from fobbing off the Admiral, Eldorado's delays and excuses had increased the pressure. There was no precedent for any of this, and now there was no way of dodging the third demand. The Director sought advice from senior colleagues in the Intelligence field. They had none to give.

'Do what you think best, old chap,' one said.

The Director grunted. 'And how do I decide that?' he asked.

'You treat the case on its merits. Just stop searching for subtleties. There aren't any.'

The Director repeated this to Freddy. 'The man's absolutely right, of course,' he said. 'If Eldorado sends a third refusal the

Abwehr will smell a rat and then the whole network may go down the pan. If Eldorado meets Canaris in Spain it may well be the last we ever see of him. The Gestapo will take him apart, the network will be blown, and what's more they'll suspect every other double-agent too.'

'Never mind the Gestapo, sir,' Freddy said. 'The Abwehr has its own interrogators. Not as messy but just as effective.'

'So whether he stays or goes, it's potentially disastrous.'

'It's virtually certain to be highly damaging if he stays, sir. If he goes, and fails . . . End of story. That, of course, is not inevitable. He might go and return. We don't know.'

The Director took out a coin and flipped it several times. 'Damn thing always comes down heads,' he said. 'I can't decide this, Freddy. I can't *order* him to go. I'm not even going to suggest it. You tell him the facts and say that whatever he decides is fine by us. It's his neck. He's the one to risk it. Or not.'

Freddy found Luis in his flat, moodily deleting all the adjectives and adverbs from a report by Wallpaper. 'Feel like a drink?' Freddy said.

'Just had one.'

Freddy sat down. 'Admiral Canaris is extremely keen to meet you at a town called Santander in northern Spain as soon as possible,' he said. 'Now here are the facts of the situation.' He went through the facts, neither exaggerating nor minimizing. 'It's your decision, Luis. Do you want to think it over?'

'No. I want to go.' He screwed up the report he had been cutting and threw it away.

'Right. I'll go and organize the flight.'

When he left, Luis telephoned Julie. 'I just wanted to hear your voice,' he said.

'I see.' He did not reply, so she said: 'Well, here it is. Sounds the same as ever.'

'I wish we could meet,' he said. 'We haven't met for a week. It's crazy, not meeting.'

'What's new about that?' she asked. 'Everything we've ever done has been crazy. Listen, you just had to *ask*, Luis. I mean, are you asking now?'

'We can't meet now,' he said. 'I'm going to Spain tonight. I'm going to meet Canaris.'

'In that case you're a complete bloody fool,' she told him.

'All in a day's work,' he said lightly. They listened to each other's breathing for a while. 'Goodbye,' he said, and hung up fast. He began packing.

As soon as Christian saw the plate of cold meats he remembered Domenik's joke about what was a hundred yards long and lived on cabbage. He wished he could cleanse his mind of such thoughts. Nobody at headquarters mentioned Domenik any more. It would be pointless and clumsy to mention him now, in Admiral Canaris's house, where Christian had been invited for supper. But he couldn't stop himself looking at the plate of rare beef and stuffed pork, and thinking: I bet nobody stood in line for that little lot.

'I hope you don't mind plain fare,' Canaris said. His family had gone to the country to escape the bombing, so he and Christian were alone. 'It's good honest sauerkraut and potato salad, and I got hold of some wheat beer from the south. Do help yourself.'

They ate. Christian was on his guard. Canaris must have a reason for this. They talked easily of unimportant, non-military matters: dogs and horses (the Admiral had some dachshunds and an Arab mare of which he was very fond), gardening, cooking – they shared a taste for wild boar – and books. Christian remarked that he was surprised the Admiral found time to read for pleasure, what with the great scope and scale of his responsibilities. Couldn't go wrong with a line like that.

'I read for distraction, especially when the English bombers make sleep impossible. Unfortunately the distraction sometimes returns to haunt me.' Canaris picked up a book. 'I thought I would be safe with this life of an English king of five hundred years ago.'

'Henry V?' Christian said. 'Shakespeare rather approved, didn't he? Agincourt. Henry made the French look silly, as I recall.'

'Yes. What Shakespeare doesn't say is that Henry spent the rest of his life trying to conquer France and succeeded only

252

in destroying what he conquered. He did it so thoroughly that its value was worthless and he made himself bankrupt.' Canaris opened the book to a portrait. 'No wonder he looked old before his time.'

Christian chewed his sauerkraut. Canaris poured some more wheat beer.

'If Henry wanted to conquer the country,' Christian said cautiously, 'why did he destroy it?'

'Well . . . I suspect that such was not his original intention. I rather think that Henry said to himself, "There's France, big country, rich country, I can get the costs of my campaign out of the French people themselves. Let the French pay for their own defeat." That's what Henry hoped.'

'But it didn't work.'

'Not according to the records. The French resisted, even after they were supposedly conquered, so the English applied the fifteenth-century equivalent of a scorched-earth policy, to teach them a lesson. Famine, slaughter, general devastation of the countryside. But of course that meant there was nothing left to pay for the military occupation!' Canaris forked a bit of pork stuffing. 'And the more Henry conquered, the poorer he became, because armies are so expensive.' He ate the pork stuffing.

'What happened in the end?' Christian asked.

'Oh, Henry died young,' Canaris said. 'And not a moment too soon.'

He went off to make coffee, and when he came back he turned on the radio. 'D'you mind?' he said. 'I've no ear for music but I do enjoy this band.' It was the Glenn Miller Orchestra, broadcasting on the BBC. Christian was briefly shocked, but he soon settled back and listened. If the Gestapo arrested him they'd have to take the head of the Abwehr too.

Christian did not stay long. As he was leaving, Canaris said, 'You've read *Mein Kampf*, of course.'

'Of course.'

'Neither have I. It's largely unreadable, rather like the Bible, but some people find it reassuring to have a copy lying about the place. Take this as a memento of a pleasant and instructive evening.'

253

It was a large presentation copy, bound in white leather with a single red swastika on the spine. Christian was touched by such generosity. He opened the book at the fly-leaf and saw the bold angular autograph, *Adolf Hitler*, all peaks and points, and he just managed to suppress a gasp. It was like being given a piece of the true Cross to keep. 'I don't know how to thank you, sir,' he said.

'Get Eldorado to Spain. That'll be enough.'

Back in his apartment, Christian examined his gift. The paper was crisp, the type was noble, and a broad silk ribbon marked somebody's place. He opened the book at that page. A passage had been marked. Christian read:

> State authority as an end in itself cannot exist, since in that case every tyranny on this earth would be sacred and unassailable. If a racial entity is being led toward its doom by means of governmental power, then the rebellion of every single member of such a Volk is not only a right, but a duty.

Christian read it and reread it. His brain felt fogged, probably the result of too much wheat beer. What on earth had the Führer been thinking of when he wrote that? The words blurred. Christian's head nodded. The book slid from his fingers and thudded to the floor. He got up and went to bed.

There were no trees in Buccleuch Avenue and that annoyed Laszlo. If it was an avenue it should have trees; that was what avenue meant. It was only a small thing but Laszlo was easily annoyed nowadays. A treeless avenue irritated him and a broken shoelace angered him and people in the street who gave him funny looks drove him into a rage. He lived on the streets and got a lot of glances when he talked to himself, so he sometimes boiled over and shouted terrible threats. He was thinner than ever and he had long since given up shaving. Or washing. Water just let the cold in. Grime was better. Grime had become part of Laszlo's armour against a hostile world.

254

He disliked 22A. It was a boxy little brick-built bungalow squeezed into a scrap of land between 22 and 23. He stared at it and wondered. Long ago, someone had planted an evergreen shrub in the tiny lawn without thinking how big it would become. Now it blocked a window and half the front door and made the house look as if it was trying to hide. Laszlo scratched his crotch and tried to make out the type of lock on the front door. A dog trotting down the middle of the road picked up a strange, exotic scent and made a detour to sniff Laszlo's legs. He hit the animal with his suitcase and sent it away, howling. Net curtains on the opposite side twitched. Laszlo scowled and moved on.

He still had a couple of tins of food left. If nothing new turned up by the time he'd eaten them, he might come back. 'Nosy old bitch!' he shouted at the net curtains. People thought they could push him around. People were dumb, and he had a gun that could make them dumber still. Permanently dumb.

'It's a tremendous honour, of course,' Christian said. 'The autograph alone must be worth thousands.'

Oster examined Hitler's signature, and handed the book back. 'No doubt about it,' he said.

'One passage puzzled me somewhat at first.' Christian showed him the lines that had been marked. 'But then I saw what the Führer was driving at. He meant Russia, didn't he? Stalin did his best to lead his people to their doom all through the twenties and thirties, and if the Russians had rebelled when we gave them the chance, in 1941, they could have overthrown the tyrant.'

'That must be it,' Oster said.

'Just think: they could have been our allies. Like Romania and Bulgaria.'

'Bloody Slavs,' Oster said. 'Let you down every time.'

He reported this conversation to Admiral Canaris. 'I rather suspect that crack on the skull he got in Madrid has scrambled his brains, sir,' he said.

'Have you read the doctor's report?' Canaris put on his spectacles, glanced at the final paragraph, and took them off. 'Not

255

a rosy outlook. Probable brain damage, various delayed effects, impairment of certain cognitive faculties, blah-blah-blah . . . Next time he lands on his head he might never get up again.'

Oster examined his right thumbnail as if it carried a message for all mankind. 'If Christian can't get his brain in gear, sir,' he said, 'do we really want to take him to Spain?'

'Have you ever seen Eldorado?' Canaris asked. Oster shook his head. 'Neither have I,' Canaris said, 'and when I meet him I want to be absolutely sure I'm talking to the right man. Christian knows him. Christian *created* him. Christian can identify him. That's all he has to do. Find him and bring him to me.'

'Of course. And Eldorado will trust Christian, too,' Oster said. 'Now why didn't I think of that?'

This time it wasn't a Sunderland flying-boat. Luis had to arrive in Lisbon like a respectable Spanish businessman, so MI5 booked him on to the scheduled BOAC service.

Right up to the moment when the car came to collect him at Knightsbridge, he worked hard on draft Eldorado reports and the outlines of ideas. After that, a kind of fatalism settled on him. He had never flown in an airliner before. The firm courtesy of the staff was soothing. There was no need to think or speak or make any decision. It was like being a child again. He was welcomed, identified, weighed, approved, smiled upon, and led into the warm womb of the aircraft. He was seated, strapped in, given a sweet to suck. They took off. Eventually the engines created a slowly surging pulse which made him think of a large animal, untroubled, at rest. While this impression was still forming, he fell asleep.

Lisbon hadn't changed, it was still the most relaxed and comfortable capital of any iron-fisted dictatorship. He took a room in an expensive hotel at the top of the Avenida da Liberdade, so that he could look down over the city, walk about it in his imagination, and save his feet. He ate grilled sardines and bananas, just to catch up on what he had been missing in wartime England. Then he told the hotel to book him a seat on the best de luxe express to Madrid next day, and he got a good night's sleep.

Madrid too looked just the same. Funny how the world had managed perfectly well without him. He took a small suite in a luxury hotel, bought a couple of silk shirts, went to the cinema. Next day he slept late, had a long hot bath, and chose some books to read on the train to Santander. He was eating lunch on this train when the future finally caught up with him and he suddenly faced the fact that he was about to meet Admiral Canaris, and he didn't know why, or what to say.

For a moment he felt sick. He put down his fork and looked out of the window. A small and barefoot boy was driving a flock of sheep across a hillside. Neither of them was in any great hurry. Lucky bastard, Luis thought.

The day after Luis left London, Julie made another prison-visit. 'If you don't water that plant it's going to die,' she said.

'Who cares?' Stephanie was sitting on the floor in a corner of the room, shoulders slumped. 'I don't care. Let it die. Everything dies sooner or later.'

'Not true. Some things live for ever.' Julie took the plant to the wash-basin and dribbled water into it. 'Truth, decency, courage, justice, that sort of stuff.' She put the plant back. 'What about beauty?' she asked. No answer. 'And what about love?' Good question, she said to herself. What about your own love? How does it compare with a potted geranium?

'I don't need love. I couldn't do anything with it if I had it,' Stephanie said. 'Why would anybody waste their love on me? Look at me. What do you see? An ugly, stupid little woman. If I died right now, like that—' she clicked her fingers ' – the world would not miss me.' She chewed a thumbnail as if it needed disciplining, and then hid her hands in her armpits. 'And I would not miss the world either.'

'Someone might miss you,' Julie said. She had planned to save this for later, when they had rebuilt their friendship, but Stephanie was a different person today: older and harder. 'Ferenc liked you. Didn't he?'

Stephanie unwrapped her hands and chewed on her other

thumbnail. Julie sat on the bed and waited. When the nail had taken its ration of gnawing, Stephanie said: 'Is that why you are here? To tell me about Ferenc?'

'Would you like to see him again?'

For the first time, a tiny flicker of happiness showed itself in Stephanie's eyes. Julie looked away. She thought: This is a really bloody shitty thing you're doing, you know, so it had better damn well work. She took some glossy ten-by-six prints from an envelope and gave them to Stephanie. 'He got washed up on the edge of the Irish Sea.' She went back and sat on the bed. After a minute she said: 'There's a close-up of the back of his head. He was shot, you can tell. Laszlo did it, didn't he?'

Stephanie sighed, and shrugged. 'Probably.'

'Never mind probably. You know damn well he did it. Laszlo killed Ferenc, Stephanie. Now he's going to kill somebody else, isn't he?'

'I don't know. I don't care.' Stephanie tore up the prints, not angrily but casually, getting rid of some old paperwork that no longer mattered. 'It's nothing to do with me.'

'Oh, horseshit! That's not true. Some poor bastard is going to get what Ferenc got, and you know who, and you sit there with your toes crossed and tell me it's got nothing to do with you?' Julie heard her voice become a rasp. She saw Stephanie flinch, and she let the rasp get harsher. 'You think I'm *dumb*, for Christ's sake? Lie to yourself all you like, Stephanie. Just don't lie to me.'

'It's the truth, it really is nothing to do with me . . .' Now her voice was higher and tighter. 'That's what I told Laszlo, I told him to leave me out of it, what he did was none of my business, I wasn't . . .' She couldn't go on. She couldn't look at Julie. It was all lies; when Laszlo had spoken to her of his secret mission she had been flattered. 'Anyway,' she said, as if that resolved everything.

'What d'you mean, "anyway"?'

Stephanie sucked her thumb. Julie took off a shoe and flung it at her. The action was vaguely familiar but she suppressed the memory. 'Don't hide behind your stupid thumb, Stephanie! You're not a baby, you're a full-grown woman with brains and you know the difference between right and wrong! You've seen

258

what Laszlo did to your pal Ferenc. Was that right or wrong?'
The thumb was still in the mouth. Julie flung the other shoe
and hit Stephanie full in the face. That brought the thumb out.
'What's Laszlo doing? You know, don't you?'

'Yes, I know!' Stephanie wiped her nose on her sleeve. 'And it
doesn't matter because it's too late, it's all over, Laszlo's done it,
that's the end.'

'Is that so?' Julie went over and picked up her shoes. 'You mean
he's killed whoever it was he got sent here to kill?' No answer. Julie
poked her in the ribs with her stockinged foot. 'If you really mean
that, then there's no secret any more, is there?' She kept poking.
'Is there?'

Finally Stephanie squirmed away. 'You don't understand! I took
an oath of loyalty and I am not a *traitor*.' She hit the word so hard
that her voice cracked.

'Of course you're not. Nobody ever said you were. Traitors are
garbage, everyone knows that. You think I'd be wasting my time
here if I thought you were a traitor?' Julie went back to the bed,
thinking That makes no sense, you're talking baloney; but the
important thing was to keep talking. 'The only reason I'm here
is I've got tremendous respect for you, Stephanie, and I know
you want to do the right thing. I know you don't want to hurt
people. Innocent people.'

'I took an oath,' she said stubbornly.

'Sure you did. You gave your word. But you didn't make
any promises to Laszlo, did you? Did Laszlo take an oath of
loyalty? How the hell could he? Laszlo's *Spanish*, for God's sake!
Isn't he?'

Stephanie gave a weak, high-pitched grunt, and almost nodded.

'Right! Damn right! The bastard's Spanish! You think he
cares about Hitler? About Germany? About *you*? Jesus Christ,
Stephanie, he knew that Ferenc was your friend and look what
he did to *him*. Blew half his brains out and tossed him in the
Irish Sea!'

Stephanie sniffed, and wiped her nose again. She picked up bits
of torn photograph and blinked at them. 'Why did he do that to
Ferenc?' she asked.

259

'Because he likes killing people. Listen, kid: you didn't take any oath of loyalty to Laszlo. The guy is not your friend. He's nobody's friend. He's scum. You'd better tell me where he's gone and why, or I'm liable to come in here tomorrow with another set of pictures just like that only worse.'

By now Stephanie couldn't make out the details of the photographs because her eyes were blurred with tears, but she went on pretending to look.

'Just say it,' Julie urged wearily. 'You want to feel lousy about yourself for the rest of your life? Just *say* it.'

'Glasgow. Laszlo went to Glasgow. He had to kill someone called Garlic. A student, a medical student from South America.' Stephanie crumpled the bits of photographs into a ball and kept squashing them as if she could reduce Ferenc's memory to nothing.

Julie took the brandy flask from her handbag and put it on the bed. She went out. Freddy Garcia was waiting. 'Now we know why Canaris has been so keen to talk to Eldorado,' he said. His face was as stiff as cardboard.

'It's not possible,' she said. 'How could Laszlo kill someone who doesn't exist?'

'In his usual way,' Freddy said. 'Very, very clumsily, I expect. Incidentally, I thought you were quite brilliant in there.'

'I don't feel quite brilliant. I feel like I've blown all my fuses.' It was true. She looked totally spent.

Sandy Hogg was fifty. He was a detective inspector in the Glasgow murder squad. Aside from the hours, which were brutal, he enjoyed his work. He would rather people didn't murder each other, just as when he had been an ordinary policeman on the beat he would have preferred drunks not to become bellicose and try to punch him; but just as he had learned how to rap the drunks on their biceps with his truncheon, thus depriving their arms of the power to punch, so he had learned how to solve murders. Usually all it called for was common sense and persistence. Hogg had long since discovered that there is nothing

260

clever about committing murder – anyone can do it: all you need is stupidity and selfishness – and there is certainly nothing glamorous about a corpse. Even when it hasn't been disfigured or mutilated, its functions usually persist after death, in particular the work of the bowel and the bladder. Corpses soon stink.

So Sandy Hogg was not impressed by murders or murderers. He put great faith in the statistic that most victims knew their killers. Unless there was evidence that pointed at a stranger, he made a list of all the friends and relatives and he questioned them, by the hour, by the day. He was good at this. Most people are bad liars and dreadful actors, especially when the howl of guilt is raging silently inside their heads. Most murders got cleared up fairly quickly. For the rest, Hogg accepted that some killers were never going to be caught: Glasgow was too big and too many people were just passing through: seamen, servicemen, deserters, derelicts. It was like a bad debt to a businessman: as long as there weren't too many it didn't bother him; after all the murderer might be in Nova Scotia or North Africa by now; might even be dead, killed in action.

Nevertheless, the death of Rosa Maria Cabezas bothered him.

There had been no reason for it. Or, at best, an absurdly inadequate reason if you accepted robbery because she couldn't have had more than a few pounds in her purse, and even in wartime you didn't shoot a woman in her own home for a couple of quid and then sleep in her bed (leaving some of your hairs to be found in her pyjamas), take a bath, open her letters, make free with the kitchen (fingerprints everywhere) and finally send a cheque to pay her gas bill, a cheque that was so badly forged the cat could have seen through it. Not to mention the fact that he must have used a silencer, or the old lady in the flat below with the bad leg and the good ears would have heard the gunfire.

A silencer. And he did the washing-up before he left. There were some funny folk in Glasgow but Sandy Hogg had never before met a murderer who stayed the night and did the dishes. When he was told that a fellow in MI5 was on the phone from London, asking about any recent death involving a South American medical student, he took the call.

261

'There was a South American lady doctor shot dead a couple of weeks since,' he said. 'Name of Cabezas. Used to be a medical student here and then she qualified. Is it her you want?'

'Venezuelan?' Freddy Garcia said.

'Bolivian.'

'Ah.' Freddy flicked through his diary. Two weeks ago. That fitted. 'May I ask what the motive was?'

'I wish I knew. Not rape, and robbery's unlikely. It was a very peculiar crime.' Hogg told him about it. 'Does any of that ring any bells with you?'

'The silencer speaks loudly. Tell me: was the ammunition foreign?'

'It was.'

'Then I think you should be looking for a man called Laszlo Martini, although he certainly won't be using that name.' He gave Hogg a description. 'Of course he may not be in Glasgow any longer . . . There's something very wrong here. We know he was looking for a person from Venezuela, specifically from Venezuela. That's all he had to go on – a medical student from Venezuela. I can see how he might think the student had become a doctor but not a *Bolivian* doctor. That must be a mistake, a blunder.'

'You're telling me that this man came to Glasgow to kill a Venezuelan student.'

'Yes.'

'Then I'd better look to see if we have any, don't you think?'

'Yes. Yes, indeed. Straight away.'

'Thank you for your help, Mr Garcia.'

Hogg telephoned the university and was transferred to Student Registration, where he got Mrs Ogilvy. 'Would you happen to know if there is anyone studying at the university who comes from Venezuela?' he asked.

'There is not,' she said promptly.

'You're absolutely sure?'

'I checked it just the other day.'

'Now why did you do that, Mrs Ogilvy?'

She suddenly remembered why, and stiffened with guilt; but it was too late, she was so deep in the mire that she might as well go on. 'They asked me,' she said wretchedly. 'What I mean is, he asked me . . . People are on the phone to us all the time, you know, it never stops ringing . . . He said the Ministry of Labour wanted—'

'Stay there,' Hogg told her. 'I'm on my way round.'

Santander survived the Civil War more or less intact. Not important enough to be a serious port, like Bilbao, and not unlucky enough to be at a crossroads, like Guernica, it missed the worst excitement, the blood and the bombs, for which the city fathers were deeply grateful. Then, in 1941, the place had the sort of fire the Luftwaffe would have been proud of starting. Half of Santander was still gutted and blackened when Admiral Canaris and his staff landed in a Heinkel of the Spanish Air Force at the airfield across the bay. The fire was one reason that they moved into a villa a couple of miles outside town.

It was backed by cool pinewoods and faced a beach that emerged newly scrubbed by the Atlantic twice a day. This was done for the benefit of the Admiral, who went riding on the beach and enjoyed the luxury of a clean track.

On their second day at Santander, Oster and Christian walked down the sand as Canaris came cantering home. They met at the water's edge. Oster handed him a piece of paper. 'Just been decoded, sir,' he said. (Canaris had brought an Abwehr radio team with him.)

It was a list of names – fourteen names. Canaris read them at a glance. 'It had to be,' he said. 'I suppose it's too much to hope that they've been shot out of hand?'

'Oh, they won't be shot for a long time yet, sir, you can be sure of that. The SD will squeeze them until the pips squeak.'

'In that case there will be more names.' Canaris nudged the horse into a walk and they strolled beside him. 'I should have seen it coming,' he said. 'I should have kept a closer eye on Domenik. Him and his damn filing cabinets. No doubt Himmler is thoroughly pleased with himself.'

'It's certainly a good time to be a long way from Berlin,' Oster said. 'Shame about Domenik's friends, but after all they are *his* friends. I mean, what Domenik got up to in his spare time is none of our business, is it?'

Canaris laughed, and shook the reins. He took off at a gallop through the shallow water. The sun made tiny rainbows in the splashes.

'He seems to be treating it very calmly,' Christian said.

'Oh, well.' Oster skipped sideways to dodge the last lunge of a dying wave. 'It's out of our hands.'

'But the Führer's bound to hear about it.'

'I wonder. Himmler has ambitions too, you know. He may not like the Admiral, but if a vacancy occurs at the top, Himmler would sooner have Canaris inside the tent pissing out than outside the tent pissing in.' Oster saw Christian suppress his distaste. 'Old Red Indian saying,' he explained. 'I got it from Domenik, so it must be true.'

All across London, air-raid sirens uncoiled their wretched noise and let it climb to a flat howl. 'Not today, Hitler,' the Director muttered, 'I'm too busy.' He was at his desk, reading a handwritten memo that Freddy Garcia had just given him. 'This is dreadful,' he said. 'I don't suppose we can stop him?'

'Too late, sir. From Lisbon onwards, we don't know how he's travelling or where he's staying.' Freddy hesitated. 'I suppose we might just conceivably grab him at Santander—'

'No, no. The place must be crawling with Abwehr by now.'

Gloomy pause. The sirens lost interest and sank, gently moaning, back into their shells.

'If we can't stop him, let's face the consequences,' the Director said, 'which are that Canaris asks a lot of ugly questions and Eldorado hasn't got any beautiful answers. Bang goes the network. Bang goes Eldorado. Literally bang, very likely.'

'That's the worst that can happen, sir. It needn't come to that if we can just get word to Eldorado about Garlic and what this blundering idiot Martini has done to him. Then maybe Eldorado can still talk his way out of it.'

264

'Get word, you say. How? Use somebody from the Madrid office?'

'Afraid not, sir. Wouldn't work.'

'He wouldn't trust them?'

'Not if he didn't know them. He's very suspicious.'

'So who does he trust? Templeton? You?'

'Templeton's in Cairo, and we know that the Abwehr knows my face from long ago. If I show myself in a little spot like Santander . . .'

'Yes, I see. So that's that, is it? Those he trusts we can't send, and those we can send he won't trust. We're snookered, or stymied, or whatever the word is. I never played tennis.'

'Of course, there is someone we could send,' Garcia said.

The Director got up and wandered over to the window. The glass was crisscrossed with anti-blast tape, and he picked at a loose end like a bored child. 'What you are about to suggest smacks of all the second-feature movies I've sat through while I was waiting for the big picture. Hero ends up in deadly danger, and who should help him out of it but his trusty girlfriend.'

'Ex-girlfriend, actually.'

'It's still a melodramatic cliché, isn't it?'

'Life is a cliché. War is a cliché. I mean to say, sir, clichés are clichés because they keep on happening, not because they're unusual.'

Away to the south, tiny black spots speckled the sky at enormous height. The Director stared and squinted, but he couldn't make out enemy aircraft among the shellbursts. 'Nuisance raid,' he said. 'A couple of Huns, a brace of bombs, and more toil for the gravedigger.' The booming of the guns at last reached them.

'There you are, then,' Garcia said. 'Another cliché.'

'What if she won't go?' the Director asked. 'Ex, you say.'

'I've been thinking about that,' Garcia said. 'How best to present our case. Why she should care enough to go anywhere near an Abwehr reunion. There are three powerful arguments which I could put to her. There's the military one: the network is a crucial weapon that could end the war more quickly and so on. Massive

265

saving of life. A huge reprieve for tens of thousands of children as yet unborn—'

'Hit that thought hard,' the Director said. 'Remember the maternal instinct. Strongest force on earth.'

'Right. Then there's the idealistic argument. This is a turning point in the crusade against Fascism.'

'Too damn right it is.'

'This is her chance not just to help win the war but to make the world a decent place to live in.'

'Life, liberty, and the pursuit of happiness,' the Director said, and cleared his throat. 'A land fit for clichés to live in.'

'And finally there's the personal angle. Eldorado's not such a bad bloke and all that. Frankly, sir, I'll have to play that one by ear.'

The Director came back to his desk. 'Why don't you try the personal angle first? Tell her you know it's all over between them. If that's true, you've reinforced her independence. Americans are very keen on independence. If it isn't, you've got a head start.'

'I'll go and see her now, sir.' Garcia turned to leave.

'There's one option we haven't discussed,' the Director said. 'Eldorado could be eliminated from the cast of characters before he comes up against Canaris.'

'Killed,' Garcia said.

'We've done it before. It has a certain logic: an Abwehr agent meets his death at the hands of who else but British Intelligence? That's how the other side would see it. And with a bit of luck we might even be able to keep the network going. Perhaps Docherty could run it.' He shrugged. 'It's an option. But don't tell the lady.'

Garcia gave the bleakest of smiles and went out. He found Julie Conroy waiting in his office. 'Are you going to Santander?' she asked him.

'I can't.'

'Then I'd better go. The silly bastard isn't going to trust anyone else, is he?'

'No.' Freddy cleared his throat. 'It really is worth the risk, you know. If we can save the network we can shorten—'

266

'Sure, sure. Save the patriotic horseshit, Freddy. Just get me on a plane.'

That process was relatively straightforward. Somebody important got bumped from the next commercial flight to Lisbon and Julie took his place. The airliner landed at dawn; an embassy official led her to a private plane, a de Havilland Rapide owned by a Portuguese millionaire whose family had sold port to England for centuries and who just happened to be flying to Madrid. Another embassy official met her at Madrid airport and drove her to the railway station. Nobody wanted to see her passport. Nobody even said very much. She was simply transported with all the speed and delicacy of urgent medical supplies or perishable flowers. By early afternoon she was sitting in the restaurant car of the Santander express, watching the Madrid suburbs slide by.

She saw the waiter's reflection in the window, waiting for her to order, and she summoned up all the Spanish she'd forgotten. What was 'hullo'? Couldn't remember. She smiled instead and he smiled back. 'I'd like a really good steak,' she said. *'Bistec, poco asado. Con una ensalada.'* Amazing how the words came back if you didn't try too hard.

Five hundred and sixteen kilometres to Santander. Say three hundred miles. According to the timetable, just under nine hours. Obviously 'express' was a relative term. But the *bistec*, when it came, was good; and without being asked he brought her a bottle of *vino tinto* that made English beer taste like a penance. Later there was *torta* and *fruta* and *queso*, and then *un poco de café*. Outside, the plains and prairies of Castile shivered under the heat. There were worse ways of travelling to Santander. The only problem was that, eventually, you arrived.

'It doesn't fit properly.' José-Carlos Coelho tapped his foot on a little pool of water on the linoleum. 'It never did fit. It's a cheap door, the rain blows in. You can see.'

'Can't you get the lock changed?' Sandy Hogg asked. 'I mean, look at it . . .'

'I agree, it's pathetic. Useless. I'm not the owner, Inspector.

I just rent the house. The owner's in the Army. Abroad, I think.'

'At least put some bolts on the door. Top and bottom. Same at the back.' They walked through the house. 'I'm not at all happy about these window-catches either,' Hogg said. 'Anyone with a thin screwdriver or a strong penknife could . . .' He shrugged.

'Let him try,' Coelho said. 'I'll help him through the window and then I'll break his neck.'

Hogg looked at him. Coelho was two inches taller and the floorboards creaked when he walked. 'No, you musn't do that, sir,' he said. 'There are legal limits in this country. Reasonable force is all you can use. I have to tell you that.'

'Of course.' Coelho smiled and nodded but Hogg could see that he wasn't really impressed.

'You do realize, don't you, sir, that this man is armed and dangerous,' Hogg said. 'I mean to say, I wouldn't be here otherwise.' He glanced into the front room. 'I don't like that big bush at the front. Hides the house too much . . . In fact to tell the truth I'd be a lot happier if you went away and lived somewhere else for a while.'

'Impossible, I'm afraid.'

They went out and Hogg got into his car. 'One of my men will check up on you from time to time,' he said. 'I don't know what more I can do. Make sure he shows his warrant-card.'

'If he doesn't,' Coelho said, 'I'll kill him.' And gave a big grin.

What it is to be twenty-two and built like a heavyweight, Hogg thought as he drove away. You're immortal.

Luis Cabrillo's train – a slightly faster express – arrived in Santander at just after four in the afternoon. He told the taxi-driver to take him to the best hotel in town. The ride took him along the Paseo Pereda, which showed him everything there was to see of the waterfront, and into a district which the driver said was El Sardinero. The best hotel in town turned out to be a wedding cake called the Wellington. Luis gave the driver money as a porter took his suitcase. 'Wellington,' he said to the driver. 'You're sure this is really the best?'

'What's wrong with it?'

'It's got a funny name, for a Spanish hotel. A wellington is an English rubber boot.'

'I could take you to the Villa Rosa Linda. That's got a nice name. Nice fleas, too.' He drove away.

The Wellington turned out to be clean and comfortable and not too full. He took a suite on the second floor, unpacked, had a bath. Room service brought him a bottle of white wine and some olives. He put on one of his new silk shirts and took a drink out on to a balcony. El Sardinero was a peninsula, so he had a fine view across the bay to old Santander. If he squinted into the setting sun he could see fishing boats painted in all the colours God created plus a few He dismissed as downright diabolical. Large, impressive waves lined up at sea and took their turn to charge the beach and make the supreme sacrifice. After Knightsbridge, the air was indecently warm. In three days Luis had consumed more than a month's ration of sunshine in war-torn England. The wine went down like a well-earned bribe. And yet he felt at a loss. There was something wrong.

He went inside, slumped in a deep easy chair that was all cane and pillows, and put his feet on a coffee table made of a slab of marble long enough to support a small corpse. Instead it supported a complimentary copy of the Santander paper. Luis flipped through it. War, war, crime, cinema, sport. Junk, all junk. Not a word about a secret, anonymous, and clandestine rendezvous between a top spymaster and his top spy. He dumped the paper.

The suite contained everything you might need and nothing you really wanted. There were mirrors. He looked at himself and decided he looked discontented. Or perhaps sceptical. Wary: was that the word? He walked away, turned back sharply and caught his reflection off-guard. Glum. That's how he looked, glum and disappointed. He rubbed his face vigorously, bullying it into brightening up. The mouth responded willingly, like the creep it was, but not the eyes. The eyes looked through him.

You found Santander, they said. Big deal. Now go out and find Canaris, because it doesn't look as if he's breaking his neck to find you, does it? He abandoned the mirror and found a small desk, its drawer full of hotel notepaper. Good time to write a letter. *Dear Julie*, he began, changed it to *My dear Julie*, changed that to *Dearest Julie* and sat for a long time thinking. Then he tore it up and burned it in an ashtray and went for a walk.

He was sitting in a clump of umbrella pine, watching seabirds do their swinging and swooping far below, when an old man with a beard approached him. 'Good to meet you again, Mr Cabrillo,' he said in English.

Luis felt his fingertips tingle with a tiny rush of blood. 'Do I know you?' he said. White shirt with short sleeves and epaulettes, blue slacks, tennis shoes: not the way a Spaniard would dress.

'Of course you do. I'm Brigadier Christian.'

'Impossible—' Luis stopped himself on the brink of saying *Christian's dead*. His brain was suddenly shrill with warning signals: he wasn't supposed to know about that, the Abwehr had never told Eldorado of Christian's death. He felt slightly sick.

'Why impossible?'

'Christian hasn't got a beard. You don't look a bit like him.'

'But I grew a beard. In any case, I recognized you at the train station. I decided to let you settle in first and then—'

'Bollocks. I've never seen you before. Mother warned me against dirty old men like you.' Luis got up and walked away. He knew by now that it really was Christian, he recognized the voice, but some instinct told him not to give in easily, to fight for a psychological advantage.

Christian followed. He tried various arguments. Luis ignored them all. 'All right, damn you,' Christian said, 'I'll shave the bloody thing off if that will make you happy.' He was furious. It was a good beard.

'Shave half,' Luis said. 'Half your face is all I need.'

The fishermen of Santander wished the cruiser *Barcelona* would go away. For nearly a week now she had been steaming slowly along the coast, always inside the three-mile limit, back and forth. It spoiled the fishing, having fifteen thousand tons of steel rumbling up and down all the time; I mean, would you like that lot overhead? Nor did the fish. It put them off their feed, they beat it to God-knew-where, the catches were lousy. The *Barcelona* was the pride of the Spanish Navy; fine, terrific, wonderful, Santander was honoured. Now let her go away and honour some other poor bastards.

To make matters worse there were two more warships prowling about: a British destroyer and an American destroyer. The day Luis Cabrillo arrived at Santander the three ships made a rendezvous in a piece of sheltered water. Launches were lowered from the *Barcelona* and they fussed about, collecting people and bringing them back to the cruiser, which retrieved its launches and departed at a modest and cautious speed so as not to spill the drinks being served at the captain's reception for his distinguished guests.

Admiral Canaris and General Oster had watched the completion of the rendezvous from the *Barcelona*'s bridge. Oster was using a borrowed pair of binoculars to study the arrivals. 'The American looks excited,' he reported, 'and he is wearing a revolver.'

'Don't they all?' Canaris said.

Oster swung the binoculars an inch or two. 'The Englishman is frowning, and he is wearing a small moustache,' he said.

'What calibre?' Canaris asked.

Oster returned the binoculars to a Spanish officer. 'You appear remarkably composed, sir,' he said. 'I mean, considering that this meeting marks the culmination of many months of difficult negotiations on your part, in the face of repeated rebuffs which would have discouraged a lesser man long ago.'

Canaris stared. 'Oster, are you trying to borrow money, or what?'

'Well, it's true, sir. This could be a turning point in the war.'

'I don't want the damn thing to turn, Hans. I want it to stop dead.' He led the way out. 'Half of it, anyway.'

The captain of the *Barcelona* met his guests as they stepped on deck. It was quite a party: the American had six men with

271

him, the Englishman four. The captain escorted them to the wardroom, where Oster was waiting at the door. The first man through it was the American. Oster made the introductions: 'Admiral Canaris, may I present General William Donovan, Head of the Office of Strategic Services of the United States of America. General Donovan, Admiral Canaris.' Donovan was big, not fat but hefty, and there was a slight twist to his lips that could have been enjoyment or perhaps appraisal. They shook hands. He stepped aside, and Oster said: 'Admiral Canaris, may I present Major-General Stewart Menzies, Head of the Secret Intelligence Service of Great Britain. General Menzies, Admiral Canaris.' Another handshake. Menzies was not tall, and he gave Canaris one brief, comprehensive glance, like a boxer meeting an opponent for the first time. Then he too stepped aside.

'I expect you two fellows know each other already,' Canaris said. It was a very small joke, but it was enough to make them all relax a little. 'There are no stewards or waiters, for obvious reasons, but I'm sure everyone can find a drink for himself.' He waved at the loaded bar. 'And later there will be food. Let me see . . . Scotch and bourbon, isn't it?' he asked Menzies and Donovan.

'Your intelligence is correct,' Menzies said, which was a slightly bigger joke and brought a chuckle from the crowd. People began to move, and talk. Canaris brought Menzies a Scotch.

'You were a cavalryman in the other war, I believe, General,' he said.

Menzies rocked his head in a yes-and-no gesture. 'I would have been, if your lot had let me,' he said. They began to talk horses.

Oster gave Donovan his bourbon, and said: 'You've seen the Italians in action, General. Abyssinia, wasn't it? 1936? Without giving away any secrets, naturally, what was your impression of that war? Cheers.' They drank.

Donovan said, 'The flies won every battle and they didn't even break sweat.' He and Oster discussed flies and other casual by-products of war.

When the first drink had gone down and the noise-level had gone up, Canaris discreetly steered Menzies and Donovan into an

272

adjacent cabin and shut the door. They sat at a table: Canaris at the head, Donovan on his left, Menzies on his right.

'Since it has never happened before and may never happen again, allow me to state the obvious and say that this is a unique occasion,' Canaris said. 'For the opposing heads of intelligence to come together to try to stop a world war is surely without precedent. To say that I am glad to meet you is a massive understatement.'

'Not the Pacific war,' Donovan said. 'That goes on until Japan's beaten. I'm here to talk about Europe.'

'If I may say so,' Menzies said to Canaris, 'you chose a funny time to put out peace feelers. Last January, Roosevelt and Churchill met at Casablanca and told the world we wouldn't accept anything less than Germany's unconditional surrender.'

'He knows that, Stewart,' Donovan said.

'I know he knows. I want to start with all the cards on the table, face-up. I don't want us to be ducking and dodging the hard questions.' Menzies still looked like a soldier: square chin, strong mouth, wide-set eyes that rarely blinked. 'So let's not pretend that Casablanca never happened.'

'It was Casablanca that changed everything for me,' Canaris said. 'Casablanca and then Hamburg.'

'You don't want to get blown to bits,' Donovan said. 'Well, I can see the force of that argument.'

'We have always had a resistance movement in Germany. Recently it has been growing stronger. I believe it could be made strong enough to take over the country.'

'Kill Hitler, you mean,' Menzies said.

'Seize, arrest, detain, eventually hand him over to the Western Allies.'

'Take Hitler out of the game,' Donovan said. 'OK, then what?'

'The war in the West comes to a halt.'

'You're talking about a ceasefire.'

'In the West, yes.'

'Get back to Hitler,' Menzies said. 'What makes you think your resistance people are up to it?'

'He's survived two attempts on his life,' Donovan pointed out.

'Let me ask you a question,' Canaris said. 'How do you think the German people will respond if their only choice is between unconditional surrender to the enemy, and following the Führer to the end, whatever that may be?'

Donovan said, 'It's not as clear-cut as that.'

'It damn well is.' Menzies turned on him. 'Don't be so bloody silly, man. I fought the German Army all through the last war, and I know that they do not give in.'

'War has changed. We have alternative strategies now.'

'I'm sure you have. Drop three thousand OSS agents into Berlin by parachute with Errol Flynn at their head. That may be your alternative strategy but it won't end the war.'

Donovan was becoming impatient. 'All I need is to get one of my boys close to Hitler.' He produced his revolver. 'Cut-and-thrust, that's what this war is about. Forget your trenches.'

'Put it away,' Menzies growled, 'before you put one of us away.'

Canaris began, 'If I might answer my own question . . .'

'Not necessary. We know the answer,' Menzies said. 'Your people will fight to the death. It's going to be a very bloody business, and you're going to lose.'

'It's the Reds you Germans are scared of, isn't it?' Donovan said. 'Well, I can understand that too.'

'Fear is only part of the formula. Fanaticism is something even stronger. Our fanaticism seems to feed upon your bombing.'

'We're not going to stop our bombing,' Donovan said sharply.

'Certainly not. You must redouble it.' The two generals stared. 'Or, if that's not possible,' Canaris said, 'you must at least *say* that you *intend* to redouble it. With that threat, that intention, as leverage, I can apply pressure to a great many influential people who wish to destroy Hitler without destroying Germany. Indeed, destroying Hitler is the only way to save Germany. But first the certainty of annihilation must be spelt out very clearly.'

'Casablanca did that.'

Canaris shook his head. 'Unconditional surrender is a plan,

a policy, an intention. Goebbels couldn't believe his luck. He knew that when the German people heard of it they would simply become even more determined *never* to surrender. You left them no room to manoeuvre and so they resolved to stand, fight, and die where they stood.'

'Well,' Menzies said, 'that's very sad, I suppose, but to use an English expression, it's their funeral.'

'It's your funeral, too,' Canaris said. 'How many young lives will you lose before you reach Berlin? One million? Two?'

'We can afford it,' Menzies said.

Canaris stood up and looked out at the glittering, blue-green Atlantic. 'I'm sure that will come as good news to Marshal Stalin. The bigger the war in the west, the easier will be his advance in the east.' He sat down. 'Perhaps his troops will be in Berlin before yours.'

Menzies and Donovan looked at each other. A ship's bell rang, dimly, in some distant quarter. Next door, in the wardroom, someone laughed, and abruptly cut his laughter short. Canaris picked up a pencil and, without actually touching the table, traced the wandering grain in the wood.

'All right,' Donovan said. 'Let's talk some more about that.'

It was the first time Brigadier Christian had grown a beard, so this was the first time he had tried to shave one off. It wasn't easy. He stood in Luis Cabrillo's bathroom, with Luis's safety razor in one hand and his shaving brush in the other, and wondered how to start. Also where.

'I don't know why you're being so bloody impossible,' he said. 'You know perfectly well who I am.'

'We live in dangerous times,' Luis said. He closed the toilet lid and sat on it. 'You might be some dreadful thug, sent to do unspeakable things to me.'

'Then I wouldn't be shaving my beard off, would I?' Christian picked a spot and rammed lather into it.

'You might be a master of disguise, for all I know.' Luis watched Christian chop away at a small patch of chin so forcefully that he cut himself. Blood dribbled down his neck. 'No, you're not a master of disguise,' Luis said. 'I can stop worrying about that.'

Christian gazed at the damage. He suddenly abandoned the razor and took out his wallet. 'Look here,' he said. 'This picture was taken only a couple of weeks after I began to grow the damn thing. You can see right through it, for God's sake.'

Luis studied the document, and sniffed. 'This identifies you as Commodore Albert Meyer.'

'Never mind the name. Look at the photograph.'

Luis did. 'Shifty,' he said. 'Eyes too close together. Not to be trusted.' He gave the document back.

Christian stood and stared at the floor as if trying to wear a hole in it. Blood gathered in his beard until a drop formed and fell. It made a miniature rose on the tiles. 'I say, do you mind?' Luis said. 'Just keep your greasy gore to yourself. This is a bathroom, not an abbatoir.'

'I should have kicked you back into the gutter, Cabrillo,' Christian muttered.

'And if you become abusive I shall have you thrown out.'

Christian went back to the mirror and tugged at his beard. 'Your razor's useless, it clogs up, I'll be here all night. Haven't you got any scissors?'

Luis gave him a pair of nail-scissors. Christian forced his blunt fingers into them and began snipping. It was going to be a long process. Luis went away and read the newspaper. Fifteen minutes later he came back. Christian had reduced much of the beard on the left-hand side of his face to stubble, lightly smeared with blood in a couple of places. His fingers hurt more than his face.

'Hold your head up,' Luis ordered. 'More to the right . . . Don't scowl, it doesn't suit you. Yes . . . In some lights I suppose there is a certain similarity. OK, you can stop now. I don't need to see the other half.' Christian said something soft and ugly in German. He fitted the nail-scissors on to his bruised fingers and went on snipping.

Luis was half-asleep on the sofa when Christian came out of the bathroom, totally clean shaven and feeling strangely pale and

276

naked. 'I hope you're satisfied,' he said. 'Now perhaps you can answer my questions.'

'I didn't come here to talk to you,' Luis said. 'Admiral Canaris sent the invitation.'

'Canaris has never met you. I'm the only person in Santander who could guarantee to identify you. You need me, Cabrillo, so watch your manners.' Christian stood over him. Luis cocked his head a fraction to see the small bits of toilet paper that marked cuts to Christian's chin and neck, and he smirked. It was an expression that had often annoyed Julie Conroy, and now it exasperated Brigadier Christian so much that he was driven to seek revenge. 'Don't you grin at me, you little crook,' he barked. 'You're in big trouble. You're in trouble right over your cheating head.'

Luis rolled on to his side, tucked up his legs and propped his head on his arm. It made him look as if he were making himself comfortable in readiness for an interesting story. 'Trouble,' he said. 'There's a word I haven't heard in a long time.' He was impressed by his own calmness. 'Are you sure you don't mean danger? I'm accustomed to being in danger.' His pulse was hammering like a jammed fire-alarm.

'I know what I mean, and so do you.' Christian knew he shouldn't be doing this; he had no authority to interrogate Eldorado; his job was simply to locate him and have him ready for Canaris. But having gone so far he couldn't back off without losing face; and anyway Eldorado was his creation, he had a right to . . . Christian couldn't define the right but he knew it existed. And he knew Eldorado had no right to be so damned off-hand, so insolent. It was time he got cut down to size. 'What about Garlic?' he said. 'How do you explain Garlic?'

Luis shrugged. 'Garlic is Garlic. What more is there to say?'

'Garlic is Garlic.' Christian found that very funny. 'You couldn't be more wrong, my foxy friend.' He laughed his way to the door. 'Tell that to Admiral Canaris when he sees you. He enjoys a good joke.' The laugh became a cackle that faded as Christian departed. There was no humour in it, and this worried Luis more than Christian's question. The man had changed since the old days in Madrid: his expression was tinged with strain, and Luis had

277

glimpsed the odd flicker of desperation too. He stretched out on the sofa, one leg hooked over the back, and worried. *Garlic is Garlic and that couldn't be more wrong . . . If Garlic wasn't Garlic, then what the hell was he?* Luis bullied his brains and got nowhere. It was all meaningless. But not to Christian. Christian had said it meant trouble.

Before dinner, each of the three heads of secret services met in private with his aides and advisers. In the case of the Abwehr it was a very small meeting. Canaris and Oster strolled on deck in the bows of the *Barcelona*. She was ambling along at four or five knots: enough to create a pleasant breeze.

'It sounds as if you made an excellent presentation, sir,' Oster said. 'I really don't see how they can refuse.'

'I do,' Canaris said.

'A million lives spared? The Allies would have to be mass murderers not to seize the chance and—'

'Please don't talk about mass murder. Our hands are not particularly clean in that respect.' Oster was silenced. 'Try and think of some other argument,' Canaris said.

'Well . . . England must be close to bankruptcy. She's spent her gold reserves, lost her overseas trade – mainly to the Americans. The sooner she stops fighting, the sooner she gets back on her feet.'

'You can play that tune backwards,' Canaris said. 'England has spent all she's got in order to win this war. She deserves her money's worth.'

'Well, she'll get it. The Allies will get all they want. We shall pull back our armies inside Germany and the Allies will liberate Europe at a stroke, without losing a man.'

'Italy, France, Belgium, Holland, Denmark, Norway.'

'Yes.'

'Poland? France and England went to war over Poland.'

'One step at a time, sir. Poland's still part of the Eastern Front.'

Canaris nodded, absently, and yawned. 'Sorry . . . I'm not

accustomed to this sea air. I wish to hell I knew what they're thinking.'

'They're thinking they could get a lot of big medals for this.'

Oster was wrong. Donovan's group was busily telling him the whole thing was a can of worms. The likeliest explanation, they said, was that it was all an Abwehr conspiracy to create mistrust and dissension between the Western Allies and Russia. Start a good strong rumour about a separate peace and Stalin would get good and mad. Anyway, what guarantee did Canaris have that the Wehrmacht would obey a Resistance Government? You might kill or capture Hitler and find German armies refusing to surrender the countries they'd fought so hard to conquer. What then? And there were war crimes. Washington had recently issued a warning that the US government would take war crimes into account when it finally settled with Germany. Was that to be quietly forgotten after a ceasefire? War criminals weren't likely to offer themselves up for trial. You'd have to go in and get them. It was a can of worms and a bag of nails. It wouldn't hold water. Donovan listened and smiled. He enjoyed a good argument.

In another part of the ship, Menzies's aides were drinking Coca-Cola (a present from Donovan's group, who had brought a couple of cases from the destroyer) and itemizing their objections to the plan.

Top of the list: Germany was playing for time. She was on the ropes, getting walloped by Russia and pounded by Allied bombers; and all her fair-weather friends were starting to backslide: Hungary and Romania were looking for ways out and Spain was hedging its bets, which explained why Franco had provided the *Barcelona* as a neutral rendezvous. So this Abwehr proposal was a device to take the pressure off and win some time. 'For what?' Menzies asked. Time to rebuild arms production, they said, time to disperse the new factories about the country where they'd be harder to hit, time to stockpile some oil, train up some pilots, but above all time to complete the secret rocket weapons that Hitler was developing on his Baltic coast.

'But Canaris tells me that Hitler will be overthrown,' Menzies said. Of course he does, they said, but if the Abwehr removes

Hitler on Monday and learns on Tuesday that they can start to devastate London whenever they like, do you seriously believe that they will feel bound by any agreement to a ceasefire? If you were a Nazi, and you could win the war in the west, or at least force an armistice, by breaking your word, what would you do?

'Canaris says that all the Nazis will be in jail,' Menzies said. The jails aren't big enough, his aides said. And another thing: if there is a ceasefire in the west, what will be the outcome in the east? Do we expect the full might of the German Army to defeat Russia? Conquer Russia? 'With any luck they'll fight each other to a standstill,' Menzies said. His aides seized upon the word *luck*. Should we base a decision with vast strategic implications upon *luck*? What if the Wehrmacht has the luck and Germany ends up the master of Russia? Would we in the west feel safe? No, we damn well would not.

'Don't forget,' Menzies countered, 'the Allies benefit immediately from a ceasefire. No more U-boats, for instance.' That's true, they agreed. But is it a coincidence that Admiral Canaris makes his offer just when the German Navy is suffering its worst U-boat losses ever? All summer we've been sinking U-boats at the rate of something like one a day. They've had to pull back their wolfpacks from our convoy routes. Just when they're losing the game they want to change the rules. Well, well, well.

'One million young lives saved,' Menzies said. 'I don't seem to have heard much about that.'

Well, let's analyse that aspect, they said. Leaving all political considerations aside, if the West agrees to a ceasefire, that leaves Russia to fight alone. Russia has been holding down two-thirds of the German Army for two years now. One thing that's kept Stalin going is the promise of a Second Front in the west. A Second Front will make Stalin's job a lot easier. Now we suddenly tell him there ain't gonna be no Second Front, Joe, and your job is gonna be a bloody sight *harder*! Uncle Joe won't like that. Uncle Joe will feel betrayed, and quite right too.

'Stalin can go to the devil,' Menzies said. 'He betrayed us in 1939. If it hadn't been for his pact with Hitler, Germany would never have invaded Poland.'

That's history, they said, but since you've raised the point, what's to stop Russia and Germany agreeing to another pact? They kissed and made up in 1939. They can do it again, if it suits them.

'We shall still have saved a million young lives,' Menzies said.

And got what for it? A strong Germany and a strong Russia; both of them far stronger now than they were when they went to war. The worst possible deal for us. We haven't won, and neither Fascism nor Communism has lost. What price a third world war, just around the corner?

The meetings broke up. Just before everyone went in to dinner, Menzies took Canaris aside for a word in private. 'You needn't pay too much attention to Donovan,' he said. 'He doesn't understand Europe; what American does? Frankly, he's a cowboy, he sees the war as a wonderful chance to have lots of exciting adventures. Did you know he has a plan to use his OSS to restore Prince Otto of Habsburg to the throne of Austria-Hungary?' Canaris did know, but he raised his eyebrows in polite amazement just the same. 'Yes, I promise you,' Menzies said. 'We have endless trouble with the OSS. If we support Tito's Communist partisans in Yugoslavia, Donovan must back Mihailovich and his royalists. For a Republican, the man seems obsessed with kings. I wouldn't be surprised if he has ambitions in that direction himself. Albania, perhaps.'

'Isn't General Donovan originally from Ireland?' Canaris asked. 'Surely even the Albanians would not wish to have an Irish king?'

'He's a millionaire Irishman,' Menzies said gloomily. 'That's the worst kind.' He turned away, and then came back. 'Not that there is a good kind, in my experience.' He left.

Donovan had seen their discussion and he drifted unhurriedly towards Canaris.

'Stewart's a great guy, isn't he?' he said. Canaris smiled his gentle sealion's smile. 'Brave,' Donovan said. 'You know he got the MC, well, they were dished out with the rations in the last show. Right? Same on your side, I expect. But the DSO . . . I mean, that's not a medal, that's an *Order*, it comes straight from the King of England. Stewart's got guts. Makes you wonder about genetics. Maybe the guy inherited a little . . . what shall we say? . . . gallantry. You know what I mean?'

'I'm afraid I don't,' said Canaris, who did.

'Oh, come on.' Donovan took half a pace back to register his amiable disbelief. 'Surely your people must have latched on to the rumour about Lady Holford? Stewart's mother? And Edward VII? Just look at that profile. I'm convinced there's a resemblance . . .' They examined Menzies's profile in silence for a moment. 'I reckon it could explain a lot,' Donovan said. 'Royal blood in his veins . . . brave as a lion . . . natural charm . . . happy on a horse . . . drinks like a king. No, make that an emperor . . . And I'll tell you the most royal quality of all: he knows he isn't clever. That's very smart. Stewart doesn't kid himself: half the time he doesn't know what's going on. So what? As long as he doesn't show it, nobody's likely to guess. And the best part is—' Donovan spread his arms in a gesture of helpless admiration '— he gets away with it!'

'Extraordinary.'

Dinner was announced. Donovan went off; and Oster, who had been watching from a distance, came over to Canaris.

'They hate each other,' Canaris said.

'Well, we knew that. And I have to say, sir, that neither man strikes me as being highly intelligent.'

'Correct. Which makes matters even more difficult.'

'Then . . .' Oster hesitated, and asked the question anyway. 'With respect, sir, why did you go to such trouble to meet them?'

'Because Menzies has Churchill's ear, just as Donovan has Roosevelt's ear. Together, those ears form a unique and invaluable collection, wouldn't you say?'

'Donovan and Menzies are just messenger-boys?'

'Not so loud,' Canaris said. 'They think they're gods, like us.'

For a drunk, he had an awful lot of pencils in the breast pocket of his jacket. That was his major problem, all those pencils. He had other minor difficulties, such as his unbuttoned flies, and his shoes which were more like slippers because of the way his feet had crushed the backs, and the three big parcels wrapped in newspaper, and the hiccups that struck as unpredictably as earth tremors; but he could have managed all that and still shuffled steadily along the street if it hadn't been for the pencils. They kept falling out.

The trouble began with the parcels. With three to carry, he had to tuck one under his arm, and when it slipped and fell he couldn't just pick it up because he still had a parcel in each hand, so he tucked one of those parcels under his left arm, bent down to pick up the fallen parcel, and all the pencils fell out of his top pocket.

Julie Conroy sat in the back of her taxi and watched him put all the parcels on the ground and start to pick up the pencils. Behind him a flickering pink neon identified the Hotel Madeira. 'This is it, huh?' she said.

'Hotel Madeira,' the driver said.

'I'm not even going to go in and ask them.'

The drunk got all his pencils safely garaged in his top pocket, and stood up. A hiccup briefly ravaged him; then he was ready to go again. He stooped to pick up his parcels and the pencils cascaded everywhere.

'Good floorshow,' Julie said. 'How many more on your list?'

'Three more. Hotel Cervantes, Hotel Goya, Villa Rosa Linda.'

'Any better than this dump?'

'Worse, I think.'

The name on his licence said Antonio Gomez. He was small and thin, and so was his moustache. He had been the only English-speaking taxi-driver at Santander station when Julie's train pulled in just after 9 p.m. A couple of porters had seemed to recognize Luis's photograph; at any rate they grinned a lot. They grinned even more when she tipped them. That's the first rule in Spain when dealing with foreigners, Julie thought: Tell them what they want to hear. Then Gomez came over and asked if he could help. 'I'm looking for this guy,' Julie said. 'Take me to the best hotel in town. He should be there.'

As they drove from the station, Gomez said: 'You speak Spanish?'

'Enough to get by.'

'Here, they speak a dialect. Catalan, it is called. Very difficult language.'

'Terrific. Just what I don't need.'

'No problem. I translate for you.'

He took her to the Hotel Marques de Salamanca. It was a rambling sprawl, and the linoleum curled round the edges of the lobby like overdone bacon. The man behind the desk had shaved, but not too recently. He didn't recognise the photograph. 'Ask him if anyone called Cabrillo has checked in,' Julie said. Gomez rattled off a question in Polish crossed with Cherokee. The man shook his head and showed them the register. No Cabrillo.

The next-best hotel was the Princesa. Its linoleum had curled up and died: Julie's shoes clicked on bare boards. The desk-man must have been clairvoyant: he shook his head and began making negative noises as soon as he saw Gomez. The photograph meant nothing to him, nor did the name. The Princesa had a distinctive atmosphere. Julie identified it on the way out. Cod. Boiled cod.

The next-next-best hotel was the Bósforo. They knew Gomez, and didn't seem too thrilled to see him, but not Luis. Julie looked around. 'They wouldn't recognize a bucket of soap and water if it walked in here,' she said.

After that they called on the Mercator, the Santa Cruz and the Escorial, before they ended up outside the Hotel Madeira. The drunk had lost his pencils for the third time, while Julie tried to think what to do next. 'He can't have vanished,' she said wearily.

'Perhaps your friend is staying with friends,' Gomez said.

At last the drunk got all his parcels and pencils under control, and he climbed the steps of the Madeira. 'That's right, chum,' Julie said, 'get your head down and sleep it off, you'll feel worse tomorrow.'

'I beg your pardon?' Gomez said.

The drunk tottered into the hotel and, as if in a revolving door,

284

was immediately flung out and went cartwheeling down the steps, all his possessions flying. A short, wide man in a collarless shirt came to the top of the steps and looked at the wreckage. When it sat up, he went back inside.

'No, I don't think that's Luis's kind of place,' Julie said. 'Are you really telling me these are the best hotels in Santander?'

'These are the *only* hotels in Santander,' Gomez said. 'Because of the big fire.'

'Let's go back to square one,' she said. He drove her to the Marques de Salamanca, and she took a room. She didn't unpack. She sat on the bed and watched a fly go round and round the ceiling light, circling, circling, endlessly circling. 'I know how you feel,' she said.

After dinner, Canaris, Menzies, and Donovan took their brandy and cigars into the adjacent cabin for another exchange of views on the Admiral's plan. This time, each man was accompanied by one top aide, who made notes of the discussion.

'War crimes,' Canaris said. 'Should we perhaps talk about that and get it out of the way?' Donovan could not suppress a grunt of surprise. 'So many of your people were talking about it at dinner,' Canaris said, 'I thought . . .'

'Sure. Go ahead.'

'Simultaneously with the ceasefire we shall close and seal the borders of Germany. Our troops will be allowed in, of course, but nobody will be allowed out. Then, as soon as possible, a special military and legal force – staffed by your people and mine – will spread out—' here Canaris made circular, outgoing gestures, vaguely Pope-like, – 'and scour and cleanse the whole country.' He turned to Menzies. 'Is that correct? Scour and cleanse?'

'Correct.' Menzies's aide was whispering in his ear. 'Good point,' Menzies said. 'We think that some of the most serious war crimes happened in Poland,' he told Canaris.

'By all means let the investigation include Poland. Please understand that our wish is to find and punish *all* war criminals.'

'And Czechoslovakia?' Donovan said. 'The sons-of-bitches who

285

executed the entire population of Lidice because your man Heydrich got bumped off? Do we go after them?'

'Certainly.'

'There have been other Lidices,' Menzies said. 'Some in Yugoslavia, many in Russia. Are you saying that our investigation of war crimes should include the Soviet Union?'

Oster said something in very rapid German. Canaris gave it a moment's thought. 'As far as military operations allow, yes,' he said.

'But the war in the east takes priority over everything,' Donovan said briskly. 'That right?'

'We see no alternative,' Canaris told him. 'Either we resist, or we allow the Russian Communist Armies to sweep over us. If they did that, they would not stop until—'

'Forget it. I'm interested in knowing exactly where your German Armies intend to call a halt in the east,' Donovan said.

'He can't answer that, Bill,' Menzies said, 'it's a military decision; a general goes as far as he has to and he doesn't stop until his men are safe. If you had any battleground experience you'd know that.'

'All the same, I'd like to hear the Admiral's answer.'

Canaris and Oster conferred in whispers. 'The best I can say is that our campaign in the east will continue until we are satisfied that the Red Armies are no longer a threat to Germany,' Canaris said.

'You want Moscow. Isn't that right?'

Canaris said nothing. There was a long pause while they all mentally redrew the map of Europe.

'You won't need your Navy to fight Russia,' Menzies observed.

'Alas, there is very little to surrender,' Canaris told him with a sad smile, 'but you are welcome to have such as there is.' Oster slid a note in front of him, and he nodded. 'As soon as the ceasefire takes effect, the Allies will of course be free to transfer ships and soldiers to the Pacific, on a very large scale.'

'That fact hadn't escaped us,' Donovan said.

'You will have calculated its effect on the Japanese war, I'm sure.

With such huge forces concentrated against her, Japan might well surrender.' Canaris glanced at the note again. 'Another million young lives saved. Perhaps two.'

'Never mind the Pacific,' Menzies said, which annoyed Donovan. 'First things first. Let's clean up Europe. What do you propose regarding your secret rocket sites at Peenemunde?'

'Not so secret any longer. Five hundred of your heavy bombers raided Peenemunde last week.'

'Glad to hear it. Do much damage?'

'Not enough. You must insist that Peenemunde be raided again and again.' Canaris leaned forward and stabbed repeatedly with a silver pencil to stress what he was saying, each stab ending so near the table that he created a sudden sense of risk. 'Germany still believes in a miracle. Hitler has a secret weapon! A death-ray will destroy the Allies. The Reich will triumph! People *believe* this! Men in important positions – men with *power* – know about Peenemunde. They tell me, "Don't worry, the Führer still has a trick up his sleeve!" You must keep hitting Peenemunde. Then they will begin to fear that the Führer's sleeve is empty and perhaps tomorrow their town will be bombed flat and suddenly now is the time to save *themselves* and save their *town* and save *Germany* and listen to what I tell them must be done.' He sat back, a little out of breath.

Nobody was in a hurry to follow that speech. The two generals waited until their aides had stopped writing, and then looked at each other. 'After you, Claude,' Menzies said.

'This is a nice little plan you've got,' Donovan said to Canaris. 'Unfortunately the weak spot is crucial. How do you grab Hitler?'

'We have made arrangements.'

'So has he, you can bet your last dollar on that. The man's a survivor. Also supreme commander of the German armed forces. He's got loyalty on his side. What have you got?'

'Treachery.' The word sounded unreal, theatrical; and yet what other word was there? 'We do not deceive ourselves,' Canaris said. 'If we fail we shall be traitors to the Third Reich. On the other hand, if we don't make this attempt we shall have betrayed the German people.'

'What are your arrangements?' Menzies asked, and when Canaris hesitated he said: 'I withdraw the question.'

'Our arrangements are best left to us. They do not involve you. But allow me to tell you how you can help. It's very straightforward. The military intelligence which is reaching the Abwehr from England is not dangerous enough. What I mean is the reports we receive are too cautious, too restrained, the threat to the Reich is still not great enough for anyone here to be seriously worried. We must be told of your RAF Bomber Command's plans to raid every German city, on the same scale as Hamburg.'

'There's a US Air Force over there, too, you know,' Donovan said sharply.

'Of course, of course. Tell us that daylight raids will be redoubled. And the Allies must have more secret weapons, things like OWCH and GABLE, only far more lethal.'

'How secret can you get?' Donovan asked the air.

'Forgive me for seeming obtuse,' Menzies said, 'but why should your High Command – who I take to be the intended audience – believe these threats?'

'They always have in the past,' Canaris said.

Menzies could make no sense of that, so he nodded.

'Why?' Donovan asked.

'Because of the source. The source is impeccable. Therefore the intelligence is treated with great respect. You know the source. You're operating it. All I ask is that you intensify the operation. Exploit your channel of communication to the utmost, and you can be sure the Abwehr will distribute the intelligence in the most profitable places.'

'I see,' Menzies said. There was a long and thoughtful silence.

Oster suggested: 'Perhaps this might be a good moment to adjourn. All of us have plenty to think about.'

'Yes indeed,' Menzies said.

The *Barcelona*'s launches carried the Allied parties back to their destroyers, and returned Canaris and Oster to Santander. They drove to the villa. Christian was waiting. 'There's something vaguely different about you,' Oster said. He ran a finger along

Christian's pale white chin. 'You've changed your eye-shadow, is that it?'

'Eldorado's arrived,' Christian said. He knew it would sound foolish, and it did. Canaris and Oster were vastly amused.

'Don't explain,' Canaris said. 'Any explanation would be an anticlimax. Just go and fetch him.'

The fly was clearly out of condition. After only seventeen hundred laps of the ceiling light, it quit and took a long rest on a curtain. 'Give up the cigarettes,' Julie advised.

She felt empty: drained of ideas, of enthusiasm, of energy. What she needed was a hot shower and a good meal. She knew that. Her room had no shower and no bath and she couldn't bring herself to go searching along the gloomy corridor. She sat on the bed, knowing that she was never going to sleep in it, knowing that she was in the wrong place, knowing that she ought to get up and go out and look for Luis, yet unable to make the first move.

It was the rank arrogance of the cockroach that got her on her feet.

She had seen plenty of cockroaches before, especially in New York when Harry had briefly rented an apartment on the Lower East Side after they got married. It was between an Irish bar and a Jewish bakery and it was steam-heated like the Brazilian jungle so the cockroaches thrived. Being in Manhattan, they acquired a lot of big-city chic. They strolled around the Conroys' apartment as if they owned it – which, in a sense, they did. Julie hadn't seen such truculence until she saw this Spanish cockroach swagger across her hotel room.

She jumped up and stamped her foot, and it turned and ambled away. Probably decided to go downstairs and buy a paper, find out what won the three-thirty at Belmont. She stamped again, and this time noticed from the corner of her eye more scuttlings and hustlings in other parts of the room. *Jesus!* she thought. What is this, a monster roach rally?

She knew from messy experience that she could never kill them all and that those too bloated to escape would die a bloody, splattering death, so she didn't even try. Instead she lay on the bed and wondered what Lois Lane would do next. A spider slightly smaller than a beer-mat was walking across the ceiling directly above her. Its feet left dirty footprints on the plaster. It had horns you could hang your hat on. Just relax, Julie told herself. Spiders never fall off ceilings. Have you ever seen a spider fall off a ceiling? Well, then. You're a grown-up woman. It's just a spider. Show it who's boss. She rolled off the bed and landed on her hands and knees, pulse pounding.

She needed something to whop the spider with. A broom would do. A Panzer division would be better. There was no broom to be found. She stood in the middle of the room, hating the spider. It stood in the middle of the ceiling, casually upside-down, and watched her, this funny American lady with the clenched teeth. That was when the couple in the next room began to fight.

It was all in Spanish, or Catalan, with a bit of Flying Ashtrays thrown in. She had a voice that was shrill and got shriller. He was gruff and grumpy, and he kept using the same words; he could have been driving cattle. What was disconcerting was the way each of them stopped in what Julie felt was the middle of a sentence; the emphasis was all wrong; the anger never found its climax. Julie listened in pity and despair and wished they would shut up or die or something. Then they began hitting each other, the woman was weeping, and Julie grabbed her purse and got out.

The desk-clerk had gone from reception. The porter who had carried her bags was in his place, reading the sports pages.

'You didn't give me a room,' she said, 'you gave me a zoo.'

He knew that word. He pointed left, down the street, and delivered a long string of bubbling Spanish advice which she broke into. 'I believe you,' she said. 'Now whatcha gonna do about my spider?' He gave a goofy smile. 'There's a spider as big as a B-17 on my ceiling and it's looking for someplace to land,' she said.

'*No comprendo.*'

'Sure, sure. That makes two of us.' She looked around for help and saw only a flyblown calendar, two months out of date. 'I need that taxi-driver,' she said. 'What's he called? The guy that . . .'

They gazed at each other, mutually baffled. Then the name came back. 'Gomez!' she said. 'Antonio Gomez.'

It had a strange and startling effect on the porter. All his amiable helpfulness vanished. He glanced up and down the lobby, and when he saw nobody he frowned hard at Julie, pursing his lips and sucking his breath: a warning in any language. Then he used his right hand to turn back the left lapel of his coat: a very deliberate gesture. Julie looked. There was nothing under the lapel. Before she could speak he had hustled away and was busy dusting the hatstand. The show was over.

She walked out of the Marques de Salamanca and turned right because it didn't lead to the zoo.

Half the streetlights were bust, and those that worked were saving their strength for winter, but that didn't discourage the population of this part of Santander: they were out in force, strolling through the gloom with their dogs and their children. There were lots of bars of the type where you could get a drink for a dime and a fight for free, several grocery stores, kids peddling newspapers, radios belting out sports commentaries, and potholes. It was like the Lower East Side without the pawn shops. Maybe Santander never had pawn shops. Maybe they all went up in the big fire. Julie weaved through the crowds, telling herself to forget about pawn shops, they didn't matter. So what mattered? Finding Luis mattered. Also finding food. She was too hungry to think straight. She passed plenty of places that were serving food but they were all too crowded, too noisy, too confusing. She wanted simple solutions to simple problems. She hurried on and gradually found herself moving out of the low-rent high-garlic quarter of Santander and into the business district. Without even trying, she saw a hotel called the Commodore that was clearly better than the Marques de Salamanca. Why hadn't Gomez brought her here? She went in and showed them the photograph. No luck. She wanted to question them about other, possibly better, hotels but the grammar was difficult and the problems of etiquette were insuperable: how do you ask a good Spanish hotel if there's a better place in town? She gave up and came out.

Her stomach wasn't speaking to her any more. It had gone on

hunger-strike: if she wouldn't feed it then it damn well wouldn't eat. She stood and watched the traffic swing by. All those cars full of smiling people who knew where they were going: she hated them. And the lights were brighter here. They showed up the foreign strangeness of the place. Julie Conroy didn't belong here and she didn't have a friend within a thousand miles, bar one, and he was lost. Loneliness stabbed, as it always does, in the back. On impulse, she turned away, seeking a corner to hide in, perhaps to cry in, and saw a priest watching her.

Well, it was a free country. If he wanted to watch her, she would watch him back. Actually it wasn't a free country, it was a Fascist dictatorship, but what the hell . . . The priest approached: tall wiry build, grey crew-cut hair, long bony nose, black suit, much worn. 'Are you in trouble?' he asked, in English; American-English. 'Can I help?'

'You could sell me a ham on rye with coleslaw.'

'Ah. Now that may be difficult, here in Santander. Would you settle for a plate of paella?' She nodded, speechless with gratitude. 'I'm on my way to dinner,' he said. 'It's a friendly little place. I'd be honoured if you'd join me.'

He was Father Desmond, a Jesuit, teaching at a nearby college. He hadn't seen America for thirty years; there was a lot he wanted to ask her about. It was a splendid meal: good food, good wine, good jokes. She had never met a priest who laughed so easily.

'Have you somewhere to stay?' he asked at the end.

'I wanted to get your advice on that. What's the best hotel around here?'

'Really the best? It's expensive.'

'Come on, Father. Where would you go if money didn't matter?'

'The Wellington. It's out at El Sardinero. That's the peninsula, you know, very pretty.' He watched her as he touched his napkin to his lips. 'You're not seriously troubled if a plate of paella and a room at the Wellington can solve all your problems,' he said. 'Or have I overlooked something?'

'No.' She had a suicidal urge to tell him everything and she quashed it fast. But it reminded her of the hotel porter. 'Yes.

Maybe. Something I don't understand. What does this mean?'
She reached across the table and turned back the left lapel of his
jacket. At once his hand came up and swept the lapel flat again.

'You'd be well advised not to do that in a place like this,' he
said. 'It could be misinterpreted.'

'As what?'

Father Desmond leaned forward. 'There are policemen everywhere in Spain,' he said softly. 'Secret police, plain-clothes police.
It's generally believed that they wear a little badge under their left
lapel, I don't know if that's true, but when someone turns back
his lapel and looks towards a man, it means that fellow's a secret
policeman, so don't trust him.'

'Ah,' Julie said. 'That explains a lot.' It explained, for a start,
why nobody had been pleased to see Gomez, and why Gomez had
steered her away from the Wellington. It also meant that Gomez
was probably working with the Abwehr, in which case the Abwehr
would know by now that she was in Santander looking for Luis.
She smiled at Father Desmond, trying not to look troubled. She
felt worse than troubled. She felt beaten.

They went Dutch on the bill. Outside, the traffic was much
thinner: it was past ten, and Santander was beginning to go home.
'You'll need a taxi to get to the Wellington,' Father Desmond said.
She nodded. 'I see one across the street,' he said, and took her
to it. A truck came to a halt for their benefit and he waved to
the driver. 'Nobody knocks down a priest in this part of Spain,'
he told her. 'It's one of the few perquisites of the job.' They
shook hands.

'Bless you,' she said.

'Hey, hey! You'll put me out of business.' He laughed and
walked away. She got into the taxi. The driver was Antonio
Gomez.

For a while neither of them spoke; they just sat and looked
at each other through the rear-view mirror. Gomez was relaxed
and expressionless, with eyes like small black pebbles. 'You're
following me around, you bum,' she said. It sounded weak. She
felt weak.

'Perhaps,' he said.

'Don't be coy with me. You're a cop, you work for the secret police.'

He examined that statement carefully. 'Perhaps,' he said.

'Yeah, you're right. Who cares?' She stretched her legs and rested her head. 'You certainly don't work for the Better Business Bureau. Why d'you take me to that dump of dumps, instead of the Wellington Hotel?'

'You did not ask—'

'Yes I did. Best hotel, I said.'

'Best, yes. Not most expensive.'

'You ever *stayed* in the Salamanca? It's bug heaven.'

'Good value for money.'

'Who runs it? Your brother-in-law?'

'Perhaps.'

'Tell him to feed the spiders more often. They've begun to eat the rats.'

He reviewed that suggestion. 'No, I think not,' he said.

'OK, let's quit horsing around. Is Señor Cabrillo at the Wellington?'

'Perhaps.'

'Let's go and see.'

Gomez drove as far as the nearest phone box, stopped, got out, made a call. When he came back, she said: 'Did you get your orders?'

'Perhaps.'

'Take my advice, never get married,' Julie said. 'She'd strangle you in your sleep before the honeymoon was over.'

He drove on. The streets became broader and soon the car was speeding past the sea on their left. Moonlight raced along the curved back of the surf as it angled towards the shore. Sometimes Julie heard the thump of a wave and smelt the tang of the Atlantic: brine laced with iodine. Very bracing. She didn't need to be braced. Her nervous system was doing a fine job all on its own. It was telling her that everything was wrong. She was trapped in this taxi. Gomez was in command and Gomez was unlikely to do what she wanted. You loused it up, she told herself, and got the angry reply: So tell me what I should have done instead. Stony silence.

The sea curved away and was hidden by trees. The road made so many turns that she gave up trying to remember the route. Suddenly and surprisingly, the sea glittered to the right. Tall white walls reflected the headlights and the taxi stopped at a pair of high wrought-iron gates, dense with metal decoration. A man came out and looked at Gomez, and went back and leaned on one half of the gates. It trundled open on rollers.

'This isn't the Wellington,' Julie said. It sounded foolish.

'Perhaps,' Gomez said. He drove in.

The moon had not yet risen when Luis was taken to the villa. The first thing that surprised him when Brigadier Christian came to fetch him was that Christian had a gun. It was perfectly obvious: he was wearing a lightweight linen jacket and the butt of the pistol was plain to see when he put his hands in his pockets and the jacket fell open. 'Goodness,' Luis said. 'Are we in danger?'

'I'm not,' Christian said. 'You might be.' And that was all he said. They drove to the villa without speaking. Luis did not enjoy the sight of the gates, or the walls. Too big, too serious. The car crunched along a gravel drive that looked as if it got raked smooth after every use and it drove into a garage big enough to play basketball in. Luis got out and met his second surprise. A man with fingers like a double-bass player searched him for weapons. Luis had been searched once or twice during the Civil War, when sentries at checkpoints patted him to see if he rattled. This man tested every part of his body except his head and his feet, and he probed the sensitive areas with professional vigour. 'Don't worry, they're all there,' Luis said. 'I counted them only this morning.' The man ignored him.

Christian led him through the villa. It was built on several levels: they went down and then up, and up again, until they reached a large semi-circular room whose straight side opened on to a dark terrace that overlooked the sea. Here was the third and final surprise. The room was empty of furniture except for a high stool, standing in the centre. The stool was spotlit. The effect was theatrical.

Christian snapped his fingers and pointed to the stool. He went on to the terrace and was lost in the darkness. Luis felt irritated. He resented being ordered about like this. He picked up the stool and flung it into the fireplace. Then he sat on the floor, under the spotlights, crosslegged, and yawned.

For three minutes nothing happened. He yawned again. The spotlights were pleasantly warm. Somewhere far away a gull made its high, querulous call. The terrace must overlook the sea.

'Tell us about Garlic,' said a voice from the terrace, not Christian's.

'No,' Luis said, flatly but politely.

'Why not?'

'Because you don't need to know.' He thought hard: Why should they be interested in Garlic? They like Garlic. They gave him a bonus. 'Simple security,' he said.

'Well, let me tell you something about Garlic. Garlic is a liar and a traitor.'

'Uh-huh.' Luis tried to locate the voice, but the terrace was too black; he could make out nothing. 'What has he lied about and whom has he betrayed?' He was quite proud of that *whom*.

'We have identified six major reports from Garlic which are contradicted by other intelligence sources – directly and completely contradicted.'

'Major reports, 'Luis said. 'Well, Garlic has certainly produced plenty of those. Convoys, troop movements, aircraft developments . . .'

'Last September.' That was Christian. 'Garlic sent some convoy sailing dates, out of the Clyde. But he wasn't even in Glasgow, was he?'

Luis braced his stomach muscles. 'Wasn't he?'

'The medical school got sent to Newcastle while three unexploded bombs were dug out of their building. Six weeks, that took. The students were away for six weeks.'

'Not Garlic.' Stout denial, always the best defence. 'Not Garlic. Garlic stayed.'

'Really?' The first voice again. 'Why?'

'Mumps. He got mumps.' There was suppressed laughter. 'I'm

glad you find it amusing,' he said stiffly. 'I can assure you that Garlic didn't. Even so, it didn't stop him working for us.'

'Was he not confined to bed?'

'There is such a thing as the telephone. And he had visitors. Garlic has a wide circle of friends.'

'But he still got the sailing dates all wrong. And the convoy numbers.'

'No, he got them right. Unfortunately . . . what with the strain of the work and the effects of his fever . . . Garlic made a simple error. He confused the dates with the numbers. He said Convoy 12 would sail on the twenty-first, instead of Convoy 21 sailing on the twelfth.' Luis shrugged. 'An agent must depend on his memory.' Luis gripped his ankles to stop his hands trembling.

'You should have reported the error,' Christian said.

'I did. Madrid didn't acknowledge.' Luis was afraid his poker-face might crack, so he looked into one of the spotlights. Now he could squint and grimace freely. 'That happens quite often,' he said.

'And then Garlic went off to the Scottish Highlands,' the first voice said, 'presumably to convalesce.'

'Is that what he said? I don't remember.'

'He said he saw a lot of Commando training.'

'Yes, that sounds familiar.'

'According to Haystack,' Christian said, 'no foreigner is permitted to travel more than thirty miles outside his place of residence without an official pass.'

'Well?' Luis raised his eyebrows and furrowed his brow like a schoolmaster trying to winkle a response from a dull class. He wrapped his arms around his legs and rested his chin on his knees and waited. Bloody Haystack, he thought, that was a damn-fool thing for Haystack to say. I'll kill the bastard.

'Well?' the first voice said.

'You surprise me,' Luis said, and immediately surprised himself by inventing a good excuse. 'Do you really expect Garlic to be frightened by that sort of regulation? He ignored it, of course. He took the risk and he came back with the intelligence.' That silenced them. 'Garlic is a brave man,' Luis said. 'You know, sometimes I think you have forgotten what courage it takes to be a good agent.' He felt himself developing an indignant pride, and shut up before he spoiled it.

Christian said, 'That's not all we found—'

'But it's enough, I think,' the first voice said. 'It's all academic anyway. Was Garlic fit and well when you left?'

'Yes.'

'Still reporting regularly and fruitfully?'

'Yes.'

'As brave and resourceful as ever, in fact?'

Luis began to feel like a rabbit dazzled by headlights: there was no way to turn. 'Yes,' he said.

'He certainly deserves a medal for resourcefulness,' the voice said evenly, 'because we had him shot dead a couple of weeks ago.'

The same man who had searched Luis now searched Julie, using the same stiff and steely fingers. 'Too late,' she told him. 'I swallowed the stolen pearls an hour ago.' But a tiny stammer almost sabotaged the word 'pearls'. The man ignored what she said and pointed to an open door.

They walked along a silent corridor, across a small courtyard with a softly bubbling fountain, and into a long room that held little more than a refectory table. There was no sound apart from their footsteps. He showed her into another, smaller room and shut the door behind him as he went out. Shut it and locked it. The lock made a soft click, no louder than a broken neck. 'Hey!' she shouted. 'What's going on? Where's Cabrillo? Gomez brought me here to meet Cabrillo!'

The walls soaked up her voice and gave back nothing.

'That's a dumb thing to say, dummy,' she said. 'You've handled this all wrong and now you're up the creek.' The outlook was fairly grim. What it all came down to was she had been dumb enough to take on the Abwehr singlehanded and she had lost. In fact when she thought of the way she had sought out defeat by trusting Gomez, disgust and despair combined to drain her of strength. She went and sat on the floor, in a corner, and waited for the world to do its worst to her.

After a while she saw herself as if from the middle of the room, and she knew what she looked like: Stephanie Schmidt. One of nature's failures. Soggy with self-pity. The image forced her to her feet. *What though the field be lost? All is not lost.* John Milton, a line from something she'd read at school. It had stuck in her memory, waiting for an emergency to drag it out. Well, this was an emergency and a half. All was not lost; there was still a slim chance she could find Luis and tell him Garlic was dead. Two seconds: that was all she needed. Get out, find Luis, tell him. Now she had a plan, or at least a purpose. Now she felt better.

The room was a bedroom. At least there was a single bed, maybe more of a couch with a yellow throw over it. She peeled back the throw and found sheets and a pillow. Might be useful. What else? No windows. Light hanging from the ceiling. Couple of upright chairs; small chest of drawers, all empty; mirror fixed to the wall; fireplace, big but empty. Strip of carpet. Wash-basin. And a piece of cord that looped around a brass shackle fixed to the wall and stretched up to the ceiling. She undid the cord from the shackle and experimented, tugging. High overhead a roller blind speedily rolled itself up and revealed the night.

Skylight.

Hope blossomed and withered. The skylight offered a possible way out except that it was impossible because it was too high, at least eleven or twelve feet above the floor.

Julie walked around the room, studying the skylight from every angle. It was always out of reach. She put one of the chairs on the chest and climbed on to the chair. Shaky and short. Far short.

Forget it. Try the fireplace.

It was one of your typical, traditional Spanish fireplaces, wide enough at the base to roast a young American but tapering fast. She crouched, eased her head and shoulders under the granite mantel and cautiously stood upright. The air smelled thick and flavoured with sulphur. She looked up. Black as a charcoal-burner's hat. She felt upwards with both hands. The chimney was wider than she was. A dusty dribble of soot tumbled on to her face.

She got out, and put one of the chairs in the fireplace. The chair was too big: she couldn't squeeze past it. She took it out, got back inside and hooked the chair forward with her foot. When she stood on it and reached up, she found that there were projecting bits of stonework to be grabbed. Even better, the chimney was narrow enough for her to press outwards with her arms and almost take her weight on her elbows. Maybe if she did the same with her feet . . .

She got down again. There was a lot of chimney to be climbed and it wasn't going to be kind to her elbows. There was bound to be a lot of soot and her eyes weren't going to like that. She was wearing a linen two-piece: skirt and short coat. Both came off. She tore a bedsheet into strips and bound them around her elbows. Tying the knots was difficult: she had to take one end in her teeth. She kicked her shoes off, got rid of her stockings, flexed her toes. There had been a boyfriend, back in her days at the University of California, who was a rockclimber. He had explained to her the technique for climbing a natural chimney in a rockface without using a rope. You pressed your feet against opposite sides, took your weight on your arms which were likewise braced and went up . . . how? Somehow. It could be done, that was the main thing. The boyfriend had done it, and he had failed archaeology and anthropology, a gut course so simpleminded that even football players sometimes passed. Climbing chimneys couldn't be too difficult.

She looked at the chimney and tried not to think of the filth and the blackness, the probably narrowing space, the possible spiders. Julie was not keen on things like cramped caves or tiny tunnels; in fact just thinking about them was like a free horror movie. Don't stand there, she told herself, do it!

She did the thing with the chair again. Standing on the chair she tied a broad strip of bedsheet over her eyes to keep the soot out. Then she reached up and fumbled until her fingers found a couple of hand-holds. She lifted herself off the chair and tried to press the soles of her feet against the opposite sides; she couldn't. Her toes scrabbled against one wall and her heel scraped the other but the damn chimney was just too wide. Also it sloped too much.

She had to let go, the chair rocked violently, panic attacked her, she ripped off the blindfold, lost her balance, banged her head, ended up straddling the chair and cursing as she waited for the pain to drain away.

More height. She needed more height.

She dragged a drawer out of the chest and placed it, upside-down, across the seat of the chair. Not enough. She laid a second drawer on top of the first. What the hell, she thought, and added the third. It made a shaky heap of wood when she dragged it after her into the chimney, but it still stood. Not for long, however. She got her feet on to the seat of the chair and tried to kneel on the top drawer but she could feel it slipping and suddenly everything overbalanced. It all went over in a clumsy crash.

Cut lip. She sucked the blood as she picked up the pieces and worked out how to do it better next time.

Turn the chair around so that its back was tight against the back of the chimney. Now at least it couldn't tip over backwards. Obvious, really.

Julie stacked the drawers on the seat. She stood on the front of the seat. She got one knee on the top drawer and levered herself up until she was standing. She tied the blindfold. The thin wood under her feet creaked, and blood trickled down her chin and fell with a faint spattering. Her hands reached up and found something to grasp. Her arms took her weight. She swung her legs and this time the soles of her feet pressed hard against the chimney walls. It worked. She felt as secure as if she were clamped in place. She began to climb.

'Shot dead, you say,' Luis said.

'Stone dead.'

Luis's mind was hunting back through what it could remember of the Garlic file, desperate for a hint of an explanation. 'That was a curious way to express your thanks,' he said softly. 'Didn't you reward Garlic with a bonus quite recently?'

'No. We asked you if Garlic deserved one.'

'For the report on OWCH, which was excellent and it certainly deserved a bonus. I was pleased to see—'

'Garlic was dead when we made the enquiry,' the voice interrupted. 'We knew he was dead. We wanted to find out whether or not *you* knew.'

Luis needed an answer, an explanation. He had nothing. His heart was jerking and jolting. His face was an old photograph, badly crumpled and flattened out. Surely the watchers on the terrace must see he was guilty as sin.

'Did you know?' That was Christian's voice. 'If you knew, why didn't you tell us?'

'Excuse me.' Luis made a little show of getting to his feet. All he had to offer was the truth. If he told them *that*, they would send for their polished jackboots and kick him to death. 'A touch of cramp,' he said, massaging his right calf. He strolled to the fireplace and picked up the stool. Stout denial would do no good. If they were wrong, he must come up with an alternative. He had about three yards, or ten seconds, to find a good, persuasive reason that they were wrong to say We knew he was dead.

He trailed the stool behind him. Then he won an extra six or seven seconds by pretending the floor was uneven, seeking out a spot where the stool didn't rock. But finally he sat on the bloody silly thing and cleared his throat.

'Why are you keeping us waiting?' That was Christian again, with a hint of gloat in his voice.

They knew he was dead, Luis thought and instantly saw the flaw in it as clearly as if it had been red-inked. 'I operate on the principle of need-to-know,' he said. 'It has helped me to survive. I have been wondering just how much you need to know. As little as possible, I hope.'

'Get on with it.'

Luis hooked his feet on the top rung of the stool and linked his hands around his knees. 'You knew he was dead,' he told the darkness, 'because you had him shot. Am I right?' He cocked his head. No answer. 'Your killer deserves a medal for marksmanship,' he said, 'because Garlic is a woman.'

He was a magician. He had whipped his silk handkerchief off

302

the birdcage and the canary was no longer there. The audience was in a slight state of shock. Their silence was total; he could hear, for the first time, the silky rustle of distant surf. By God, Luis promised himself, I'll be an actor when this war is over and I'll act the socks off all of you.

The shock wore off. There were murmurings in the night. Then the voice which was not Christian's said: 'Garlic's sex is not relevant.'

Luis allowed himself the luxury of a twisted grin, which they could see, to balance his twisted guts, which they could not. 'Garlic would not agree,' he said.

'Do you deny that Garlic is dead?'

'She was very much alive last week. No sign of bullet-holes.'

More murmurings.

'May I ask a question?' Luis slowly drew the tip of his forefinger down the left side of his jaw and up the right. 'Did your alleged assassin report that he had shot a man?'

Oster told Canaris: 'It was a coded message. Mission accomplished, that's all it said. That's all we needed.'

'Correct me if I am mistaken,' Luis said. His fingers found an earlobe and stroked it, which felt wonderfully comforting. 'You sent your agent to shoot a man, is that right? He claims to have shot Garlic, who is undoubtedly not a man. Yet your agent did not report this surprising information. Therefore it seems to me very likely that he did not shoot Garlic.'

'You *are* mistaken.' This was Christian, and from the tone of his voice he had recovered his confidence. 'We did *not* send our agent to kill a man, we sent him to kill a Venezuelan medical student at the University of Glasgow School of Medicine. He signalled success.'

'Then either he lied, or he killed the wrong Venezuelan medical student.'

Oster had been waiting for that. 'He killed *all* the Venezuelan medical students,' he said.

'That's . . . incredible.'

'In war many things are incredible,' Christian said. 'You, Cabrillo, are hard to believe. What does it matter if Garlic was

303

male, female, or hermaphrodite? We know that he, she, or it is dead. So what is your motive in trying to persuade us the opposite is true? How does your behaviour serve the Third Reich?'

'Oh dear,' Luis said. The canary was back in the birdcage and he had canary-shit over both his hands. All the optimism drained out of him and despair galloped in to fill the space.

'We need to know,' Canaris said.

With every fresh hand-hold, fresh soot fell on her arms and head and, sometimes, hit her in the face and mouth. She spat it out. The stuff felt disgusting – powdery yet greasy – but it didn't taste too bad. After all, what was it? No different from burnt toast. At least her eyes were safe. It was odd that she kept them tightly closed behind the blindfold. Enhanced the sense of feel, perhaps.

The first five or six feet were easy. Her fingers found new places to grip, her feet moved and clamped, moved and clamped. Then the chimney narrowed again. She hung by her arms and tried to reach new places to press her feet against, and she banged her right knee on the stonework. She scrabbled about and managed to secure her right toes in front and her left heel behind, but she was gasping for breath and her arms felt like old string. She rested them and wondered what her Californian boyfriend would have done now.

In fact there was no alternative. Her toes were beginning to stiffen and her heel was slippery with soot. 'Move, Julie!' she said. 'Shift your butt.' The words echoed gloomily. She put her fingers to work, and climbed.

The chimney continued to narrow. She was bumping her elbows and shoulders and her backside, and her knees were losing skin. Should have bandaged them. Too late now. The hand-holds were getting worse: smaller and tighter and further apart. What if the damn chimney poked up high in the sky? What if it came to a point? She searched with her toes, twitched her hips, gained a few more inches and both her shoulders rubbed against stone. This felt like the end of the road. It also felt like sweet fresh air:

304

something pleasant was blowing in her face. She released one hand and groped. Her hand went through a hole. She clung to the edge of it and used the other hand to drag off her blindfold. The moon glared at her.

That was the good news. The bad news was that she was looking at it through a six-inch-square gap in some sort of elaborate chimneypot.

After she'd got some strength back she hit the chimneypot as hard as she could with her fist, and hurt her fist. That chimneypot was built to withstand hurricane winds. Weary American ladies could pound it day and night and it wouldn't budge.

It was easier to climb down without the blindfold; easier, that is, until the chimney really widened and the sole of one foot, slick with soot, lost its grip. The sudden strain was too much for her overworked fingers and she fell six feet on to the chair and its stack of drawers. Pain blazed in a dozen parts of her body. She lay in the wreckage, looking up through her tears at the glimmer of moonlight high above.

'Need to know,' Luis said quietly. 'Need to know, need to know.' He did a bit more earlobe-tugging.

'Garlic is dead,' the first voice said. 'Secrecy isn't going to protect him. Or her. Is it?'

'I'm not so sure. Appearances can be deceptive.' Luis had no idea what he meant by that.

'The appearance of death? Or the appearance of Garlic?'

'I think he means the appearance of loyalty,' Christian said. 'That is certainly deceptive.'

The moon had risen; Luis could make out the soft outlines of the figures on the terrace. 'What I mean is,' he said, 'people are not always what they seem. Brigadier Christian, for instance, turns out to be Commodore Meyer. Or is it the other way round?' He spread his arms, the picture of innocent bewilderment. 'Whom should I trust?'

'Trust me,' said the first voice. 'And stop waffling.'

'You want the truth about Garlic.'

305

'Without delay.'

'But which one? That's the difficulty.'

'You mean there is a second Garlic? We killed one and you met the other last week? Fine. Tell us about the other. *All* about the other.'

'No, no, no.' Luis shook his head, like a piano teacher whose pupil keeps missing the B flat. 'There isn't *another* Garlic. There are *six* other Garlics. You shot the seventh.'

Utter silence.

'One for every day of the week,' Luis said. 'Except Sundays, thanks to you.'

This no longer had anything to do with the great big war. It wasn't even part of the contest between the Double-Cross System and the Abwehr. Now it was just Mrs Julie Conroy versus The Room. She hated its blank, silent stupidity more than the people who had shut her inside, and she was going to get out if she had to chew a hole through the wall.

The skylight looked easier.

She dragged the bed to the middle of the room and stood the chest of drawers on top of it. The chest was less than steady: the mattress did not make a solid base. There were two chairs. She stood one of them on the chest. Its legs reached to the very edge; there was nothing to spare. If it slid an inch it would fall.

That left the second chair. Fix the second chair on the first and it just might add enough height for her to stand on top and reach the skylight. Unfortunately their design made this impossible: the legs splayed out too much, they contained too many struts and braces in awkward places. 'Come on, you little bastard, *help* me,' Julie urged as she stood on the bed and struggled. The little bastard refused to help and the whole heap of furniture wobbled. 'Sweet suffering Christ!' she said, and gave up and got down before it all collapsed. Then, in a fit of fury and frustration, she seized the bed and tipped it, and spilt her gimcrack creation all over the floor with a gratifying crash.

Nobody came to investigate. Nobody cared.

The mattress had fallen off the bed.

The bed had a wooden frame that held together a strong wire mesh with the help of a lot of little springs around the edge. Its legs were very stubby and attached exactly at the corners.

Julie sat on the floor and picked bits of soot off her arms and legs while she thought. Her hair was full of the stuff; it was in her ears, up her nose . . . She was wearing her slip, which was torn and filthy; bits of her body must be cut or bruised because they made her wince when she accidentally touched them. It was all irrelevant. Only escape mattered. The bed must be six feet long. Six feet: that was more than half the height she needed.

She shoved the wreckage to one side and stood the bed on its end. Its little legs held it perfectly vertical.

By now she was getting to be an old hand at this escaping racket. She looked at the bed and worked out in her blackened, battered head that if she climbed up one side – the side with no legs – her weight would pull it over. But if she went up the side with the legs sticking out she might get to the top.

The wire mesh did her toes no favours but as long as she kept going the pain never caught up. She got to the top and sat shakily on the wooden frame. It was a hell of a view. When her feet had forgiven her, she brought them to the top and, slowly and carefully, she stood. Her head was level with the bottom of the skylight. She could see out. It was a fine, moonlit night. She could see the sky and the stars and the steel clasp on the outside of the skylight and the padlock through the clasp.

She went back down, got a shoe, climbed up with it in her teeth, and attacked the glass with the heel. After a couple of minutes her arm was exhausted and the glass had lost a very small chip. It was too bad to be true. The moon had risen in the sky. She looked hard at the place she had chipped and the moonlight showed her a fine filament of wires criss-crossing the glass. No way out here. She was so weary that on her way down she lost her balance and fell, but she landed on the mattress, so it scarcely hurt at all.

'Seven sub-agents,' Christian said, his voice stretched with disbelief. 'All called Garlic.'

'Well, you didn't really think I got all that intelligence out of one person, did you?' Luis said. 'Good gracious, no. Garlic One was my first sub-agent in Glasgow, and jolly good she was too, but when she had to sit her medical exams she introduced me to Garlic Two.'

'And what does Garlic Two do?'

'Works for the railways. Manager. Arranges troop trains. Key man.'

'Garlic Three?'

'Tugboat captain. I recruited him. Daughter got made pregnant by an American soldier. Very bitter.'

'Garlic Four?'

'Pest control officer, gets him into all sorts of offices. Five is a woman typist for the Army, Six is a crook. Steals documents. God knows which Garlic your gangster has shot. I only hope it's not Garlic Five, she's just got promotion, works for a lieutenant-general now, if you've shot her he'll be heartbroken, they were starting to be really close friends if you know what I mean—'

'We killed Garlic One,' the first voice said. 'We killed the Venezuelan medical student.'

Luis yawned, and rubbed his eyes. 'Do it more often,' he said. 'She looks very well on it. I told you she'd moved to Cambridge, didn't I? Works for Churchill's heart specialist now. Clever woman. Should go far. No, I bet you shot Garlic Five, and she's irreplaceable.'

'You're lying,' Christian said. 'Give me one reason why our agent might have shot Garlic Five instead of Garlic One.'

'Garlic Five moved into Garlic One's flat when Garlic One went to Cambridge,' Luis said. 'And now there's blood all over the carpet. Sloppy. Very sloppy.' Watch it! he warned himself. You're getting so you couldn't tell the truth if you tried.

Forget the chimney. Forget the skylight. The room had no windows, no ventilation grills, no secret trapdoors under the carpet. It was a stone box with a door, and the door was solid mahogany with heavy brass fittings. Julie Conroy had hit it with the chair and she had bust the chair. Forget the door.

She lay on the mattress, staring at the light fitting and hunting for the solution that must exist; otherwise she was beaten. Not the chimney; not the skylight. It *must* be the door, which was locked from the outside and couldn't be broken down from the inside. Given those facts, escape was obviously impossible.

So get out and find some new facts, she told herself.

Well, there was the mirror. Smash that and you've got a cutting edge. Anything you can think of that's worth cutting? No.

So.

The bed had lots of metal bits – springs, wire mesh. Rip a bit off, straighten it, pick the lock. She rolled on to her side and looked at the lock. Massive. Poke a wire in there and the lock would eat it for breakfast and belch in your face.

Wash-basin?

Turn on the taps, flood the room, sooner or later someone would see water pouring out under the door and do something.

Like what?

Like open the door and reproach her with a straight left to the chops.

Which were already cut. Her lower lip felt as big as a banana.

Light fitting?

There was electricity waiting up there. An invaluable aid to modern living, so the power companies said. No light bulb should be without it. Julie stared at the light bulb until its glare was imprinted on the backs of her eyeballs.

She looked at the door and saw it through a kaleidoscope of red and purple and green. She looked back at the light. How far? Twelve, thirteen feet?

The springs that attached the wire mesh to the frame of the bed would not come off. She damaged a couple of fingernails wrestling with them before she quit and bashed the frame with the chest of drawers instead. This took all her strength, hoisting

309

the chest and then bringing it crashing down so that an edge hit the frame midway between its legs. After three blows it cracked. The effort left her slightly giddy. She sat on the floor, sucking in deep lungfuls of air until she felt strong enough to stand up and try again. She managed one more attack with the chest; then her arms refused. She put her shoes on and jumped on the bedframe repeatedly until it snapped.

That took the tension off the springs, and off the wire mesh. She unclipped all the springs down two sides. The wires zigzagged, interlocking to make a wide diamond pattern. It took five finger-bruising minutes to extract three bed-lengths of wire: fifteen or sixteen feet in all. She hooked them together and wrapped one end round the brass door knob. She took the other end, stood on the chest, and wound it around the flex above the light bulb, leaving a foot of wire to spare.

She got dressed, thinking hard about all the high-school physics she had forgotten. She took a thin strip of bedsheet, soaked it in water, put it in her pocket, dried her hands. She turned off the light. The moonlight let her see enough to get back on the chest and, with her handkerchief, remove the light bulb. She made a hook out of the end of the wire and shoved it deep inside the socket. Then she stuffed the wet bit of bedsheet all around it and rammed the cloth home. Water dribbled down her thumb.

She eased herself to the floor. She put the plug in the wash-basin and turned the taps full on. She found the surviving chair and carried it to the light switch, taking care to avoid the loop of wire. She stood on the chair. After a while, water began to lap over the wash-basin and spread across the floor. She put her finger on the switch.

'All right,' said the first voice, 'let's put Garlic aside for the moment.'

'I thought you'd already done that,' Luis remarked.

'You arrived in Santander alone. Is that correct?'

'Yes.'

'But not for long. One of your colleagues is here.'

310

'No. I mean, not as far as I know.'

'I assure you it's true. I hoped you would have an explanation.'

Luis was silent. Anything he said might be dangerous. He scratched his nose; that was safe. This interrogation was turning into an ordeal; he was beginning to feel mentally bruised.

'I'm surprised you don't want to know the name of this visitor,' the first voice said.

'I'm surprised you haven't told me.'

'Mrs Conroy,' Christian said.

'Good God Almighty.' Luis didn't need to fake his astonishment. 'What on earth does she want here?'

'You.'

Luis put his head in his hands. Dismay struck hard. He felt like a juggler struggling with three oranges who suddenly finds a flaming torch added to his act.

'She is very anxious to meet you,' Christian said. 'Why is that?'

Oh Christ, Luis thought, something must have gone horribly wrong, something really crucial . . . He raised his head but kept his fingers cupped over the bottom half of his face. 'It's an infatuation,' he said, making his voice as flat as a plank. 'The silly woman thinks she's in love with me, I can't get rid of her. Everywhere I go she follows. She's rich, she's infatuated and she won't listen. It's like a disease.'

'She's also an American.'

'But she suspects nothing. I keep her at arm's length. Further, if possible.'

'Tell us more,' the first voice said. 'Tell us everything.'

The water found the gap under the door remarkably quickly. Julie Conroy couldn't see it going through but she could hear it seethe and bubble at the corners. The sound was very different from the steady splatter of the overflowing basin. Moonlight shimmered on the thin flood rippling across the middle of the room. The water had no way out except under the door, and soon it was more than the narrow gap could take. The seething and the bubbling were drowned.

After that a surprisingly long time passed and nobody outside noticed anything. Julie worried, and then remembered: the room she was in was at the end of a bigger room, the one with a refectory table. So the water would have to escape from *that* room too, before it did her any good.

Someone cried out. Julie took a deep breath, and flexed her fingers. A distant door banged, light drew a thin white line around her door, footsteps came splashing towards her, someone pounded on the door so violently that she flinched. He shouted, furiously, in German. Her mouth was bone-dry; she swallowed, uncomfortably. A key rattled, the door opened and the instant she saw the hand on the doorknob she pressed the switch. A bang like a small handgun seemed to shake the air. The door swung open in a rush of spray, dragging with it a man bent like a bow, eyes gaping, fist welded to the brass knob, mouth screaming. By then Julie was out and running.

Luis Cabrillo spoke for the best part of ten minutes about the sufferings of unrequited love as experienced by the loved one. He spoke with a mounting eloquence and, in the end, a passion that surprised him. 'There is no escape,' he said. 'One's life becomes dominated by the woman. The harder you kick her the more she adores you.' He had second thoughts about 'adores' but it was too late, he had said it. 'It's more like hero-worship than love,' he said. 'Ten seconds in my presence is enough to excite her for a week. That's what drives her to follow me everywhere. It's a disease, an addiction, and I'm the victim too.' They heard all this in silence. 'She has no scruples,' he said bleakly. 'I don't know how many times she's bribed her way into my hotel bedroom. I'm her obsession.' He took them on a pilgrimage of the hotels of Great Britain where Mrs Conroy had pursued him, cornered him, offered him eternal devotion combined with immediate erotic gratifications of such variety and intensity that he would have had no strength left to serve the Abwehr . . . Luis took them from the

Savoy in London to the Waverley in Edinburgh, the Rougemont in Exeter, the University Arms in Cambridge, and a dozen others before ending up back in London at the Dorchester. He had never seen them but he knew them well: they figured on the expenses charged by his network when they travelled on Abwehr business. 'I can't go to the police,' he said at the end. 'For obvious reasons.'

There was no response from the gloom of the terrace but he sensed that his remarks had gone down rather well. He slumped on his stool and tried to remember what it was like to enjoy erotic exhaustion in the arms of Julie Conroy. It had never slowed down his Eldorado work, he knew that. Quite the reverse. He missed that. He missed her. He wished very much that she *would* chase him everywhere, or even somewhere. Anywhere. Thus his mind was wandering unhappily through no man's land when she flung open the door and staggered in, soot-blackened, wild-eyed, bloody-faced, her clothes ruined. 'Holy shit,' Luis said. 'Not you again.'

It was simultaneously the best and the worst thing to say. She went over to him and punched him in the face as hard as she could. His feet were hooked inside the stool. He and it fell like a broken drawbridge.

'Damn, damn,' she said, hiding her raging knuckles in her armpits, 'I didn't mean to do that. I'm sorry.'

The lights went up on the terrace. 'True love,' Canaris told Oster. 'It's what makes the world go flat.'

The beach was moonstruck. Luis had found the word in a book of English poetry long ago and saved it up for a suitable occasion. The sand was crisp as sugar; the surf was silver-plated. The moonlight was so rich and pure and tranquil that it seemed to leave a silent tingle in the air. 'How many would you have hanged, then?' Luis asked mildly.

'I would have hanged one in three, as a minimum,' Canaris said. 'In Germany we hanged at least half the Allied agents we caught.'

'And the other half?'

'We turned them, of course. They work for us.'

After Luis had disentangled his legs from the stool and got
to his feet, Canaris had come forward and introduced himself.
In a quietly courteous and considerate manner he had offered
Julie the use of a bathroom, the help of a doctor, and a change
of clothes. She was bewildered by this civility and she turned to
Luis. Luis, gingerly testing his jaw, said: 'Take it. You look like
the sole survivor of a ten-alarm fire.'

Julie began to speak but then changed her mind. 'Perhaps,' she
said. Oster escorted her from the room.

'Well, now,' Canaris said, and smiled benevolently. 'Are you
hungry? There are sandwiches and drinks . . .' He indicated the
terrace.

Luis drank a fast glass of red wine and chewed a ham sandwich
while Canaris admired the stars and Christian frowned and
fidgeted.

'Let us stroll on the beach, you and I,' Canaris said. Luis took
two more sandwiches and followed him. Christian watched them
go. He couldn't understand why this was happening. It baffled
and angered him. Cabrillo had obviously lied, and lied again: first
about Garlic, then about Mrs Conroy. Clearly he was a traitor to
the Abwehr; he should be taken out and shot; they should both
be shot, the woman was a menace . . . It hurt to think. Christian
had a permanent headache nowadays. At times his brain throbbed
so violently that he wanted to kill someone; then the dead man
would have his headache. That made no sense, but nothing made
sense any more, did it? When everyone was crazy nobody was
crazy. It couldn't be allowed to continue. Christian scowled at the
diminishing figures strolling down the beach.

Canaris had opened the conversation by congratulating Luis
on the calibre of his intelligence reports; Eldorado, he said, was
well named. Luis munched his sandwich and made some vague
remarks about the contribution of teamwork. Canaris agreed. Of
course, he said, there were teams and teams. Lots of teams. Some
good, some less good. But all of them reporting regularly from
England. Dozens and dozens and dozens of Abwehr agents. Of
all the spies sent by the Abwehr to England, Canaris said, only

314

about ten per cent were caught and hanged. Now that was a great mistake. It didn't ring true. If he (Canaris) had been running MI5, the figure would have been much higher.

That was the point at which Luis asked him how many he would have hanged, and Canaris said one in three; as compared with Germany where they hanged half and turned half. 'That's realistic, isn't it?' Canaris said. 'After all, espionage is a precarious and hazardous trade; otherwise it wouldn't be so well paid. The suggestion that nine out of ten Abwehr agents escape capture is absurd. Quite absurd.'

'Some do,' Luis said.

'And it seems they never make mistakes! They're always taking terrible chances, hanging about secret military sites, asking peculiar questions, but they hardly ever get arrested, do they? If I were running MI5 I'd have a lot more arrests.'

'You wouldn't like it if your best agents spent half their time in jail.'

'And another thing: none of our agents in Britain gets married. Not even a girlfriend or boyfriend.'

'Think of the risk,' Luis said.

'Think of Mrs Conroy.' When Luis did not reply the Admiral said: 'Think of life *without* Mrs Conroy.'

Dull, Luis thought, dull duller dullest. 'Just to satisfy my curiosity,' he said, 'did you bring me all the way to Santander to argue about whether or not Garlic is a woman and to prove how much more of a woman Mrs Conroy is?'

'I don't care about Garlic. That was a small crisis, long since overtaken by events. I brought you here because I want you to tell your masters in British Intelligence to increase the pressure. Pile on the bad news. Create more armies! More armoured divisions! Discover new airfields crowded with super-bombers! Why aren't the Allies developing monster tanks as fast as motor-cars? New fighter aircraft that make our Focke-Wulf 190 look like an old tin can? Tell them to help me strike terror into the hearts of enough German people and we can stop this stupid, pointless war *now*.'

'You can?' Luis suddenly woke up. 'How?'

'The details need not concern you.'

Luis silently concerned himself with the details. 'Adolf Hitler would have to go,' he said.

'That is self-evident.'

'Crikey.' Freddy Garcia's word slipped out before he knew it. 'It's a coup. You want to lead a coup.'

'There's still time to save the German people.'

'Is there really?' Luis finished his second sandwich and brushed crumbs from his lips. 'I rather think people in England have made up their minds about that.'

'Everybody's real enemy is Russia. While we in the West fight each other, Stalin wins. He wants world dominance. Churchill and Roosevelt must know that.'

They reached the end of the beach and turned back. Luis saw his own footprints stamped blackly in the wet sand, and he trod carefully in them, fitting his feet to the marks.

'That's no good,' Canaris said. 'You can't delete the past.'

Luis laughed. 'How can you be so sure that the entire Eldorado Network has been turned by British Intelligence? It's preposterous. You might as well say that it doesn't exist, that I sit in an office in London and invent everything.'

'My dear Cabrillo, I don't give a damn if you sit in Stratford-on-Avon and write your reports in blank verse with a quill pen. What matters is that the OKW trusts you. They don't trust *me*. For a start I'm an admiral, and this is a land war. What can I, a sailor, tell those generals and field-marshals? But if it comes with *Source: Eldorado* stamped on the cover, they pay attention. They stand up and salute. Eldorado is our masterspy lighting Churchill's cigar, pushing Roosevelt's wheelchair, answering the telephone for Eisenhower. They like that. It gives them a chance to cheat, you see. Generals hate to fight fair, Cabrillo. Hate it.'

'I can understand that,' Luis said. 'When I was a boy I used to trip my opponents on the football field. They were frightfully cross.'

'Did you win?'

'I got sent off and went to the cinema. Was that winning?'

Canaris put an arm around his shoulders. 'Hitler frightens the German people,' he said, 'so you and I must do more than frighten

316

them. We must utterly terrify them. Go home and tell your masters in British Intelligence.'

'Naturally, I shall do my best,' Luis said, 'but I really haven't the slightest idea what you're talking about.'

'Of course not.' Canaris squeezed his shoulder. 'It's a mystery to me too.'

Oster left Julie being sponged down and patched up by the Admiral's doctor and his nurse, who had found a Spanish maid's uniform for her to change into. He went back to the terrace. He was very tired; it was past 2 a.m. and it had been a hard day; but as long as Canaris was awake, so was Oster.

He got himself an iced lager and some spicy Spanish sausage, and slumped in a wicker chair.

Christian was at the other end of the terrace, watching the walkers on the beach. He did not seem at all tired. His shoulders were square. His hands were behind his back, the right fist grasping the left wrist as if it were a prisoner.

Oster had almost finished his lager when Christian walked over to him.

'Domenik told me something that I didn't understand, back in Berlin,' he said. 'Now I think I do.'

'Forget it,' Oster said, 'before you regret it.'

'It was on the day of your champagne party, when I collapsed on the balcony. I don't remember exactly what Domenik said, not word for word, but it came down to one man being willing to kill another *and* himself, in order to save the nation. It's patriotic sacrifice, isn't it? That's what Domenik was offering me, and all the more gallant and patriotic and triumphal because nobody will know, except me, and I'll be dead.'

'I see. You are proposing to kill our great and glorious leader, is that it?'

'I have no choice. The man has betrayed the nation.'

'Let's get this absolutely straight,' Oster said. 'You plan to save the nation by killing whom, exactly?'

'That traitor on the beach. The traitor who is using Eldorado to make deals with British Intelligence. God, I've been extremely stupid.'

Oster began: 'What evidence—'

'I used to think Domenik was a traitor! How unbelievably stupid . . . All the time, Domenik was trying to show me that the leader I must kill is here, in front of me! It's destiny. Mine, his, yours.'

'I see.' Oster cleared his throat. 'And who is going to kill you?'

'Oh, you are. You have no choice either.'

Oster's eyes flared wide, but no other part of him moved. He remained slouched on the wicker chair, the lager glass propped between the extended fingers of each hand.

'We all have to die,' Christian said.

'You say you got all this from Stefan Domenik?'

'The big thing is finding something worth dying for.'

'And you've found it?'

'It was in front of my nose all the time.' Christian went to the front of the terrace, looked at the beach, and came back. 'There will be a cover-up, of course. You'll do that, won't you? Heart attack or something. I don't care. I'm technically dead anyway, so you won't have any difficulty getting rid of me, will you? I take it you've got a gun?'

'No.'

'Use mine. It's fully loaded.' Christian took the pistol from its shoulder holster and pulled out the clip of ammunition. 'See?' He shoved the clip home. 'Plenty left for you.'

Oster sighed. He drank the last mouthful of lager and put the glass on the floor. 'Don't you think you're taking Domenik too seriously?' he asked.

Christian shook his head. 'How can anyone take patriotic self-sacrifice too seriously?' he said.

Oster stood up. 'Have a drink,' he said. 'Have a glass of wine, for God's sake. Relax.' He showed Christian the bottle. 'Have you tried this?'

'Here they come now,' Christian said. He turned to face the beach. Oster took a good look at the back of Christian's head. The scar made by Adler formed a white zigzag in the close-cropped hair.

The Admiral and his agent came strolling up the beach, chatting easily of this and that. 'I never thought I'd miss eggs as much as I do,' Luis said. 'The ration is one a month. One develops a craving.'

'With me it's coffee,' Canaris said. 'Not so much the taste as the smell. Ersatz coffee is like sawdust.'

'That's a very unpatriotic remark.'

'No, it's very *good* sawdust. No complaints about that.'

'D'you get oranges? I suppose not. Neither do we.'

'The place to go is Brussels. I don't know how, but the Belgians can lay their hands on anything.'

'Swiss chocolate?'

'Crates of it.'

They climbed the steps to the terrace. 'Hullo!' Canaris said. Brigadier Christian lay sprawled on the floor, face-down, as if he had just been unloaded from the back of a truck. The stink of wine soaked the air. 'Be careful where you walk,' Oster said, 'there's broken glass everywhere.'

Canaris circled the body from a distance. 'He looks dead,' he said.

'He is dead,' Oster said.

Canaris leaned forward. There was a lot of blood mixed in with the wine. 'That head of his is a nasty mess,' he said. The label from the wine bottle was on a fragment of glass attached to the scalp. 'Rioja 1940,' Canaris read aloud. 'A decent year.'

'What happened?' Luis asked. Nobody else seemed interested but he was.

'Poor Christian was opening the bottle when he had another of his blackouts. Landed on his head.' Oster shrugged. 'Must have been the last straw. He's fallen on that head quite a lot lately.'

Luis nudged the broken-off neck of the bottle with his foot. The cork was in place, and there was no sign of a corkscrew. 'Sudden death, was it?' he said. 'No warning?'

'Very little,' Oster said. 'Came as a surprise to me, I can tell you.'

Spain under Franco was in some respects like England under Cromwell. Both men were generals. Both believed in the virtues of discipline and in the discipline of virtue. Both believed that they had won a civil war because God was on their side, and Franco let it be known that the least Spain could do in appreciation of this was to live by God's holy standards in future. That meant no sexual hanky-panky.

Thus the desk clerk at the Wellington was never in doubt when Luis Cabrillo turned up at three in the morning in the company of a slightly damaged chambermaid who had no luggage. He gave Luis his key and he gave Julie the key to a different room, on a different floor, in a different wing.

They had not talked in the car that had brought them from the villa: too risky, with the driver listening. Now Julie spun the room-key on her finger and laughed. It was a laughable situation, to come all this way and be separated by hotel propriety. 'See you at breakfast,' she said.

In fact by the time Luis got down for breakfast she was in Santander, shopping for clothes. He was on his third coffee when she came through the hotel dining-room in a lime-green outfit with a lemon-yellow blouse and a cherry-red beret.

'You look like a fruit salad,' he said. 'I think I preferred you as a maid.'

'Your bags are in the taxi, I've paid the bills, and there's an express to Madrid in half an hour.' Her lip was still swollen and it gave her a slight lisp. 'Come on, let's go.'

'Jesus!' he said. 'You American women can be so *bossy*.'

'Life is too short to horse around, Luis. *Mañana* never comes.'

When they got into the taxi she said: 'This is Antonio Gomez. He's a secret policeman, aren't you, Tony?'

'Perhaps.'

'Friend of yours?' Luis asked.

'Very old friend. Aren't we very old friends, Tony?'

320

'Perhaps.

'That's all he ever says,' she explained. 'He never says anything else.'

'What else is there to say?' Luis asked.

'Nevertheless,' she suggested. 'In so far as. Notwithstanding. You like those words, Tony?'

'Perhaps.'

'I see what you mean,' Luis said. 'He doesn't sparkle.'

The rest of the journey was silent; and it wasn't until they were on the train, in the restaurant car, each with a drink and a view of the passing wheatfields, that she said: 'By the way . . . Garlic's dead.'

'Yes, I know. It doesn't matter. They don't care.'

'Oh. Well, that's all right, then.' She fingered her lip. 'So I bust a gut to find you, I got captured, I bust several other guts to escape, and it was all for nothing. Is that right?'

'Um . . .' The train was making two pieces of cutlery rattle. Luis separated them. 'Well . . . Yes, I suppose it is.'

'Fine,' she said. 'Terrific. Next time I'll stay home and do something really useful, like clean the typewriter.'

'Ah, but you were brilliant last night. Canaris said he thought you were sensational. Fabulous.'

'Did he really?' she asked. Luis nodded. 'You're lying,' she said.

'Of course I'm lying. Lying is what I do best.' He took her right hand, very cautiously, and examined the bruises. 'Who told you about Garlic?'

'Stephanie Schmidt.' Julie gave him the story.

'Glasgow,' Luis said. 'Glasgow . . . They really sent somebody all the way to Glasgow. And he actually shot this poor South American lady doctor dead? Because he thought she was Garlic?'

'Don't blame yourself. She wasn't even from Venezuela.' Julie linked little fingers with him. 'Sounds like a Noel Coward song, doesn't it? "She wasn't even from Venezuela . . ." Don't squeeze, please. It hurts.'

'Tell me all about last night,' Luis said. 'And I'll tell you all about poor old Christian.'

321

Laszlo Martini became so desperate that he took work. He was deeply ashamed. It had never happened before, and now only the acid nag of hunger drove him to it. He got a job in a fish and chip shop, preparing the potatoes. First he knocked off the worst of the mud, then he filled a machine which he hand-cranked until it had tumbled and scraped the potatoes more or less white. Then he picked out the biggest eyes with the point of a knife. Then, one by one, he fed the potatoes into the chipping machine, which he worked by pulling down a lever time and time and time again until his right arm twitched and flexed long after the last potato had dropped in strips into the bucket. Then it was time to start again, knocking off the mud.

The pay was insulting but he could eat all the fish and chips he wanted, and the owners let him sleep on a pile of potato sacks at the back of the shop. He told them he was a seaman who had missed his boat and was waiting for it to return. They didn't care. As long as he chipped half a ton of spuds a day nothing else mattered. His beard was quite thick by now, so he was confident that no policeman would recognize him from the descriptions given by the people he had robbed.

With a full belly again, he began to think more clearly. There were hours and hours available for thought, while his hands and arms did the work of a machine. Always his thoughts drew him to the same conclusion. He had killed the wrong person. Dr Rosa Maria What's-her-name could not have been Garlic. That explained the Abwehr's silence. They had not responded to his signals in the *Glasgow Herald* because . . . Well, why hadn't they?

It had taken Laszlo a long time to work that out. He had been sitting on an upturned bucket, taking out eyes, when the truth, the enormously obvious truth, burst upon him so suddenly that he pronged his hand. The next few dozen potatoes were tinged pink. Laszlo was too absorbed in his revelation to notice. The Abwehr had not responded because *they knew that Garlic was still alive.* How did they know? *Because they were still getting reports from Garlic!* It was dazzlingly, blindingly obvious. By its silence, the Abwehr was sending Laszlo the loudest possible signal.

Next day he quit his job. He had had it for nearly a week. He hated the sight and smell and feel of potatoes. He was operating the chipping machine when two drunken sailors standing in the queue began making fun of him. They made obscene jokes which he didn't completely understand but he knew enough to be insulted. Nobody in the shop told the sailors to be quiet. Laszlo quit on the spot. He took his pay, he took his suitcase with his gun locked inside it, and he walked away.

He kept walking until he reached Buccleuch Avenue. By then it was about four in the afternoon. He walked past 22A and gave it only the briefest glance. Nothing had changed. He walked to the end of the road, turned, walked back. Now that he had money he knew exactly what to do. He had to kill the other Garlic, the *real* Garlic, this one, and signal Oster via the *Herald* that Happy Days Are Here Again, Just You Wait And See. Or something like that.

He had stopped at a public lavatory and taken from his suitcase the cavernous shoulder-holster and the pistol with the silencer like a beer bottle. He felt a different man with that comforting weight under his left armpit. He strolled up to the front door of 22A but ignored it and followed the path around the side of the building, glancing in at windows and also secretly watching the next-door houses for signs of life. Nothing showed, either way. He reached the back door and it was open. Only an inch, but so what? Open is open. Laszlo touched it and it swung wide. Creaked wide.

Now that scared him. It was a weekday afternoon, he expected what's-his-name . . . Coelho . . . to be at work or college or somewhere.

Unless he'd gone out and forgotten to shut the back door.

Laszlo took a pace inside so that he could bring out his pistol without the neighbours seeing it.

The house was silent: no ticking clocks, no dripping taps, no simmering saucepans. It *felt* empty. Laszlo was convinced it was empty. He walked in.

The first room was the kitchen. Half a loaf on the bread board, a sink full of dirty cups and plates, spent matches scattered on and round the gas stove. Smell of kippers.

Opposite the kitchen was a big bedroom-cum-study. Books and papers everywhere, desk, wardrobe, single bed by the window. The bed had been made and somebody had been lying on it. The imprint of a body was clear. Laszlo put his hand on the bed. It was still warm. That shocked him far more than the open back door.

He searched the rest of the house in a rush of fright. Guest bedroom: only a camp-bed and a gaping cabin-trunk. Bathroom: empty. That left the front room. He kicked the door open and found no enemies to shoot. He looked behind the sofa and the curtains. Nothing. Nobody. Nil.

Laszlo walked slowly back to the passageway that linked the rooms and he thought hard. He was very unhappy; something here was extremely wrong. Those bedclothes were warm. How long did bedclothes stay warm after someone got off the bed? Ten minutes? Two minutes? It made a difference. He was beginning to hate this house. He hurried back into the bedroom and felt the bedclothes again. They were cool. Damn it, they were nearly cold! So Garlic had been lying here only minutes ago. Now he was gone. Where could he have gone? There was nowhere to go.

The bed was covered by a large quilted bedspread. It reached almost to the floor. Laszlo took a handful in his left fist and ripped the bedspread away. Papers fluttered in the breeze; a china lamp got knocked over and it shattered like a small bomb. Laszlo stood, legs apart, braced for action. No action offered itself.

He knelt and peered under the bed. Empty. Dark but empty. He sat on his heels and smiled in relief. The whole house really was empty. A silky slithering made him turn his head and he took a thunderous blow in front of his right ear, a blow that smashed his smile into a gaping, lopsided grin and lifted him off his knees and sent him skidding on his rump across the shiny linoleum and thudding into the wall. Pain flowered hugely, hotter and redder than any blast furnace, and it faded as fast to a wretched semi-darkness. When he could feel again there was a burning balloon inside his head and it was threatening to burst and split

324

his skull. He had to open his mouth and let the balloon escape but his mouth was full of splintered rubbish. Whenever he breathed, he choked. When he choked, pain savaged his broken face.

The blow came from José-Carlos Coelho. He had been lying on his bed, reading a pathology textbook, when he caught a glimpse of this stunted, bearded stranger in his back garden. At once he rolled off, landing softly on his hands and stockinged feet, and slid under the bed. Half a minute later the bed-springs above him moved as Laszlo prodded. Laszlo muttered and mumbled, and then ran from the room. Coelho took a chance, slid out from under the bed and hid behind the door. When Laszlo came back, Coelho saw the gun and knew he would probably have only one chance; so as soon as Laszlo sat back on his heels Coelho made two huge strides and punched Laszlo so hard that Coelho came away with bits of beard and skin on his knuckles, cursing at the pain. He had boxed as a heavyweight for the university for three years, but he had never hit anyone as hard as that, especially without gloves. When Julie Conroy socked Luis Cabrillo she was exasperated and she didn't know how to make a proper fist. When José-Carlos Coelho punched Laszlo Martini he wanted to take his head off with one good shot. Laszlo's head would never be the same again. His jaw was broken in three places and the splintered rubbish inside his mouth was bits of teeth.

Coelho found the pistol and stuffed it in a pocket. He put on his shoes. He kicked Laszlo across the bedroom and into the bathroom. He closed the lavatory seat and dumped Laszlo on it. Laszlo wavered and moaned. He dribbled a mixture so foul that even Coelho the pathologist did not want to see it. Coelho got an old necktie and fastened Laszlo's hands behind him; then he picked up Laszlo by his armpits. He made him stand on the seat and he knotted Laszlo's hands to the ring in the end of the lavatory chain. 'Don't fall or you'll break your arms,' he warned. He took the key from the bathroom door and locked it on the outside. He went in search of a telephone and the police.

Laszlo did fall. He fainted. He did not weigh a lot but all that there was of him snatched at the chain with a sudden shock that was too much for the elderly plumbing. The cistern was already cracked; now it split, fell apart, dumping gallons of cold water on or around Laszlo's body and then continuing to pump water over it.

Laszlo recovered a bit. He crawled to the other end of the bathroom, dragging behind him the chain with a jagged chunk of cistern still attached. He knelt, and gripped the chunk between his heels, and began sawing at the necktie around his wrists. It was the sort of thing he'd seen done on the movies dozens of times. It always worked. The necktie was old and frayed. Laszlo didn't care how much skin went with it. He hacked hard.

When the police car arrived, water was pulsing under the bathroom door and Laszlo had gone. José-Carlos Coelho looked at the bathroom window in disbelief. It was the size of a shoebox. 'Nobody could get through that,' he said. 'Could they?' He was talking to himself. The police were off and running.

'I don't believe any of it,' the Director said. Freddy Garcia looked startled. 'Not *your* stuff, Freddy,' the Director said, waving a thick typescript. 'I believe all *this*. You've debriefed the pair of them very well, it's a model of its kind. I don't believe what Canaris says. I think Canaris is lying. I think he's got a racket going. That's the only way this makes sense.'

'What in particular is Canaris lying about?'

'Well, his knowledge of the Double-Cross System, for a start. He wants Eldorado to believe that the Abwehr knows we've turned all their agents, for heaven's sake.'

'Most, not all.'

'All right, most. But *we* know perfectly well the Abwehr has the greatest confidence in those agents. Has had for years. Many of their reports go straight to the top. We know that for a fact. Canaris wouldn't let that go on happening if he knew the contents were counterfeit, would he? I mean to say, the man's not a suicide.'

'Could he be a peacemaker, sir? Eldorado says he rambled a bit, got slightly emotional, but the general drift was clear enough.'

'I'm sure it was. Ceasefire in the west, keep up the good work in the east. Right? I've heard that song before. Altruistic

326

Germans are constantly popping up in highminded places like Berne or Stockholm or the Vatican and offering us painless ways of avoiding an invasion of Europe. Dust in the eyes, old chap, dust in the eyes.'

'But Canaris claims there is now a genuine anti-Nazi resistance party, or . . . Well, not a party, more of a group, or—'

'Or two men and a dog. Listen: if they hate their dreadful Führer so much, why don't they simply shoot him?'

'Canaris says he needs—'

'Canaris says, Canaris says. Suppose we give him what he asks for. Suppose we use Eldorado to pump up the Allied threat. What will be the consequence? Militarily?'

'They'll reinforce their defences in the west,' Freddy said.

'We don't want that. That's the last thing we want. What chance will our invasion stand if Canaris persuades Hitler to stuff France full of troops?'

Freddy flicked thoughtfully through his own copy of the debriefing. 'Even assuming he was lying, sir, why on earth would Canaris tell Eldorado that he knew some of his agents had been turned? Where's his racket?'

'Of course he's lying about it.' The Director put his feet on the desk: for him, a wildly extravagant gesture. 'If Canaris isn't lying then we might as well all shut up shop and go home. I'll tell you what I think happened. Canaris got badly shaken by the Garlic affair. First, somebody on his staff persuades him that Garlic is unreliable and must be removed. When that's done – or so he believes – Canaris has to face the awful possibility that Eldorado is crooked too. *Then* it turns out that Garlic's death was an Abwehr blunder! So Eldorado is a splendid fellow after all. Well, Canaris can't apologize, he's incapable of that, so he goes to the other extreme. He brags. He lets Eldorado know that he, Canaris, is a masterspy! He knows of every double-agent being run by British Intelligence. In other words he tells a whopping great lie in order to cover his embarrassment over his little mistake.'

Freddy had been listening carefully to all this. 'Yes,' he said. 'I see what you mean, sir. So Canaris knew he was lying.'

'Well of course he knew.'

327

'Yes . . . All the same, sir, he couldn't be sure whether or not Eldorado knew he was lying, could he?'

An ankle was getting stiff. The Director switched his feet around. 'Couldn't he?'

'No, sir. I mean, for all Canaris knew, Eldorado might have been convinced that nobody had been turned. In that case Eldorado would have assumed that Canaris was lying to him.'

The Director stared. 'Canaris *was* lying. I thought that was the one thing we were all agreed on.'

'Oh, absolutely. Except that I can't help wondering what Canaris made of Eldorado's response.'

'What response? He made no response.'

'Exactly, sir. Eldorado should have made a response if Canaris was lying. He should have told Canaris he was wrong, that no agent had been turned as far as he knew. When Eldorado failed to deny that suggestion, surely Canaris must have realized that he was telling the truth.'

'Well of course he was telling the truth,' the Director said. 'He was lying *and* he was telling the truth.'

'Yes,' Freddy said. 'Well, thank you for straightening that out, sir. I think we can put the whole business aside now, don't you?'

'Not that it matters,' the Director said. 'From what I hear, nobody gives a damn what Canaris says anyway.'

After their debriefing, Julie and Luis discussed the Santander expedition only once.

'All that fuss,' he said. 'And what difference has it made to anything?'

'Absolutely none.'

'Garlic's dead. Christian's dead. Doesn't change anything, does it?'

They were walking in the park. Luis clapped his hands to drive away some pigeons clustered in their path. 'Bloody birds,' he said. 'Tell me, which is worse? Pigeons or chimneys?'

She stopped and leaned against a tree. He sat on the grass where he could get a better view of her legs.

'I must have thought I was on some Commando mission,' she said. 'Here goes the plucky gal Commando to rescue her trapped buddy. Straight out of the comic strips.'

'At least you didn't do any harm.'

'Didn't do any good.'

'According to Freddy, half of all the war effort doesn't do any good.'

'That so? Which half?'

'Ah, there's the difficulty. He says you've got to win the war before you can decide.'

'And by then it doesn't matter,' she said.

They walked on, and that was the end of it.

Nobody could end the war. General Sir Stewart Menzies conferred with General William Donovan after their meetings on board the cruiser *Barcelona*; and they found themselves in broad agreement: Communism was the greater threat, and if Germany (without Hitler) could keep Russia at bay, then it would surely be possible and desirable to negotiate a ceasefire in the west. They reported all this to their respective masters and they walked into a pair of brick walls. The only ceasefire that Churchill and Roosevelt would consider was German unconditional surrender. The fact that Russia was Communist was, for the moment, irrelevant; what mattered was the way a succession of vast and violent land battles kept two-thirds of the German Army tied down in the east. The Western allies needed their Eastern partner to help them get an invasion army ashore in Europe. In the face of that massive fact, all the hopes and plans of Canaris and his fellow-conspirators were just chatter.

General Oster chattered too loudly. Canaris sacked him. The move came too late to save the Abwehr from constant scrutiny by Himmler's Gestapo. It wasn't just a matter of plotting to replace the regime. Down through the years, the Abwehr had been weakened by a whole series of acts of minor corruption, some of them linked with political attempts to bring the war to an end. For Abwehr agents who did a lot of travelling into and out of neutral countries – Switzerland, for instance – currency smuggling was an attractive sideline. There were all sorts of rackets in wartime Germany which could be hidden under the cloak of Abwehr activity. Inevitably, the cloak slipped and one or two rackets were investigated by civil or military police. The Abwehr did not come well out of these investigations. Canaris had to use all his political leverage to contain them.

By February 1944 his organization had lost Hitler's respect and Canaris himself was a tired and troubled man. The Gestapo missed no chance to point out the Abwehr's failings, and when a senior Abwehr officer and his wife walked into the British Legation in Istanbul and defected, it was the end of Canaris and the end of the Abwehr. Hitler dismissed the head and merged the agency with the Gestapo under Himmler's overall leadership, thus creating one wide-reaching national intelligence agency.

The former Abwehr operations continued. Himmler had not coveted Canaris's department in order to dismantle it. He valued its established networks of agents and the rich and various strands of military intelligence which they reported. The Eldorado Network went on working and earning. Many of the reports which Himmler's new organization took and paid for concerned preparations for the Allied invasion of Europe. Everyone knew it was coming; the great debate was about when and where it would go ashore. The possible landing sites stretched from the Belgian coast westward through the Pas de Calais and along the coast of northern France, around the peninsula of Normandy to Brittany and down to the Bay of Biscay: more than a thousand miles of shoreline to be defended.

Not that there was any guarantee that the Allies would strike at any of it.

They might invade the south of France. There were good arguments in favour of that, what with Allied control of the Mediterranean and a solid base in Italy. Or maybe the invasion route would be via Greece and Yugoslavia, where great help could be expected from Tito's partisans and there was the promise of an early link-up with the Russian advance. This was the 'soft underbelly' of Europe for which Churchill had such a liking, as if the Continent could be attacked like an animal; although anyone who had fought in or around Greece in 1941 could have told him (as some did) that there was nothing soft about that bit of Europe; quite the reverse.

Scandinavia had its supporters too. Since the Wehrmacht had seized Norway so quickly and easily, perhaps it could be thrown out just as fast. Think what that would do to the German Navy's attacks on the Arctic convoys to Russia! And from Norway it was just a short hop into Denmark, and Germany was around the corner . . .

The speculation was endless; but those who talked didn't know, while those who knew didn't talk. Luis and Julie didn't know, but that didn't stop them arguing the Second Front all around the coastline of Europe. It was a national sport, trying to second-guess the warlords. 'No, it's got to be the short route,' Luis said. 'Damn it all, you can *see* France from the cliffs at Dover.'

'But that's exactly what Eldorado's been telling Madrid,' Julie objected. For many months, the network had reported an accelerating build-up of troops and ships and aircraft in south-east England. Essex and Kent, Sussex and Surrey were so crammed with American and Canadian and British infantry and armour that – according to Knickers and Nutmeg – space had had to be found for a whole new American Army Group in the flatlands of Suffolk, Norfolk, and Lincolnshire. 'Why are we always pointing at the Pas de Calais if it's the truth?' she asked.

'Double-bluff. The enemy expects a deception plan. When we make so much fuss about the obvious invasion route he thinks it can't be true, it's a deception, Eldorado's sub-agents are being shown what Allied Intelligence wants them to see, so the landings must be planned for elsewhere.'

She waited. 'Like where else?'

Luis shrugged. 'Somewhere a long way off, probably. My money's on the French Riviera. If I was Hitler that's where I'd be looking.'

'And maybe Hitler's right,' she said.

'No.'

'What makes you so sure? There's a lot to be said for the

Med. The tide doesn't rush in and out like the Channel, for a start.'

'Sure. Nice weather, too. But it's a double-bluff. He's looking for a deception plan, isn't he? Fine. He's found it. What he doesn't know is that the phoney attack is also the real attack.'

'OK, Luis. OK. For the sake of argument. But what if he doesn't buy the double-bluff? What if he buys the deception plan pure and simple?'

'Then he's an idiot.'

'He's an idiot with an awful lot of guns waiting in the Pas de Calais area.'

They stared at each other, Julie half-smiling, Luis frowning as his mind picked its way through this phantom maze.

'Maybe I should talk to Freddy,' he said. 'Maybe it's time Eldorado told Madrid about the possibility of a double-bluff.'

'Madrid might not believe Eldorado,' she said. 'Madrid might suspect that Eldorado has been sold a brand-new deception plan by British Intelligence. That would make it a triple-bluff. Look: our invasion build-up opposite the Pas de Calais is so obvious that the Germans know they're meant to ignore it, so that's what they *don't* do, because the last thing they're going to do is what *they* know *we* want them to do, except that in this case they know that we know what it is *they* think *we* want them to think, and then when Eldorado spells all that out to them they reckon his warning is just a further layer of deception. Therefore they do the opposite.'

Luis's head had sunk lower and lower under the weight of her reasoning. 'They do the opposite,' he repeated. 'What's that?'

'I can't go through it all again,' she said. 'You'll just have to wait and see.'

He got out of her bed and began putting on his clothes. 'I can't be expected to make love to you *and* organize the Second Front,' he said. 'Are you wearing my socks? I can't find my socks . . . Look, why can't we live together? It would save all this dressing and undressing.'

'We can't live together,' Julie said, 'because you're such a tremendous pain in the ass, Luis.'

'That's a double-bluff,' he said. 'When you get to know me better you'll discover that I'm really a tremendous pain in the ass.' He found his socks and put them on. 'Back to work,' he said.

Larbert 17 was a three-man pillbox made of concrete. It was one of a chain of pillboxes that guarded a valley through which roads and railways ran between Glasgow and Edinburgh. The chain had been built in a hurry in 1940 when it seemed more than possible that a German invasion fleet might steam up the Firth of Forth and put ashore a horde of infantry in field-grey and coalscuttle helmets who would seize Falkirk and Larbert, stream down the A80 to Dumbarton, Muirhead, Stepps, and Carntyne, from where they could take a tram to anywhere in Glasgow they pleased. It was the sort of thing that had happened to Poland, Norway, Denmark, Holland, Belgium, Luxembourg, and France, so why not to Scotland? Hence the pillboxes: chunky, five-sided concrete cells with narrow gun slits.

Larbert 17 was set on a hillside that overlooked a road bridge. In 1940 it was camouflaged green and brown but by the spring of 1943 nature had done a much better job. Moss, lichens, brambles and ivy left little of the concrete exposed. The pillbox blended gently into the hillside, forgotten and ignored by everyone except the farmer's dog.

The farmer raised sheep in the fields beyond the hillside. By springtime his ewes had lambed but that didn't mean they couldn't get into trouble. They wandered off, found (or made) gaps in the hedge, fell over, got their fleece trapped in brambles or thorn trees, struggled, exhausted themselves, sometimes died. Or they might plunge a leg in a rabbit-hole and be stuck. Those were the ewes. The lambs, of course, were twice as daft. So the dog – a border collie with a bit of spaniel somewhere in his ancestry – had a nose for accidents. He could smell distress or injury a long way off. Especially he could smell death. One day he let his master know it. The dog led him to Larbert 17. The farmer took one look inside and went to Larbert police.

That was in the morning. At mid-afternoon Inspector Hogg

picked up José-Carlos Coelho at the Department of Pathology and drove him the thirty-odd miles to Larbert 17, which was being guarded by a local constable.

'I thought this might be useful experience for you,' Hogg said to Coelho. 'Assuming it's the same man, of course.' They had to duck to get through the cramped entrance at the rear.

It was the same man. Laszlo Martini lay in a corner under a couple of sacks. Hogg had a flashlight. 'He looks smaller,' Coelho said.

Laszlo was smaller. He looked like a child: a bearded child, a circus freak. His face was turned to the gun-slits. Presumably he had been looking at the sky.

After he had squirmed through the bathroom window he had escaped the police by no more than a minute; but as he was on a bus, a minute was plenty. Laszlo had earned the rewards of daring and (considering the pain he was in) of courage. He had crossed Coelho's back garden, found a gate into an alley, and instead of running along the alley he had found another gate into another back garden, off the next street. It could have been full of large and angry men with spades or hoes, ready to challenge him. He was lucky: it was empty. As he made his way to the street he wrapped a woollen muffler around his battered face. What he needed was a bus, any bus, going anywhere, and obligingly one trundled around the corner.

He could only mumble and gesture to the conductress; in the end she lost patience and gave him a ticket to the end of the ride. Laszlo was trembling, and he dropped his ticket. She thought maybe he had the flu and that's why he was all wrapped up. Anyway, he got off the bus long before the end of the ride, as she told the police when they questioned her. But that was next day. Laszlo had taken several more bus rides by then. He was out in the countryside, slowly starving to death.

He could not chew. Anything like chewing set up a chain of pain in his shattered jaw that made him cry out. In any case he had little food and no ration book to buy more, even if he had the money. Most of his coins had spilled from his pockets in various parts of 22A Buccleuch Avenue.

He found the pillbox while he still had enough strength to climb to it and to drag open the small steel door at the back. He left it only once, to steal potatoes from a clamp. On his way back he washed them in a stream and drank from the stream too, sucking up the cold water with the unbroken half of his mouth. He paused for breath and saw himself reflected. He looked like his father in the year he died.

Half a mile upstream from the place where Laszlo drank, the water was used by pigs. He carried his potatoes back to Larbert 17, picking up a couple of ripped and useless sacks on the way. Inside the pillbox he examined the potatoes. They were not big. If he could cook them he might be able to swallow the soft centres. He had no matches. It was a very difficult problem, an exhaustingly difficult problem. He fell asleep.

What woke him was the burning ache in his belly. That and the lunging throb in his head. It was night. He was shuddering from the cold and sometimes he could not find the strength even to shudder. He lay under the sacks for three days. Once, a field mouse came in and took a very long look at him. On the fourth day Laszlo died.

José-Carlos Coelho squatted and examined the face. He ran his forefinger down the jawline, tracing the zigzags of the fractures. 'I find it utterly astonishing that he got through that window,' he said. 'I thought I'd killed him when I hit him.'

'Desperate fellow,' Hogg said. 'He was certainly out to kill you. The gun was loaded.'

'If you'd caught him, what would have happened to him? Eventually?'

'He would have been hanged.'

'I see he left his trademark,' Coelho said. 'Small potatoes.' He looked up at Hogg. 'Joke,' he said.

D-Day was 6 June 1944. The event came as a great surprise to Luis and Julie, as it did to most people. 'It's a ruse,' Luis said. He had only recently discovered this word and he enjoyed it. 'You watch. This is a tremendous ruse. Invading Normandy is absurd, it's far too far away and we haven't even tried to capture a port, so there's no hope of reinforcing the first wave of troops fast enough. Normandy . . .' He shook his head. 'It's got to be a ruse.'

'You're just pissed off because Eisenhower hasn't taken your famous short route,' Julie said. They were in Freddy's office, drinking tea.

'Not at all. The ruse will serve its purpose, you watch.'

'What is that?' Freddy asked.

'Hitler will detach some of his defensive units from the Pas de Calais area and send them off to Normandy,' Luis declared. 'When this so-called invasion, which is really a ruse, has distracted a large amount of German tanks and artillery, Eisenhower will make his *real* move. You wait and see.'

'I don't think you should wait,' Freddy said. 'Not too long, anyway.'

The following day, Eldorado signalled Madrid that the Normandy landings were only a diversion, a ruse. He warned that the real attack was poised to be launched against the Pas de Calais area at any moment. He repeated this warning twice in the next seven days, with supporting evidence from Haystack and Pinetree.

'I thought you hated Haystack,' Julie said. 'I thought you told me he was an idiot.'

'Can we discuss this in bed?' Luis asked. 'I'm feeling rather weary. It's very tiring, holding back half the German Army.'

Two weeks after D-Day, Freddy told him to forget about the Pas de Calais landings. 'It seems Hitler is now convinced that it's Normandy after all,' he said. 'He's just taken six or seven divisions out of the Pas de Calais and sent them westward.'

'Very ill-advised,' Luis said. 'He'll regret it.'

'Lucky for us he didn't do it on D-Day. Our chaps might have been booted off the beaches.'

Luis took Julie out to lunch. 'Eisenhower was lucky. Freddy told me as much. The Allies never expected to be so successful in Normandy, that was just supposed to be a decoy landing to confuse the Hun. When it went so well, Eisenhower cancelled his main attack. Obvious, isn't it?'

'I don't suppose Freddy told you where the main attack was going to be,' she said.

'I told Freddy.'

'Fine. Now you can tell me.'

'Dieppe. Hitler would never in a million years expect us to attack twice in the same place . . . Anyway, none of that matters any more. There's obviously no future in working for the Abwehr, is there? So I've found a new client. Well, two new clients, actually. The Russians and the Americans. They each think they've turned me.'

For a moment Julie thought he was joking; then she recognized the suppressed pleasure in his voice. 'How did you do it?' she asked.

'Usual way. Walked into their embassies and made a deal. The pay's good. Especially from the Reds.'

She sipped her drink while she studied his contented face. 'Haven't you any sense of loyalty at all, Luis? I mean, how can you go on working for Freddy while you're betraying MI5?'

'It was Freddy who suggested it. He said the Yanks have started spying on the British, the Russians have been spying on them for years, and since neither of them trusts anyone to tell the truth, Eldorado could be a useful way of passing information which they'll believe because they know they shouldn't have it.'

'Now you're a quadruple-agent,' she said.

'And very strenuous it is. A chap has to keep his strength up. I wonder if they have any roly-poly pudding today? If there's one thing in this dreadful country worth fighting for, it's roly-poly pudding.'

'You don't really mean that.'

'No,' Luis said. 'It's a double-bluff. I really want apple pie.'

At last, on 20 July 1944, somebody had the courage and the competence to blow up Adolf Hitler. The man was Colonel Count Claus von Stauffenberg, not only a regular officer and a Catholic but a patriot who had lost one eye and two fingers while fighting for his country. He was now involved in the raising of new divisions – urgently needed following catastrophes on the Eastern Front – and he came to a conference at the Führer's headquarters at Rastenburg in East Prussia in order to present his report. This was in his briefcase along with a packet of British plastic explosive, captured the previous year.

The first thing he did when he reached Hitler's headquarters was to visit the lavatory. There he broke open the tiny container of acid which activated his time bomb. He entered the conference room and was briefly presented to Hitler. An officer then continued describing the latest grim developments in the east. Hitler stood at a map table. Von Stauffenberg put his briefcase under the table, near to Hitler. After a few moments he murmured that he had to make a telephone call, and he left.

Hitler was six feet from the bomb when it exploded. The blast was so violent that an adjutant got flung through a window. One general had a foot blown off. Two generals were injured so badly that they died. By then von Stauffenberg was in a fast car to the plane that would take him to Berlin and Operation Valkyrie, code name for the state of emergency that should ensure the success of the coup. But Hitler was not dead.

He was deafened, his face was cut, and he was badly peppered about the legs with splinters; but after treatment he ate lunch as usual, and in the afternoon he went ahead with a scheduled visit from the Italian dictator Mussolini. Hitler even showed Mussolini the ruins of the bombed hut. Meanwhile his orders were going everywhere to reverse Valkyrie. By evening the coup was dead (as was von Stauffenberg) and all over Occupied Europe, men were hastening to reaffirm their loyalty to Hitler and the Nazi regime.

One such was Admiral Canaris. In fact Canaris had not known in advance of von Stauffenberg's attempt. That did not save him. He escaped the first wave of arrests but was detained on 23 July. Oster had been taken two days earlier. They were part of a round-up that went on and on, circles ever-widening, until perhaps five thousand had been arrested. Few survived. Canaris and Oster lasted longer than most. They were hanged on 9 April 1945.

AFTERWORD

There is much fiction in this novel, but it is built on a framework of fact. The reader is entitled to know which is which.

Artillery of Lies is a sequel to *The Eldorado Network*, now reissued in Pan paperback. Luis Cabrillo, the central character of both books, is based on a young Spaniard who in fact went into hiding at the end of the Spanish Civil War, emerged in January 1941 and offered himself to the British as an intelligence agent, was rejected, and thereupon joined the Germans – meaning (he later claimed) to double-cross them in order to improve his prospects of employment by the British.

The Abwehr code-named him 'Arabel', trained him in Madrid, and in July sent him to spy in Britain. He arranged to travel there on a Spanish diplomatic mission. Actually he went to Lisbon where, with the help of a few books and a skilled imagination, he supplied Madrid Abwehr with long reports (all supposedly sent from England) which they came to value highly. As his efforts increased he created sub-agents to help him.

Once established, Arabel again approached the British. Again they rejected him. Then, in February 1942, British Intelligence learned that the enemy was wasting his time trying to intercept a non-existent convoy from Liverpool to Malta. Arabel had invented it. At last they recognized his value. He was smuggled to England, given the code name 'Garbo', and made part of MI5's Double-Cross section, which operated German agents who had been caught and 'turned'.

Starting with this improbable but historically true outline, I wrote *The Eldorado Network*. It is a bizarre yarn, and even more surprising was the discovery that Garbo/Arabel was still alive. Juan Pujol – his real name – made his home in Venezuela after the war. He visited London in 1984, and revealed details of his wartime network of phantom agents and sub-agents. Readers who find Eldorado's code names a little fanciful – Nutmeg, Wallpaper, Knickers and so on – might like to know that two of Garbo's agents were called Moonbeam and Dagobert. Another agent, Benedict, was a Venezuelan student in Glasgow.

When I wrote *The Eldorado Network*, my slim knowledge of Garbo came from J. C. Masterman's excellent book, *The Double-Cross System in the War of 1939–1945* (Yale, 1972), which describes Garbo as 'the most highly developed example of the art' of double-cross. Masterman also said: 'By means of the double-agent system we actively ran and controlled the German espionage system in this country.' MI5 operated about 120 double-agents; certainly the operation was a considerable triumph.

However, it has been suggested more recently that maybe the enemy was not as gullible as he seemed. Did the Abwehr really believe that so many of its spies survived for so long, never got caught, and were able to uncover and transmit so much secret information? Or did some Abwehr officers know very well that their agents had been turned by MI5, but preferred to let this arrangement continue because they could exploit it to their own advantage? We know that Admiral Canaris, General Oster, and other senior Abwehr officers were involved in plans to overthrow Hitler, in which case a direct line to MI5 would have been very useful. Heinz Höhne, the biographer of Canaris, gives evidence of a meeting in the summer of 1943 between the Admiral and the heads of Allied Intelligence – Menzies for Britain, Donovan for the United States – at Santander, in northern Spain, where the Abwehr leader argued for a separate peace in the west. Stranger things have happened.

My account of Eldorado's prolific skill is true to the facts of Garbo's phenomenal output. By 1944 Garbo headed a network of fourteen active agents and eleven valuable contacts. He had sent four hundred secret letters and transmitted about two thousand radio reports, for which the Abwehr paid some £20,000. Since I completed *Artillery of Lies*, the final volume of the official history of British Intelligence in the Second World War has been published.* Its author, Michael Howard, describes Garbo as the agent 'who was almost single-handed to provide a justification for the existence of the Twenty Committee'. Probably his greatest contribution to the Allied cause was to help persuade the Germans that the main D-Day landings would take place in the Pas de Calais area, and that the Normandy attack was only a diversion. Michael Howard quotes a message from Berlin to Garbo's Abwehr case officer on 11 June, five days after the landings: 'The reports received in the last week from Garbo have been confirmed almost without exception and are to be described as especially valuable.' To the end, it seems, the Germans were convinced that the only reason the Pas de Calais attack never took place was because the Normandy landings were unexpectedly successful. Not surprisingly, Arabel/Garbo was awarded both the Iron Cross and the MBE.

Historical facts such as these I was happy to incorporate in *Artillery of Lies*. Similarly, details of the anti-Nazi conspiracies, of rivalry between the Abwehr and the SD, of Albert Speer's colossal architectural plans, of the Hamburg firestorm, and of Jeschonnek's suicide are all authentic. The Double-Cross System operated broadly as described. Some of Eldorado's military 'secrets' had their roots in reality. For instance, the US Air Force experimented with remote-controlled Flying Fortresses, each packed with TNT and directed to crash on its target – the basis of OWCH – and the idea of GABLE (a ski-jump take-off for bombers) was confidently reported by a wartime magazine. The rest I made up; which is not to say that it could not have happened.

DR

*Michael Howard, *British Intelligence in the Second World War*, HMSO, 1990

DEREK ROBINSON
War Story
£3.50

"There is going to be the most enormous battle, and the war will be over by Christmas. Which Christmas, God alone knows. . ."

Lieutenant Oliver Paxton was eighteen years old and desperately keen to help win the war when he was posted to France in June, 1916.

In the war-streaked skies over the Western Front, his education was hurried and painful. The rest of Hornet Squadron thought him a pompous idiot, but a very available lady behind the lines thought him the loveliest killer she'd danced with all night, while he could hardly wait to get a Hun in his sights when the order came for the Big Push.

And the fearsome first day of the Somme waited gaunt in the wings of history. . .

'This book is marvelous in technical detail on the first fragile days of kites in conflict – and by far the sweetest, most cynical modern story of that "lovely war".'

Mail on Sunday

'Ther is a tremendous humour, a rich assortment of characters and. . . an unstated tribute to the bravery of those going down over the front line like "spiders under a lawnmower".'

Daily Telegraph

DEREK ROBINSON
Eldorado Network

£4.99

Bestselling author of Piece of Cake
and The Goshawk Squadron

MADRID, 1941.
LAUNCH PAD FOR A MILLION-DOLLAR SPY. . .

Eldorado was the code name for a young, inexperienced
Spaniard sent to England in 1941 to spy for the Third Reich.

Luis Cabrillo had no right to survive, let alone succeed.

Yet against all the odds Eldorado set up a network of agents
whose information was valuble enough to alter the course of
the war.

He made a lot of money. He also made a lot of dangerous
enemies.

Could Eldorado turn himself into a millionaire before his
enemies could turn him into a corpse?

*'Eldorado' really existed, under another code name. This
book was inspired by the known facts about his astonishing
wartime career.*

'Original and dazzling'
Sunday Times

'A sharp and ironic footnote to the Second World War'
New Yorker

All Pan books are available at your local bookshop or newsagent, or can be ordered direct from the publisher. Indicate the number of copies required and fill in the form below.

Send to: **CS Department, Pan Books Ltd., P.O. Box 40, Basingstoke, Hants.   RG21 2YT.**

or phone: 0256 469551 (Ansaphone), quoting title, author and Credit Card number.

Please enclose a remittance* to the value of the cover price plus: 60p for the first book plus 30p per copy for each additional book ordered to a maximum charge of £2.40 to cover postage and packing.

*Payment may be made in sterling by UK personal cheque, postal order, sterling draft or international money order, made payable to Pan Books Ltd.

Alternatively by Barclaycard/Access:

Card No.

Signature:

Applicable only in the UK and Republic of Ireland.

While every effort is made to keep prices low, it is sometimes necessary to increase prices at short notice. Pan Books reserve the right to show on covers and charge new retail prices which may differ from those advertised in the text or elsewhere.

NAME AND ADDRESS IN BLOCK LETTERS PLEASE:

....

Name ————————————————————————————

Address ————————————————————————————

————————————————————————————

————————————————————————————

————————————————————————————

3/87